"Engrossi[ng]..."

"Gritty..."

**Praise for the *Goodreads*-nominated
and *Romantic Times* award-winning
Elemental Assassin series**

UNRAVELED

"*Unraveled* . . . packs a generous punch of adventure, suspense, mystery, and humor."

—*Smexy Books*

BITTER BITE

"Estep's street-smart characters, lively narrative, and ever-evolving stories keep this series alive and kicking."

—*Library Journal*

"The fourteenth title in the Elemental Assassin series is a fast, furious, and entertaining romp."

—*Kirkus Reviews*

SPIDER'S TRAP

"The continued evolution of not only Gin but all the rest of the core characters as well is what keeps this series fresh and immensely entertaining. These relationships give such rich depth and emotional heft to the otherwise nonstop action."

—*RT Book Reviews* (Top Pick!)

"Nonstop action, great characters, humor, and even some moments where your heart is in your throat."

—*Dark Faerie Tales*

BLACK WIDOW

"Everything that I adore about this series is right here and more so in *Black Widow*. There's expertly crafted fights, banter, and suspense that continued to keep me on the edge of my seat. I can't recommend this book enough and love being on the rollercoaster ride that is Gin Blanco's life."

—*All Things Urban Fantasy*

"*Black Widow* is crazy good and Gin Blanco is still one of the best-written heroines in urban fantasy. I was riveted from beginning to end."

—*Fiction Vixen*

POISON PROMISE

"A knockout. . . . Lots of vividly depicted battles, a high body count, and high-octane escapes worthy of a James Bond movie keep the pages turning."

—*Booklist*

"A quick-moving plot and characters that jump off the page. . . . Estep finely balances a confident, tough-edged personality with an inner life filled with doubts and emotions, making Gin a surprisingly down-to-earth heroine whom readers will root for."

—*Publishers Weekly*

THE SPIDER

"By virtue of her enormous skill, Estep keeps this amazing series fresh and unputdownable!"

—*RT Book Reviews* (Top Pick!)

"Made me fall in love with Gin all over again."

—*All Things Urban Fantasy*

HEART OF VENOM

"Amazing. . . . Estep is one of those rare authors who excels at both action set pieces and layered character development."

—*RT Book Reviews* (Top Pick!)

"Action-packed with tons of character growth. . . . One of the best books in the series, which says a lot because Estep's writing rarely, if ever, disappoints."

—*Fall Into Books*

DEADLY STING

"Classic Estep with breathtaking thrills, coolly executed fights, and a punch of humor, which all add up to unbeatable entertainment!"

—*RT Book Reviews* (Top Pick!)

"I've been hooked on this series from the first word of the first book. I can't get enough."

—*Fiction Vixen*

WIDOW'S WEB

"Estep has found the perfect recipe for combining kick-butt action and high-stakes danger with emotional resonance."

—*RT Book Reviews* (Top Pick!)

"Filled with such emotional and physical intensity that it leaves you happily exhausted by the end."

—*All Things Urban Fantasy*

SPIDER'S REVENGE

"Explosive. . . . Hang on, this is one smackdown you won't want to miss!"

—*RT Book Reviews* (Top Pick!)

"A whirlwind of tension, intrigue, and mind-blowing action that leaves your heart pounding."

—*Smexy Books*

VENOM

"Estep has really hit her stride with this gritty and compelling series. . . . Brisk pacing and knife-edged danger make this an exciting page-turner."

—*RT Book Reviews* (Top Pick!)

"Gin is a compelling and complicated character whose story is only made better by the lovable band of merry misfits she calls her family."

—*Fresh Fiction*

SPIDER'S BITE

"The series [has] plenty of bite. . . . Kudos to Estep for the knife-edged suspense!"

—*RT Book Reviews*

"Fast pace, clever dialogue, and an intriguing heroine."

—*Library Journal*

BOOKS IN THE ELEMENTAL ASSASSIN SERIES
BY JENNIFER ESTEP

Spider's Bite

Web of Lies

Venom

Tangled Threads

Spider's Revenge

By a Thread

Widow's Web

Deadly Sting

Heart of Venom

The Spider

Poison Promise

Black Widow

Spider's Trap

Bitter Bite

Unraveled

Snared

E-NOVELLAS

Thread of Death

Parlor Tricks

Kiss of Venom

Unwanted

Nice Guys Bite

Snared

AN ELEMENTAL ASSASSIN BOOK

JENNIFER ESTEP

POCKET BOOKS

New York   London   Toronto   Sydney   New Delhi

Pocket Books
An Imprint of Simon & Schuster, Inc.
1230 Avenue of the Americas
New York, NY 10020

This book is a work of fiction. Any references to historical events, real
people, or real places are used fictitiously. Other names, characters,
places, and events are products of the author's imagination, and any
resemblance to actual events or places or persons, living or dead, is
entirely coincidental.

First Pocket Books paperback edition May 2017

POCKET and colophon are registered trademarks of
Simon & Schuster, Inc.

For information about special discounts for bulk purchases, please
contact Simon & Schuster Special Sales at 1-866-506-1949
or business@simonandschuster.com.

The Simon & Schuster Speakers Bureau can bring authors to your
live event. For more information or to book an event, contact the
Simon & Schuster Speakers Bureau at 1-866-248-3049 or visit
our website at www.simonspeakers.com.

Manufactured in the United States of America

10 9 8 7 6 5 4 3 2

ISBN 978-1-5011-4227-7
ISBN 978-1-5011-4228-4 (ebook)

To my mom, my grandma, and Andre—
for your love, patience, and everything else
that you've given me over the years

Acknowledgments

Once again, my heartfelt thanks go out to all the folks who help turn my words into a book.

Thanks go to my agent, Annelise Robey, and my editor, Adam Wilson, for all their helpful advice, support, and encouragement. Thanks also to Melissa Bendixen.

Thanks to Tony Mauro for designing another terrific cover, and thanks to Louise Burke, Lisa Litwack, and everyone else at Pocket Books and Simon & Schuster for their work on the cover, the book, and the series.

And finally, a big thanks to all the readers. Knowing that folks read and enjoy my books is truly humbling, and I'm glad that you are all enjoying Gin and her adventures.

I appreciate you all more than you will ever know.

Happy reading!

✵ 1 ✵

Being an assassin meant knowing when to kill—and when *not* to kill.

Unfortunately.

I stood in a pool of midnight shadows, my boots, jeans, turtleneck, and fleece jacket as black as the night around me. My dark brown hair was stuffed up underneath a black toboggan that matched the rest of my clothes, and I'd swiped some black greasepaint under my eyes to reduce the paleness of my face. The only bit of color on my body was the silverstone knife that glinted in my right hand. I even inhaled and exhaled through my nose, so that my breath wouldn't frost too much in the chilly January air and give away my position.

Not that anyone was actually looking for me.

Oh, a dwarf on guard duty was patrolling the vast estate. Supposedly, he was here to keep an eye out and make sure that no one snuck out of the woods, sprinted across the lawn, and broke into the mansion off in the distance. But he was doing a piss-poor job of it. I'd been watching him amble around for more than three minutes now, making an exceptionally slow circuit of this part of the landscaped grounds.

Every once in a while, the dwarf would raise his head and look around, scanning the twisted shadows cast by the trees and ornamental bushes that dotted the rolling lawn. But most of the time, he was far more interested in playing a game on his phone, judging from the beeps and chimes that continually emanated from it. He didn't even have the sound muted—or his gun drawn.

I shook my head. It was so hard to find good help these days.

Still, I tensed as the guard wandered closer to my position. I was standing at the corner of a gray stone house, set in the very back corner of the yard, several hundred feet from the main building. Trees were clustered all around the house, their branches arching over the black slate roof and making the shadows here particularly dark, giving me the perfect hiding spot to watch and wait out the guard.

No doubt the man who lived in the mansion charitably referred to this house as a caretaker's cottage or something else equally dismissive, even if it was almost large enough to be its own separate manor. Even Finnegan Lane, my foster brother, would have been impressed by the spacious rooms and expensive antique furniture that I'd glimpsed through the windows when I was sneaking around the cottage and getting into position—

"So are you actually going to break into the mansion,

or are we just going to stand around out here all night in the dark?" a snide voice murmured in my ear.

Speak of the devil, and he will annoy you.

I looked to my right. Fifty feet away, a tall man-shaped shadow hovered at the edge of the tree line. Like me, Finn was dressed all in black, although I could just make out the glimmer of his eyes, like a cat's in the darkness.

"I'm waiting for the guard to turn around and go back in the other direction," I hissed. "As you can bloody well see for yourself."

The transmitter in my ear crackled from the force of Finn's snort. "Mr. Cell-Phone Video Game?" He snorted again. "Please. You could do naked cartwheels across the lawn right in front of him, and he still wouldn't notice."

Finn was probably right, but with the guard only about thirty feet from me now, I couldn't risk responding. Instead, I slid back a little deeper into the shadows, pressing myself up against the side of the cottage. My body touched the wall, and I reached out with my elemental Stone magic, listening to the gray rocks that made up the structure.

Dark, malicious whispers echoed back to me, punctuated by high, shrill, screaming notes of fear and agony, as the stone muttered about all the blood and violence it had witnessed over the years and all the people who had died within its walls.

The mutterings didn't surprise me, considering where I was, but their deep, harsh intensity made me frown. I wouldn't have thought that the caretaker's cottage would have been this affected by the man in the mansion, given the distance between the two structures.

Then again, anything was possible when dealing with the Circle.

I shut the stone's mutterings out of my mind and focused on the guard. Like most dwarves, he was short and stocky, with bulging biceps that threatened to pop through the sleeves of his suit jacket. Your typical enforcer, save for the thin, scraggly wisps of black hair that lined his upper lip. Someone was trying to grow a mustache with little success.

Stopping about ten feet away from me, the guard raised his gaze from his phone and glanced at the front of the house. He tilted his head to the side, listening to the whistle of the winter wind as it made the tree branches above the cottage scrape together like dry, brittle bones.

I tightened my grip on my knife, the symbol stamped into the hilt pressing into the larger, matching scar embedded in my palm, both of them a circle surrounded by eight thin rays, a spider rune, the symbol for patience.

Something that the guard had little of. Five seconds later, he turned his attention back to his phone and resumed his slow, ambling walk, taking him right past my hiding spot. I could easily have reached out of the shadows, sunk my hand into the dwarf's hair, yanked his head back, and cut his throat. He would have been dead before he'd even realized what was happening. But I couldn't kill him—or anyone else here—tonight.

Unfortunately.

Once I started dropping bodies, the members of the Circle, a secret society responsible for much of the crime and corruption in Ashland, would realize that I was onto them. They would close ranks, increase their security, and come after me. Or worse: target my friends. Something that I wasn't ready for.

So as easy as it would have been for me to kill the guard, I let him wander away, never knowing how close he'd come to playing his last video game.

Once the guard had moved far enough away, I relaxed and looked over at Finn, who flashed me a thumbs-up, then raised the gun in his other hand and saluted me with it. His voice crackled in my ear again. "I'll be here waiting but with gun drawn instead of bells on. Just in case you need the cavalry to ride to your rescue."

I rolled my eyes. "Please. I'm Gin Blanco, fearsome assassin and underworld queen, remember? The only thing I need rescuing from is you and your bad puns."

Finn grinned, his white teeth flashing in the darkness. "You know you love me and my bad puns."

"Oh, yeah. Like a toothache that I can't get rid of."

"That's me, baby. Finnegan Lane, rotten as they come."

He saluted me with his gun a second time, proud that he'd gotten the last word in. I rolled my eyes again.

But I was smiling as I turned away from him, left the shadows behind, and hurried toward the mansion.

Being early January, the holidays were officially over, but someone was a little slow about putting away the decorations. White twinkle lights were still wrapped around the thick columns that supported the sprawling, two-story, gray stone mansion, along with strands of illuminated snowflakes that glowed a pale blue. Still more lights and snowflakes curved over the stone archways and outlined all of the windows, which also had white velvet bows hanging in them.

New year, new targets for the Spider.

I crossed the wide lawn, stepped onto a stone patio, and hunkered down behind some lounge chairs that ringed the heated pool, staying as far away from the cheery glow of the holiday lights as I could get. Then I peered around the chairs and over at the mansion.

It was after ten o'clock, and lights burned in every room on the first floor. I spotted several servants moving back and forth, tidying up and doing their final chores for the night. Through the windows closest to me, I saw two women plucking red and green glass balls off a massive Christmas tree that took up most of that room.

I watched the women and some other servants work for a little while longer, but no one moved toward the windows and looked outside. No one had seen me approach, so I raised my gaze to a particular window on the second floor. Lights burned in that room too, but I didn't spot anyone moving around inside. Excellent.

I glanced over my shoulder, but the guard was at the very back of the lawn now, several hundred feet from me, still playing his game. I wouldn't get a better chance than this. I slid my knife up my sleeve so as to have both hands free. Then I surged to my feet, got a running start, leaped up, and grabbed hold of a trellis that was attached to the side of the building.

The wood creaked and groaned under my weight, more accustomed to holding up pretty roses than a deadly assassin, but the slats didn't crack, and I felt safe enough to keep climbing. It took me only about ten seconds to scale the trellis, hook my leg onto the first-story roof, and pull myself up. I lay flat on my stomach for several seconds, listening, but no surprised shouts or alarms sounded. I also glanced at the guard again, but he was a murky, indistinct shape in the night. No one had seen my quick spider climb.

Even though lying on the cold roof chilled my body from head to toe, I held my position, once again reaching out with my magic. Just like the ones at the caretaker's cottage, the stones of the mansion whispered of dark, malicious intent, along with blood, violence, pain, and death. The mutterings were much fainter here, more sloppy slurs than clear, distinct notes, as though the stones themselves had been thoroughly soaked in all the alcohol that their owner so famously imbibed. Still, I could pick out the lingering emotional vibrations from all the evil deeds that had been committed here over the years. Exactly what I would expect to find in the home of a member of the Circle.

Sadly, though, the stones' mutterings weren't as disturbing as those of many of the other places I'd been, and the noise certainly wasn't going to stop me from completing my mission. So I got to my feet and hurried over to the window that I wanted, the same one I'd looked at earlier. After a quick glance through the glass to make sure the room was still empty, I reached out and tried the window, which slid up easily.

I waited a few seconds, but no alarms blared. I shook my head. You'd think that someone who was part of a decades-old criminal conspiracy would have enough common sense to lock the windows of his fancy mansion or at least order his staff to do it for him. But the mansion's owner thought that he was well protected, anonymous, and untouchable, just like the rest of the Circle.

Well, they weren't. Not anymore. Not from me.

I pushed aside the dangling white velvet bow, ducked down, and shimmied in through the open window, making sure to close it behind me. Then I turned and looked over the room.

The office was the inner sanctum of Damian Rivera, the first member of the Circle on my hit list. Several generations ago, the ancestors of Maria Rivera, Damian's mother, had made a fortune in coal before selling off their mines and branching out into other areas. Maria herself had been big into real estate, buying and selling property all over Ashland and renovating crumbling old homes that she decked out with antique furniture and family heirlooms that she got for a song at estate sales.

Damian had definitely inherited his mother's flair for both decorating and dramatic spaces. The office was enormous, taking up this entire side of the mansion. Dark brown leather chairs and couches filled the decidedly masculine area, along with tables covered with all sorts of expensive knickknacks. Porcelain vases, crystal figurines, wooden carvings, stone statues. All perfectly in place and all perfectly highlighted by the three gold-plated chandeliers hanging from the ceiling.

But the centerpiece of the office was an elaborate bar that took up one entire wall, complete with several red padded barstools lined up in front of it. A wide assortment of liquor bottles perched prettily on the wooden shelves behind the brass-railed bar, along with rows of gleaming glassware. I eyed the bottles, recognizing them all as being well out of my price range but fitting right in with the rest of the luxe furnishings. The air reeked of expensive floral cologne and even more expensive cigar smoke, adding to the feel of a gentlemen's club. I had to wrinkle my nose to hold back a sneeze.

But I wasn't here to gawk at the expensive furnishings, so I moved over to the desk in the back of the room near the window that I'd just slithered through. To my disappointment, the golden wood was spotless, as though it had never been touched, much less actually used, and not so much as a pen or a paper clip littered the smooth, shiny surface. Then again, I shouldn't have been surprised. Damian Rivera didn't have to do something as common as *work*. From what I knew of him, his favorite hobbies were drinking, smoking, shopping for antiques, and flitting from one woman to the next. Not necessarily in that order.

Still, I'd come here to search for information about the Circle, so I opened all the drawers and tapped all around the desk, looking for hidden compartments. But the drawers were empty, except for some stacks of cocktail napkins and paper coasters, and no secret hidey-holes were carved into the wood.

Strike one.

Since nothing was in the desk, I moved over to the bar, perusing the shelves underneath it and the wooden ones behind it. But all I found were more napkins and coasters, along with several sterling-silver martini shakers and other old-fashioned drink-making accoutrements.

Strike two.

Frustration surged through me, but I forced myself to stay calm and search the rest of the office. I ran my hands over all of the furniture, looking for any secret compartments. Examined all of the vases, carvings, and statues for false bottoms. Tapped on the walls, searching for hidden panels. I even rolled back the thick rugs and used my magic to listen to the flagstones, just in case a safe was hidden in the floor.

But there was nothing. No secret compartments, no hidden panels, no floor safes.

Strike three, and I was out.

My frustration mixed with disappointment, both burning through my veins like bitter acid. A couple of weeks ago, I'd found several safety-deposit boxes full of information on the Circle that Fletcher Lane, my mentor, had compiled. For some reason that I didn't understand, Fletcher had only photos of the group's members, but it had been simple enough for me to get their names, especially since many of them were such wealthy, prominent Ashland citizens.

I'd scouted several of the Circle members, and Damian Rivera proved to be the easiest target with the least amount of security. So I'd broken in here tonight in hopes of learning more about the group, especially the identity of the mystery man who headed the organization, the bastard who'd ordered my mother's murder. But maybe there was a reason Rivera's security was so lax. Maybe he wasn't as important or as involved as I'd thought.

Still frustrated, I turned to the fireplace, which took up most of the wall across from the bar. Since any little bit of information could be important, I pulled out my phone and snapped shots of all the framed photos propped on the mantel, hoping that one of them might hold some small clue.

Not only did Damian Rivera love the finer things in life, but he also loved himself, since most of the photos were softly lit glamour shots showing off his wavy black hair, dark brown eyes, bronze skin, and startlingly white teeth. Rivera was in his prime, in his early thirties, and he was an exceptionally handsome man—and a thoroughly disgusting individual, even by Ashland's admittedly low, low standards. Not only was he a trust-fund baby, living off his family's wealth, never having worked a day in his life, but he'd also never faced any consequences for any of the despicable things he'd done.

And he had done plenty.

Silvio Sanchez, my personal assistant, had been looking into Rivera for only a few days, but he'd already found several arrests, mostly for DUIs, stretching all the way back to when Damian was a teenager. Rivera also had a violent temper and some serious anger-management issues. He'd beaten more than one girlfriend over the years, servants too, and had even put a couple of them in the hospital with broken bones and other serious injuries.

But all of that was nothing compared with the woman he'd killed.

One night during his college years, Rivera had gotten into his SUV and decided to see how fast he could drunkenly navigate Ashland's mountain roads. He'd come around one curve, crossed the center line, and plowed head-on into a sedan being driven by a single mother of two. She died instantly, but Rivera walked away from the crash with only minor injuries. He never was charged in the woman's death, thanks to his own mother, who pulled all the right strings and paid off all the right people to cover the whole thing up.

But Damian hadn't learned his lesson. He hadn't learned *anything*, since he'd been arrested for several more DUIs over the years, including his most recent offense on New Year's Eve just a few days ago. Not that he would face any consequences for that one either. His mama was long dead, but Damian still had someone to clean up his messes: Bruce Porter, a dwarf who'd been the Rivera family's head of security for years.

I stopped in front of a picture of Maria Rivera, a beautiful woman with long golden hair, brown eyes, and red lips. In the photo, she was smiling and standing between Damian and his father, Richard Rivera, with a dour-looking Bruce Porter hovering behind them in the distance. I raised my phone and snapped a shot of them—

"You've been in there a while now." Finn's voice sounded in my ear. "Does that mean you've finally found something good?"

"No," I muttered. "Just a lot of liquor, antiques, and photos."

"What kind of liquor?" Finn chirped with obvious interest. "Anything I would drink?"

I slid my phone into my jacket pocket and took a closer look at the rows of gleaming bottles behind the bar. "Oh, I think that you would drink them all, especially since Rivera's tastes are even more expensive than yours. Why, you would cackle with glee if you could see all the spirits he has in here."

"Well, why don't you bring me a bottle or two so I can cackle in person?" Finn chirped again. "I might as well get *something* for standing out here in the cold."

Even though he was in the woods outside and couldn't see me, I still rolled my eyes. "I came here for information on the Circle. Not to pilfer Daddy's booze like some naughty teenager."

"You say potato, I say *opportunity*."

I had started to respond when a faint *creak* sounded in the hallway outside, as though someone had stepped on a floorboard. I froze. The *creak* came again, louder and closer this time, and it was followed by something far, far worse: the distinctive *snick* of a key sliding in a lock.

"Let's have a drink," a faint, muffled voice said on the other side of the door.

✵ 2 ✵

I bolted for the window, intending to yank it up and dive through the opening. Otherwise, I'd be caught, and all of my careful surveillance of Damian Rivera and the other Circle members would have been for nothing.

But I'd forgotten about the white velvet bow hanging from the window frame, and I ran straight into it. Even worse, the fabric decided to stick to me, like an octopus clutching at my clothes.

"Shit," I hissed, trying to peel off the clinging velvet and open the window at the same time. "Shit, shit, shit!"

"Gin?" Finn's voice rang in my ear, sharp with worry. "What's wrong?"

I finally slapped the bow away and grabbed hold of the frame. "I thought you said that Rivera was attending some charity dinner tonight?"

"He is. According to my sources, he RSVP'd several

weeks ago. It didn't even start until eight o'clock, so the dinner shouldn't be anywhere close to being finished."

"Well, tell that to Rivera," I muttered. "Because he's right outside the office."

"Get out of there, Gin." Finn's voice crackled with even more worry. "Get out of there *right now*."

I hoisted up the window, wincing at the faint *screech* it made. "Way ahead of you."

As soon as the glass was out of the way, I ducked through the opening and stepped out onto the roof.

At least, I tried to.

My foot caught on that stupid bow again, and my leg stuck straight out in midair, as though I were doing a complicated yoga pose. I ground my teeth and yanked my foot free of the clutching fabric. The sudden, violent jerking motion pitched me forward, but I managed to stagger away from the window and catch myself before I did a header onto the roof or, worse, fell off it completely.

The second I regained my balance, I whipped around and hurried back over to the window, reaching for the frame to push it down.

Across the office, the antique crystal knob turned, and the door rattled, as though someone was putting his shoulder into the wood to force it open.

"Damn door always sticks," a deep male voice said.

The crystal knob turned again, and the door finally swung open. I grabbed the frame and shoved the window down as fast as I could. But I didn't have the best grip on it, and I didn't manage to close it all the way. I grunted, trying to force the window down that final inch, even as a man stepped into the office.

If I could see him, then he could see me, so I abandoned the window and lurched to the side to get out of sight. My heart hammered in my chest, beating up into my throat, and I snapped my hand down to my side, palming a knife and waiting for the inevitable shouts of surprise and discovery.

One . . . two . . . three . . . four . . . five . . .

Ten . . . twenty . . . thirty . . .

Forty-five . . . sixty . . . ninety . . .

I counted off the seconds in my head, but more than a minute passed, and no alarms blared. Instead, something else echoed out of the office and through the slightly open window to me.

Tinkle-tinkle.

The distinctive sound of ice cubes dropping into a glass, followed by the *crack* of a bottle opening and a steady *glug-glug-glug* of liquid, eased some of my worry. Still gripping my knife, I dropped into a low crouch, crept forward, and peered through the glass.

Sure enough, Damian Rivera had come home early from his charity dinner. He looked the same as in all the glamour shots on the fireplace mantel—black hair, perfect teeth, trim figure poured into an expensive gray suit. The only things that the airbrushed photos didn't show were the red flush that stained his bronze cheeks and his slow, exaggerated movements. Someone had already had a few too many.

And he was intent on having even more. Rivera tossed back his Scotch and poured himself another, filling his glass almost to the top, like he was *dying* of thirst. He took another healthy swallow, draining half of the Scotch, before turning and gesturing at someone.

"Well, don't just stand out there," he said, his voice a suave purr. "Come in and have a drink."

A long-suffering sigh sounded, and another man stepped into my line of sight. With his black hair and expensive suit, he could have been an older, fifty-something clone of Damian Rivera, if not for the black goatee that clung to his chin and the displeased pucker of his lips. And unlike Rivera's sloppy state, this man's black eyes were sharp and clear and fixed in a cold, flat stare that I knew all too well.

Hugh Tucker, the Circle's number one vampire enforcer and my nemesis.

I sucked in a breath, my fingers curling even tighter around the knife in my hand.

"Gin?" I heard Finn's voice in my ear again. "What's going on? Are you okay?"

"I'm fine," I whispered. "I got back out onto the roof in time. Rivera's inside the office now. Tucker's with him."

"Be careful," Finn said. "If Tucker sees you—"

"I know, I know. Quiet now. I want to hear what they're saying."

A faint sound came through my transmitter, as though Finn had started to deliver another warning, but he fell silent. I scooted forward, tilting my head so that my ear was close to the window opening for optimal eavesdropping.

Tucker joined Rivera at the bar, although he didn't sit down on one of the padded stools. Instead, he watched his companion grab a second glass and fill it with ice and Scotch. Rivera pushed the glass across the bar to Tucker, but the vampire didn't deign to pick it up.

Rivera grinned, not bothered in the least by the other man's obvious hostility. He raised his own glass in a silent, mocking toast, drained all of the amber liquor inside, and smacked his lips. "You really should try the Scotch. It's Brighton's Best, straight from Bigtime, New York. Costs a fortune, but it's worth it."

Tucker's reply was a decidedly noncommittal "Mmm."

Rivera poured himself a third Scotch and moved away from the bar. He staggered across the office and flung himself down onto one of the brown leather couches, making it creak under his weight.

"So, Hugh," Rivera said, his voice slurring just a bit. "What was *so* important that I had to leave my dinner and my lovely lady and rush back to meet you?"

Instead of answering, Tucker headed over to the fireplace, moving down the line of photos and staring at each one in turn, just as I had done. His nostrils flared with disgust as he eyed all of Rivera's glamour shots, but he quickly moved past those, stopping at that picture of Richard and Maria Rivera standing with their son. Tucker's nostrils flared again, as though something about the photo greatly displeased him, and he nudged the frame with his index finger, so that it was crooked and out of line with the others.

"You know exactly why I'm here." Tucker crossed his arms over his chest and turned to face Rivera. "It's the same problem that I brought to your attention several weeks ago. One that you have done absolutely *nothing* to correct."

Rivera shrugged. "That's because I don't see it as a problem."

"Well, you should," Tucker snapped. "Since it is entirely your fault."

Rivera leaned back against the couch, settling himself even deeper into the plush leather. He toed off his black wing tips and propped his socked feet on an overstuffed ottoman that matched the couch.

"So what if it's my fault? No one knows about it, which means that no one's going to do anything about it. That means that it's not really a problem at all."

Tucker's eyes narrowed at Rivera's breezy tone, but the other man was too boozed up to notice the vampire's clenched jaw and how his index finger tapped impatiently against his opposite elbow. I got the impression that Hugh Tucker was one more cavalier dismissal away from crossing the office, snatching Damian Rivera up off the couch, and snapping his neck.

Well, that would have been fine and dandy with me. I didn't much care exactly how the members of the Circle died, only that their reign of terror ended and that they finally paid for ordering my mother's murder. For once, I actually found myself rooting for Tucker, hoping that he would give in to his anger and take care of Rivera once and for all.

But of course that didn't happen.

Tucker uncrossed his arms and smoothed his gray tie and matching suit jacket, using the motions to help get his anger and annoyance under control. His voice was as cold as the winter wind tangling my hair when he spoke again. "Well, *I* know about it, which means that *he* knows about it. You know as well as I do that he doesn't like complications, and he certainly doesn't need them, especially not now."

My eyes narrowed. *He?* Tucker had to be talking about his boss, the mysterious leader of the Circle who pulled the rest of the group's evil strings. Maybe tonight wouldn't be a complete bust after all.

Come on, Tuck. Say his name. That's all I need you to do. Say his name, say his name, say his name . . .

Rivera snorted. "Really? He doesn't want complications? You mean like all the ones you've caused by not killing Gin Blanco yet?"

Tucker stiffened at the insult.

Rivera gave him a smug smile, knowing that he'd scored a direct hit. "You know how our little group loves to gossip. I heard *all* about it. How you thought that you'd forced Blanco into finding and handing over those jewels from Deirdre's tourist-trap theme park. But Blanco hoodwinked you instead, didn't she? Gave you a bag full of fakes, and you were too stupid to know the difference. Why, the way *I* heard it, you proudly handed those fake jewels over to our fearless leader, and he was so angry that he crushed them all with his bare hands right in front of you, then made you clean up the mess."

Tucker's lips pressed into a tight line, but he didn't say anything.

"Face it, Hugh." Rivera's voice took on a sneering, mocking tone. "You might work for him, but you'll never be one of *us*. Not really. Never again. Not only did your father squander your family's wealth, but he also ruined your position in the group. You'll never get back that standing, that respect, no matter how hard you try."

Tucker's face remained flat and expressionless, but he couldn't hide the faint red blush creeping up his neck, almost as if he was embarrassed by Rivera's revelations.

I frowned. I'd thought that Hugh Tucker was second-in-command of the Circle, right below the mysterious *he*. But Rivera was making Tucker sound like some castoff, some poor country cousin who had fallen on hard times. Some servant the members of the Circle charitably let do their dirty work in exchange for the privilege of hovering in their highfalutin orbit. It almost made me feel sorry for the vampire.

Almost.

"And then, of course, there was your unfortunate choice of a woman back then, which only compounds all your many mistakes with Blanco now." Rivera's lips curved up into a cruel smile. "Tell me, Hugh, are you still carrying a torch for Eira Snow after all these years?"

I gasped, shock jolting through my body like a lightning bolt. I lurched back from the window, causing one of my feet to slip out from under me. My other foot went flying, and my ass hit the roof a second later.

Thud.

For a moment, I just sat there, eyes wide, mouth gaping open, arms and legs splayed out at awkward angles, knife dangling from my fingertips, as though someone had just shot me in the heart and let my body drop wherever it might. My mind struggled to process Rivera's words, as if I were trying to translate some foreign language that I'd never heard before.

Hugh Tucker and my mother?

No—no, no, no, no, no.

As soon as the horrible thought formed in my mind, I forced it away. There was *no way* that Tucker had loved my mother. Not when he'd stood by and let Mab Monroe kill her. But my mind kept churning, and another equally horrible thought popped into my head.

My mother couldn't have possibly *loved* Tucker in return . . . could she?

No—no, no, no, no, no.

Bile rose in my throat, and I thought that I was going to vomit all over the roof—

Soft scuffs sounded, penetrating my sick shock, and I noticed a shadow growing larger and larger next to me, as though someone was walking toward the window and blocking the light from inside the office. I hadn't made a lot of noise falling on my ass, but Tucker was a vampire, and the blood he drank was more than enough to give him enhanced senses, including supersharp hearing.

Years of Fletcher's training took over, cutting through the last of my shock, and I scrambled to my feet, lunged forward, and pressed myself up against the side of the mansion, leaning my head forward just enough so that I could still see in through the glass.

Not a moment too soon.

Tucker appeared in the window. The vampire pushed the white velvet bow out of the way and stepped forward, his nose almost pressed up against the glass, peering out into the darkness beyond. No doubt his sight was as sharp as his hearing, and I didn't dare move a muscle for fear that he would notice me out of the corner of his eye.

Even though my heart was pounding, I forced myself to take slow, deep breaths through my nose and exhale the same way, not making any more noise than absolutely necessary.

After several long, tense seconds, Tucker relaxed and drew back, although his gaze dropped to the window, which was still cracked open. His eyebrows drew together, as though he was puzzled about why the window would be open at all on such a cold night.

"Well?" Rivera called out, his voice still snide. "You didn't answer my question about Eira. Still missing your little lovebird? From what I've been told, the two of you made quite the handsome couple back in the day."

Couple?

No—no, no, no, no, no.

The denial rose up in me again, along with that bile in my throat, but I forced myself to swallow it all down. Now was not the time to let my emotions get the best of me.

Tucker's face twisted at Rivera's mocking tone, and his black eyes practically glowed with murderous rage. Whatever had happened between him and my mother, whatever *feelings* he might have had for her, it was a chink in his armor, and Rivera had scored another bull's-eye.

Once again, I thought that Tucker might give in to his rage, whirl around, and attack the other man, but instead he tilted his head to the side, studying the open window again, as though it held some great secret. A second later, his face smoothed out, and his lips lifted into a faint smile, as though he was pleased by something. I stayed anchored in place, scarcely daring to breathe, thinking that the vampire had spotted me after all and expecting him to yell out that there was an intruder on the roof.

But Tucker left the window open, turned around, and strode out of my line of sight. "I didn't come here tonight to talk about the past. Only your future, Damian. Which will be decidedly short and unpleasant if you don't take care of things the way that he wants you to."

Rivera scoffed, and the ice *tinkle-tinkle*d in his glass again as he downed the rest of his Scotch.

I waited several seconds, giving Tucker plenty of time to move away from the window, then sidled forward and peered through the glass again. The vampire was back standing beside the fireplace, his arms crossed over his chest, staring at Rivera, who had set aside his empty glass and was now yanking off his tie, completely unconcerned by Tucker's threats.

Tap-tap-tap.

A soft knock sounded on the door, and a third man stepped into the office: Bruce Porter, Rivera's head of security.

Porter was a dwarf, five feet tall with a compact, muscled body that looked even harder than the stones that made up the fireplace. He too wore a suit, although it wasn't nearly as expensive as his boss's. His eyes were a pale blue, while his gunmetal-gray hair had been buzz-cut so short that it was barely more than bristle covering his head. His fifty-something face bore the deep lines and perpetual ruddy skin of someone who'd spent years standing in the sun waiting for other people to tell him what to do.

Porter moved with stiff, military precision as he strode

over and snapped to attention at Rivera's elbow. "Sir," he said in a deep, soft voice. "As requested, I escorted your lady friend to the estate. She's waiting in your bedroom."

Rivera bared his teeth in a predatory grin. "Good man, Porter."

The dwarf nodded at Rivera, then politely tipped his head to Tucker too. For a moment, the vampire's gaze flitted from Porter over to the photos on the mantel. Then Tucker looked at the dwarf and returned his nod before focusing on Rivera again.

"You have exactly one week to take care of your problem," Tucker said. "And not a second longer."

Rivera chuckled, squirmed even deeper into the couch cushions, and laced his fingers behind his head. "I might actually be frightened if it were anyone but you threatening me. Face it, Hugh. We both know that you're just a barking dog on a chain. There's no real *bite* to you at all."

Once again, that thin, pleased smile played across Tucker's lips, as if the other man's sneering dismissal was exactly what he wanted to hear. "Don't say that I didn't warn you."

His final threat delivered, Tucker strode out of the office.

* 3 *

For a mad, mad moment, I thought about chasing after Tucker.

Leaping off the roof, running around to the front of the mansion, and attacking the vampire before he got into his car and drove away. Or at least following him back to his lair so that I could decide what to do next. Maybe even capture, question, and kill him, if the circumstances were right.

Damian Rivera wasn't going anywhere, but I still had no clue where Tucker hung his hat when he wasn't skulking around Ashland threatening people. Plus, if I got my hands on the vampire, I could make him tell me what was going on with Rivera and who the leader of the Circle was.

And what, if any, relationship he'd had with my mother.

Hugh Tucker and my mother. Together. A couple.

The thought had never occurred to me before tonight.

Never. But Rivera's mocking words had made it sound like the two of them had been involved in some sort of romantic relationship. So had Tucker's reactions to Rivera's taunts. There had to be some other explanation—please, *please*, let there be some other explanation—but try as I might, I couldn't come up with one. Neither man had had any reason to lie about something like that.

Hugh Tucker and my mother.

The words kept running through my head like a really bad song lyric that I couldn't forget no matter how hard I tried. The mere idea of them together boggled my mind. No, it was worse than that. It was like an elemental Fire bomb had exploded in my heart, obliterating everything that I thought I knew, burning away all of the clues, puzzle pieces, and broken threads that I'd spent so much time, energy, and effort uncovering, arranging, and stringing into some kind of order. Every time I got some answers about the Circle, they only raised more questions about the shadowy group members, their twisted motives, and why they had killed my mother.

But as much as I wanted answers, as much as I *needed* them for my own sanity, I couldn't go after Tucker. More guards were stationed at the front of the mansion, and attacking him here would tell the Circle that I'd identified Rivera as one of the group's members. It would destroy my slim advantage.

So I had to let Tucker go.

Unfortunately.

Dammit.

"What was that about?" Porter asked, still standing by his boss's elbow.

Rivera eyed the dwarf, a bit of annoyance flashing in his dark gaze, and waved his hand. "Nothing. Just Hugh trying to exert what little power he thinks he has. I've already forgotten all about him."

He got to his feet, grabbed his empty glass, and shoved it at Porter, like a child asking his father to put away his favorite toy. The dwarf stepped forward and whisked the glass away from Rivera with a smooth, practiced motion, as though he'd done the same thing a hundred times before. No doubt he had.

"Send the usual bottles of champagne to my bedroom," Rivera commanded, heading toward the door, his body listing from side to side like a ship bobbing along on the waves.

I couldn't see how he was still standing, given all the Scotch he'd drunk in the office, in addition to whatever other liquor he must have downed earlier. But I supposed that he'd built up a considerable tolerance. Damian Rivera could probably drink ten men under the table and still be thirsty for more.

Porter nodded. "Of course."

Rivera staggered out the open door without a backward glance.

Porter moved around the office, putting away the glass, grabbing Rivera's discarded wing tips, and tidying up. The only mildly interesting thing he did was go over to the fireplace, walk down the row of photos on the mantel, and nudge each one a few centimeters to the left and right, even though they were already as straight as could be. Someone was a little obsessive about having everything perfectly in place. Or perhaps Porter knew that Damian would take his wrath out on him if anything in the office was the slightest bit askew.

Porter frowned when he came to the family photo of the Riveras, the one that Tucker had nudged out of place, and he spent the better part of a minute fussing with it, sliding the frame back and forth until it was just where he wanted it.

Finally satisfied, Porter nodded to himself and glanced around the office, as if checking to make sure that there was nothing else he needed to do in here tonight. His gaze slid past the window, and he did a double take and looked back at the frame, as if he'd finally noticed that the window was cracked open.

Time to go.

Even as Porter walked toward the window, I moved away from it, slid my knife back up my sleeve, and darted across the roof. I lowered myself onto the trellis and quickly climbed down to the ground.

The guard patrolling the back side of the mansion was still engrossed in his video game, making it easy for me to sneak across the lawn and back into the woods, where Finn was waiting. Judging from the faint path he'd worn in the leaves, it looked as though he'd spent the last several minutes pacing back and forth.

"What took you so long?" Finn groused, holstering his gun. "I was getting worried."

I arched my eyebrows. "You? Worried about me? Aw, I'm touched."

"Well, you should be," he groused again, pushing his

black toboggan out of the way so he could reach up and massage his forehead. "You just gave me a whole new set of wrinkles."

"Poor baby," I crooned. "Then again, you aren't getting any younger. Maybe you should let Jo-Jo give you some Air elemental facials. Before all those wrinkles and nasty crow's-feet get any worse than they already are."

"Crow's-feet!" Finn hissed in an indignant tone, slapping his hands on his hips. "I do *not* have crow's-feet!"

I just smiled and walked away, knowing that this time I'd gotten the last word in.

Finn and I left Damian Rivera's mansion and hiked through the woods, our breath steaming out around us in eerie white vapor trails. When the lights of the mansion faded away, we pulled small flashlights out of our pockets and clicked them on. We were the only things moving in the night, besides the sluggish water. The back side of the Rivera estate butted up against the Aneirin River, and the woods ended in a series of high, rocky cliffs that overlooked the water far, far below.

Finn stopped, shone his flashlight over the side of the cliffs, and let out a low whistle. "Wouldn't want to fall off here."

I had started to snipe that if he didn't want to fall, then he should probably get away from the edge when a series of low, harsh mutters drifted over to my ears. For a moment, I thought that someone was at the bottom of the steep cliffs, moaning for help, but then I noticed a glint of glass out of the corner of my eye. I turned in its direction, shining my flashlight into the darkness, and spotted the faint outlines of a small, crumbling stone cottage off in the distance.

The cottage was hidden back in the trees and covered with thick strands of dead kudzu, camouflaging it almost entirely. I studied the structure, wondering if some homeless person might have set up camp inside, but no lights or lanterns flickered in the windows, and no smoke drifted up out of the kudzu-covered chimney.

Despite the fact that the cottage was obviously abandoned and had been for quite some time, the stones still muttered with notes of blood, violence, pain, and death. Odd. I wouldn't think that enough people would be around way out here to leave any emotional vibrations behind in the rocks. But I supposed that more than one unwary hiker had slipped off the cliffs and fallen to their death on the rocky riverbank below. Perhaps those sounds had drifted over to the cottage and slowly permeated the stones over the years.

"What is it?" Finn asked, scanning the woods with his flashlight, his hand dropping to the gun holstered at his waist. "What's wrong?"

I shook my head to clear the disturbing mutterings out of my mind. "Nothing. Let's go."

We walked on and left the cliffs, the cottage, and the river behind. While we hiked back to the car, I told Finn everything that Tucker had said, including his threats to Rivera about cleaning up whatever mess he'd made. The only thing I left out was Rivera's mocking words about Tucker's supposed relationship with my mother. I still needed some time to process that bombshell before I shared it with anyone else.

"What do you think Damian's done that has the rest of the Circle so worried?" Finn mused. "From your surveillance and all the info that Silvio and I have dug up, Damian Rivera seems perfectly content to spend his mama's money and drink himself to death. I wouldn't think him sober or ambitious enough to stir up any kind of trouble. At least, not the kind of trouble that would bring a guy like Hugh Tucker to his door to tell him to knock it off—or else."

I shrugged. "Who knows? Probably something to do with money. That seems to be a major concern of the Circle. The group has probably been hurting for cash ever since Deirdre Shaw lost a good chunk of their resources. Rivera's fortune is still intact, though, and he seems to have more money than any of the other members we've identified so far. Maybe he's not paying his dues or helping them build their reserves back up. I just wish the two of them had dropped the big boss's name. I still haven't been able to figure out who he is, despite all the photos Fletcher left in those safety-deposit boxes."

Finn gave me a sympathetic look. He knew how important it was to me to track down the man who'd ordered my mother's murder, and he, Silvio, and the rest of our friends had been working right alongside me the past few weeks to uncover the information. Thanks to Fletcher's photos, we'd managed to identify who we thought were the major players in the Circle—at least the ones who were still alive—but I wanted *more*.

I wanted the ringleader, the man who was in charge of this monstrous hydra. I wanted to know exactly what my mother's role in the group had been. What they had made her do and why. What my mother had been plotting, what move she'd made against the Circle that was such a threat that the ringleader had ordered Mab Monroe to burn her to death.

But most of all, I wanted to confront—and then kill—the source of so many nightmares in my life.

"Don't worry, Gin. We'll find the bastard sooner or later, and then you can carve him up to your heart's delight." Finn slung his arm around my shoulder in a reassuring hug. "But in the meantime, don't frown. It makes your face scrunch up."

"Worried about *my* wrinkles now?" I teased.

He flashed me a charming, devilish grin, his green eyes as bright as holiday lights in the darkness. "Got to keep my deadliest girl looking young and beautiful."

I snorted and elbowed him in the ribs. "I am not *your* girl. I am my *own* girl."

"Damn skippy you are."

Finn hugged me again, silently offering his brotherly love and support the way he had since this whole mess with the Circle had started. I hugged him back, and we walked on.

Thirty minutes later, we reached the edge of the woods and stepped out into a ritzy subdivision, one of many in Northtown, the part of Ashland where the social, magical, and monetary elite lived. Cookie-cutter mansions dotted the gently rolling lawns in front of us. Finn and I headed over to the curb where his Aston Martin sat in front of a mansion that was currently under construction. The expensive car seamlessly blended in with all the

Audis, BMWs, and Mercedes that were parked in the spacious driveways up and down the street.

Finn and I slid into the vehicle, and he cranked the engine and blasted the heat. We both sat there in silence for a few minutes, slowly thawing out after our long, cold trek through the woods.

"Where to?" Finn asked. "Our supersecret hideout?"

He was referring to our current base of operations, a battered old metal container that was parked in a shipping yard several miles down the river from our current location. Lorelei Parker, one of Ashland's many underworld bosses, ran the shipping yard, but she'd given me a container, and I'd made it my own personal safety-deposit box, storing all the information I had about the Circle inside it. Hugh Tucker already knew far too much about me and my friends, but he hadn't sniffed out the hideout yet or the fact that I'd identified several members of the Circle—and I wanted to keep it that way.

I shook my head. "Nah. Not tonight. I didn't learn anything earth-shattering."

Of course that wasn't true, but I wasn't ready to talk about Tucker's relationship—or whatever had been going on—with my mother. "Besides, it's late, it's cold, and I'm too tired and cranky to think about conspiracies any more tonight. Home, Finn. Home."

He winked at me. "As my lady wishes," he crooned in a really bad English accent.

"Are you going to talk like that the entire ride home?"

"But of course, my lady," he said, thickening the cheesy accent. "Since I'm acting as your personal driver and chauffeur tonight, I really insist on sounding the part. Anything less would be unseemly. Don't you think?"

I groaned, but Finn grinned, reached up, and tipped an imaginary hat to me. Then he threw the car into gear, steered away from the curb, and drove out of the subdivision.

❊ 4 ❊

Finn drove me to Fletcher's house—my house now—and dropped me off. A familiar car was sitting in the driveway next to mine, and the front porch light was on.

"What's Owen doing here?" Finn asked, waggling his eyebrows at me. "You guys having a hot late-night date? A little *bow-chicka-wow-wow* time?"

I punched him in the shoulder. "Your maturity never ceases to amaze me."

He snickered and started to tease me some more, but I drew my fist back again in a clear warning about what would happen if he kept on yapping.

Finn threw up his own hands in mock surrender. "Fine, fine. I'll keep my mouth shut." He grinned. "Just don't do anything that I wouldn't do."

I snorted. "You would do anything and everything."

His grin widened. "I know. That's what makes life fun."

And just like that, Finnegan Lane triumphantly got the last word in, beating me two to one tonight.

Finn promised to let me know if he found out anything else about Damian Rivera or what he might have done. I got out of the car, stood on the front porch, and watched until his taillights disappeared down the driveway, then went inside and locked the door behind me.

"Honey, I'm home!" I called out, singing the old cliché.

"In the den!" Owen called back.

I toed off my boots, yanked off my toboggan, and shrugged out of my fleece jacket before walking down the long hallway to the back of the house. I reached the doorway to the den and stopped, my eyes widening at the sight in front of me.

Normally, the den was, well, just a den, with a couch, television, tables, and other well-worn furniture. But tonight it had been transformed into a cozy, romantic space. White and red candles covered the end tables, casting out a warm, soft, flickering light. Thick pillows large enough to sit on had been positioned all around the coffee table in the center of the room, adding to the intimate feel.

Fine china and silverware covered the table alongside crystal wineglasses. Dinner had already been served, and steak and mashed potatoes were on the menu, along with a garden salad and a basket of bread that had just been taken out of the oven, given the delicious curls of steam wisping up from it. Even better, a chocolate cheesecake topped with fresh raspberries sat perched off to one side of the table, just begging to be cut into. My stomach growled in anticipation.

"Do you like it?" a low, husky voice asked.

I looked over at Owen Grayson, my significant other, who was arranging a few more candles on the fireplace mantel. He was a little more than six feet tall, with a body that was all strong, delicious muscle. He struck a match, and the resulting glow highlighted his black hair and rugged features, including his slightly crooked nose and the faint white scar that slashed across his chin.

"What's all this?"

Owen finished lighting the last candle, blew out the match, and set it aside. A teasing grin lifted his lips. "Not what you were expecting?"

I shook my head. "When you called and said that you wanted to come over tonight, I expected pizza and a movie. Not all this."

"Well, with all of us working nonstop to learn more about the Circle, we haven't exactly had time for a proper date these past few weeks." Owen gestured at the candles, pillows, and gourmet food. "So I thought I'd change that."

I went over and looped my arms around his neck, staring up into his violet eyes. "Have I told you lately that you're the best?"

"Right back at you, babe." He grinned and drew me closer. "Right back at you."

I stood on my tiptoes and kissed him, opening my mouth and seeking his tongue with my own. Owen kissed me back, holding me tight. My fingers started to roam down his chest, but he caught my hands, brought them up to his lips, and kissed the spider rune scar branded into each of my palms.

"No funny business," he teased. "Not yet anyway. I spent way too much time cooking dinner for it to go to waste."

I peeked around his broad shoulder at the take-out containers stacked by the trash can in the corner. "Really? Because those containers make it look like the fine folks at Underwood's spent way too much time cooking dinner."

Owen laughed. "Okay, okay, you got me. But I did painstakingly reheat everything."

I clasped his hands to my heart and batted my eyelashes at him. "My hero."

He laughed again and pulled me over to the table. We sat down on the pillows on the floor and dug into our meal. Underwood's was the most expensive restaurant in the city, and the food matched its excellent reputation. The steak, mashed potatoes, and garden salad might have been simple dishes, but they'd been made with the very best ingredients, elevating them to new heights. And the cheesecake was a chocolate dream, melting in my mouth bite after sinfully rich bite, along with the tart, refreshing bursts of the raspberries.

After dinner, we lay down on the pillows on the floor, Owen with his arm around my shoulder and me with my head on his chest, and I told him everything that had happened at the Rivera estate, including Damian's dig at Tucker about his feelings for my mother. I'd gotten over my initial shock and denial, and Owen was the perfect person, the perfect sounding board, to help me work through all my turbulent feelings about the startling revelation.

"Hugh Tucker and your mother?" Owen asked. "You really think they were an item way back when?"

"I don't know. I don't remember Eira ever mentioning him, not even in passing. The only memory I have of them together is when Tucker threatened her in her office the night of her last Christmas party."

Ever since I'd found out about the Circle, I'd been desperately trying to remember every single thing I could about my mother, searching my mind for the smallest, faintest images of her face, smile, laugh, words. The memory of Tucker threatening Eira had bubbled up to the surface of my brain a few weeks ago when I was sleeping, dreaming, as did so many of the bad things in my past.

"Maybe you'll remember more about them," Owen said. "Or at least about your mom."

"I hope so. I still don't know what she did for the Circle or why they had her killed."

My gray gaze drifted up to a series of framed drawings behind the candles on the mantel. I focused on the first drawing, of a snowflake, my mother Eira Snow's rune, the symbol for icy calm. Her matching pendant was draped over the frame, and the flickering candlelight made the silverstone snowflake necklace gleam as though it had just been freshly minted. The pain of her loss knifed through my heart, as it had a thousand times before, still as sharp and bright as her rune pendant, along with equally strong stabs of cold rage and icy determination.

"If my mother and Tucker were involved at some point . . ." My voice trailed off for a moment. "Well, that just makes me even more determined to kill him."

"Why is that?"

I propped myself up on my elbow so that I could look at Owen. "Let's say that Tucker had feelings for my mom, cared about her in some way, like Rivera claimed. Let's say that Tucker even loved her at one point."

"Okay . . ." Owen said, not quite sure where I was going with this.

"Then why didn't he help her? Why didn't he warn her that his boss wanted her dead and was sending Mab Monroe to do the job? Why didn't he fucking *save* her?"

My voice cracked on the last few words, and I had to blink back the tears suddenly stinging my eyes. My heart ached and ached, each beat bringing a fresh wave of loss and longing with it, as though I were stabbing myself in the chest over and over again with one of my own knives.

"Oh, Gin," Owen whispered, sympathy filling his face. "I'm sorry. So sorry."

I shook my head. "It's not your fault. It's *his* fault. And I'm going to make him pay for it—all of it."

"I know you will," he whispered again. "I know you will."

Owen pressed his lips to mine in a sweet, comforting kiss, and I slowly lost myself in him. I couldn't do anything about Hugh Tucker tonight, and I didn't want to waste another second of my time with Owen thinking about the past.

So I focused on the man I loved, on the feel of his lips against mine, the warm brush of his breath on my face, the faint taste of chocolate and raspberries that lingered on his tongue from the cheesecake we'd eaten. I concentrated on each sensation, along with the slow slide of his hands up and down my back, until my heartache and rage faded away, melted by the growing heat between us.

We finally broke apart, and I nuzzled my nose up against his. "So . . . think we can finally get down to that funny business now?"

Owen laughed, his violet eyes gleaming with anticipation. "Oh, I think that can be arranged."

Our lips met again, and the familiar fire ignited between us. We kissed again, and again, and again, each meeting of our tongues longer and more intense than the last. We rolled around on the pillows, scattering them all over the floor, our hands roaming up and down each other's body.

And that's when we met the first bits of resistance.

"Stupid winter clothes," I grumbled, yanking at the buttons on his jeans, trying to get them open. "Why are you wearing so many of them?"

"I could say the same thing about you," Owen muttered, fumbling with my turtleneck, trying to shove it up out of the way.

We stopped, looked at each other, and started laughing. Our chuckles rang out through the den, growing louder and louder, and we collapsed onto the pillows again, both of us laughing as hard as we could.

"Okay, okay," I said, when the last of our chuckles had faded away. "Take two."

This time, we were far more sensible about things. We both stripped off our clothes, then came together in the middle of the floor again. But our laughter was gone now, and we were ready—*hungry*—for a different kind of teasing.

Owen grabbed a condom from his wallet and put it on, since we always used extra protection in addition to the little white pills that I took. I admired the rippling of muscle in his arms and shoulders, the sprinkling of dark hair that arrowed down his abs, and especially the hot, fierce light in his eyes as he turned toward me.

I got up on my knees, and we met in the middle of the floor, our lips and tongues thrusting together, our hands roaming, kneading and caressing all the sweet spots that each of us knew that the other liked. Hot, electric desire sizzled through my veins, and I couldn't kiss him enough, couldn't touch him enough, couldn't get close enough to him.

Owen let out a low, primal growl deep in his throat, picked me up, and set me on the edge of the coffee table. I leaned back, and he feasted on my breasts, licking and teasing my nipples with his tongue and teeth. More heat spiked through me, and I groaned and pulled him down on top of me.

Owen's hand slid down my stomach, and I opened my legs. He eased a finger inside me, drawing those slow, deliberate patterns that he knew drove me crazy. He pulled back ever so slightly, his tongue darting in and out of my mouth in time with his finger. I moaned with each glide of him against me.

I didn't want to wait any longer, and neither did he. I put my hands on his shoulders and rolled us both off the coffee table and onto the floor. The pillows broke our fall, and we crashed together once more. I locked my legs around his waist and pulled him deep inside me, moaning at how good he felt sliding against me.

Back and forth, we rolled on the floor, kissing, caressing, and thrusting against each other, trying to wring as much pleasure out of this moment as possible. Our movements became more and more frantic, our kisses longer, our thrusts harder and deeper, until finally we both reached the peak of our pleasure and went over the edge together.

Bow-chicka-wow-wow indeed.

I woke up a couple of hours later, my arms still wrapped around Owen, the two of us cuddled together in the mounds of pillows on the floor. He was snoring, the sound vibrating out of his chest like a low, rolling drumbeat. I lay there for a minute, enjoying the feel of his warm, strong body next to mine and the steady, soothing *thump-thump-thump* of his heart under my fingertips.

But as wonderful as tonight had been, I was too restless and had too many things on my mind to just relax and lie there next to Owen. So I slipped out of his arms and covered him with a blanket from the couch. Then I grabbed another blanket, wrapped it around myself, and left the den.

I headed into Fletcher's office—my office now—snapped on the lights, and went over to his battered wooden desk. Ever since the old man's murder more than a year ago, I'd slowly been going through several decades' worth of papers, photos, and other information that he'd collected and squirreled away in here. Now, finally, everything was organized and neatly filed away, and I could find info on just about anyone in the Ashland underworld in a matter of minutes. I'd even been updating and adding to the files myself, with Silvio's help. But tonight I only had eyes for the bottle of gin and the glass perched on the center of the desk.

I plopped into Fletcher's chair, poured myself a healthy amount of gin, and drank it down, relishing the sweet burn of the liquor sliding down my throat. I poured a second glass, leaned back in the chair, and eyed the photo of the old man that I had placed on the corner of the desk.

Walnut-brown hair, green eyes, tan wrinkled features. Fletcher smiled as he looked out over the scenic landscape of Bone Mountain, where we'd gone hiking together so many times over the years. This photo was one of my favorite shots of him, and now that I'd cleaned out his office and made it my own, I often found myself coming in here and looking at the picture for guidance, even if he was dead and buried.

"Did you know about Tucker and my mother?" I asked. "Did you have any clue about the two of them? Because it was certainly news to me."

Of course, Fletcher didn't answer. He just kept looking out over the mountain view and grinning his sly grin, as if he knew all these secrets and was silently telling me that I'd have to find the answers myself.

Fletcher had set this whole thing up like an enormous treasure hunt, with one clue leading to another clue, all of them slowly revealing more and more information about the Circle, its members, and my mother. Not for the first time, I wondered why he'd done things this way, instead of just leaving all the information in one place for me to find. Specifically, why he hadn't included a photo of the leader of the Circle with all the other pictures that had been in his safety-deposit boxes. What was so special, terrifying, or horrifying about this man that Fletcher had deliberately left him out?

It was almost like Fletcher was building up to something—some secret that he knew would further rock my world—and he was trying to get me ready for it, trying to prepare me for the shocking truth, trying to soften the blow by only giving me small dribs and drabs of information along the way. I had the sinking feeling that my mother and Tucker being involved wasn't the worst of it. Not by a long shot.

The old man might have thought he was protecting me, but it was damn frustrating to always have more questions than answers.

"Well, Fletcher?" I asked, still staring at his picture, the office walls soaking up my soft words. "Care to tell me what you were thinking? What am I going to find out when I finally get to the bottom of this crazy rabbit hole?"

Just saying the words made me feel better, like the old man was sitting here with me, like we were discussing a new assignment, a new mission, the way we had so many times in the past. And it also calmed some of my turbulent emotions, although it left more questions in their wake.

If Damian Rivera's mocking works were true, then Hugh Tucker had been sweet on my mother. At some point, he had cared about her, enough for other people to notice and remember it, even now, all these years later. Maybe the two of them had even had a romantic relationship before my mother met and married my father, Tristan. I could accept all those possibilities, although they still boggled my mind. Try as I might, I just couldn't picture Eira, who'd always been so warm, caring, and considerate, with someone like Tucker. Someone so cold, heartless, and ruthless.

Someone so much like, well, *me*.

Then again, it had taken me years to get to this point. I hadn't started out as a stone-cold killer. Once upon a time, I'd been a sweet, innocent little girl without a care in the world. But that little girl had burned to ash right alongside Eira and my older sister, Annabella, the night Mab Monroe murdered them and tortured me.

Every single step I'd taken since then had seemed perfectly logical, necessary, and right at the time for my own protection, survival, and self-interest. Living on the streets, hiding my true identity, taking Fletcher up on his offer to train me, becoming the Spider. Now I was a notorious assassin with a perpetual target on my back. Not exactly where I'd thought I'd wind up, but it was my life, for better or worse, and I was going to make the best of it.

For the first time, I wondered what had happened to Hugh Tucker to turn him into the man he was today. The one who did so many bad things on someone else's orders. I wondered how fast the vampire's downward spiral had been. I wondered what the tipping point had been, the one thing that had dragged him down, down, down into the darkness, never to surface into the light again.

My own downward spiral had started with the murders of my mother and Annabella. But what had been Tucker's trigger? The loss of his family's wealth, power, position, and prestige? His own ruthless ambition to get it all back? Helping to orchestrate my mother's death? Or perhaps all the dirty deeds he'd done for the Circle since then? The ones that had chipped away at his soul a little bit at a time until now there was nothing left?

In the end, Tucker's reasons were his own, and I doubted that I would ever learn them. And however sad and tragic his motives, however they might pluck the heartstrings, they still didn't change everything the bastard had done to me and my friends. Tucker's rationale didn't change how he'd stood by and watched Deirdre Shaw weasel her way into Finn's life, pretending to be a doting mother, when all she really wanted was to rob the First Trust bank. It didn't change how Tucker had drugged and kidnapped Finn, Bria, and Owen so that I would hand over some precious jewels that Deirdre had hidden from him and the Circle. And it certainly didn't change how many times he'd tried to kill me.

Or the fact that I would kill him, when the time came.

Because that sweet, innocent little girl was long gone, and this stone-cold killer would do whatever it took to protect the friends and family that she had left.

Feeling much calmer, I raised my glass in a toast to Fletcher's photo. "Good talk."

I downed the gin and set the empty glass aside. Then I got to my feet, turned off the lights, and went back to Owen to try to get what sleep I could tonight.

✲ 5 ✲

I didn't think that I would sleep, but eventually my questions faded away, and I snuggled up next to Owen and slipped into a soothing blackness.

I woke up the next morning feeling refreshed and already plotting how I could find out what Damian Rivera had done that had upset Tucker. Maybe I could kidnap and put the squeeze on Rivera, threaten to go public with his many sins, unless he told me who the leader of the Circle was. After that, well, I would have to keep Rivera from ratting me out to Tucker.

Of course, the obvious answer was to kill him. I didn't have any problem with that, but I couldn't just stab him to death the way I normally would. Tucker would realize that it was me and that I was onto him and the rest of the Circle, and then I'd totally lose the element of surprise. No, I'd have to figure out some other way to silence Rivera, something that looked like a plausible accident. I hadn't done many of those sorts of jobs as the Spider, but I'd think of something.

I always did.

Owen and I chowed down on a light but filling breakfast of egg-white omelets loaded with spinach, cheddar cheese, and ham, along with whipped vanilla Greek yogurt topped with crunchy homemade granola and fresh fruit. Once we'd finished eating, we went our separate ways for the day.

I headed upstairs, showered, and changed into a pair of black boots and jeans, topped by a royal-blue sweater. My spider rune pendant glinted brightly against the fabric, while a matching ring glimmered on my right index finger. Normally, I wore my rune tucked away inside my clothes, but today I wanted it out for everyone to see. I wasn't quite sure why. Maybe it was my own small way of officially declaring war on Rivera and Tucker.

Whatever it was, it felt good.

It was almost nine thirty by the time I drove downtown, parked my car, and made my way to the Pork Pit, my barbecue restaurant. I stood at the corner of the brick building and eyed the flow of traffic on the street and sidewalks, but the air was bitterly cold, with a few flurries fluttering on the breeze, and people all ducked their heads and hurried on toward their destinations.

No one gave me a second glance, so I did my usual check for rune traps and bombs on the front door and windows. Finding everything clean, I headed inside to do another equally thorough check. But no one had broken into the restaurant overnight, so I pulled a blue apron on over my clothes and got to work.

The first thing I did was mix a big vat of Fletcher's secret barbecue sauce and let it simmer away on one of the back burners. The rich, heady smell of cumin, black pepper, and other spices permeated the restaurant, making it feel warm and inviting. Once the sauce was cooking, I moved on to my other chores, including wiping down all the tables and the long counter that ran along the back wall.

About ten o'clock, a loud knock sounded on the front door, followed by the *click* of a key turning in the lock. Silvio Sanchez, my personal assistant, stepped inside and shut and locked the door behind him. The vampire sighed as he took off his hat and jacket and unwound the thick gray scarf from around his neck.

"Days like this make me glad that you work out of a restaurant," he said. "No matter how cold the weather, it's always nice and toasty-warm in here."

"Happy to oblige," I drawled.

I finished wiping down the counter, then moved over to the stove to stir the still-simmering sauce. Silvio sat on his usual stool at the counter, pulled out his phone and tablet, and fired everything up for the morning briefing.

"So I got your texts last night, and I have to admit that I'm as baffled as Finn is," Silvio said, swiping through some screens on his tablet. "I can't imagine what Damian Rivera has possibly done to warrant a personal visit from Hugh Tucker. Apart from his recent DUI arrest and general boorish and drunken state, Rivera's been behaving himself lately."

"Well, he's done something wrong, and I want to

know what it is. Especially since he seems like the easiest member of the Circle to interrogate and then eliminate."

"Agreed," Silvio said. "Rivera does seem to be the weak link in this chain of evil. I'll keep digging into him."

While Silvio texted and emailed his contacts, I took the barbecue sauce off the burner to let it cool and started on something new. Milk and dark cocoa powder went into a small pot, along with a splash of vanilla extract and a cinnamon stick. A few minutes later, I pushed a steaming mug of hot chocolate, topped with a large dollop of vanilla whipped cream, mini marshmallows, and a generous drizzle of homemade chocolate sauce, across the counter to Silvio.

He took a sip and sighed with pleasure. "You know, I'm starting to get spoiled with all the hot chocolate and cookies and food all the time," he grumbled. "I've had to add five miles to my workout routine every week just to burn off all the extra calories."

"I do try." I grinned. "And all that grumbling would sound a whole lot more convincing if you didn't have a whipped cream mustache right now."

Silvio gave me a sour look and wiped away the offensive whipped cream with a napkin, but he kept right on sipping his hot chocolate, and he took the refill that I gave him several minutes later.

By the time Catalina Vasquez, Silvio's niece and my best waitress, and Sophia Deveraux, my head cook, came into the restaurant, the vampire was on his third mug of hot chocolate. Catalina rolled silverware into napkins, while Sophia and I started on the day's cooking. The rest of the waitstaff trickled in one by one, and as soon as I opened the front door at eleven o'clock sharp, customers streamed in, eager to get somewhere warm and cozy, just like Silvio.

The lunch rush passed in a busy blur, although I kept an eye on everyone, always alert for potential trouble. More than a few underworld bosses came into the Pork Pit to eat and pay their respects to me, and to bend Silvio's ear, hoping to set up a meeting with yours truly so they could gripe about their rivals, the general lack of respect for their territories and boundaries, and all the other petty problems that they expected me to solve.

Complain, complain, complain. That was all the other bosses did to me, and why any of them thought that it would actually be fun or fulfilling to be the head of the underworld was beyond my comprehension. They shouldn't be plotting to murder me. They should all be down on bended knee, profusely thanking me for putting up with the whole sorry, corrupt lot of them instead of stabbing them all to death the way that I so often dreamed of. Now, that would be fun *and* fulfilling.

Every time some boss tipped his head at me or had one of his minions sidle up to Silvio, I had to grind my teeth to keep a bland smile fixed on my face. Everyone thought that I was in charge, that I was the head honcho, that I was in complete control, but that couldn't be further from the truth.

For weeks now, Hugh Tucker had been leading me around like I was some cute little kitten playing with the strings that he kept dangling in front of me. Sure, I knew who some of the Circle members were, and I even knew the group's rune, a circle of sharp swords pointing outward. But none of the members was going to be easy to get to, much less take out, especially not the still-unidentified mystery man in charge of the whole she-bang. But all I could do was build my own web of death one strand at a time, starting with Damian Rivera.

Annoying underworld bosses aside, lunchtime went by with no problems, and I finally had a chance to relax and eat my own lunch at around two o'clock. Since it was so cold outside, I wanted some warm, hearty comfort food, so I whipped up a pot of chili, along with a couple of ooey-gooey grilled cheese sandwiches. The chili was a fantastic mix of meat, beans, and spices, all in a rich, thick, tomato-based sauce, while the grilled cheese sandwiches were buttery, melty, and perfect for dunking into the chili. I finished off my meal with some chocolate chip cookies and a tart, refreshing raspberry lemonade.

By the time I finished, I was actually in a good mood, despite last night's shocking revelations about Tucker and my mother. I'd just wiped the last of the cookie crumbs off my hands when the bell over the front door chimed, and a woman dressed in a long crimson coat trimmed with black faux fur entered the restaurant. Her blond hair gleamed under the lights, and a pair of oversize black sunglasses perched on her face, like she was a movie star trying not so successfully to go incognito.

Jade Jamison was a minor underworld boss with big-time ambitions who was always looking to climb higher and get richer. Jade had helped me out in the past, and I considered her a friend, one of the few that I had among the city's criminals. I smiled as she hurried over to the counter, her black stiletto ankle boots *clack*ing against the blue and pink pig tracks on the floor.

"Jade."

"Gin."

She slid her sunglasses on top of her head, pushing her blond bob of hair out of the way. Jade was a beautiful woman, and her makeup was as smooth and flawless as ever. But the expertly applied lipstick, powder, and shadow didn't quite hide the tired lines around her mouth, the purple streaks under her eyes, or, especially, the fear and worry glimmering in her green gaze.

Something was wrong.

The longer I stared at her, the more certain I was. Jade had come to the Pork Pit not as a friend but as an underworld boss, which only meant one thing: she had a problem that she wanted me to solve.

Sure enough, Jade drew in a deep breath, then slowly let it out. "You owe me a favor, and I'm here to collect."

I raised my eyebrows at her pronouncement. "Well, that sounds rather ominous."

Her lips tightened into a grim slash. "Believe me, it is." She glanced around the restaurant, then turned back to me. "Can we go somewhere private and talk?"

"Sure. Step into my office. You too, Silvio."

I motioned for Jade to walk around the counter and over to the swinging double doors that opened into the back of the restaurant. Silvio grabbed his phone and followed us. I led the two of them past the metal shelves full of sugar, ketchup, cornmeal, napkins, silverware, and other restaurant necessities and opened the back door of the restaurant. I stuck my head outside, just to make sure that no one was lurking in the alley foolishly hoping to kill me, but the coast was clear, and the three of us stepped outside. Silvio shut the door behind him.

Jade looked up and down the alley, taking in the dirty, broken pavement, the overflowing trash cans, and the battered metal Dumpsters hugging the walls. The air wasn't nearly cold enough to kill the stench of rotten meat, putrid vegetables, and other spoiled food mixed with the sticky-sweet and sour scents of crushed soda cans and broken beer bottles. Her crimson lips curled up with disgust, and she made sure to keep her boots out of the puddles of oily water that had filled in the cracks in the asphalt.

"Some office," she muttered.

I shrugged and leaned a shoulder against the brick wall of the Pork Pit. "What's up?"

Jade looked at Silvio, who was standing off to my right, his phone in his hands, ready to take down notes of our meeting.

"Does he have to be here for this?" she asked.

"Yes. He's my assistant. He gets rather cranky when I don't let him actually assist me."

Silvio's gray eyes narrowed, and he let out a little huff of disapproval, not liking my quip, especially since it was true. I winked back at him, teasing him a little more.

Jade bit her lower lip and glanced around the alley again, as if she was afraid that someone was going to overhear us. Of course, that wasn't the case, since no one else was back here, and I got the sense that she was stalling, trying to work up to delivering whatever bad news she had. I wondered if the delay was for my benefit or for hers.

"Spit it out, Jade. What's wrong?"

She let out a long sigh and finally raised her green eyes to mine. "One of my girls is missing."

My eyebrows rose. Jade Jamison ran a variety of businesses, everything from temp services to cleaning groups to coin laundries to hookers.

"What kind of girl? Do you mean—"

Jade shook her head. "No, she's not a hooker. She's one of my talkers."

My eyebrows rose a little more. "Talkers?"

"Yeah," she replied. "Talkers. Women who go out with someone for the night and provide companionship only. No sex."

"Who would pay for something like that?" Silvio asked.

Jade shrugged. "Older men mostly, ones who've lost their wives. Folks who need a plus-one for some charity event or party but don't want the bother of finding someone to go with them. So they call me up and arrange a date."

"And what exactly do these dates do?" I asked.

She shrugged again. "Most of the time, it's just simple companionship, like I said. A young, pretty, friendly face by your side with no pressure of it being a real date. Lots of, well, *talking*. Hence the name. Talkers also help to keep the vultures and gold diggers away, especially at society events. I have some guys who are talkers too, who go out with older women, widows, and the like."

"And one of your talkers is missing?" I asked.

She nodded. "Her name is Elissa Daniels, and she's been missing since last night."

Jade pulled her phone out of her jacket pocket and called up a photo. Her fingers trailed over the screen for a few seconds before she passed the phone over to me.

Elissa Daniels looked to be in her early twenties, and I was guessing that she was a student, given her dark blue Ashland Community College sweatshirt. She was a pretty girl, with a long blond ponytail, green eyes, and a shy smile. But what was most interesting about the photo was that her arm was slung around Jade's shoulder and their heads were tilted together as though the two of them were best friends. No, it was more than that. Despite the fact that Jade was at least a decade older than Elissa, the two of them could have been twins, with their blond hair, green eyes, and matching features.

And I suddenly realized exactly why this was so important to Jade.

I passed the phone over to Silvio, who blinked and then brought the device closer to his face so he could get a better look at the photo.

"Elissa's not just a missing worker, is she?" I asked in a sympathetic voice.

Jade's lips pressed together, as though she was having trouble answering, as if actually saying her fears out loud would make them that much more real. After a few seconds, she cleared her throat and forced out the words. "She's my little sister."

✵ 6 ✵

Jade's confession echoed down the alley, colder than the winter wind whistling between the buildings. Despite her coat, she shivered and wrapped her arms around herself, as if just saying the words out loud had chilled her more than the weather ever could.

"Elissa is my sister, and she's missing," Jade whispered, her voice cracking like the asphalt under our feet. "Will you help me find her? Please, Gin?"

Before I could answer, she started pacing back and forth across the alley, her stiletto boots clicking against the pavement. "I know that I have no right to ask you this. It's not a *business* favor like Silvio and I agreed on, not at all, not even close. Believe me, I didn't want to come here. I didn't want to bother you with this. I'm a professional, and I don't expect you to solve all my problems for me. Not like the other bosses. But I can't find Elissa anywhere. I just can't *find* her . . ."

Jade kept talking, the words, fear, and worry spilling out of her even faster than her short, staccato pacing. I let her keep talking, expecting her to wind down once she got it all out of her system. Silvio stepped back against the restaurant wall, giving her a wide berth. But after the better part of a minute came and went and she showed no signs of slowing her rapid-fire movements, I stepped in front of her.

"Stop—please *stop*."

Jade froze at the sharp command in my voice. She dropped her head and closed her eyes, as if bracing herself for my rejection.

"Of course I'll help you find your sister. All you had to do was ask."

She shuddered out a breath, the air frosting around her, then staggered forward and wrapped me up in a tight, fierce hug. I got the feeling that if she'd had the strength, she would have lifted me clear off my feet and swung me around. Even as it was, her shoulder dug into my neck so hard that I could feel my spider rune pendant pressing against my throat even through my heavy sweater. But I didn't mind the uncomfortable sensation. Jade wanted the Spider to find her sister, and that's exactly what I was going to do.

Silvio cleared his throat, and the soft sound made Jade freeze again. She abruptly let go of me and lurched back, worry twisting her face, as though she'd just hugged all the help right out of me.

"Come on," I said in a gentle voice. "Let's go back inside where it's warm, and you can tell me all about your sister."

• • •

The three of us left the alley and went back into the front of the restaurant, where Silvio escorted Jade over to an empty corner booth.

By this point, it was almost two thirty, and the last of the lunch-rush customers were gone, with only a few stragglers still chowing down on their burgers, barbecue sandwiches, and side dishes. As soon as the last customer had eaten, paid up, and left, I flipped the sign on the front door over to *Closed* and taped up a piece of paper saying that we would reopen in an hour. Sophia and Catalina herded the waitstaff into the back so they could all take an extended break, leaving me alone out front with Jade and Silvio.

The vampire perched on his stool at the counter, his fingers tapping on his tablet, already trying to find out everything he could about Elissa Daniels. Jade sat in the booth, her shoulders slumped, staring out the storefront windows with a blank expression on her face, as though she wasn't actually seeing anything on the street outside. I worked behind the counter, making a grilled cheese sandwich just like the ones I'd had for lunch. I also dished up a bowl of steaming chili, along with some chocolate chip cookies and a sweet iced tea, put everything on a tray, and took it over to Jade. After setting the tray on her side of the table, I slid into the booth across from her. Silvio pulled a chair up to my side of the booth, propped his tablet on the table, and hooked a small keyboard to it so he could type faster and take better, more detailed notes.

Jade stared at the food, then shook her head and

pushed the tray away. "That looks and smells great, but I can't eat anything right now. I'm sorry."

I leaned forward and pushed the tray right back where it had been before. "Just have a few bites. You need to keep your strength up. How long has it been since you've eaten anything?"

"I don't know. Maybe dinner last night? That's how long Elissa has been missing."

"What happened?" I asked. "Tell me everything."

Jade drew in a deep breath and slowly let it out. Her hand crept forward, and she picked up the spoon from the tray. She dug the utensil into the chili and started moving it from one side of the bowl to the other, not because she had any intention of eating it but just to have something to do with all her nervous worry and energy.

"Elissa and I are half sisters. Same mother, different fathers. Kelsey, our mother . . ." Her voice trailed off for a few seconds. "Well, let's just say that she never won any Mother of the Year awards. She was a society broad who flitted from man to man, always looking to trade one guy in for a newer, richer model. She and my dad got divorced when I was five. She took him to the cleaner's."

"Where's your dad now?"

"He lives in Arizona with some yoga instructor." Jade scoffed. "She's younger than I am."

She stirred the chili again. "Anyway, after that, my mom moved from man to man, until she got pregnant with Elissa. Stephen, Elissa's dad, actually married my mom. He was a great guy, and he deserved much better than my mother. I was thirteen when Elissa was born, and I loved her from the moment I saw her. Despite the age difference, the two of us were always close . . ."

She trailed off again and put down her spoon. She reached out, grabbed the glass, and took a sip of iced tea. Then she put the glass down and started sliding it back and forth on the tray, making the ice inside *tinkle-tinkle* together. After several seconds, Jade's hand stilled, and her fingers curled around the glass.

"Stephen and my mom died in a boating accident when Elissa was ten, so I finished raising her. Luckily, Elissa took after her dad. She's a great kid. Smart, polite, thoughtful, always wanting to help other people." Jade's face softened. "She's everything to me. Surely you can understand that, Gin."

I did understand that, far more than she realized. For years I'd thought that my younger sister, Detective Bria Coolidge, was gone forever, crushed to death in the falling rubble of our mansion the night Mab Monroe murdered our mother and our other sister. I'd used my Stone magic to collapse our house to try to save Bria, and I'd thought that I'd killed her in the process. That burden, grief, and guilt had weighed down my heart for years, until Bria came back to Ashland looking for me. So I knew exactly how Jade felt when she talked about how precious her sister was to her.

"What happened when Elissa went missing?" I asked. "Was she out on a job?"

Jade shook her head. "No, not exactly. Elissa went to meet one of her regular clients at a charity event in Northtown last night. She loves getting dressed up and going out and meeting people. It's one of the reasons she works for me, and she says it's good practice for her marketing degree."

I nodded. "And the event?"

"Dinner, dancing, speeches, the usual. Nothing out of the ordinary and absolutely nothing dangerous."

"So what happened?"

"The client came down with the flu, so he called and canceled at the last minute. Elissa was already at the dinner, though, so he told her to stay and have a good time and put everything on his tab. She texted me from the party to let me know what was going on. That was about seven o'clock last night." Jade paused. "And that's the last that I heard from her."

Her fingers curled a little tighter around the glass still in her hand, and she started twisting it around and around on the tray. I could tell that something else was bothering her, so I kept quiet and let her work up to telling me what it was.

"Elissa asked if I wanted to come and have a drink. She even sent me a photo of her champagne glass, trying to convince me. But I had work to do, so I texted her back, told her to have a good time, and went right back to work." Jade's lips pressed together, and anguish pinched her face. "This . . . this is all my fault. If I'd just told her yes, if I'd just met her for one lousy drink, she would be here, she would be *safe*—" Her voice choked off, and she blinked back tears.

I shook my head. "Don't—don't go there. You can't let yourself think like that. It's not your fault, Jade."

"Yes, it is," she whispered. "Yes, it is."

I knew exactly what she was feeling—the guilt, the shame, the sickening self-loathing. I also knew that nothing I said would change her mind, so I focused on the one thing that would help her right now: finding her sister.

"Tell me the rest of it. When did you first realize that Elissa was missing?"

"When I woke up this morning and she wasn't home," Jade said. "I called her, but she didn't answer. That's when I started to get worried. I kept calling and texting. I tried all of her friends, including her boyfriend, thinking that maybe she'd crashed with one of them. But no one's seen or heard from her since last night. She's finishing up her marketing degree at the community college, so I even went over there this morning, checking to see if she was in class and had just turned her phone off. But she wasn't there. She never misses class—*never*."

More anguish glinted in Jade's eyes, as bright and sharp as shards of glass. "I can't find her anywhere. She's gone. She's just—*gone*." She blinked and blinked, but this time she couldn't stop the tears from streaking down her face.

"Have you gone to the police yet?" I asked in a gentle voice.

Jade nodded and wiped away her tears. "As soon as I realized that Elissa wasn't in class, I went over to the campus police office. But they said that there was nothing they could do, especially since I didn't know if she'd even been on campus this morning. They told me to go see the regular police, so that's what I did. But when they realized who I was, the cops assumed she was one of my regular working girls. You can imagine how concerned they were about what they thought was a missing hooker."

"Not very."

The majority of the cops in Ashland were as corrupt as the day was long. Most of the time, the only way to get them to actually do their jobs was to offer them a hefty financial incentive. But there were a few good men and women on the force, my own sister being one of them.

"Did you ask for Bria? Or Xavier, her partner?" I asked. "They would have helped you."

Jade nodded again. "Of course I did. But they were both out on assignment, and I couldn't get anyone to tell me when they would be back. So I filed a missing person report and left. I've been searching for Elissa ever since then, checking in with the college and her friends again, but it's like she's vanished off the face of the earth. I can't find her *anywhere*."

I leaned back and crossed my arms over my chest, thinking about all of the facts and everything that she'd done so far. I looked over at Silvio, and he nodded back, telling me that he was doing the same, even as he kept on typing.

"What about the client Elissa was supposed to meet?" I asked. "What's his name? Have you talked to him?"

"That was the first thing I did when I realized that Elissa wasn't home this morning," Jade said. "But he sounded awful on the phone. He really was sick, and he said that he never made it to the dinner last night. His name is Stuart Mosley. He's the president of First Trust bank. Do you know him?"

The name startled me, but I didn't let any of my surprise show. First Trust was the bank where Finn worked, and Stuart Mosley was his boss. Silvio shifted in his chair, and his fingers slowed their quick, relentless rhythm. He'd recognized the name too.

"Yeah, I know Mosley," I murmured. "Small world."

Sometimes it was a little too small for my peace of mind. Suspicion filled me. Stuart Mosley didn't seem like the kind of man who would be involved in a young woman's disappearance, but I couldn't overlook him either. Fletcher had taught me that people, even those you considered potential allies, could always surprise you.

"Why did Mosley need a date for this charity dinner?"

"His wife died almost two years ago, and he's used my service ever since," Jade said. "I've never had a problem with him, and neither have any of my girls. He's always been a perfect gentleman. For the past year, he's only used Elissa. Mosley told her once that she reminds him of one of his great-granddaughters who passed away."

"What happened to his granddaughter?"

She shook her head. "I don't know. He's never said."

Dwarves lived a long time, hundreds of years in some cases, so it wasn't unusual that Mosley had a great-granddaughter who had passed on before him. Any number of things could have happened to her, including just dying of old age if she had been a regular human. Still, I looked over at Silvio and raised my eyebrows, silently asking him to add Mosley's granddaughter to his list of things to check on. He nodded back at me, his fingers picking up speed on his keyboard again.

Jade chewed on her lower lip. "Actually, Mr. Mosley is the one who suggested that I contact you. I don't know why I didn't think of it myself. He said that if anyone could find Elissa, it would be you."

My eyes narrowed. "Did he now?"

Stuart Mosley knew all about my being the assassin the Spider, especially since he had been friends—or something—with Fletcher back when the old man was still alive. I didn't know exactly what their relationship was, but Fletcher had trusted Mosley to look after all those safety-deposit boxes full of information on the Circle. The dwarf knew far more about Fletcher than he'd ever told me or Finn, and he might know more about Elissa Daniels too.

I'd pay him a visit and find out.

"Is something wrong?" Jade asked. "Why are you asking so many questions about Mr. Mosley?"

I shook my head. "Just being thorough. Where was the charity event? Tell me everything, no matter how small and insignificant it might seem."

Jade let go of her glass, picked up her spoon, and started stirring her chili again, but she gave me all the details about the event, who had sponsored it, and some folks who might have attended. But it sounded like your typical charity dinner, so she moved on to Elissa's friends, classes, and life in general. I listened carefully, absorbing everything she said, while Silvio typed copious notes.

"Then there's Anthony." Jade rolled her eyes. "Anthony Fenton, Elissa's boyfriend."

"What's wrong with him?"

"Nothing, except for the fact that his rich parents have spoiled him rotten his entire life. Elissa thinks that he's the perfect guy." She rolled her eyes again. "I think he's a self-entitled jackass."

I chose my next words carefully. "Do you think that Anthony could be involved in this?"

Jade snorted. "Anthony's too lazy and self-absorbed to hurt anyone, if that's what you're asking. He can't even be bothered to crawl out of bed before noon. All he cares about is looking good and partying."

Silvio asked Jade to spell out the names of Elissa's friends so he could be sure that he was focusing on the right people. He also got Jade to text him a headshot of Elissa, and then asked her about the dinner again, trying to jog her memory and see if she remembered anything else. While they worked, I thought back over everything Jade had told me.

I could see why she was so worried. Nice, smart, responsible, dependable girls like Elissa didn't just vanish for no reason. Something had happened to her—something bad. And in a city as dirty, violent, and corrupt as Ashland, the longer she was missing, the worse it most likely was.

If she wasn't already dead.

Walking down the wrong street at the wrong time of day. Smiling at the wrong person. Carrying a designer purse. Wearing a pretty necklace or sporting a cool leather jacket. Sometimes that was all it took to make you a target, especially in this city. And all too often, death struck in an instant. All it took was one punch, one bullet, one slice of a knife to end someone's life.

I didn't share my dark thoughts with Jade because I knew that they had already occurred to her, no doubt a hundred times since she'd started her frantic search. Silvio's face remained carefully neutral while he questioned Jade, but I could see the pity in his eyes. He thought that Elissa might already be dead too.

Finally, Jade had answered all of Silvio's questions and told us every little detail that she could think of. She hadn't touched any of her food, except for the iced tea, and she took one more sip of it before setting the glass down, along with her spoon.

"I know that I don't have any right to ask you this," she repeated, looking at me again. "This wasn't the kind of favor we agreed on. That was all business between us, and my favor should be that way too."

"But?"

"But Stuart Mosley is right. You're the strongest, toughest, most dangerous person I know," Jade said in a shaking voice. "If anyone can find Elissa, it's you, Gin. So please. *Please* do this for me. If you want money, I will gladly pay you whatever you want. I will do anything to get my sister back. *Anything*. Just name your price. Anything that I have or that's in my power to give you, it's yours. And if I don't have it, then I will lie and cheat and steal until I do get it for you—as long as it takes."

I reached across the table and took her cold, trembling hands in my own. "There's no need for any of that. I owe you a favor, and I am happy to pay up. Favors or not, business or not, I would have helped you anyway."

Jade stared at me, a mixture of relief and gratitude filling her face. She exhaled, and some of the tension left her body, although she curled her fingers into mine and squeezed them tight. "Thank you, Gin. You don't know how much this means to me." More tears glimmered in her green eyes before streaking down her cheeks. "Just . . . just find her. Please, please find her."

Before it's too late.

She didn't say the words. She didn't have to. We could all hear the clock ticking, counting down what might be left of Elissa's life—if it hadn't stopped already. The faint, hopeful note in Jade's voice made my stomach clench, but I forced myself to nod at her.

"I'll find your sister. I'll find Elissa. Wherever she is at. I promise you."

7

Jade wanted to leave the Pork Pit to continue searching, but I convinced her to sit in the booth and at least pretend to eat some food. While Jade once again moved chili from one side of her bowl to the other, I went over to the swinging double doors and opened one of them. Most of the waitstaff had left, probably to go over to the Cake Walk to get some coffee and doughnuts during their break, but Sophia Deveraux was still in the back.

The dwarf was standing in front of the metal shelves, doing inventory of the ketchup, sugar, cornmeal, and other foodstuffs, with a clipboard in one hand and a hot-pink pencil in the other. The pencil matched the neon color of the lace spiderwebs that decorated her black T-shirt, along with her metal spiderweb earrings. She'd also dusted hot-pink glitter all over her black hair, making the strands shimmer under the lights.

Sophia checked a final box on her clipboard sheet and

turned to me. "What's wrong?" she rasped in her eerie, broken voice.

"Jade's sister is missing, and she wants me to find her."

"How long?"

"Since last night."

Understanding and sympathy flashed in her black eyes. "What do you need me to do?"

"Go home with Jade," I said. "She shouldn't be alone right now. Help her call all of Elissa's friends again, just in case. And keep an eye out too. Jade has her share of enemies, just like all the underworld bosses do. Someone may have grabbed Elissa to get at her. A ransom demand might be coming."

Sophia nodded, but disbelief filled her face, and I could tell that she was thinking the same thing I was, that there wouldn't be any ransom demand because Elissa Daniels was most likely already dead.

The dwarf had known Fletcher even longer than I had, and I knew that she had absorbed more than a few of the old man's nuggets of wisdom over the years. Fletcher had always told us to brace ourselves for the absolute worst. That way, anything better was a pleasant surprise. The realistic, if pessimistic, sentiment had helped me through more than one bad situation, and I was hoping that it would help me through this one too.

Sophia put down her clipboard and pencil and grabbed her long black trench coat from the rack in the corner. She shrugged into the coat, making the sequined silver skull on the back wink at me. I'd always liked Sophia's Goth style, but right now, the skull seemed more like a portent of doom than anything else.

I had a bad, bad feeling about all this.

But I plastered a calm, neutral expression on my face as Sophia followed me into the front of the restaurant and over to the booth where Jade was still sitting. I told Jade that Sophia was going to drive her home and stay with her for a while, just in case Elissa came home or someone called with new information. Jade brightened briefly at my ransom-demand theory, but the more she thought about it—and how unlikely it was—the more her features crumpled back into a pale, worried mask.

At this point, though, she was too tired and heartsick to argue, so she got to her feet and let Sophia lead her out of the restaurant. The bell over the front door chimed at their passage, ringing out like a low, mournful dirge.

Silvio moved over to stand beside me. "You know that girl is probably already dead. Or if she's not dead, she probably wishes that she was."

I sighed. "I know. But a favor is a favor, and I'm going to do my best to find her. What have you found out so far?"

Silvio started swiping through screens on his tablet. "It looks like Jade told you the truth about her sister. Elissa Daniels is squeaky clean as far as I can see. No arrests and no criminal record of any kind. She's never gotten so much as a parking ticket. If she got into trouble last night, it probably wasn't of her own making."

I nodded. "What about her friends? Anyone that Jade didn't know about? Maybe another boyfriend besides Anthony Fenton?"

He shook his head. "Not that I've been able to find by examining her social media, but that doesn't mean anything. I'll start looking more closely at her and her friends' sites right now."

"Good. You stay here and do that. And text me that headshot of Elissa that Jade sent you." I grabbed my jacket off the rack behind the counter, shrugged into the black fleece, and zipped it up.

"What are you going to do?" Silvio asked.

"Start at the beginning. I'm going to the club where the charity dinner was held last night. I'll get the security footage and see if I can spot Elissa on it. I'm also going to nose around the building and see if I can pick up anything with my Stone magic. If someone snatched Elissa from the dinner, then maybe he left some sort of clue behind."

Silvio nodded. "I'll call you if I learn anything new."

"I'll do the same." I sighed again. "Although I don't think that either one of us is going to like what we find."

The waitstaff came back from their extended break, and I left the Pork Pit in Catalina's capable hands for the rest of the day. After checking to make sure that no one had booby-trapped my car while it was parked on the street, I got inside and headed toward Northtown. While I drove, I called my friends to fill them in on the situation.

First up was Bria.

"Detective Coolidge," she said through the sound system in my car.

"Hey, it's Gin. Are you at your desk? I need a favor . . ."

I told her everything that Jade had told me, including about her less-than-helpful trip to the police station earlier today. After I finished, I could hear Bria typing on the other end of the line.

"I don't see a missing person report on Elissa Daniels filed anywhere in our system," Bria said. "Who did Jade talk to?"

"Some cop named Sykes."

"Sykes," she snarled, a note of disgust creeping into her voice. "That lazy slob. All he does is sit around, eat doughnuts, and misfile paperwork. He probably just wadded up Jade's report and tossed it into the trash the way he does all the others."

"Sounds like a charming guy," I said. "Real dedicated to protecting and serving."

"You have no idea," Bria muttered. "Anyway, give me all the info, and I'll see what I can dig up."

I repeated everything I knew about Elissa and her disappearance and suggested that Bria call Silvio so the two of them could pool their resources and exchange information. Bria agreed to get right on it and also to tell Xavier what was going on. She promised to call with any updates, and we both hung up.

Next on my contact list was Finn.

"Why, hello there, darling," he drawled in a deep, suave voice. "You have reached the always awesome and ever-charming Finnegan Lane. How may I be of service to you today?"

"It's Gin. Does Stuart Mosley really have the flu?"

Silence. I didn't often throw Finn for a loop, but that wasn't the response he'd expected.

"How do you know that Mosley is sick?" he asked. "And why are you so interested in my boss's sniffles?"

I filled him in on the missing girl. "Did you know that

your boss likes to squire sweet young things around Ashland?"

"Well, yeah," Finn said. "It's no secret. He's done it for a while now. Ever since his wife died. He told me once that it helps to keep the society sharks at bay. The ones who want to take a big bite out of all his money. Do you actually think that Mosley might be involved in this girl's disappearance?"

Worry rippled through Finn's voice. He liked Mosley a lot and thought of him as a mentor the same way I thought of Fletcher. Finn didn't want to think ill of his boss. Neither did I, but Mosley was far too mysterious for my liking.

"I don't know, but he was the one she was supposed to meet last night. Mosley definitely has his secrets, and I want to be sure that kidnapping college girls isn't one of them," I said. "Can you find out if he really was sick at home last night?"

"I'm on it," Finn said.

He also promised to contact Silvio and Bria and see what he could do to help them drill down into information on Elissa and anyone she might have had any contact with.

Last but definitely not least, I dialed Owen and told him what was going on.

"That's awful. I can't imagine what Jade must be going through. If Eva was missing . . ." His voice trailed off at the thought of his own younger sister, and I could tell he was thinking how horrible things were for Jade right now. "What can I do?"

Even though he couldn't see me, I still smiled. Owen's willingness to help, no matter how ugly or desperate the situation, always warmed my heart. "I was hoping you'd say that. Talk to Eva. See if she or Violet knows anything about Elissa and her friends. They all go to the community college. Maybe they have some classes together. Elissa seems like a good kid, but even good kids can have hidden depths."

"Roger that," Owen said. "And Gin?"

"Yeah?"

"Be careful. I don't know what I would do if you were the one missing either."

I smiled again. "That's something that you'll never have to worry about."

"Promise?"

"Promise."

By the time I finished my call with Owen, I'd reached my destination: the Five Oaks Country Club.

Five large, circular buildings made up the club, which featured all of your usual amenities, including tennis courts, swimming pools, and more. Given the cold, most of the outdoor areas were deserted, although I could see a few hardy souls off in the distance, bundled up from head to toe, walking across one of the golf greens. A couple of miserable-looking caddies with heavy bags of clubs slung over their shoulders trudged along behind the golfers. A gust of wind swept over the land, and they all stopped and tucked their chins down into the tops of their puffy parkas until the blustery breeze had subsided.

I parked my car and headed for the center building,

an elegant structure of pale gray stone and gleaming glass that served as the club's main social area. I pushed through the double doors and walked down a long ivory-carpeted hallway, listening to the hushed whispers of the stones as they murmured about money, manners, station, and all the other things that were so important to the people here. I reached out with my magic, focusing on their soft, sly mutterings, but no loud, obvious notes of danger or violence trilled through the stones. Whatever had happened to Elissa Daniels, I didn't think that it had started here.

Only one way to find out for sure.

The hallway led into a large corridor with several sets of double doors set into its walls. The two doors in front of me were standing wide open, and the trill of more than a dozen conversations drifted over to me. No one was standing at the nearby host's station, so I stepped up and peered inside the club's main ballroom.

Round tables covered with pale peach linens filled the massive space from one end to the other. An acorn—the country club's rune—shimmered in gold thread in the center of each tablecloth and napkin and was also engraved into all the silverware. A glass dome curved over the ballroom four stories above, letting in the weak winter sunlight, as did the floor-to-ceiling windows that lined the back wall. Multiple sets of stairs led to the upper levels of the ballroom, where more tables were situated.

The ballroom served as the country club's restaurant, offering gourmet brunch, lunch, dinner, and drinks to its wealthy members and their guests. Given the cold outside, everyone wanted to be warm and comfortable inside, and people had flocked to the club to eat, drink, socialize, and scheme against their frenemies.

Being a Five Oaks member was a status symbol that told everyone exactly how obscenely wealthy you were, and I recognized more than a few faces in the crowd: the mayor, the police chief, a couple of local congressmen, and, of course, several underworld bosses, all dressed in their best business suits. My gaze roamed over them all in turn, men and women, seeing who was sitting with whom, who was pointedly ignoring their companions, and who had more martini glasses on their tables than plates of food. Despite their nice clothes, understated jewels, and benign smiles, more than one killer lurked in this crowd. I wondered if Elissa had had the misfortune to find that out for herself.

A particularly loud guffaw caught my attention, and my gaze flicked to a table in the center of the ballroom where a man with wavy black hair was using a large glass of wine to gesture at his companions.

Damian Rivera.

I blinked, wondering if it was really him, but yes sir-ree, the Circle member was here and holding court, like he was the king of the country club. Several women were sitting at his table, all leaning forward and hanging on to his every word. Rivera might be a notorious drunk, but he was an extremely rich notorious drunk, and the soci-ety sharks, as Finn called them, would be eager to make themselves available to a man like him to try to pry some of his money loose for themselves.

I scanned the crowd again, but I didn't see Hugh Tucker or any of the other Circle members in the ballroom. Perhaps they knew better than to draw such attention to themselves.

But Rivera wasn't alone. Bruce Porter stood against the wall, looking bored and texting on his phone, knowing that his boss was in absolutely no danger from anything other than gold diggers. Still, Porter was a professional, and he glanced up from his phone every few seconds, scanning the ballroom and making sure that his boss was still secure. The dwarf must have sensed my stare because he looked in my direction.

I ducked my head, pivoted away, and stepped back into the corridor, out of Porter's line of sight. I couldn't afford to let him know that I was onto his boss. Not until I was ready to make my move against Rivera and the rest of the Circle.

I peered through the crack between the open door and the wall. Porter was still staring in this direction, his middle-aged face pinched into a frown, but he didn't start across the ballroom to come investigate. He must not have spotted me after all—

"Who are *you*, and *what* are *you* doing *here*?" a snide voice asked.

I turned around to find a man standing behind me, his arms crossed over his chest. He was wearing an expensive but subdued navy suit that was tailored to his tall, skinny frame. Everything about him was perfect, from the way his dark brown hair curled over his forehead, to his square gold cuff links, to the small gold acorn glinting in the exact center of his light blue tie. A gold name badge glimmered on his jacket: *Marco, Club Manager*.

Marco's dark brown gaze drifted over my black fleece

jacket, jeans, and boots, and his lips curled with disgust. "I'm sorry," he said in an arrogant tone that indicated that he was not sorry at all. "This is a private club. We are not open to the public."

He said the word *public* as though it were some sort of horrendous plague upon all mankind. Or at least upon those with money.

"Good thing I'm not the mere *public*, then," I said, giving him a razor-thin smile.

Marco blinked, as if he weren't used to having his authority challenged, but I ignored his confusion, pulled out my phone, and showed him Elissa's photo.

"This girl was here at the charity dinner that the club hosted last night. Do you remember seeing her?"

Marco let out a delicate huff, as though I'd greatly offended him by daring to ask a question. "We do not give out information to *commoners* who just wander in off the street. If you don't leave right now, I'm going to call the police."

I laughed. "Oh, sugar. You go right ahead and call the cops. Unless you've got a couple of them on your payroll, I can't imagine that they'll be too eager to rush all the way up here just to remove some *commoner* like me from the premises."

Marco's lips curled again at my easy dismissal of his empty threat. "Well, then, it's a good thing that the club employs its own private security force to deal with certain . . . problems."

He looked down the hallway, raised his hand, and snapped his fingers a couple of times. Footsteps scuffed on the carpet, and three giants wearing navy suits stepped up and flanked me. Ah, reinforcements. The men weren't carrying guns, but they didn't need them, given their solid seven-foot frames and massive fists. Besides, it wasn't like we were in Southtown. The most dangerous things these guys faced down on a regular basis were drunken businessmen and tipsy debutantes.

Marco gave me a triumphant sneer. "Please escort this woman off the property. And *don't* be gentle about it."

I could have stopped this before it got started. I could have pulled my spider rune pendant out from under my jacket, flashed it at Marco and the giants, and told them exactly who I was. My being the Spider would have been enough to get them to back off.

Probably.

Maybe.

Okay, okay, so probably not.

Folks had a very peculiar—and *bad*—habit of not believing me when I claimed to be an assassin, and that one mistake almost always led to their deaths. Their disbelief killed them, right along with my knives.

Two of the giants stepped forward and clamped their hands on my arms, deliberately, painfully digging their fingers into my skin, but I still didn't reach for my spider rune. If Marco and his minions wanted to play rough, then I would be happy to oblige them.

I liked playing rough too.

I looked at Marco. "What's the matter? Not manager enough to throw me out yourself?"

His dark eyes narrowed at my mockery. "You know what, guys? Let's take her to the security office for a more . . . private conversation."

The three giants grinned at their boss. This was probably the most excitement they'd had in ages, and they were all looking forward to the pleasure of beating me—or worse.

Oh, it was going to be worse, all right—for them.

Marco led the way, and the two giants strong-armed me down the hallway, with the third man following along behind us, just in case I decided to make a break for it. But I didn't protest or try to wrench away or even dig my heels into the carpet to slow our progress.

After all, they were taking me exactly where I wanted to go.

We wound through a couple of different hallways, heading away from the crowd in the ballroom toward the far side of the building. We passed a few staff members, mostly janitors and housekeepers mopping, dusting, and making sure that the inside of the club was spick-and-span. At the sight of Marco and the giants, they all stopped what they were doing and snapped to attention. The second Marco's back was to them, they all relaxed again, and a few folks even winced, shook their heads, and gave me sympathetic looks. Some of them must have taken this same forced walk to the security office.

I wondered what their infractions had been. Forgetting to put enough toilet paper in the restrooms? Not getting the last speck of dust off the gilded mirrors on the walls? Or perhaps it was something even more serious, like not bowing down to Marco in what he considered to be his own little fiefdom.

A minute later, we reached the end of this hallway, and

Marco used a key card to open a door marked *Security Personnel Only*. He held out his hand, and the two giants shoved me through the doorway. I stumbled forward and hit a table, pretending to be far more off balance than I really was. All the while, my gaze flicked around the room, taking in the security monitors that lined the opposite wall, the poker cards on the table in front of me, and the half-full coffee cups that littered the messy desk in the corner. Three cups, to be exact, which meant that these three giants were probably the full extent of the club's security force.

Excellent. Wouldn't want any stragglers to miss this.

The two giants trooped into the room behind me, along with Marco and the third giant, who closed the door behind him. I grinned at the sound of the lock *snick*-ing home, then straightened up and turned to face the men.

Marco crossed his arms over his chest. "Not so mouthy now, are you?"

"Oh, sugar. I've always thought that actions speak far louder than words."

He frowned at my cryptic comment, but I ignored him and stared at the three giants standing in front of me.

"I hope you boys didn't pay too much for those fancy suits," I drawled.

"Why is that?" one of the giants asked.

My grin widened. "Because I'm going to have a lot of fun splattering your blood all over that pretty, pretty fabric."

The giant snorted. Another disbeliever. His loss.

"Enough talk," Marco said in a bored tone. "I have a

club to run, so get on with it. Slap her around and then throw her outside."

"Yes, sir," the giants said in unison.

The first two men came at me with outstretched arms, thinking that they could latch on to me again and hold me still while the third man hit me.

I actually did let the first giant grab my shoulder, just so I could snap up my fist and sucker-punch him in the throat. He choked and started to stagger backward, but I grabbed hold of his silk tie, yanked it down, and slammed his face into the table beside me. His nose busted open, and blood flew through the air, along with the poker cards. The giant screamed, but I whipped around and drove my knee into the side of his head. He collapsed to the floor unconscious.

The second giant growled, pissed that I'd hurt his buddy, and he too came at me with outstretched arms. I whirled around him, grabbed one of the coffee cups from the desk in the corner, and tossed the contents into his face. Luckily for him, the coffee had cooled, but it still blinded him. He yelped in surprise and batted at his face, as if he expected the liquid to start burning him at any second. I rammed my foot into the side of his knee, making it give way with a sickening *pop!* He yelped again, his leg buckling. I darted forward, dug my fingers into his hair, and slammed his head into the table. Once, twice, three times, until his screams cut off, and he too dropped to the floor unconscious, landing right on top of his friend.

Two down, two to go.

The third giant was a little smarter or had at least been

in a few more fights than his friends. He raised his fists and gave me a wary look, but he didn't actually attack.

"What are you waiting for?" Marco demanded, his voice sounding higher and more panicked with every word. "Get her! Now!"

The giant ignored his boss and stared at me, waiting for me to make the first move. With my left hand, I feinted like I was going for another cup of coffee on the desk. Even as the giant moved in that direction, I reached out with my right hand, grabbed the landline phone off the desk, and smashed it into the side of his head. The giant screamed and staggered away, but I grabbed his suit jacket, pulled him right back to me, and smashed the phone into his head again. The plastic broke apart in my hands, and the giant screamed again.

I tossed away the ruined phone and went low, sweeping my right leg out and catching the giant around his ankles. His legs flew out from under him, and his head hit the floor with a resounding *crack*. He didn't move after that.

I straightened up and eyed the giants, but they were all out cold, sprawled all over the floor, and bleeding all over their fancy suits just like I'd warned. I could have palmed a knife and killed them, but that would have been a whole other headache to deal with, one that I just didn't have time for right now. So I turned to Marco, who had pressed himself up against the wall, his eyes wide, his hand clamped over his mouth, as if he was going to be sick.

"Let me guess," I drawled. "Your boys can dish it out, but you can't take it yourself, right?"

Marco made a choking sound and ran for the door,

but I beat him to it. I wrapped my hand around the knob and blasted it with my Ice magic, further sealing us inside the security office.

"Now, now," I said. "We wouldn't want anyone to interrupt us. We have important business to discuss. That private conversation you were so eager to have with me—remember?"

Marco stumbled away and tripped over one of the unconscious giants. I reached out and grabbed the back of his suit jacket so that he wouldn't fall down and accidentally knock himself out. The manager quickly regained his balance, although he scuttled away from me, pressing his tall, thin body into the corner, as if that would somehow protect him.

"What—what do you want?" he whispered.

This time when I stepped forward, I did finally reach under my jacket and pull out my silverstone pendant. Marco's eyes locked onto the spider rune symbol, and his mouth gaped open. Now he knew exactly who I was. What a nice surprise.

"Now that the pleasantries are over with, I want to look at your security footage."

✢ 8 ✢

Marco was *so* much more helpful after that.

He spent the next thirty minutes downloading the club's security footage from last night onto some DVDs, along with emailing me the information. I used my phone to forward the footage on to Silvio, Bria, and Finn so they could review it too. DVDs in hand, I used another round of my Ice magic to blast open the office door and left the Five Oaks Country Club.

By this point, it was after four o'clock, and I headed home to plan my next move. Beating down giants was hard work, so I grabbed some dark chocolate brownies from the kitchen, put them on a napkin, and carried them into the den. While I ate, I popped the first DVD into the TV.

These security cameras showed the outside of Five Oaks, and the footage was exactly what I'd expected: limos, sedans, and SUVs pulling up to the front of the club and dropping off rich, important, powerful, and dangerous folks. The low resolution on the cameras made the images a bit grainy, but I still recognized several faces, including some underworld bosses. People got out of their cars, handed off their keys to the valets, and hurried into the waiting warmth of the club. Nothing unusual or suspicious.

Finally, a yellow cab pulled up to the club, and Elissa Daniels got out, paid the driver, and headed inside. I stopped the footage so I could get a better look at her. Elissa was just as pretty on camera as in the photo Jade had shown me, and she'd dressed up for the dinner. Her blond hair hung in loose waves around her shoulders, and she was wearing a long black coat over a short, fitted red dress, along with matching red stilettos.

I looked at the time stamp on the bottom corner of the video. Six fifty-five. Right before Elissa was due to meet Stuart Mosley at seven. I scanned through the rest of the footage on the disc, but Mosley never appeared. It looked as if he'd been telling the truth about being sick and skipping the dinner. So I switched DVDs, moving on to the footage from inside the club.

Once I knew what time Elissa had arrived and what she was wearing, it was easy to track her through the footage on the other discs, specifically as she entered the country club ballroom, since several security cameras were trained on that area. She looked around the ballroom, searching for Mosley, then headed over to the bar and ordered a glass of champagne. She sat there sipping her drink for about ten minutes before she got a call, most likely from

Mosley. Elissa nodded and talked for about a minute before ending the call.

After that, she snapped a photo of her champagne glass and texted it to someone, most likely asking her sister to come have a drink. Of course, Jade didn't come, but Elissa continued to sit at the bar, sip her champagne, and people-watch, content to enjoy the rest of the evening just as Mosley had told her to.

Until she got a message, apparently.

Elissa had just finished her champagne when her phone lit up. She stared at the screen for a moment, then signaled the bartender that she wanted to pay her tab. Five minutes later, she left the ballroom, so I popped in another DVD that showed the outside of the club again. Sure enough, Elissa was standing by the entrance, pacing back and forth, and checking her phone over and over again.

A cab arrived just after seven thirty, and Elissa slid into the backseat. I froze the footage again so I could get the cab's number—227—and texted it to Silvio and Finn, asking them to find out who the driver was and where he'd taken Elissa. I also sent them both another text asking if they could hack into Elissa's phone records. I wanted to know what message had gotten her upset enough to rush out of the country club and head off to parts unknown.

After that, there was nothing for me to do but wait, so I called Sophia, checking on how things were going with Jade.

"She's wearing a path in the floor," Sophia rumbled. "Woman won't sit still. She's making me dizzy."

"Just keep an eye on her. Try to get her to eat something and lie down for a few minutes. She needs to rest. She's no help to anyone if she's an exhausted bundle of nerves."

"Will do." Sophia paused. "I feel sorry for her. Hard to lose your sister. Hard to be the one who's lost too."

Sympathy and sadness rippled through her raspy voice. Years ago, Sophia had been kidnapped by a couple of sadistic Fire elementals who'd delighted in torturing her, and they had come back and taken her again last summer. The things that she'd endured . . . They made me sick to think about, and I still didn't know how she'd found the strength to survive them not once but twice. Sophia knew better than anyone how horrifying it was to be ripped away from your family, with no hope of escaping or ever seeing them again. I wondered if that was what Elissa was feeling right now. That sickening misery, that dark despair, that utter hopelessness.

But more than that, I wondered if she was still feeling anything at all—or if she was already dead.

"Gin?" Sophia asked, breaking into my turbulent thoughts.

"Yeah," I murmured. "It is hard to lose your sister."

The two of us hung up, and I got to my feet and walked over to the rune drawings on the mantel. Sophia's comments made me think about my own lost sister, and I ran my fingers over the ivy vine pendant that was draped over the matching drawing. My sister Annabella's rune, the symbol for elegance.

I wondered what Annabella would be like today if she'd gotten the chance to grow up. She would have been thirty-six, five years older than me, maybe married, maybe even with a kid or two. I could almost picture her standing before me, with the same blond hair, blue eyes, and pretty features that Bria and our mother had.

My gaze moved over to my mother's snowflake pendant and drawing. Eira would have been in her fifties now, no doubt with some gray hair and a few wrinkles, but still a distinguished beauty.

But I would never know the answers to my questions.

Mab Monroe had burned my sister and mother to death, right in front of me, and I hadn't been able to do a damn thing to save either one of them. Even now, all these years later, I still remembered the intense heat of Mab's elemental Fire searing the air. The red-hot flames of her magic streaking toward Eira, almost in slow motion. My mother mouthing the words *I'm sorry* to Annabella and me before disappearing into that ball of Fire. Then Annabella rushing downstairs to meet the exact same fate.

Watching them die had been horrible enough, but it was all the other sensations that truly haunted me. My mother's blackened, smoking husk of a body hitting the floor with a dull thud. Annabella's nightgown crackling like a match that had just been lit. My mother's skin crumbling to ash. The stench of their charred flesh filling my nose. The hot, acrid odor of fire, smoke, and cooked skin sliding down my throat, making my stomach heave, and poisoning me from the inside out as I realized that my mother and sister were dead, dead, dead—

My phone rang, snapping me back to the here and now.

My hand had fisted so tightly around Annabella's ivy vine that her symbol pressed into the spider rune branded into my palm, another parting gift from Mab. I forced my fingers open and backed away from the rune pendants and matching drawings, trying to clear the morbid memories out of my mind and ignore the pain pulsing in my heart.

Easier said than done, but I went over to the coffee table and picked up my phone. The caller ID said that it was Finn.

"Please tell me that you found something on that cab Elissa got into," I said immediately upon answering.

"What?" Finn said. "No hello? No small talk? No chit-chat?"

"Not when a girl is missing. So what did you find out?"

"According to the cabdriver's log, Elissa paid with a credit card," Finn said. "Guess where the cabbie dropped her off at last night, around eight o'clock?"

"I have no idea," I snapped, not in the mood to play along right now.

"Northern Aggression," he said in a smug voice.

Well, that was actually a bit of good news. Unlike with Marco, I wouldn't have any problems getting this security footage; Roslyn Phillips, the owner of Northern Aggression, was a good friend.

"Feel like calling Owen and going over there?" Finn asked.

"Absolutely."

"Good," he said. "Because I've already called Roslyn. So put on your dancing shoes, Gin. We're going out tonight."

• • •

An hour later, a sharp knock sounded on my front door, which I opened to find Finn standing outside on the porch.

My eyes widened. "*What* are you wearing?"

Instead of his usual dark, subdued banker's suit, Finn was sporting a light gray coat over a powder-blue bow tie, shirt, vest, and pants, along with shiny, white patent-leather wing tips. His dark brown hair was slicked back into an artful style, he was freshly shaven, and a bit of spicy cologne wafted off him.

He grinned. "Isn't it great? It's winter chic, the newest style from Fiona Fine."

"You look like a bad prom date."

He arched his eyebrows, his green gaze taking in the boots, jeans, blue sweater, and black fleece jacket that I'd had on all day. "And you look like you beat up some guys earlier and forgot to wash their blood out of your jacket." He stabbed his finger at the dime-size stains on the fleece. "I know what those dark spots *really* are."

I shrugged. "It was only three guys, and they didn't bleed all that much."

Finn's eyebrows rose a little higher in disbelief.

"Well, they didn't bleed all that much on *me*," I amended. "Certainly not enough for me to change jackets."

He shook his head. "Your lack of fashion sense always confounds me. But blood-spattered jacket aside, there is another issue."

I crossed my arms over my chest. "And what would that be?"

He sniffed the air. "You still smell like barbecue from the restaurant."

"You once told me that smelling like barbecue was a total aphrodisiac."

"And it usually is," Finn said. "Women and barbecue are two of my favorite things. But not when we're going out clubbing."

"We are not going *clubbing*. We're looking for a missing girl. They are not the same thing. Not at all. Not even a little bit."

He grinned. "You say potato . . ."

I rolled my eyes. "I know, I know. You say *opportunity*. Let's go, Prom King. Owen is meeting us there. Bria has to work tonight, but she said that she'd call if she had any news."

I shut and locked the front door behind me, then drove us over to the nightclub.

Northern Aggression was Ashland's most decadent club, known near and far for its many hedonistic pleasures. You could get just about anything you wanted in the club—drinks, smokes, blood, sex—in just about any amount and combination, as long as you had enough cash or credit to pay your tab at the end of the night. Even though it was just after seven o'clock on a Wednesday night, dozens of people were already standing in line, waiting to get past the giant bouncers and the red velvet rope so they could go inside and get their party started.

The nightclub was located in a featureless building that looked like it could have housed a call center or some other anonymous corporate endeavor. The only thing that set the club apart from the surrounding Northtown buildings was the sign over the front door: a heart with an arrow shooting straight through it, Roslyn Phillips's rune for her club and all the pleasure and pain that could be had inside. The sign glowed a bright neon red, then orange, and finally yellow, highlighting the eager faces of all the people milling around below.

Finn, being Finn, naturally strutted past everyone and went straight to the front of the line. Normally, I would have scoffed at his swagger and told him to wait his turn, but tonight I followed him. I wanted to get inside as quickly as possible and find out what had happened to Elissa.

Finn shook hands with first one bouncer, then the other. "Gerald, Tim, nice to see you guys again."

The giants nodded and murmured their thanks, since Finn had just slipped each one of them a C-note to further expedite our entrance into the club. They undid the red velvet rope and let us pass, much to the muttered annoyance of everyone else still waiting in line in the cold.

I followed Finn inside, and we made our way to the main dance floor. The outside of Northern Aggression might be plain and featureless, but the inside was all luxe decadence. The dance floor was made of a springy bamboo, and thick red velvet curtains covered the walls. And most important to those partying hard, a large elemental Ice bar ran along one wall.

The bar had been updated a bit since the last time I'd been here, with the shapes of martini glasses, cherries, and other drink paraphernalia carved into the pale, glittering surface. Behind the bar, a guy mixed drink after drink, his eyes glowing a bright blue as he steadily fed his magic into the thick sheet of Ice to keep it frozen, solid, and in one piece amid the heat from all the bodies gathered around it and grooving out on the dance floor.

The music pulsed with a low, thumping beat, and Finn started shaking his ass in time to it as we pushed through the throngs of people and headed deeper into the club. A hand rose in the air, waving, and I spotted Owen standing at the far end of the bar. I waved back, put my hands against Finn's shoulders, and steered him in that direction.

Unlike Finn, who'd dressed up, Owen had dressed down in a pair of black corduroy pants and a dark gray sweater that outlined his broad shoulders. His black hair gleamed under the flashing strobe lights, which also made his violet eyes shimmer. I wasn't the only one who noticed him. Several women gave Owen appreciative, come-hither looks, but his gaze met mine and stayed there. I went over, wound my arms around his neck, and gave him a long, lingering kiss, marking my territory. The women in question all pouted into their drinks and drifted off in search of easier prey.

Owen looked at me, an amused smile playing across his lips. "What was that for?"

"No reason, really. Maybe because it's Wednesday?"

"Wednesday, huh?" He leaned down and murmured in my ear. "Then you'll have to come over later tonight, and we'll really make it memorable. Why, Wednesday might even become my new favorite day of the week."

His low, husky voice sent shivers down my spine, and I kissed him again. "Deal."

Owen winked back at me, and then we both turned to the woman standing beside him.

With her short black hair, toffee eyes and skin, and perfect features, she was quite simply one of the most beautiful women I'd ever seen. Supermodels would be jealous of her lush, curvy figure. Even when she was just standing at the bar and sipping a drink, she was the sort of woman who drew everyone's eye—and envy.

Roslyn Phillips gave me a warm, welcoming smile. "Hey, Gin."

"Roslyn." I stepped forward and hugged her. "It's good to see you. I just wish it was under better circumstances."

She nodded. "Yeah, Finn called and told me about Jade's sister being missing. I've got the security footage all queued up for you in the back, but I don't know how much help it's going to be. I've already asked the staff, but no one remembers any kind of disturbance, fight, or major trouble last night."

I nodded back at her, then turned to Finn and Owen. "You guys stay out here. Show Elissa's picture to the bartender and other workers, and see if anyone remembers seeing her."

Finn grinned at a passing redhead. "With pleasure."

Despite the fact that he was in love with Bria, my foster brother still liked to flirt with anything that moved. I was happy to see him getting his groove back after all the horrible things that had happened with Deirdre Shaw, but I still defended Bria's honor, the way I always did.

I elbowed him in the side. "Try to keep the partying to a minimum, okay?"

Owen clapped his hand on Finn's shoulder. "Don't worry. I'll keep him in line."

"You're no fun, Grayson." Finn pouted for a few seconds before his face brightened. "But you know what? That makes you the *perfect* wingman. C'mon. This is going to be good."

Owen blinked and opened his mouth to protest, but Finn slung his arm around Owen's shoulder and steered them both out onto the crowded dance floor. Owen looked back at me, a panicked expression on his face, but I just waggled my fingers at him.

"You boys have fun!" I called out over the pulsing music.

Roslyn laughed and finished off her martini. "C'mon. I've got everything ready for you."

She led me toward the back of the club. It was slow going, not only because of the dancers and the drinkers but also because of the workers who stopped to get Roslyn's advice or orders about this or that. Finally, we made it to a door in the back wall, and Roslyn opened it and ushered me through to the other side.

She shut the door behind us, cutting off some of the noise and commotion from the main part of the club, and I followed her down a series of hallways. Several waiters moved past us, returning to work after their breaks, and a few giant bouncers were stationed back here too, keeping an eye on things in the VIP rooms through various spy holes cut into the walls.

Roslyn led me into her office and gestured for me to sit in her desk chair. When I was settled, she leaned over me and logged into her computer.

"I've got the security footage ready to roll," she said. "Each camera is on a different tab so you can toggle back and forth between all of them."

"Thanks. I really appreciate this."

Roslyn nodded. "Anytime. And please tell Jade that I'm sorry and that I hope Elissa turns up soon."

"Do you know Elissa?"

"Not personally, but she's a college kid. Sometimes I think that they *live* here at the club." Roslyn smiled, but her expression quickly turned serious again. "I can't imagine what Jade's going through right now. If anything happened to Lisa or Catherine . . ."

Her voice trailed off at the thought of her sister and young niece. Roslyn shook her head. "Anyway, just holler if you need anything."

"I will. Thanks, Roslyn."

"Good luck." She smiled at me again, left the office, and closed the door behind her.

I pulled the keyboard a little closer, grabbed hold of the mouse, and started going through the footage.

Roslyn's state-of-the-art security cameras had a much higher resolution than the grainy ones from the country club, and she had a lot more of them showing both the inside and outside of Northern Aggression, plus some of the surrounding parking lots. Roslyn had fast-forwarded yesterday's footage to about ten minutes before the cab had dropped off Elissa, so I watched the ebb and flow of people in, out, and around the club, looking for anything suspicious, unusual, or out of place.

Northern Aggression attracted all ages, from those barely old enough to drink to folks who'd spent a lifetime partying hard. Young, old, and every age in between moved through the footage, along with humans, elementals, vampires, giants, dwarves, and every combination thereof. The club also catered to a wide range of incomes, everyone from poor college students looking to have a few cheap beers to wealthy businessmen who only imbibed the most expensive liquors. The nightclub truly was Ashland's melting pot.

The footage unspooled, and time passed, until at last a yellow cab cruised up to the club entrance. Elissa got out, paid the driver, and waited her turn in line to get inside. A few folks, men and women alike, tried to chat her up, but Elissa kept her eyes glued to her phone. Other than that, nothing out of the ordinary happened, and no one suspicious approached her.

Once Elissa actually got inside the club at around eight thirty, I switched to the interior footage so I could track her movements. Instead of heading out onto the dance floor or over to the bar, she hugged the wall, keeping to the fringes of the crowd, her head moving back and forth. She was obviously searching for someone. But who? Maybe Silvio was wrong, and she had a guy on the sly, someone other than her official boyfriend.

I followed her through the footage. Elissa glanced down at her phone, then back out into the crowd. She started to move closer to the dance floor, but something caught her attention, and she turned toward the elemental Ice bar instead. She stopped short, her entire body stiff with shock, her mouth wide open in a silent *O* of surprise. She stayed like that for several seconds before a passing waiter bumped into her, jostling her out of her daze. Her face crumpled, her shoulders sagged, and she whirled around and started pushing her way back out of the club.

I stopped the footage and called up another angle, trying to see what had upset her. It took me a few minutes, but I realized that Elissa was staring at a guy and a girl at the end of the bar. On the footage, the two clinked their beers together before downing their drinks. Then the guy pulled the girl over onto his lap, and the two of them started doing things that were better left unseen. I zoomed in on the amorous couple, took a photo of their faces with my phone, and texted it to Silvio: *Who are these people?*

My trusty assistant texted me back less than a minute later. *Guy is definitely Anthony Fenton, Elissa's boyfriend. Girl looks like Rose Sears, one of Elissa's friends.*

And just like that, everything made sense. Maybe Elissa had suspected that Anthony was cheating on her. Maybe another friend had seen Anthony and Rose at the club and had tipped her off. Maybe she'd even put a tracking app on his phone, like Silvio had on mine. Either way, Elissa had found out that Anthony was at Northern Aggression last night, and she'd come here to see what he was up to—which was basically screwing another girl in plain sight.

And just to twist the knife in a little deeper, it hadn't been some random girl but one of Elissa's friends, someone who knew exactly how much Elissa liked Anthony. No wonder Elissa had rushed outside. I wouldn't have wanted to stick around for that kind of betrayal either.

I put my phone aside and went back to the security footage. Elissa hurried out of the club, stumbled into the closest parking lot, and leaned up against the side of the first car she came to. Given the way her head was bowed and her shoulders were shaking, I could tell that she was crying her eyes out, something that she did for a good ten minutes. Lots of people walked by her, heading to and from the club, but a crying girl wasn't an uncommon sight at Northern Aggression, and no one stopped to ask her what was wrong or offer any kind of help.

Finally, Elissa straightened up, wiped off her face, and made a call, probably for another cab. Then she started pacing back and forth in the parking lot, blowing her nose and wiping away a few more tears while she waited. Eventually, though, something caught her attention, something that made her stop pacing. She looked over to her right and stood there for several seconds, frowning.

And then Elissa slowly started walking in that direction. A minute later, she disappeared around the far corner of the club, as though she was going around to the back of the building.

And she never returned.

I watched the rest of the security footage, both inside and outside the club, but the minutes turned into an hour, then two, then three, and Elissa never reappeared. So I went back and called up some different angles, but the cameras only covered so much space, and I couldn't see what might have caught her eye.

I double-checked all the footage and angles, with the same result. Elissa had just vanished into thin air, and no one had seen her since.

Not good. Not good at all.

I leaned back in the chair, drumming my fingers on Roslyn's desk. Three things could have happened to Elissa.

One: a cab could have shown up and taken her somewhere else.

Two: she could have found someone willing to give her a ride to her next destination, wherever that might have been.

Three: she could have been kidnapped right here at Northern Aggression, conveniently out of view of any of the security cameras.

Since Elissa hadn't come home and hadn't responded to any of her sister's frantic texts or calls, I was betting on option number three. And if that was the case, then I had no idea how I was going to find her. Hundreds of people, cars, and cabs came and went every single night at Northern Aggression. Sure, some people might dimly remember seeing Elissa crying in the parking lot, but once folks' money ran out and their party was over, they were focused on getting to their cars and going home—not what anyone else around them was doing.

Either way, Elissa was still gone and most likely in serious, serious trouble.

If she wasn't already dead.

I hated jumping to that scenario again, but I was an assassin, and I'd seen plenty of the worst of human nature up close and personal—including my own.

But I'd promised Jade that I would do everything I could, so I rewound all the security footage and watched it for a third time, focusing on everyone close to Elissa. So many people were crammed into the club that it was hard to keep track of everyone, much less pick out anyone who might have wanted to hurt her. No one paid her any special attention, and no one followed her outside. The most obvious suspect was Anthony, the sleazeball cheating boy-friend, but he'd been so busy macking on Rose that he'd never even realized that Elissa was here and watching the two of them break her heart.

I drummed my fingers on the desk again, thinking about the surrounding area. Parking lots flanked North-ern Aggression, and the nearest businesses were several hundred yards away. Those businesses' security cameras would be aimed at their own properties, not farther down the street at the club. It was probably a dead end, but I grabbed my phone and texted Silvio anyway. He texted back a few minutes later, saying that he would look into getting all the security footage from the surrounding busi-nesses. I thanked him and emailed copies of the Northern Aggression footage to myself, Silvio, Finn, and Bria, just in case they might see something that I'd missed.

Once I'd finished, I left Roslyn's office, strode down the hallways, and slipped out the club's rear exit. There was one more thing I wanted to check.

The back door opened into another paved lot, al-though no one parked back here, not even the staff, since the asphalt was so cracked and pitted with potholes. Dumpsters and trash cans overflowing with cigarette butts, used cocktail napkins, and empty liquor bottles ringed the area, forming a haphazard maze of rusted metal and rotten garbage. Shards of glass glinted like di-amonds against the broken blacktop, and the stench of sour spilled beer permeated the air. A few lights glowed at the corners of the building, but they did little to drive back the darkness. Even the loud, continually pulsing music faded to a faint hush back here, and the relative quiet was somewhat shocking after the constant noise inside the club.

All put together, it was the perfect place to kidnap a girl—or kill her.

I looked up at the security camera above the back door. It was pointed out at the parking lot, just like it should have been, but the plastic case was busted open on one side, revealing several frayed, disconnected, dangling wires. Well, that explained why there was no footage from back here. I wondered how long the camera had been out of commission and if it had been broken by some drunk asshole chucking beer bottles at it or by someone with far more sinister motives.

My phone beeped, and I pulled it out and read the message from Owen: *No one remembers seeing Elissa last night. Trying to herd Finn toward the front door.*

I smiled, knowing that he wouldn't have any luck with that, and texted him back, saying that I would meet them at the front of the club in ten minutes. That would give me enough time to search the parking lot. Oh, I didn't expect to find anything, but I had to make the effort for Jade's sake and my own conscience. I wasn't leaving here without doing every single thing possible to find her sister.

I had just put my phone away when I realized that the stones all around me were muttering—dark, dark mutterings that whispered of blood, violence, pain, and death.

Now, that was nothing new, since I'd actually killed more than a few people myself in this very parking lot. But these mutterings were high and sharp, meaning that they were fresh and that someone had been up to no good here very recently.

Maybe even last night, when Elissa had wandered back here.

I reached out with my magic, listening to the stones, and realized that it wasn't the walls of the club muttering so much as it was the broken pavement under my feet. So I palmed a knife and walked forward, scanning the shadows and slowly following the violent mutterings to their source, as though they were musical notes dancing on the breeze in front of me. The mutterings led straight into the maze of Dumpsters and trash cans. Naturally. I wrinkled my nose, trying to ignore the stench of rotting garbage, and kept going. The farther I walked and the closer I got to the origin of the violence, the darker and harsher the sounds became.

Something very, very bad had happened here.

I skirted around a pile of empty cardboard boxes and found myself staring at a cluster of old, dented Dumpsters. Unlike the others, these Dumpsters had been emptied recently and pushed together like the three sides of a triangle, although wide gaps still remained at the corners. The formation created a hollow space in the center, one that was largely blocked from sight until you stepped up to the space where the corners didn't quite meet. The mutterings intensified, growing harsher and louder, as though the musical notes I'd been following were building to a final, roaring crescendo.

My stomach twisted. I knew exactly what those sounds meant.

I eased forward. I took one step, then another, then another . . . until I could finally look through one of the gaps in between the Dumpsters.

The first thing that came into view was her long blond hair, shining like dull gold against the cracked, dirty asphalt.

My heart dropped, and my stomach twisted again, but I kept moving forward, even though I knew exactly what I would find.

Her arm was next, flung out behind her, the torn sleeve of her red dress fluttering like a feather in the winter wind. Then the curve of her back. Her long, lean, bare legs. And finally, scuffed red stilettos that barely clung to her feet.

I blinked and blinked, as if that would change the horrible image in front of me. But of course it didn't. It never did.

A dead woman sprawled across the pavement, discarded right along with the rest of the trash.

***

I tiptoed forward and crouched down beside the woman.

Her blond hair was strewn all over her face, obscuring her features, but she seemed young and pretty, in her early twenties, just like Elissa. She was also wearing a red dress, just like Elissa had been last night.

The color perfectly matched the blood on her face.

Even through the strands of her hair, I could tell that someone had beaten the young woman to a pulp. Her face was a swollen, bloody mess, with a broken nose, two blackened eyes, and more cuts and bruises than I could count.

And those weren't her only injuries.

Deep, ugly bruises circled her wrists, and matching ones marred her ankles, as though she'd been tied down to a chair. Still more bruises ringed her throat, each one a dark purple against her pale skin, almost looking like an expensive amethyst necklace instead of marks of death. I recognized the brutal pattern. As if beating her hadn't been enough, someone had wrapped his hands around the young woman's neck and squeezed, squeezed, squeezed.

Oddly enough, her hands were lying flat on the pavement, her fingers spread wide, as though she were trying to push herself away from her attacker.

I glanced around, but the surrounding pavement was empty. No purse, no phone, no coat, no sign of any personal possessions anywhere around her. She looked like a doll that a child had broken in a fit of rage and then tossed aside because it wasn't fun to play with anymore.

Even though I didn't want to, I forced myself to lean in even closer and study the woman's face. I still couldn't positively identify her, given the brutal beating, but the longer I stared at her, the more my heart sank. Blond hair, right age, red dress, last place she'd been seen. There was no denying those facts—and what they meant.

I'd wanted to find Elissa Daniels, but not like *this*. I might have assumed the absolute worst, the way I always did, but I'd still been hoping deep down inside that I was wrong and that things would turn out okay.

But Elissa was dead, and there was only one thing that I could do for her—and her sister—now.

I pulled my phone out of my pocket and hit a number in the speed dial.

She answered on the second ring. "Detective Bria Coolidge."

"It's Gin."

"What's wrong?" Bria's voice sharpened, picking up on my sad tone. "Have you found Elissa?"

"Yeah. You and Xavier need to come over to Northern

Aggression as soon as you can." I sighed, more sadness creeping into my voice. "And bring the coroner with you."

I hung up with Bria, stepped inside the club, found Roslyn, and told her what was going on. Then I grabbed Finn and Owen, and we all went back outside to wait for Bria, Xavier, and the rest of the police to arrive.

The four of us stared down at the body, careful not to touch her or disturb any evidence. Still not touching anything, we also searched the area around the three Dumpsters, looking for her purse, phone, or anything else that she—or her killer—might have left behind, but the only things we found were crumpled fast-food bags, smushed cigarettes, and broken beer bottles.

I also reached out with my magic again, hoping that the stones might give me some clue to who had done this, but the cracked sections of pavement only muttered about the blood, violence, and death that they had witnessed. Nothing more, nothing less.

I also pointed out the busted security camera to Roslyn. It had been broken for more than two weeks, although she didn't know by whom. She'd been trying to get the repair company to come fix it, but they'd been backed up with other jobs. Another dead end.

Thirty minutes later, a woman walked out of the back door of Northern Aggression. Given the cold, a toboggan covered most of her shaggy blond hair, although the dark blue fabric brought out the matching color of her eyes. Her cheeks were already pleasantly pink from the chill, and a silverstone primrose rune glinted against her dark blue jacket.

A few seconds later, the door opened again, revealing a giant who was around seven feet tall, with a strong, muscled body. Despite the frosty air, his shaved head was bare, and his ebony skin and dark eyes gleamed under the lights on the back of the building.

Detective Bria Coolidge, my baby sister, and Xavier, her partner on the force and Roslyn's significant other.

"What do you have?" Bria called out.

"Nothing good," I replied.

Finn, Owen, Roslyn, and I all stepped back out of the way so that Bria and Xavier could do their thing. The two cops crouched down and moved all around the body, studying the woman, their faces flat and expressionless. As cops, Bria and Xavier had seen a lot of bodies in their time, but you never quite got used to it, especially something like this, where a young woman had been so viciously assaulted.

Finally, after making pages of notes and taking tons of photos, Bria and Xavier straightened back up. Xavier went over to talk to Roslyn, Finn, and Owen, while Bria pulled me aside.

Bria's mouth tightened into a grim slash. "You think this is Elissa Daniels?"

"Unfortunately. She fits Elissa's description, right down to the dress and heels, and this was the last place she was seen."

I told her about the security footage that showed Elissa heading in this direction. "You can watch it for yourself. I emailed it to you earlier."

"I'll do that. The coroner's assistants are on their way. I've already got some men inside, talking to the bartender and other workers, but . . ." Bria shrugged. She didn't have to tell me how unlikely it was that someone had seen or heard anything.

"Xavier and I will stay with the body." She hesitated. "After we wrap up here, do you want to call Jade and ask her to meet us at the coroner's office?"

My heart squeezed with dread. "Yeah. I can do that. Just tell me when you're ready."

Bria gave me a sympathetic look and laid her hand on my shoulder. Then she shifted into full-fledged detective mode, examining the body again, along with the surrounding area, and taking more pictures. At her request, Roslyn brought out several large trash bags, and Bria and Xavier pulled on black crime-scene gloves and started collecting the garbage closest to the empty Dumpsters, hoping that it might hold some clue.

Fifteen minutes later, the patrol cops had roped off the area with yellow crime-scene tape and had rigged up portable lights all around the three Dumpsters. Blue lights flashed on the police cars in the parking lots and on all the surrounding side streets, but the sight of the po-po didn't stop people from entering the club. Instead, most folks simply ignored their presence. A dead body, even one that had been violently murdered, wasn't an uncommon occurrence in Ashland, not even in this part of Northtown. It certainly wasn't going to stop people from partying.

There was nothing else my friends could do, so Owen agreed to take Finn back to his car at my house, then check in with Eva, to see if his sister or Violet had learned anything about Elissa, her friends, or who might have done this to her. Finn said that he would coordinate with

Silvio and start reviewing the nightclub's security footage again. Roslyn went back into the club to tell her staff what was going on and question them again herself, on the off chance that someone had seen something after all. They were more likely to talk to their boss in confidence than to the cops.

Me? I stayed until the bitter, bitter end, watching Bria and Xavier slowly, methodically bag up trash and search the area yet again.

Finally, a large black van arrived, pulling as close to the back of the club as possible, given all the potholes, and a couple of guys wearing dark coveralls got out of the vehicle, pushing a stretcher along in front of them. The cops were finished with the scene, and now Elissa would be taken to the coroner's office for an autopsy.

Bria pulled off her gloves and nodded at me, finally ready for me to make the call I'd been dreading ever since I found the body.

With a heavy heart, I pulled out my phone and dialed Sophia.

"News?" she rasped.

"Yeah. Let me talk to Jade, please."

A second later, Jade's voice flooded the line. "What's going on, Gin? Have you found Elissa? Please, *please* tell me that you've found her."

The raw, naked desperation in her voice made my stomach drop like a lead weight. It took me several seconds to force out the very last words that she wanted to hear. "I need you to meet me downtown at the police station." I paused. "At the coroner's office."

Jade sucked in a breath. "What—why—"

Now she was the one who couldn't speak, but I made myself keep talking.

"I tracked Elissa to Northern Aggression. A little while ago, I found a body in the parking lot behind the club," I said, my own voice rough with regret. "It's a young blond woman. Bria wants you to come down to the coroner's office. Please."

"No! No! It can't be her! It can't be her—" Jade's voice went from a wail to a sob in a heartbeat.

I didn't say anything else. Nothing I could say would change the cold, cruel facts or make this any better.

A loud clatter sounded, as though Jade had dropped the phone, although I could hear her still sobbing *no-no-no* in the background. Each one of her cries shattered another piece of my heart. The better part of a minute passed before someone picked up the phone again.

"Don't worry," Sophia rasped. "I'll drive her."

"Thanks. I'll meet you there."

We hung up, and I looked over at the crime scene. The workers from the coroner's office had loaded Elissa onto the stretcher, and I watched while they slowly zipped the black body bag over her, hiding her bruised, bloody, battered face.

Out of sight but not out of mind.

Never, ever that.

And a hard, inescapable truth punched me in the gut, the way it always did whenever something like this happened.

This might be the end of Elissa Daniels, but it was just the beginning of her sister's pain.

✳ 10 ✳

I left Northern Aggression, drove through the downtown loop, and fell into the flow of traffic a few blocks away from the main police station. It was after ten o'clock now, and the mean streets of Southtown were open for business.

Hookers wearing as little as they could without freezing to death ambled up and down the sidewalks, stamping their feet and trying to stay warm between customers, while cars slowly cruised by, the drivers debating who they wanted to take for a spin. Pimps bundled up in puffy parkas lurked in the dark alleys beyond, ready to make their presence known if someone tried to leave without paying for services rendered. Still more folks gathered at the street corners under the flickering lights, buying and selling everything from pills to pot to bags of fresh blood for the vampires. At least, that's what the dealers claimed it was. I had my doubts, though, especially since it looked more like colored corn syrup than actual O-negative.

I pulled into the first empty parking space on the street that I saw, got out of my car, and locked it. I hadn't taken three steps down the sidewalk before a couple of guys sporting flashy gold chains over neon-green jackets broke away from their posse of friends at the corner and stopped in front of me. The guys looked to be in their early twenties, and they both grinned like fools as they cracked their knuckles and gave me a leering once-over.

"Hey there, honey," one of them crooned in a high, twangy voice. "What's a sweet little thing like you doing out on the dark, dangerous streets tonight?"

I rolled my eyes. Sweet little thing? Please. I'd already been killing people when these idiots were still in middle school.

I could have done the whole song and dance about how they needed to move out of my way, how they didn't know who they were messing with, and how they would deeply, painfully, and permanently regret hassling me. They would be stupid enough to attack me, and I would kick their asses into next week, just like I'd done with the giants at the country club earlier today. The same scenario had played out dozens of times over the past year.

Part of me wanted all of that to happen just so I could beat somebody down. Just so I could let out some of my simmering anger and frustration that I hadn't been able to find and save Elissa. But this wasn't about what I wanted, not anymore. It was about helping Jade as best I could. I needed to get to the coroner's office before she did, and I just didn't have time to deal with these fools. So I reached underneath my jacket, pulled out my spider rune pendant, and held it out where the two goons could see it.

"Any more questions?" I snarled.

Their eyes bulged, and their mouths opened and closed and opened and closed again, but no sounds came out. They knew exactly who this rune belonged to and just how dead I could make them.

"I didn't think so."

I strode forward, and the two guys practically tripped over each other to get out of my way. And not just them. Everyone on the block had seen our confrontation. All conversation abruptly cut off, and everyone on the sidewalk stopped what they were doing and stared at me. No one else blocked my path, and I got the distinct impression that several people were holding their breath. Of course, I knew that they would all start talking about me the second I turned the corner, wondering what I was doing here tonight, but I didn't care. Let them gossip all they wanted.

It didn't much matter when a girl was dead.

A few minutes later, I reached the police station, which was located in a prewar building made of dark gray granite that took up its own block. Despite the late hour, light spilled out of every window, highlighting the columns, crenellations, and curlicued carvings of vines and leaves that covered much of the stone. I'd always thought it highly ironic that the station was housed in such a beautiful building when so much ugliness passed through its doors on a daily basis.

A bored-looking cop was working a metal detector that had been installed just inside the main entrance. The machine *beep-beep-beep*ed out a sharp, high-pitched warning when I went through, but I didn't want to deal with the cop any more than I had wanted to deal with the thugs outside, so I *tap-tap-tapp*ed my fingernail against my spider rune, making it ring like a bell. The cop knew what the symbol meant just like the thugs had, and he swallowed and waved me through.

Sometimes being feared was quite helpful.

Fifty feet later, the corridor opened up into the main part of the station, an enormous room of lovely gray marble with silver flecks running through it. Crystal and brass chandeliers dropped down from the ceiling, highlighting the people below. Uniformed cops carrying paperwork from one side of the room to the other, suited detectives gossiping around a water cooler, criminals slouching on wooden benches along the walls waiting to be processed and taken to their cells for the night. The murmur of a dozen conversations echoed through the room, punctuated by the constant *jingle-jangle* of one phone after another, and the air reeked of black coffee, burned popcorn, and sour sweat.

I skirted around the uniformed cops, ignored the detectives, walked by the criminals, and headed toward the back of the room, where several desks were clustered. Xavier was already here, sitting at his desk and scribbling on a notepad, a phone wedged in the crook of his neck. He spotted me and waved me over.

"Yeah . . . yeah," Xavier said. "Gin just walked in the door. I'll send her down to you."

He hung up, then threw down his pen, leaned back in his chair, and ran his fingers over his shaved head in a sharp, scrubbing motion, as if he were trying to wipe something particularly horrible out of his mind. Curious. Xavier was rock-solid, one of the strongest, toughest, most dependable guys I knew. I wondered what had upset him so much.

Xavier dropped his hands, leaned forward in his chair, and looked at me.

"Rough night?" I asked.

He gave me a faint smile, but his gaze remained dark and troubled. "Aren't they all?"

Couldn't argue with that.

He gestured at his phone. "That was Bria. She's downstairs with Ryan. He's just finished his preliminary examination."

I nodded. Dr. Ryan Colson was the head coroner and a friend to both Bria and Xavier.

Xavier's mouth twisted, and he stared at me like he wanted to tell me something. After a second, he shook his head, as if banishing the thought. "Ryan will clean up her face as best he can so that Jade can officially identify her. Try to make her look a little less . . ."

"Beaten, strangled, and dead?"

He winced. "Yeah. But there's no softening a blow like that, is there?"

"Not in my experience."

Once again, he gave me a strange, almost pitying look. I wondered what he knew about Elissa Daniels's murder that I didn't.

"Did you guys find anything at the scene?" I asked. "Anything in the trash you collected? Any clue to who might have done this?"

He shook his head. "Nope. Nothing obvious. Just a bunch of soggy cardboard boxes, empty bottles, and broken glass, which isn't unusual, given the location. Bria and I will go through all the trash again later, but I'm not holding out much hope of finding anything useful."

I nodded. "Thanks for trying, though."

Xavier shrugged his massive shoulders. "Just doing my job." His gaze flicked over to the detectives, who were still standing around the water cooler, watching a video on one of their phones. "Someone around here has to, right?"

"Right."

Xavier jerked his thumb over toward the elevators. "You go on down to the coroner's office. I'll stay here and keep an eye out for Sophia and Jade."

"Thanks, Xavier."

He nodded at me and picked up his phone to make another call.

I got into one of the elevators, punched the button, and rode down to the basement. The elevator doors opened, revealing a long, empty hallway. After the constant noise and motion upstairs, the lack of sound and people was a bit jarring, as if I'd been transported to a distant, deserted planet, instead of just another floor in the same building.

I walked down the corridor, my boots whispering against the floor, and opened the door to the waiting room that fronted the coroner's office. Padded chairs against the walls, dusty plastic palm trees in the corners, a glass table topped with several tissue boxes. The functional furniture was nice enough, but it was still a thoroughly depressing place. Even worse, I could hear the walls wailing with the cries of everyone who'd been unfortunate enough to come here and identify a dead loved one. Soon Jade's sobs would be added to the ones already here. The mournful notes made my own heart squeeze tight.

The frosted-glass door at the back of the waiting room buzzed open, and Bria stuck her head out. "There you are. Ryan's ready for you."

I walked through the opening and stepped into a room that was mostly made of metal. Stainless-steel vaults, each one fronted with its own door, lined two of the walls, while several long metal tables took up the center of the room, each positioned above a drain in the floor. It was several degrees cooler in here, and goose bumps rippled down my spine, despite my heavy winter clothes. A sharp tang of lemony antiseptic hung in the air, as though someone had just cleaned out a refrigerator.

Dr. Ryan Colson, the coroner, stood beside one of the tables, his blue scrubs looking shockingly bright against the dull metal. The soft lights made his black hair and goatee gleam like wet ink against his ebony skin, and his dark hazel eyes were kind and sympathetic behind his round silver glasses.

"Dr. Colson."

"Please," he said. "Call me Ryan."

"Okay, Ryan. But only if you call me Gin."

He nodded. "Gin."

My gaze flicked past him to the table. Elissa's body had already been stretched out on the metal, with a blue sheet draped over everything but her face and her toes, whose nails were painted a fun, flirty pink. My stomach turned over again.

"I haven't started my official autopsy yet, but the causes of death are pretty obvious," Ryan said in a low, somber voice. "Blunt-force trauma to the head, face, and torso, along with manual strangulation. One of the blows to the head probably knocked her out before the strangulation occurred. That's my hope, anyway."

He reached out and rested his hand on the table beside Elissa's head, almost as if he were trying to comfort her, even though she was far beyond anyone's reach now.

"It's a bit hard to tell with the cold weather, but I'd estimate that she's been dead at least twenty-four hours. I'll know more when I do the full autopsy, but that's not why you're here."

I shook my head. "I wish none of us were here tonight."

A sharp knock sounded on the door, and we turned toward the frosted glass. Ryan went over and opened the door. Jade stood in the waiting room, with Sophia hovering behind her.

Jade was wearing the same crimson coat she'd had on at the Pork Pit earlier today, but her face had been scrubbed free of its usual makeup, and her blond hair had been pulled back into a messy ponytail, making her look younger and far more vulnerable than she had at the restaurant. Her puffy eyes were bloodshot, and she twisted a white silk handkerchief around in her hands. She'd probably been crying ever since I called.

Jade looked at me a moment before her green gaze locked onto the body on the table. She froze, as if she were as dead as Elissa. No one moved or spoke, giving her time to process the ugly, ugly scene. Jade stayed ramrod-still for the better part of a minute before a single, violent tremor shook her body. Then she started shaking and couldn't stop. Her lips trembled, her fingers spasmed, her legs wobbled, and she would have crumpled to the floor if Sophia hadn't reached out and steadied her.

To my surprise, Ryan stepped forward and gently took hold of Jade's elbow. "It's all right," he said in a soft, soothing, sympathetic voice. "I know how hard this is. Whenever you're ready, Ms. Jamison. Just take your time."

Jade stared back at him with a blank expression, so far down in her grief that she wasn't really seeing him. After several seconds, she nodded and let him slowly lead her over to the table. Sophia stayed by the door, while Bria and I both stepped back away from the table.

Ryan had combed out Elissa's long blond hair and had cleaned the blood off her face, trying to make her look as normal as possible, but her features were still a bruised, battered mess.

Jade gasped and pressed her fist to her mouth, shocked by the sight of her dead, beaten, strangled sister. Another violent tremor ripped through her body, as though she was going to collapse under the weight of her emotions. Jade reached out and grabbed Ryan's hand, squeezing his fingers as if to push back her own feelings and steady herself. Ryan winced at her tight, bruising grip, but he didn't remove his hand from hers.

"Can—can I see a little bit more of her?" Jade whispered. "Just down to her shoulders? Please?"

Ryan nodded. "Of course."

He gave Jade's hand a little pat with his free one, and she finally realized that she was still holding on to him.

Jade grimaced and let go. Ryan nodded his thanks, then stepped forward and lowered the blue sheet a few more inches, revealing Elissa's collarbones and the curve of her shoulders.

Jade leaned over the table, her gaze roaming over Elissa's face, trying to see her sister through all the bruises, swelling, and broken bones.

Bria opened her mouth to ask for a positive ID, but Ryan shook his head, telling her to wait.

I looked at Jade, expecting tears to start pooling in her eyes and more tremors to start shaking her body as the hard, inescapable truth sank in. She braced her hands on the side of the table and dropped her head, her gaze locked onto Elissa's left shoulder, as if she couldn't bear to look at her sister's battered face any longer.

After several seconds, Jade shuddered out a long, slow breath. I tensed. This was it—this was the moment when the tears, sobs, and heartbreak would truly begin.

Jade drew in another breath and slowly let it out. I stepped forward to put my arm around her shoulder, to try to comfort her in whatever small way I could, but she lifted her head, her lips stretching up into an enormous smile, despite the tears cascading down her face. She held out her hand, stopping me.

"That's not her," Jade said. "That's not Elissa. That's not my sister."

Jade's words echoed through the room, bouncing off the walls and freezing me in place, as though I were as cold, dead, and stiff as the bodies inside the metal vaults.

For a moment, I just stared at Jade, not sure that I'd

heard her right. Bria and Ryan were doing the same thing, shocked expressions on their faces. Then her words sank in, and my brain started functioning again.

I looked at Jade, then at the body, then back at Jade. "Are you sure? Maybe you should take another look——"

Jade shook her head. "I don't need to take another look. That's not Elissa. My sister has a small birthmark on her left shoulder. It looks like a little half-moon." She pointed to the dead woman's shoulder. "This woman doesn't have a birthmark. I don't know who that is, but it's not Elissa. I'm sure of it."

More tears streamed down her face, and her entire body sagged with relief. Once again, Jade would have fallen to the floor if Ryan hadn't grabbed her elbow. She looked up at him, then grabbed his face in her hands, pulled his head down to hers, and pressed a loud, smacking kiss to his lips.

"Thank you!" she said, her voice high and giddy. "Thank you, thank you, thank you!"

She kissed him again, once on either cheek, before finally letting him go. This time, it was Ryan who reached out and grabbed the table to keep from dropping to the floor.

"Um . . . thank you too?" he mumbled, his silver glasses a bit crooked from Jade's enthusiastic smooches.

She beamed at him for several more seconds before reality slowly set back in. Jade frowned and looked at the dead woman again. "That poor, poor girl. But . . . if that's not Elissa, then where *is* she?"

And just like that, the last of Jade's euphoria vanished, and misery filled her face again. Her shoulders slumped, and her breath escaped in harsh rasps that made her whole body tremble.

"That could still be Elissa," Jade whispered in a grief-stricken voice. "That could still be her . . . She could still be *dead* . . ."

Her voice trailed off, and fresh tears streaked down her cheeks. Jade whirled around and hurried away from the table, as if she couldn't stand to be in here a second longer. Sophia was still waiting by the door, and she put her arm around Jade's shaking shoulders and steered the other woman back out into the waiting room. Sophia nodded, telling me that she would stay with Jade, and shut the door behind them.

That left Bria, Ryan, and me alone in the morgue with the body. Bria bent back down over the woman, studying her face again and trying to see her true features through all the bruises and swelling. I did the same, although after a few seconds, the girl's face blurred in front of my eyes, and I found myself thinking about Elissa again.

Jade was right: Elissa could still end up here dead on a slab if I didn't find her.

And I had no idea how to do that.

Bria finally straightened up and shook her head, making her blond hair fly around her shoulders. "This woman didn't have any ID on her. No purse, no wallet, no phone. If her fingerprints or DNA aren't in our system, it'll be difficult to figure out who she is. Much less where she came from and who might have killed her."

"You don't think it happened at Northern Aggression?" Ryan asked.

Bria shook her head again. "No. There was no blood

anywhere around the body. Not pooled on the ground underneath her and not spattered on any of the Dumpsters around her. She was definitely murdered somewhere else. The killer just used the club to get rid of her body. He probably thought that she wouldn't be discovered for a couple of days, until the next time the trash got picked up."

I'd never envied Bria her job of dealing with all the crime in Ashland, especially when it came to something like this, a young life cut short in such a brutal, violent fashion. If the girl wasn't in any of the police databases and no one had filed a missing person report on her, it could take Bria days, if not weeks, to figure out who she was. That sort of delay would most likely ruin any chance that she and Xavier had of finding out who had done this.

"There's something else," Ryan said. "Something you need to see, Gin."

I looked at him.

The coroner straightened his glasses and stared back at me, his hazel gaze sympathetic, as if I were the one who'd come here to identify a dead relative instead of Jade. "I noticed something in my initial examination of the body. Something that was impossible to miss." He cleared his throat, suddenly uncomfortable. "You're not going to like it."

"What is it?" I asked, wondering what this dead girl could possibly have to do with me.

Ryan hesitated, obviously not wanting to deliver whatever bad news he had, and glanced over at Bria. She crossed her arms over her chest, her lips tightening into a grim slash in her pretty face. They kept staring at each other, having some silent conversation and debate that I couldn't follow. It reminded me of the strange look Xavier had given me upstairs. The three of them knew something that I didn't.

Something bad.

"Spit it out," I said. "No matter how horrible it is, I can take it. Trust me."

Ryan kept staring at Bria. Finally, my sister sighed and nodded, giving him permission. He nodded back at her, then reached down and gently pulled the dead woman's arms out from underneath the blue sheet. He looked at me again, then slowly turned the woman's hands over so that her palms faced up where we could all see them.

He was right. It was impossible to miss.

Something had been drawn on both of the woman's palms in what looked like bright red blood, a distinctive symbol that was as familiar to me as my own face: a small circle surrounded by eight thin rays.

I sucked in a breath.

My spider runes were on the dead woman's palms.

✳ 11 ✳

For a moment, I couldn't speak. My heart, my breath, every small tic, twitch, and tremor in my entire body just *stopped*, shocked into stillness by the sickening sight before me.

Then, in the next instant, movement, breath, and sensation all rushed back into my body, and I could feel my eyes slowly growing wider and wider, until it seemed like those two spider runes filled my entire field of vision.

The longer I stared at them, the more the symbols actually seemed to *move*, to quiver, to pulse, as though the bloody circles were connected to my own heart, frantically pounding in my chest. All I could do was stare and stare at those two spider runes—*my runes*—peering up at me like evil eyes and mocking me from a dead woman's hands.

"Are those runes . . . were they made with . . . her blood?" I asked, my voice as shocked and breathless as I still felt.

"Actually, they were drawn with lipstick," Ryan said. "But yes, those are definitely spider runes. I told Bria and Xavier the second I saw them."

"But how—who—*why*—" The words sputtered out of my mouth, but I couldn't get them to form a coherent sentence. Just like I couldn't form a coherent thought right now.

No, that wasn't true. Too many thoughts flashed through my mind one after another, all of them lightning strikes scorching my heart to ash. What connection, if any, could I possibly have to this woman? And why draw my spider runes on her palms? Was it a warning that I was next? That the killer wanted to make me as bloody, broken, and dead as this poor girl?

The questions just kept coming and coming, with no answers in sight. I felt like I was standing in a dark tunnel, and all I could see were the bright lights of the oncoming train, about to mow me down.

Bria shook her head, making her hair fly out around her shoulders again, as if she were trying to rattle this horrible sight right out of her mind the same way that I was. She laid a comforting hand on my shoulder. "Gin, are you sure that you don't know this woman? Take another look at her."

Ironically enough, she was treating me the same way I had treated Jade a few minutes ago, trying to soften the stinging, sickening blow of something that could never, ever *be* softened. Anger roared through me that my own sister was trying to handle me like I was some sort of *victim*.

I started to snap at Bria that of course I didn't know

this girl, but I forced myself to rein in my rage. None of this was Bria's fault, and lashing out at her wouldn't help anything, especially not the dead girl. So I forced myself to bend down and take another look at her, just as my sister had asked.

I carefully examined the girl, once again trying to look past the beating, bruises, and swelling and see her as she had been in life—her eyes, her nose, her smile. But her features remained as strange to me as before. I didn't know this girl. I had never seen her before. I was sure of it.

So I moved on to what I did know: my spider runes.

My stomach squeezed, but I ignored the hot, bitter bile rising in my throat, bent down, and peered at the runes. Now that I was looking more closely at them, I could see that they'd been drawn with bright red lipstick, not blood, just like Ryan had said.

And I noticed something else odd. The rest of her was a bruised, battered mess, but her palms were absolutely pristine, with no blood, dirt, grime, or anything else marring the surface of her skin there, except for the two symbols. And it wasn't just that she had my spider runes drawn on her palms; it was how clear, precise, and neat they were, each one essentially a carbon copy of the other.

Someone had taken his slow, sweet time marking her up.

My own hands snapped into tight fists, my knuckles cracking from the sudden, intense pressure, and the spider rune scars embedded deep in my own palms started itching and burning, almost as if someone was tracing over them with a tube of lipstick. The scars pounded in time with my heart, until I thought that blood was going to come bursting out of the marks, forced out by my own rage, disgust, horror, and shock.

Slowly, I forced myself to relax my fists, unclenching them one finger at a time, and my right hand crept up to the spider rune pendant hanging around my neck. It had been a present from Owen, one that I'd always loved wearing, along with the matching ring on my finger, a gift from Bria.

Until this moment.

Now the pendant felt as heavy as an anchor, dragging me down, down, down, and the ring was a circle of rot around my finger, spreading out to infect and destroy every single part of me. Just feeling the pendant and the ring touching my body, along with my Ice and Stone magic rippling through the surface of the silverstone jewelry, made me sick to my stomach again.

The spider rune pendant slipped through my cold, numb fingers and thumped against my chest, as hard as a sledgehammer beating against my heart, and I had to clench my hands into fists again to keep from ripping off the jewelry and trying to tear the scars out of my own palms.

"Gin?" Bria asked in a soft voice, cutting into my turbulent emotions. "Do you know her?"

I shook my head. "No. I've never seen her before. I'm sure of it. But the spider runes . . ." My voice trailed off, and it took me a moment to finish my thought. "They're *exactly* like mine."

Even though it was the very last thing that I wanted to do, I forced myself to uncurl my fists again and held out my hands, palms up, so that Bria and Ryan could see my scars. They both bent down, comparing the marks on the dead girl's hands to the ones branded into my palms. I made myself keep my hands open, even though I felt completely exposed, as if I had been stripped naked and staked out in a public square for everyone to gawk at.

After about a minute, Ryan straightened up and cleared his throat. "It would seem that whoever drew the runes on the girl is familiar with your actual scars. Or at the very least your pendant. You wear that necklace quite a bit, don't you?"

"All the time now," I muttered. "All the damn time now. Out in the open where everyone can see it. What a fucking fool I am."

Ever since Owen had given it to me, I'd always been so proud of the pendant, since it was something from my childhood that I'd thought was lost forever. Even more than that, ever since I'd become head of the underworld, a small part of me had liked people knowing my sym-bol—and especially fearing it. I just never thought that someone would take my spider rune and do something so horribly sick and disgusting with it.

And I still couldn't puzzle out what it really *meant*. If someone wanted to warn me that I was on their hit list, that they were coming for me, that they wanted me dead, there were far easier ways to do it. Why not spray-paint the symbol on the front door of the Pork Pit? Why not scratch it on the hood of my car while it was parked near the restaurant? Why not just burn it into the front lawn at Fletcher's house, if they wanted to be truly dramatic?

Any one of those things would have immediately got-ten my attention. So why put the symbols on a dead woman instead? Was he just mocking me? Or was something else entirely going on here?

I didn't know—but I was going to find out.

The killer might think that he was taunting me, using my runes in such a sick, disgusting fashion, but all he had really done was piss me off. He wanted to get my attention? Well, he had it now, in fucking spades. I was going to hunt down this blackhearted son of a bitch, and he was going to pay for what he'd done to this poor, innocent girl.

More than he'd ever imagined.

"Gin," Bria said in a low, warning voice. "Take it easy."

I looked at her, and she pointed at the table. Ice crystals flowed out of my fingertips and ran across the metal table, quickly creeping toward the girl's body like a tidal wave of frost. A sign of my own cold, cold rage.

I yanked my fingers off the table and forced myself to tap down my magic, pulling it back inside my own body where it belonged. "Sorry." I looked at Ryan. "I didn't mean to hurt anything or destroy any evidence."

"You didn't." He gave me a sad smile. "Besides, she's well beyond any sort of physical hurt or pain now."

He looked down at the woman, his face creasing with more sadness. Like most people in Ashland, Dr. Ryan Colson had had his own share of tragedy. His younger brother had been shot and killed right in front of him when they were both just kids. I wondered if he was thinking about the brothers and sisters who might be missing this girl, whoever she was.

After several seconds, Ryan shook his head, as if chasing away his own bad memories and heartache. He raised his gaze to mine again, his face even more somber than before. "There's something else you need to see, Gin. Something to do with this girl."

My heart clenched, and my gut twisted. What now?

Bria frowned. "Do you mean . . ."

Ryan gave a sharp nod. "Yeah."

"And you think that this girl . . ."

"Yes. Unfortunately."

I looked back and forth between the two of them, not understanding their shorthand sentences, but they stared at each other instead of me, once again having some silent conversation that I couldn't follow.

"What's going on?" I asked.

Bria sighed. "Nothing good."

Ryan turned to me. "Follow me, please, and I'll explain it all."

Curious and more than a little wary, I followed Ryan out of his office and through the waiting room, with Bria trailing along behind me. Sophia and Jade were gone, although Sophia had left a note on the waiting room table saying that they were in the restroom and would be back in a few minutes.

Ryan left the waiting room and led us down a couple of hallways before stopping in front of an old wooden door that was set in the very back corner of this level. I looked over at Bria, but her face was grim, and she stood right alongside Ryan like the two of them were soldiers in some battle that no one else even knew about.

There was no sound this far back in the basement, not even the faint hum of the distant elevators or the gurgle of water running through the overhead pipes. The air was absolutely still and even colder here than it had been in his office, as though this part of the basement was completely cut off from all heat, life, and ventilation.

Ryan pulled out a ring of keys, flipped through them, and stuck one of them into the lock. He opened the door and stepped aside so that Bria and I could enter first. Then he slipped into the room behind us, closed the door, and hit the switch on the wall.

The overhead lights slowly winked on one by one, as if waking up from a long winter's nap. I blinked against the harsh glare and studied the area before me. Floor-to-ceiling metal shelves covered all the walls, and several more free-standing shelves took up a good portion of the back of the room. Heavy-duty cardboard boxes lined each shelf from top to bottom and side to side, and each box had its own unique numbers and names written on the cardboard in permanent black marker. The air smelled old and musty, and a heavy coating of dust covered many of the boxes and shelves, as though they'd been brought down here years ago and totally forgotten.

"This is the cold-case storage room," Bria said. "One of them, anyway. For crimes that go unsolved. Lots of those in Ashland."

I nodded. I'd heard her talk about this room in passing, about sending evidence down here for safekeeping or bringing up the boxes when she got a long-awaited break in a case, but I'd never been here myself. Then again, I wasn't a frequent visitor to the police station; it was one of the few places in Ashland that I avoided like the plague.

Ryan disappeared back behind a row of shelves. Several faint *scrape-scrape-scrape*s sounded, as though he was pulling a cardboard box down from up high on one of the shelves. A few seconds later, he reappeared with a box in his arms, walked over, and set it down on a metal table in the center of the room. He looked at Bria, who nodded. Ryan pulled a small knife out of his pants pocket and used it to carefully slice through the red evidence tape that was wrapped around the box.

"A knife in your pocket? You're a man after my own heart, Colson," I drawled, trying to lighten the mood.

He flashed me a grin and continued his work. A few seconds later, he slid the knife back into his pocket, pulled the lid off the box, and set it aside. I stepped forward and peered down inside, not quite sure what to expect, but all I saw were thick manila file folders.

One by one, Ryan pulled out the folders and carefully, neatly arranged them on the table. Once all the folders were out of the box, he flipped them open and drew out a photo from the top of each file. He turned the photos around so that I could see them and lined them up side by side. There were a dozen of them, and they all showed the exact same thing.

A dead woman.

At first, I wondered what the point was, but then I took a closer look at the photos, and I began to see the similarities. Each woman was lying on a metal slab in the coroner's office, cold and still in death. Each one had long blond hair and had probably been young and pretty— until someone had beaten her face to an unrecogniz- able pulp. Ugly, purple bruises also ringed each woman's throat from where she had been strangled.

I moved down the row of photos, staring at them all in turn. But they were all so similar that they could have been carbon copies, and one face melted into the next and the next until they all seemed to solidify into a single dead woman. My breath caught in my throat, and my stomach churned as I realized exactly what I was looking at.

"All these photos, all these women. You're saying that this girl tonight and all the rest of these poor women are connected . . ." My voice trailed off for a moment. "You're saying that there's a serial killer in Ashland."

❋ 12 ❋

For the second time in the last ten minutes, my mind spun around and around, trying to make sense of this startling new revelation.

Even in Ashland, where violence was sadly so very common, serial killers were exceptionally rare. The only one that I knew of recently had been Harley Grimes, the Fire elemental who'd kidnapped and tortured Sophia, and had done the same to dozens of other men and women before Sophia had finally killed him last year. But even then, Grimes had just been a mean son of a bitch who liked to hurt everyone who crossed his path. He hadn't been a true serial killer, driven to hunt, abduct, torture, and murder the same kind of person over and over again.

But all these young women, all roughly the same age, with roughly the same features, and all killed in roughly the same way. It was a stunning new horror.

"How many?" I whispered. "How many women?"

Bria looked at Ryan, letting him take the lead.

"The dozen women before you are all the ones that I know of, that I've done the autopsies for," he said, gesturing at the files and photos on the table. "There could be more victims—many more victims. I've been going through the cold-case files, trying to figure out if there are others and how long the killer has been active, but I haven't found anything conclusive yet. All of these women have been murdered over the past two years. All of them badly beaten and strangled, with their bodies dumped in locations all over Ashland."

"What made you connect the deaths? What ties them all together? Besides how they look and how he kills them?" I asked, part of me not wanting to know the answer. "Because it sounds like there's something else. Something *worse*, if that's even possible."

Ryan reached back into the box and drew out a large plastic bag that I hadn't noticed before. Several small compacts, all different colors, shapes, and sizes, rattled around inside, along with pots of eye shadow, sticks of eyeliner, and tubes of mascara. "Makeup."

"Makeup?"

He nodded. "Makeup. Foundation, powder, eye shadow, eyeliner, mascara. I've found quite a lot of it on all the victims' faces. Far more than anyone would normally wear, and all of it in these bright, gaudy colors that look more like paint than makeup." He shifted on his feet. "It looks like the killer . . . dolls them up, for lack of a better term. That he either makes the women put on the makeup or he does it himself before he, ah, well, you know."

"Kills them," Bria finished in a harsh voice.

Ryan winced and nodded again. He set the bag down on the table, making the compacts and other items inside rattle together again. The harsh sound reminded me of bones breaking.

"My resources are limited, but I've been working on it in my free time," he said. "I'm certainly no expert, but so far, I haven't found one brand or type of makeup that seems to be used more than any other."

I glanced down at the photos of the dead women spread out on the table. I didn't want to ask the question, but I had to know more. "What about lipstick? Like the blood-red lipstick he used for my spider runes?" A horrible thought occurred to me, and I had to clear my throat before I could force out my next words. "Has he . . . drawn my spider runes on any of the other women?"

"No," Ryan said. "This is the first time that he's put any sort of runes on his victims."

I exhaled. It didn't change anything, and it certainly didn't help any of the dead women, but at least he'd only used my runes this one time. I didn't know what I would have done if he'd marked them on all his victims. Probably felt even more sick guilt than I already did. Although I wondered why he had drawn them on this girl and not any of the others. Why mark her up? Why now?

"As for the lipstick, I have found that on all the victims. Their lips are the one thing that he actually seems to use the same color on from woman to woman," Ryan said. "I've been trying to determine exactly what color and brand of lipstick it is, but it's been hard to get a good, clean sample, given how badly he beats the women, and their subsequent exposure to the elements."

I barked out a short, brittle laugh. "Well, now you have a clean sample, thanks to my spider runes."

He gave me a grim look. "Yes, I do."

I curled my hands around the edge of the table, feeling the cold metal dig into the still itching and burning spider rune scars on my own palms. Fletcher had been wrong. Sometimes you just couldn't brace yourself for the worst. Because I had never expected something like this to happen, not even in Ashland.

"So he kidnaps them, puts makeup on them, and kills them," I said. "What else does he do to them?"

Ryan shook his head. "Nothing. He doesn't do anything else to them. At least, not before the end."

"What do you mean he doesn't do anything else to them?" I asked. "Surely there has to be more to this than some creep painting women's faces. He has to take them and make them up for some reason."

He waved his hand over the photos. "There are no signs of physical abuse. No cuts, no burns, nothing like that. He restrains them, probably with a heavy rope, judging from the bruises around their wrists and ankles, but he doesn't torture them." His mouth twisted. "The beatings the women endure are horrific enough all on their own."

Ryan looked at Bria, and she nodded, telling him to continue.

"If I had to guess, I would say that he ties them down to a chair. But he takes care of them. He feeds and bathes them on a regular basis, judging from my examination of the bodies."

"So he kidnaps these women and holds them hostage. How long?" I asked. "How long does he keep them?"

"That's a bit harder to determine. But judging from when some of the women were reported missing and when their bodies were found, the weather and the temperature at the time, and the varying rates of decomposition, I would say that he keeps them for at least four days. Sometimes a week or longer."

So all of these women had endured at least four horrific days of being tied down, knowing that they would never see their friends and family again, knowing that they were going to be killed sooner or later, whenever the urge struck the monster who'd taken them.

That sort of helplessness was its own kind of cruel, cruel torture.

My gaze dropped to the photos of the dead women again, and for a moment, I could hear each and every one of their frantic cries ringing in my ears, screaming, begging, pleading for their captor to release them. Promising to do whatever he wanted if only he would let them live. If only he would let them go home to their families. A cold shiver crawled down my spine. I shook my head, but I couldn't get rid of those dark, wailing echoes.

"But why even take them in the first place if he doesn't actually do anything to them?" I asked. "If he just wanted to kill women, he could do that easily enough. Snatch them off the street, drag them into some dark alley, beat them, and leave their bodies behind. Not keep them prisoner for days on end."

Ryan raised his hands in a helpless gesture. "I don't know why he chooses these women, what they represent to him. My theory is that they remind him of someone close to him, someone he maybe even loved once upon a time. Whatever happened to that woman, and if he killed her too, well, that's anyone's guess. But I think that he's trying to replace this person in his life. And when the women don't measure up to his standards or don't act the way he wants them to, that's when he flies into a rage and kills them." He hesitated again. "I think that he paints their lips last, right before he starts beating them. Then, of course, the strangulation is the final death act."

"Why do you think that he paints their lips last?" I asked.

He grimaced. "Because I've found traces of lipstick on all of the women, especially in and around the wounds on their faces. Like it transferred from their lips to the fists of the man beating them and back again first thing, before he did anything else to them, before he strangled them."

That made sense, but there was another question that I needed to ask. "Are you sure that it's a man?"

Ryan nodded. "Yes. Most serial killers are men, and the size and the pattern of the strangulation marks around the women's necks also indicate a man. A very strong man, judging from the fractured bones in the victims' faces."

"So you think that it's most likely a giant or a dwarf," I said, picking up on his train of thought.

"I do. Or perhaps even a vampire who drinks giant or dwarven blood on a regular basis. Whatever else he is, this man is exceptionally strong."

My gaze moved from one woman's photo to the next, their faces all cold, still, and frozen in death. Not just strong but smart too—a dangerous, devious kind of smart that had let him kidnap and murder a dozen women, maybe more, without getting caught.

I turned to Bria. "How long have you known about this?"

"About six months," she answered.

"And why didn't you tell me about it before now?"

"Because you've got enough on your plate dealing with the underworld and everything else. You didn't need to be worried about a serial killer too." Bria crossed her arms over her chest and gave me a pointed look. "Besides, I know you, Gin. You would somehow think that it was your fault that this guy was kidnapping and killing women."

"Isn't it my fault?" I growled. "He's doing it in *my* city. What's the point of being the big boss if I can't stop horrible things like this from happening?"

She shook her head. "No, it is *not* your fault. You are not personally responsible for all the crime in Ashland, especially not something this terrible."

I knew that she was right, that people made their own choices, including whether to hurt other people, but anger and frustration filled me all the same. Maybe if I had known sooner, I could have done something to help Bria, Xavier, and Ryan catch this guy. Maybe I could have put the word out on the street about this killer. Maybe I could have offered a reward for information. I glanced at the photos again. Maybe I could have saved some of these poor dead girls.

"I've worked several of these cases, but Ryan was the one who first noticed the similarities between the victims, especially the makeup," Bria said. "He started going back through his files and compiling a list of similar cases. Xavier's been helping too, and this is what the three of us have come up with so far."

"A jackpot of evil," I muttered.

"Yeah," Bria said. "That about sums it up."

"So if you know that there's a serial killer on the loose in Ashland, then why are all of these cases down here in storage?"

Bria and Ryan shared a grim look.

"Our superiors aren't as convinced," she said. "They think that the cases are unrelated. Or rather, they don't *want* them to be related. They think that Ashland has enough crime and corruption without adding a serial killer to the mix."

Well, that was certainly true. For as violent as Ashland was, there was usually a method to the madness. Somebody had something that someone else wanted, so they took it by force. Or somebody screwed someone else over in some other way, and the wronged party came back for revenge. Not to mention all the territorial disputes between gangs, criminals jacking their rivals' shipments of guns and drugs and money, and desperate folks knocking over convenience stores for petty cash. And of course there were the old traditional standbys: people hurting each other because of money, love, jealousy, or all three.

But a serial killer, someone whose dark motives and even darker desires were known only to him, who could strike at any time and in any place without any rhyme, reason, or warning . . . That was truly frightening, even in Ashland.

"And of course the higher-ups are worried about the

media attention," Bria continued. "They can just see the headlines. *Dollmaker strikes again. Dollmaker claims another victim. Dollmaker still on the loose.*"

"Dollmaker?" I asked.

She shrugged. "We had to call him something. But his name doesn't really matter, just the headlines he could generate. At least, that's what our bosses think. They want to avoid the bad press at all costs, along with the resulting panic it would create."

I snorted. "You mean the esteemed members of the po-po just want to cover their own asses because they haven't been able to catch this guy yet."

Bria nodded. "Yeah. That too."

The three of us fell silent, although my gaze locked onto that plastic bag full of compacts, eye shadow, and mascara again. Out of all the things you could do to someone, why put makeup on them? And why paint every woman's lips the exact same shade of red? Why not pink or purple or even black? Why not just use the woman's favorite lipstick from her own purse?

Ryan was right. How these women looked—the young pretty faces, the long blond hair, the makeup—it all had to mean *something* to the killer. But what? Maybe it was all tied to some woman he'd once loved, like Ryan thought. Maybe he was Dr. Frankenstein trying to create—or recreate—his own perfect mate. Or maybe it was something else entirely. No way to know for sure.

Until I caught the bastard.

"So you two think that the dead woman tonight, the one with my spider runes lipsticked on her palms, is another one of the Dollmaker's victims?" I asked.

"I do," Ryan said. "Her injuries are consistent with the other women's, and she has traces of makeup all over her face. Beaten, strangled, and dumped in Ashland. It's the same guy. The only thing that's different are your spider runes drawn on her palms. He's never done that before. Never left any sort of runes or symbols behind on the bodies."

"What do you think it means?" Bria asked, looking at me. "Do you think that it's some sort of challenge to you? To catch him before he kills again?"

My head started pounding from all the unanswered questions. "I have no idea. I'm not blond, though, so why would he even care about me? Besides, I'm not known as a crime fighter. More like a crime killer. But whatever the runes mean, we have to find and stop this guy before he kidnaps his next victim."

Ryan cleared his throat. "I hate to point out the obvious, but I think it's already too late for that. Bria showed me a photo of that missing girl you're searching for. Young, pretty, long blond hair. She fits his type to a T."

With the sickening spider rune and serial killer revelations, I'd momentarily forgotten that Elissa Daniels was still missing. The ache in my head intensified.

"Plus, he's been escalating," Ryan said in a somber voice. "Kidnapping and killing the women closer together. Going from months between kills down to weeks. And it will only get worse."

I glanced down at the photos laid out on the table again. Ryan was right. Elissa looked exactly like all the other victims. Young, blond, pretty. More important, she'd been at Northern Aggression last night.

I thought back to the security footage I'd watched. Something had caught Elissa's attention and made her walk around to the back of the nightclub. Maybe she'd seen the killer messing around back there. Maybe the killer had realized that Elissa spotted him. Maybe he'd even called out to her, asking her to come help with his sick friend or some other ruse like that. Either way, the Dollmaker had just gotten rid of his latest victim, and he would have probably leaped at the opportunity to snatch up a new plaything. Elissa had been in the wrong place at the wrong time, and she was suffering horribly for it.

"I want all your files," I told Ryan. "Every note you've made, every scrap of evidence you've collected, every theory you've ever dreamed up about this guy. I want copies of all of it. And I want to know everything you find out when you autopsy this latest woman, especially when it comes to my spider runes on her hands."

He nodded at me.

I turned to Bria. "And I want all of your notes, Xavier's too. Info on every victim you've identified, background on all their friends and family, every time, date, and place this guy has dropped a body in Ashland, if there are any similar cases outside the city. Everything."

She nodded too.

"What are you going to do, Gin?" Ryan asked, even though he already knew the answer.

"What I do best." I gave him a grim smile. "I'm going to find this bastard and put him in the ground."

❖ 13 ❖

Bria stayed behind in the cold-case room with Ryan, pulling out her phone and asking Xavier to come help them make copies of the files. I went back to the coroner's office. Jade was slumped against the wall outside the office, with Sophia standing by her side.

Jade gave me a weary look, but she straightened up and pushed herself away from the wall. "Do you know anything else about that dead girl? Or Elissa?"

I shook my head. "Nothing concrete right now. I'm sure that Dr. Colson will do the autopsy tonight, so we might know more in the morning. Maybe he'll find something that will at least help identify the woman, so her family can be notified."

Jade nodded, although disappointment pinched her face. Elissa still being missing was bad enough, but my heart twisted at the thought of what I had to tell her about the Dollmaker and how he most likely had her sister.

I turned to Sophia. "You've been great today. I'll take Jade home now. Thank you, Sophia."

"Keep me posted," she rasped.

"Of course."

The Goth dwarf nodded at me, gently squeezed Jade's arm, and walked off down the hallway, leaving me alone with the other woman.

Jade studied my face, her gaze sharpening. "There's something you're not telling me. Something bad. What is it?"

My heart twisted a little more. "Not here. I've had enough of this place for one night, and I'm sure you have too. I'll tell you everything I know when we get to your house."

Jade and I left the coroner's office and walked over to my car. Even though it was creeping up on midnight now, the streets between the police station and my car were even busier than before, but all the hookers, pimps, and dealers gave us a wide berth.

Jade glanced around, watching everyone duck their heads, step back into the shadows, and do their best not to catch my attention. "I see that they know you around here."

The image of those blood-red spider runes on the dead girl's hands flashed through my mind. My heart twisted. "Yeah. You might say that."

We reached my car. After making sure that no one had left any rune traps or bombs on the vehicle, we got inside. Jade rattled off her address, and I left the downtown loop behind and steered in that direction. She lived in a subdivision close to Jo-Jo Deveraux's, although her sprawling, one-story, gray brick house was far more modest than the dwarf's elegant antebellum home.

Jade unlocked the front door, and we stepped into an office that took up the front half of the house. Several workstations were spread throughout the area, each featuring an all-in-one computer and monitor, along with a phone, pens, notepads, paper clips, and other office paraphernalia. Since it was so late, no one was working, although red lights blinked on several of the phones, indicating a multitude of messages.

Jade saw my surprised look, and a faint grin lifted her lips. "What did you think it would look like? Some Old West bordello swathed in black lace? Roslyn Phillips might go in for red velvet at her club, but I do things a little differently."

I shook my head. "I didn't know what to expect. It's a bit more high-tech than I anticipated."

Jade shrugged. "It's not just sending folks out on paid dates. That's only a small part of my business these days, one that I'm slowly phasing out. I actually make a lot more money from my cleaning, temp, and other service businesses."

"You're quite the entrepreneur."

She shrugged again. "I never wanted to be like my mother and have to depend on anyone else to support me. I never wanted to have to play all of the games that she did, and I especially never wanted to be as desperate as she was."

"So you built your own business empire instead. Smart."

For a moment, a spark of pride flashed in her eyes, but

the light was quickly snuffed out. "Not smart enough. Not to protect Elissa."

I didn't respond. Nothing I could say would make the situation any better. And what I had to tell her about the Dollmaker . . . that was another blow that couldn't be softened.

Jade gestured for me to follow her, and we left the high-tech office behind and walked down a long hallway that opened into a kitchen. Unlike the sleek professionalism of the front of the house, this area was much more lived-in, with bills and junk mail piled on the countertop, a bowl of soggy cereal sitting on the kitchen table, and an enormous cookie jar shaped like a giant chocolate cake perched next to the stove.

Jade caught me staring at the cookie jar, and her face brightened. "That was a Christmas present from Elissa. Going out and getting dessert is one of our traditions. We've done it ever since she was a little girl. Every time we go on vacation, we try to find a new dessert to try . . ."

Jade stared at the cookie jar a second longer, then went over to one of the cabinets, yanked it open, and pulled out a large bottle of gin, along with two glasses. She poured a regular amount of liquor into one glass and held it out to me. I took it from her, and she turned her attention to the second glass, which she filled all the way to the brim. Jade downed half of the liquid in one gulp, shuddering a little, as though it burned her throat, before she looked at me again.

"You've put it off long enough. Tell me what you found out." Her fingers curled tightly around the glass. "I want to hear it, no matter how bad it is."

I downed my own gin, fortifying myself with a bit of liquid courage, and told her everything that Bria and Ryan had told me about the Dollmaker.

Jade's eyes grew wider and wider, and her face went paler and paler the longer I talked. By the time I finished, her pretty features were twisted into one of the most horrified expressions I'd ever seen. She started to raise her glass to her lips again to down the rest of her drink, but it slipped from her trembling hand and shattered on the floor, spraying shards and liquid everywhere. She clapped her hand over her mouth, whirled around, and ran out of the kitchen. A few seconds later, I heard her retching.

Yeah, I felt sick to my stomach too.

I put my own empty glass down on the counter. I found Jade slumped beside a toilet in a bathroom down the hall. She'd already emptied her stomach and flushed the contents away. Now she just sat there, curled up against the toilet, her body sagging against the cold white porcelain, tears streaming down her face.

"A serial killer," she said, her voice coming in ragged gasps. "A fucking *serial killer* has my sister. Why? Why is this happening? Why Elissa? She never hurt anybody. She doesn't deserve this. No one deserves this."

"I don't know. I just don't know. I'm sorry, Jade. So sorry."

She looked up at me, and her face just crumpled. More tears rolled down her cheeks, and she cradled her head in her hands and started sobbing.

I went over and sat down beside her, wedging myself between her and the sink. Jade kept right on crying, so I slung my arm around her shoulders and held her tight, trying to offer what little comfort I could, even though each one of her gasping, heaving, choking sobs ripped at the black threads of my heart, tearing them to shreds.

Jade's heartbreak and exhaustion finally caught up with her, and her tears slowed and finally stopped—for now.

I helped her to her room, tucked her into bed, and waited until she'd fallen asleep before I slipped back out into the kitchen. By this point, it was after one o'clock in the morning, but I didn't want to leave her alone, so I called Owen and told him that I was spending the night at Jade's house. He was waiting up for me and as support- ive as always, which warmed my heart despite everything that had happened.

"Do me a favor," I said.

"Anything." Owen's voice rumbled in my ear.

"Go hug Eva for me. And Violet too, if she's there."

"You got it," he said, his tone suddenly thick with emotion. "Do you think . . . do you think that you can find Elissa before it's too late?"

I closed my eyes and rubbed my aching forehead. "I don't know. I just don't know. But I'm going to try my best."

"Well, I have faith in you," Owen said. "If anyone can find and stop this guy, it's you, Gin."

My throat closed up at his strong, unwavering belief in me, especially since it was a belief that I didn't have. Not right now. Not with the pictures of all those dead, beaten, strangled women running through my mind, mixed with the blood-red spider runes on the most recent victim's hands.

"I love you," I whispered.

"I love you back," Owen murmured in my ear.

I promised to call with any updates, and we hung up.

I checked on Jade, and she was still sleeping, so I wandered around the house, searching for a place to crash for the night. I opened a closed door down the hall to find another bedroom, Elissa's bedroom.

I hesitated, my hand on the knob, wondering if I should go inside, but my curiosity got the best of me, the way it always did. So I turned on the light and slipped into the room.

It was your typical college girl's room. Colorful clothes were strewn all over the unmade bed, while plastic baskets full of fresh, clean laundry sat in front of the open closet, waiting to be hung up and put away. A stuffed brown bear wearing a blue T-shirt with the words *Ashland Community College* on it perched on the corner of a white vanity table cluttered with textbooks, pens, notepads, jewelry, and nail polish. Photos were stuck in all around the edges of the vanity table mirror, showing Elissa with her friends. I leaned in for a better look.

In every single photo, Elissa was grinning and looking into the camera, as though she were staring directly at me. After a few seconds, I shivered and dropped my gaze. I couldn't bear to look at her smiling face right now, not when I knew how much danger she was in and how very slim my chances were of finding her.

I shifted on my feet, feeling like I was trespassing again and expecting Jade to come barging into the room at any second, demanding to know what I was doing in here. I even glanced out into the hallway, but the house was as dark and quiet as before. Jade was still sleeping. I'd already violated her and Elissa's privacy by coming in here, so I pushed my guilt aside and decided to do something useful.

I searched Elissa's room.

Slowly, carefully, quietly, I opened all the nightstand and vanity table drawers, rifled through all the clothes in her closet, and checked every single place where she might have hidden something that she didn't want her big sister to see. But there was nothing. No hidden stashes of cigarettes, no drugs or alcohol, not even so much as an old-fashioned diary with a locked heart for a clasp. Elissa Daniels was exactly what she appeared to be in all the photos—a happy college girl with big plans, dreams, and hopes for her future.

A future that was rapidly running out unless I found her.

Frustrated, I plopped down on her bed and looked around the room again, but everything was the same as before. Clothes, books, furniture. Nothing that would tell me anything about Elissa that I didn't already know and absolutely nothing that would lead me to her kidnapper—

Rattle-rattle.

The sound was soft, no louder than a whisper. But as an assassin, I'd slipped into enough places to recognize the sound of someone jimmying a lock.

Someone was breaking into Jade's house.

14

In an instant, I was up off the bed, a knife in my hand. I hurried over to the open bedroom door and peered out into the hallway beyond. I looked toward the front of the house, but the office was dark and still.

Crunch-crunch.

Another sound came from the back of the house, but it wasn't the doorknob turning again. No, this sounded more like someone stepping on broken glass—like the shards that littered the kitchen floor where Jade had dropped her drink earlier.

I slipped out of Elissa's room and headed in that direction, tiptoeing past the bedroom where Jade was still sleeping. I didn't know who might be breaking into her house, but she'd been through enough already, and she needed her rest. I just hoped that I could kill the intruder quietly enough not to wake her up—

Creak.

Of course, I stepped on a loose floorboard, one that seemed to screech as loudly as an owl in the dark quiet. I winced, realizing that I'd lost the element of surprise, and hurried on.

I reached the end of the hallway and stopped, peering into the kitchen beyond. A nightlight was plugged into an outlet on the kitchen counter, and the soft pink glow illuminated the area, including the scattered shards in front of the glass double doors that took up the back wall.

But no one was there.

No one was in the kitchen. No cat burglar dressed all in black, no low-level thug sporting a cheap suit and a cheaper gun, no guy wearing a hockey mask and clutching an overly large knife.

So who—or what—had made that telltale noise?

My knife still in my hand, I sidled over to the doors and looked out through the glass—

Rattle-rattle.

I froze at the sound, and it took me a second to realize that one of the doors was cracked open. The winter wind gusted in through the opening, making the glass rattle in its frame and sliding some of the broken shards across the floor. Well, that explained the noises.

Still, I frowned. I was almost certain that the door had been closed and locked when Jade and I were in the kitchen earlier, but now here it was, standing open. Perhaps someone had gotten inside after all and had been scared off when I stepped on that loose floorboard. Only one way to find out. I eased the door open, wincing at the *rattle-rattle* that it made, and slipped outside.

The doors opened onto a stone patio, which gave way

to a large backyard, before the woods took over fifty feet away. I slipped off the patio and crouched down in the shadows at the corner of the house. The moon and stars shone big and bright in the night sky, painting everything a ghostly silver, from the white wicker patio furniture, to the short, stubby grass, to the tops of the bare, skeletal trees in the distance. A heavy frost had already crusted the ground, gleaming like metallic snow, and the cold wind cut through my clothes, chilling me from head to toe.

I scanned the patio, the yard, and the woods beyond, but I didn't see or hear anything, not so much as a stray cat padding through the grass, searching for shelter for the night. In the distance, the houses on either side of Jade's were also dark, and no cars rumbled down the street. Everyone was in bed, except for me.

Still, I couldn't help but feel like someone was here, watching me.

It wasn't anything I could put my finger on. No trampled patches of grass, no man-shaped shadows that shouldn't be here, not even someone's breath steaming in the chilly night air. But an uneasy finger of dread crept down my spine all the same, and I pressed my back up against the wall so that no one could sneak up on me from behind and take me by surprise.

My knife still in my hand, I held my position and waited, scanning the landscape again. One minute passed, then two, then three, and nothing moved or stirred.

But I couldn't shake the feeling that someone was out here—maybe even the Dollmaker himself.

It wasn't out of the realm of possibility. If the killer

had Elissa, then he had her purse, driver's license, address, phone, everything. Maybe creeping around his victims' houses and witnessing the anguish of their loved ones gave him another sick thrill. Maybe it was all part of his twisted ritual. Or maybe he was here for me, since he'd drawn my spider runes on his latest victim.

I didn't know, but if the Dollmaker was here, I was going to end him. So I tightened my grip on my knife and waited—just waited. All he had to do was move one fucking *inch*, make one more fucking *sound*, and he'd be *mine*.

But nothing happened.

No movement, no noises, nothing.

After about five minutes, even that creepy feeling of being watched faded away. If the Dollmaker—or any-one else—had been here, he was gone now, and I was all alone. I scanned the yard one more time, but it was as cold and empty as before, so I finally admitted defeat, went back inside the house, and locked the kitchen door behind me.

I spent the next several minutes cleaning up the broken glass and liquid from Jade's dropped drink. I also lined up all the kitchen chairs in a row in front of the glass doors, creating a crude barricade. The whole time, I kept one eye on the backyard, but it remained as empty as before.

Once that was done, there was nothing more I could do tonight, so I curled up on a couch in the den, which was located off the kitchen, and slid one of my knives under my pillow. If the Dollmaker or anyone else tried to break into Jade's house again tonight, I would hear him and respond accordingly.

I grabbed a fleece blanket from the back of the couch, covered myself up with it, and settled down to get some sleep. Even though it had been a long, long day with all sorts of emotional ups and downs, I still had trouble falling asleep. The image of those blood-red spider runes loomed in my mind, making me toss and turn.

Eventually, my exhaustion caught up with me, the same way it had caught up with Jade, and I fell asleep. Although sometime after that, the blackness receded, and I found myself in the land of dreams, memories, and nightmares from my past . . .

My world was on fire.

My childhood home was fully ablaze, the flames streaking up into the night sky like rockets being fired one after another. Ash fluttered like confetti spraying everywhere, and the acrid stench of smoke overpowered everything, even the stench of my own charred flesh. Even though I was in the woods, fifty feet away from the mansion, I could still feel the intense, searing heat from the flames.

Not just regular flames—elemental Fire.

The same Fire that had engulfed my mom. That had consumed Annabella. That had been used to torture me. I could still feel the foreign magic burning inside my own skin, a constant, throbbing, intense agony that seemed like it would never, ever stop.

Despite the sweat soaking my body, I still shivered. I would have wrapped my arms around myself to ward off the chill, if it wouldn't have made my hands hurt more than they already did. But I couldn't stop myself from unwrapping one of the crude bandages from around my palm. I held my shaking hand up to the flickering light, knowing and dreading what I would see.

The mark, the wound, the burn was the same as before— a small circle with eight thin rays. Half of my spider rune pendant, superheated and melted into my flesh. Even though it was made of silverstone, just like my necklace had been, the mark was a vivid blood-red. The pain of it blazed as harsh and bright as my house, and the sensation made me just as sick. I quickly wrapped the bandage back around my hand, hiding the rune from sight.

I couldn't stand to look at it right now. I just couldn't stand it.

I'd staggered away from our house ten minutes ago and had been standing in the woods ever since, aimlessly wandering up and down along the tree line, unable to tear my eyes away from the sight of the ruined, rocky rubble of the Snow family mansion. But the flames were only part of the damage. I'd caused the rest when I'd used my Ice and Stone magic to collapse the structure, in a last-ditch effort to save Bria from the Fire elemental and her men who had stormed into our home.

But I'd collapsed all of that stone, wood, and glass right on top of my baby sister, crushing her to death.

That horrible knowledge pushed me over the edge. I bent over double and heaved and heaved, until my stomach was as empty as my heart. After several minutes, I straightened up and wiped my mouth off on one of my makeshift bandages, ripped from the bottom of my nightgown. I knew that I should leave, walk, get away from the mansion, but I couldn't make my legs move. I couldn't do anything but stare at the destruction, destruction that I was more than a little responsible for—

"What did you do?" a loud, harsh male voice demanded. "What did you do?"

I blinked, wondering if I'd only imagined the booming voice. But then, a second later, a low, satisfied laugh rang out, floating through the trees right along with all the ash.

"You know exactly what I did, Hugh," a lighter feminine voice said. "I killed Eira. Finally, finally killed her. Just like the others wanted. Just like I wanted."

I froze. I recognized that soft, silky, sinister tone. It belonged to the Fire elemental who had killed my mom and Annabella and tortured me with her terrible magic. I'd thought—hoped—that she was dead, crushed by the falling rubble. The sound of her smug, satisfied voice made a fresh wave of heat spike through my burns, reminding me just how much I had lost tonight. I had to bite my lip to keep from screaming from the pain, both in my hands and especially in my heart.

"You killed Eira?" Hugh's voice rang out, harsher than before. "You actually killed her?"

"Oh, yes," the elemental purred again. "No doubt about it. She never had a chance against my Fire magic. I got one of her little brats too."

Even though I wanted to run, run, run away from that voice, from her, from this living, waking nightmare, I made myself creep forward, hunker down, and peer around a tree. Through the dense, boiling smoke, I could just make out two figures standing in what had been our backyard garden before part of the house had toppled over and landed on it, burying all the trees and flowers in jagged, broken stones.

One of them was a man—Hugh—although he seemed more like a shadow than a tangible person. Hair, eyes, goatee, suit. Everything about him was blacker than the night itself. He paced back and forth, staring at first one burning, crumbled section of the mansion, then the next.

Someone was standing beyond him, backlit by the flames. All I could make out was her slender shape, but I knew who she was—the Fire elemental who'd just destroyed my entire world.

Hugh stopped pacing, stormed over to the elemental, and stabbed his finger at her. "You enjoyed this."

The Fire elemental let out another deep, throaty laugh. "Of course I did. I've wanted Eira dead for years, and the Circle finally let me take care of that meddlesome bitch once and for all."

"She was one of us!" he hissed back. "You always were jealous of her."

"Aw, what's the matter, Hugh? Upset that your precious Eira is dead? You didn't really think that she'd come crawling back to you, did you?" She clucked her tongue, mocking him. "We all knew that wasn't going to happen. Not after Tristan's . . . accident."

I frowned, wondering if I was hearing them right over the continuous popping, cracking, and sizzling of the flames. Tristan? Why were they talking about my dad? He'd died in a car accident several years ago. What did that have to do with any of this?

Hugh turned away from the Fire elemental and stared at the burning house again.

"Oh, you did. You really did think that Eira would fall in

line and come back to you." She let out another loud, pealing laugh. "You sad, stupid little fool."

"Shut up," he growled. "Just shut your fucking mouth."

"Or you'll do what?" She sneered. "What will you do, Hugh? Everyone knows that you can't even tie your shoes without his permission——"

Her words were abruptly cut off, and it took me a second to realize why. From one heartbeat to the next, Hugh had crossed the distance between them, wrapped his hand around the elemental's throat, and hoisted her up off the ground as easily as I could pick up one of Bria's dolls. I'd never seen someone move that fast. He bared his teeth at her, a telltale gleam of white flashing in his mouth. Not just teeth—fangs.

The vampire tightened his grip and gave the elemental a vicious shake. She let out a little squeak of fear, like a mouse caught in a cat's sharp claws. Dark satisfaction filled me. In that moment, I wanted the vampire to bite her, to snap her neck, to hurt her the same way that she'd hurt me.

Do it, *I thought.* Make her suffer. Kill her just like she killed my family.

But instead, he gave her another hard shake, slammed her back down onto her feet, and shoved her away. The Fire elemental staggered back, clutching her throat.

"You said that you killed one of the girls," Hugh snapped. "Which one?"

She coughed and coughed, trying to get her breath back.

"Which one?" he growled again.

"The . . . oldest . . . Annabella . . ." she wheezed.

"What happened to the other two girls?"

She kept wheezing, and he stepped forward, as though

he was going to throttle her again. She staggered back and snapped up her hand. Flames erupted on her fingertips, momentarily stopping him. But as fast as the vampire was, he could easily snap her neck before she even had a chance to blast him with her magic.

"I don't know. They were still in the mansion when it all came tumbling down. I assume that they're both buried in the rubble."

Hugh looked back at the burning mansion. "But you don't know for sure. You didn't kill them yourself. You didn't actually see them die."

The Fire elemental cleared her throat and straightened up, trying to regain her composure. "I didn't have time. But you're right. We should check and make sure that they didn't escape. We wouldn't want any loose ends coming back to strangle us later, would we?"

She stepped behind a pile of rubble, out of my line of sight, but I heard her voice ring out loud and clear. "Barry! Chuck! Carlos! Get over here! Start searching the woods for survivors!"

"Sure thing, boss!" a male voice called back.

A few seconds later, three giants jogged into view. They stopped long enough to nod their heads respectfully at Hugh, the vampire, and then headed toward the tree line—toward me.

Heart pounding, I lurched to my feet, whipped around, and stumbled deeper into the woods. I had to hide. I had to run, or I'd be as dead as the rest of my family . . .

I woke up grinding my teeth, my fingers clenching the blanket, my spider rune scars itching and burning as though Mab Monroe had just freshly branded them into my palms, just like she had on that horrible night so long ago.

For a moment, I didn't remember where I was, but then last night came rushing back to me. Finding the dead girl at Northern Aggression. The trip to the coroner's office. All the ugly revelations about my spider rune and the Dollmaker. Driving Jade home and destroying her world with the news that the serial killer had her sister.

I forced myself to let go of the blanket and take deep, slow, calming breaths as I dug my fingers into first one scar, then the other, trying to massage the memories out of the marks, as well as my mind. But it didn't work.

It never did.

I might have gotten some sleep, but it hadn't been restful. Not at all. And the memory that it had brought along with it . . . So many awful things had happened that night, and I'd been in so much pain that it was hard to keep track of them all. Oh, I dimly remembered staggering away from our burning mansion, trekking through the woods in the dark, and eventually making my way down into the city. But I hadn't remembered Hugh Tucker being there, talking to Mab, not until tonight. And he'd actually been upset that she'd murdered my mother. Distraught enough to consider killing Mab with his bare hands.

I thought back to how Damian Rivera had mocked Tucker by bringing up my mother. My memory seemed to confirm that the two of them had had *some* sort of relationship. I wondered exactly what had happened between them, what had gone so wrong that it had ended with my mother's murder.

But that was a question for another day. There was no more time to rest, so I threw off the blanket, swung my feet over the side of the couch, and got up, ready to start the day and face whatever new danger, despair, and heartbreak it might bring.

* 15 *

Jade was still asleep, so I went into the kitchen and raided her refrigerator and cabinets, determined to make her a hearty breakfast. Even though she didn't feel like it, she needed to eat to keep her strength up, and so did I.

But the kitchen was depressingly empty, except for all the containers of take-out food in the fridge, including several from the Pork Pit. I opened one and sniffed the contents. My nose wrinkled at the sour stench. Even I couldn't do anything with two-week-old baked beans, so I tossed them into the garbage, along with some old Thai food, a couple of half-eaten burritos, and a lasagna that was pea-green with mold.

Luckily, Jade had some fresh eggs, milk, and cheddar cheese in her fridge, and I found a couple of potatoes tucked away in a cabinet, along with some dill weed and other spices. So I whipped up some cheesy scrambled eggs with a side of fried, seasoned breakfast potatoes.

I was dishing up a plate of food for myself when Jade stumbled into the kitchen. She looked slightly less exhausted than she had last night, and her eyes weren't quite as red this morning. She hadn't been crying today. Yet.

"Just in time," I said, keeping my voice light. "Sit down, and eat up."

Jade staggered over to the table, plopped down, and stared with bleary eyes at the plate that I slid in front of her. "How can you even function without coffee?" she mumbled.

I thought of my memory of Hugh Tucker and Mab Monroe watching my childhood home burn to the ground. "Trust me," I muttered. "I don't need a jolt of java to start my day."

I poured Jade a cup of the coffee that I'd brewed and set it in front of her. She leaned over and breathed in the rich fumes, waking up a bit more, before grabbing the cup and taking a sip of the hot, dark liquid.

She gagged, almost spitting it right back out again. "What—what *is* this? Because it is most certainly not *coffee*."

"Sure it is. Chicory coffee. I had a bag of it stashed in the emergency supplies in my trunk. You were out of your regular brew, so I had to use it instead."

She frowned. "You keep coffee in your car?"

"Sure. Coffee, granola bars, bottled water, knives, healing ointment. The usual."

"But why coffee?" she asked. "What kind of assassin emergency requires chicory coffee?"

"Finnegan Lane."

Jade gave me a puzzled look.

"You do *not* want to talk to Finn in the morning before he's had his coffee. It's like trying to communicate with a bear that's just woken up from hibernating. Glares, grumbling, and gnashing teeth. It's not pretty, not pretty at all."

I sat down with my own plate and nudged hers a little closer to her elbow. "Now, eat up."

Jade stared at the food. After a moment, she shook her head. "Sorry, but I just don't feel like eating. Not when I know that Elissa is out there somewhere, that she probably hasn't had a meal in hours . . ." Her voice trailed off, and she blinked back the tears in her eyes. "So what's our next move?"

"*Our* next move?"

"*Our* next move," she repeated. "I'm with you on this, Gin. Every single step of the way."

I shoveled some food into my mouth, giving myself time to think. Despite the few ingredients that I'd had to work with, the scrambled eggs were light and fluffy, with a sharp, gooey tang from the cheese, while the potatoes had the perfect amount of spices and crispy brown edges. Normally, I would have thoroughly enjoyed the food, but thinking about Elissa and what she might be going through made everything taste like burned toast—dry, brittle, and utterly unappealing. Still, I forced myself to take bite after bite. No doubt today would be another long day, and I would need all the energy I could get to keep going.

Jade stared at me, wanting an answer, so I sighed and put down my fork.

"I know you want to be there for Elissa. I know you

want to find her more than anything else. I know that you would give anything for that to happen."

"But?"

I let out a breath and made my voice as gentle as I could. "But we might not find Elissa. We might not find her alive. We might not find her at all—ever."

Jade flinched, as though I'd slapped her. She dropped her head, leaned back in her seat, and crossed her arms over her chest, as if she were trying to shield herself from the ugly truth of my words. After several long, tense seconds, she raised her head and looked at me again, tears shimmering in her eyes.

"I know that." Her voice was as soft and serious as mine had been. "I don't like it, but I know it. I know that she could already be . . . dead." Her voice cracked on the last word, and she had to clear her throat before she could continue. "But she's my sister, and if I don't do everything that I can to find her, then I will never be able to live with myself. Surely you can understand that, Gin."

"I do understand that." I gave her a hard, serious look. "But if you want to be involved, then you have to play by my rules, and you have to do what I say, when I say it. I might have to do some nasty things to find Elissa. Things that would turn anyone's stomach. If you don't want to be involved in those things, I understand."

Jade's mouth tightened, and her chin lifted. "I don't care who you have to hurt or what you have to do to them. I'll stand right by your side and hand you the damn knives myself if it means getting my sister back."

Determination flashed in her eyes, and I knew that she meant every single word. Jade would do whatever it took to find Elissa. Still, she would be emotional and vulnerable, no matter how much she tried to keep her worry and fear in check. But I could be cold, hard, and strong enough for both of us. And Jade was right. I couldn't shut her out. I wouldn't have been able to stand aside if Bria was missing.

"All right, then," I said, picking up my fork again. "Gin's first rule. Eat your breakfast."

Jade opened her mouth like she was going to protest that she couldn't possibly eat a single bite, but I stabbed my fork at her.

"Gin's second rule. Do not argue with assassins carrying multiple knives. Ever."

For a second, a ghost of a smile pulled up her lips. "Yes, ma'am."

I nodded. "Now, that's more like it."

I forced myself to finish the rest of my food. Jade merely picked at hers, but at least she ate a few bites and grudgingly sipped the chicory coffee. Better than nothing.

After breakfast, we both got to work. Jade called her employees, telling them that she had a personal matter and they should all take the day off. I made a call of my own, then went outside, grabbed a fresh set of clothes out of the supplies in the trunk of my car, and took a shower.

At nine o'clock sharp, a polite knock sounded at the front door. Jade and I were back in the kitchen, and she almost jumped up out of her chair at the sudden noise.

"Who could that be?" Jade asked.

"Reinforcements."

We went into the office in the front of the house.

The knock came again, a little louder and more insistent than before. I rolled my eyes at his impatience, but I still double-checked to make sure that it was him before I unlocked and opened the door.

Silvio was waiting outside, his phone in one hand and his tablet case resting in the crook of his other elbow. "Finally. I was wondering if you were going to make me stand outside all morning."

"The thought never crossed my mind," I quipped.

"Uh-huh." He arched his eyebrows and stepped inside the house. "Jade."

"Silvio." She nodded at him.

My assistant looked around, his gray eyes brightening with appreciation as he took in all the desks, computers, and other equipment. "Finally. A *real* office. This will do quite nicely."

He went over to the closest desk and put down his phone and tablet case. Then he headed back outside, returning a minute later with a large cardboard box. Back and forth Silvio went, until a dozen cardboard boxes were stacked in the corner.

"What's all this?" Jade asked in a puzzled voice.

Silvio set down the last box. "Everything that the Ashland Police Department has on the Dollmaker."

Jade stared at all the boxes, her face creasing into a frown. "All those boxes, all those files inside. It would take an army to go through all of that information."

He flashed her a smile. "Don't worry. Help is on the way."

Sure enough, less than five minutes later, another knock sounded at the front door. Jade opened it to find

Finn, Bria, and Owen standing outside. They all trooped into the house and murmured their hellos to us.

The fourth and final person at the back of the pack surprised me: Dr. Ryan Colson. He'd changed out of his blue scrubs and was now wearing black boots, black corduroy pants, and a dark blue sweater under a black leather jacket. Despite the fact that he'd probably been up all night, performing an autopsy on the Dollmaker's latest victim, he looked as calm and steady as always. Then again, I supposed that he was used to working hard, long, and odd hours, given his job.

"I'm sorry to just barge in like this, but Bria told me what you were doing." He looked over at Jade, who was staring at the boxes of information again. Sympathy and understanding filled his face. "I'd like to help, if you'll let me."

"Of course, Ryan. Come on in."

He stepped inside, took off his jacket, and hung it up on a rack in the corner.

"Any news on the dead woman?" I asked.

"We got an ID on her—Lacey Lawrence," he said. "Missing since last week. Vanished after working her shift at a clothing store in Northtown. Xavier's tracking down her family so they can be notified."

"What about your autopsy? Any new clues there?"

He shook his head. "Nothing that I haven't seen before with the other victims. She had been dead at least twenty-four hours before you found her, just like I thought. I also sent off a sample of the lipstick to a lab guy who owes me a favor. I'm hoping that he gets back to me today with the color and brand. Maybe I'll know more then."

"Thanks, Ryan."

He nodded at me and looked at Jade again. He hesitated, then went over and said something to her that I couldn't hear. She nodded back at him before her gaze locked onto the boxes again.

"Now that we're all here," Silvio said, rubbing his hands together in anticipation, "let's get cracking."

There were few things that my assistant loved more than organizing, whether it was people, information, or both, as in this case. Silvio made us each take a separate desk, and he assigned each of us a single box to start with. We all settled down and got to work, cracking open our boxes, digging into the files inside, and reading through the information, trying to find some clue that would lead us to the Dollmaker and where he might be holding Elissa.

My box was about Sandra Reeves, the killer's very first victim, two years ago. At least, she was the first victim Ryan knew of so far. Twenty-three, blond, pretty. Sandra had worked as a waitress at the Cake Walk, another downtown Ashland restaurant, before she'd disappeared one night after her shift. Her body had been found two weeks later dumped in a park that fronted the Aneirin River, not too far away from Lorelei Parker's shipping yard. Beaten and strangled, with traces of makeup and blood-red lipstick all over her bruised, battered face.

And that was it. That was all the pertinent information in the file. The police had interviewed Sandra's friends and family and had taken a long, hard look at her boyfriend, but none of them seemed likely to have killed her, and the cops didn't have any other leads. No one with a grudge against Sandra, no one she owed money to, no one with any reason to hurt her.

I flipped back to the beginning of the file and read through all the info again, but nothing changed, and I didn't get any brilliant new insights.

I examined a photo of Sandra's swollen face that was included in the file. Young, blond, pretty. At least before the Dollmaker had gotten his hands on her. I knew rage when I saw it, and this bastard was chock-full of it. Once he'd started beating Sandra, he hadn't stopped until she was dead, and he hadn't been too particular about where or how hard he hit her. He'd broken her nose, her ribs, and both of her collarbones.

But there was no real clue in anything that the killer had done to Sandra. In fact, the only real, tangible clue we had was the spider runes that had been drawn on the palms of Lacey Lawrence, the latest victim.

Silvio had given me photos of the marks, and I picked them up and studied them. But in each one, I saw the exact same thing as before: a circle with eight thin rays radiating out of it, all done in blood-red lipstick.

Disgusted, I threw down the photos, and they both glided to a stop right next to that photo of Sandra Reeves's beaten face. I glared at all three pictures, but then I noticed the one, single, striking difference between them.

How battered and broken the girl was compared with how very neat and precise the spider runes were.

At some point during his sadistic ritual, the Dollmaker had flown into a deadly rage and killed the poor girl he'd abducted. Girl after girl beaten and strangled, with no change in the pattern at all.

But the spider runes were different. These marks had been drawn with a cold, steady, dispassionate hand. No smudges, no hesitation lines, no places where he'd stopped and started or traced over the runes. It was almost as if . . . maybe . . . possibly . . . the symbols had been drawn by someone *other* than the Dollmaker.

I frowned and rocked back in my chair, mulling over that disturbing new possibility. But how could that have even happened? The Dollmaker had dumped Lacey Lawrence at Northern Aggression and had kidnapped Elissa to take her place. So if a second person was involved, he would have had to come across Lacey's body at Northern Aggression sometime after the killer had left it there, pulled out a tube of lipstick, and drawn the marks on her palms. What kind of person would do that? And who went around carrying blood-red lipstick in their pocket?

But if there was a second person involved and he knew who the Dollmaker was and had maybe even followed the killer to Northern Aggression, then why didn't he call in an anonymous tip to the police? Why not try to save Elissa himself? Why draw my runes on the dead girl instead?

My head pounded with all the questions, speculations, and what-ifs. I felt like I was snared in someone else's spiderweb, and everything I did only made the sticky threads twist and tangle tighter and tighter around me. Nothing about this made any sense, and Elissa was running out of time for me to figure it out.

"Does anyone have anything useful?" Finn growled, throwing down a stack of papers on top of his desk. "Because I have fuck-all nothing. No fingerprints, no DNA, nothing that could lead us back to the killer. This guy is a ghost. He's a sick fucking *ghost*, and I have no idea how we're going to find him."

Owen shook his head. "I don't have anything either. Nothing that would tell us who or where this guy is."

Silvio shook his head too. "Nor do I."

Ryan sighed. "Nothing here that I haven't seen a dozen times before."

Bria also tossed her papers down, as disgusted and frustrated as everyone else. "How do you think Ryan, Xavier, and I feel? We've been looking into this guy for months now, and he's killed several more women in that time span. Soon he'll have another murder on his résumé, and we'll be getting a call about Elissa's body being found somewhere."

A tense, heavy silence dropped over the office. Bria winced, knowing that she'd said the wrong thing. Jade slowly pushed back from her desk and got to her feet, a sick, stricken look on her face. Bria opened her mouth to apologize, but Jade held out her hand and shook her head. She left the office and went into the back of the house. A second later, a door banged shut, making all of us flinch.

"Dammit," Bria snarled, massaging her temples. "I wasn't thinking."

To my surprise, Ryan got to his feet. "It's okay. Jade knows that. We all know that. I'll go talk to her." A grim smile twisted his lips. "I'm good at dealing with grieving folks."

He too disappeared into the back of the house. A soft knock sounded, and a few seconds later, a door creaked open. A short, muffled conversation took place, and the door shut much more quietly than it had before.

That left Bria, Finn, Owen, Silvio, and me in the office. That tense, heavy silence fell over us for a second time, but Bria sighed and picked up her files again. So did Finn, Owen, and Silvio, and we all went back to work.

Since I hadn't found anything in the first box of information, I grabbed a second one from the stacks in the corner, took it over to my desk, and cracked it open. The very first thing that caught my eye was the victim's name: Joanna Mosley.

Mosley? As in Stuart Mosley, the president of First Trust bank? The man who'd hired Elissa to be his date the night she disappeared? No, no way. It couldn't be.

But it *was*.

Sure enough, Stuart Mosley was listed as Joanna's great-grandfather, and he'd leaned on the police hard, demanding that they find out who'd murdered her, according to the detectives' notes. But those detectives hadn't had any more luck than Bria and Xavier, and the case had gone unsolved, much to Mosley's frustration and disappointment.

Even though I knew exactly what I would find, I still flipped through the file until I came to some photos of Joanna, both before and after her murder. Young, blond, pretty—at least until she'd been beaten and strangled. No wonder Mosley had told Elissa that she reminded him of his granddaughter. Joanna could have been Elissa's sister, along with the rest of the Dollmaker's victims.

"Finn," I said. "Come take a look at this."

He and the others gathered around my desk, and I showed them the file.

Owen let out a low whistle. "It really is a small world, isn't it?"

"When it comes to crime in Ashland?" Silvio sighed. "Unfortunately so."

Finn picked up a headshot of Joanna that showed her before she'd been murdered. "I remember when Mosley's granddaughter died, since he took a leave of absence, but he kept it quiet, and I never heard exactly what happened to her. His wife passed away just a few months later, and he took another leave of absence then."

"You don't really think that Mosley knows anything about Elissa, do you?" Bria asked. "Xavier and I have looked into him and all the other victims' families. We didn't find anything suspicious."

"No. He's not the killer. His alibi checks out, and he was nowhere near Northern Aggression when Elissa was taken." I looked at Finn. "But I still want to talk to him."

"What do you think Mosley will tell you that this file doesn't?" Finn asked.

"I don't know. Mosley probably doesn't know any more than any of the other victims' families do, but it's worth a shot," I said. "It's not even a real lead—it's a coincidence, perhaps—but it's all we have right now. And like Bria said, Elissa is running out of time."

For the third time, that somber silence swept over us.

Finn nodded. "I'll make the call."

✴ 16 ✴

Finn called Mosley and asked if we could come over. Mosley agreed, even though Finn didn't tell him exactly what we wanted. Bria got a text from Xavier, saying that he'd found Lacey Lawrence's parents and asking her to come help him do the death notification and follow-up interviews. So we all decided to take a break for a couple of hours, attend to our business, and come back and look at the files with fresh eyes.

To my surprise, Ryan agreed to stay with Jade until I returned. Apparently, the two of them had bonded while the rest of us were going through the files. While the others grabbed their coats and left, I pulled Ryan aside and gave him my cell phone number.

"You see or hear anything suspicious—anything at all— you call me immediately. No matter what it is. Got it?"

Ryan nodded. "Got it. But you don't really think that the killer will come here, do you? He's never made contact with any of the victims' families before. That we know of, anyway."

I thought of the odd noises and the open door in the kitchen last night, along with that creepy sensation of being watched. I'd done a thorough sweep of the back-yard before breakfast, but I hadn't found any evidence that anyone had been lurking outside the house. Still, I didn't want to leave Jade here alone. Someone had drawn my spider runes on a dead girl, and I didn't want Jade to be the next victim.

"Better to be safe than sorry," I said.

Ryan nodded again and went into the kitchen to check on Jade, who was brewing a fresh pot of coffee. She might not like the strong chicory brew, but apparently, any coffee was better than no coffee at all.

Thirty minutes later, I steered my car up a steep drive-way only a couple of miles from Fletcher's place. And just like there, the gravel driveway snaked up to a sprawling home perched on top of a rocky ridge. Unlike Fletcher's old ramshackle house, which was an odd mishmash of tin, brick, and stone, Mosley's abode was a brand-new construction of gleaming glass, dark wood, and gray river rock that gave it the look and feel of a rustic cabin. If a rustic cabin could be several thousand square feet and feature a pool, a hot tub, and a tennis court.

Up ahead, Finn parked in the paved driveway in front of the house and got out of his car. I pulled in behind him and did the same. Together, the two of us approached the mansion. A breeze gusted over the ridge, bringing the smell of fresh sawdust along with it.

"Not what I expected," I said.

"Mosley has to deal with people all day every day at the bank. He used to live in a luxury apartment in the city, but folks would drop by his place at all hours. He finally decided that he wanted to leave work at work. That's why he built way out here in the middle of nowhere," Finn said. "Plus, after his wife, Jane, passed away, I think that he wanted to get away from all the memories in their apartment. He's only been moved in here a couple of weeks."

"Well, you'd certainly have to work to find this place," I said.

Finn grabbed hold of the metal knocker and let it thump against the front door. Several seconds later, the door opened, revealing a thoroughly miserable-looking individual.

He was a dwarf, right at five feet tall, with a thick, stocky body, who was wearing a pair of dark blue plaid flannel pajamas and matching slippers. His wavy silver hair stuck up in crazy tufts, and a deep pillow crease ran along the left side of his head, from where he'd been napping. His hazel eyes were dull and watery, although his nose was a bright red spot in his face. He was carrying a half-empty box of tissues like it was a life preserver that would keep him from drowning in a sea of snot.

I'd never seen Stuart Mosley look so disheveled, unkempt, and all-around sickly before. Whatever cold, flu, or sinus infection he had was really doing a number on him, further convincing me that he'd had nothing to do with Elissa's disappearance. People who felt that miserable didn't go around kidnapping other folks. They didn't have the energy for it.

"Hello, Finn," Mosley rasped, congestion making his

voice even deeper and throatier than normal. "And I see that you brought a guest. Ms. Blanco, welcome to my humble home."

"You probably wouldn't say that if you knew why I was here," I replied.

Mosley held up a finger. His eyes watered, his nose crinkled, and he let out a violent sneeze that had both Finn and me stepping back.

"I knew I should have brought some hand sanitizer," Finn muttered. "And a mask."

Mosley ignored his snide remark, plucked a tissue out of his box, and blew his nose as violently as he'd just sneezed. He stuffed the used tissue into the pocket of his pajama pants and gestured for us to come in.

The inside of the house continued the rustic cabin motif, with lots of stone floors, exposed wooden beams overhead, and floor-to-ceiling windows to take advantage of the sweeping views from the top of the ridge. Mosley shuffled down a hallway and into a living room before collapsing onto a large sectional sofa. Tissues littered the coffee table in front of the sofa, along with bottles of half-drunk ginger ale, empty cough drop wrappers, and several open boxes of over-the-counter medication. The entire room reeked of sharp, minty menthol, and I spotted several open tins of ointment lying on the floor in front of the sofa.

The common cold was one of the few illnesses that Air elementals just couldn't heal. At least, not very well. So it was one of those things that you just had to suffer through, and it looked like Mosley was suffering plenty.

He pulled a blanket over his lap and settled himself

back against the couch cushions. "So what was so urgent that you two drove all the way out here to see a sick old man?"

"I want to talk to you about Joanna, your great-granddaughter," I said.

He blinked. "How do you know about . . ." His voice trailed off, and his face hardened. "What's wrong? What's happened? Have you finally found the son of a bitch who killed her?"

I shook my head. "No. But he's kidnapped another girl. Someone you know. Elissa Daniels . . ."

I recapped everything that had happened and everything that we thought we knew about the Dollmaker. Mosley sneezed, coughed, and blew his nose the whole time I talked, but I knew that he was listening to every single word.

"So we came here hoping that you might know something about the killer," I finished. "Anything you can remember, any detail, no matter how small, might be helpful."

Mosley pointed over at the fireplace mantel. "You can see Joanna for yourself."

I got up and looked at the framed photos. Young, blond, pretty, nice smile. I recognized Joanna Mosley from the pictures I'd seen in her murder file. The photo in the center of the mantel had been taken at a graduation ceremony, and Joanna was wearing a dark blue cap and gown. She had her arms around her grandfather's shoulders, and both of them were beaming into the camera.

"She was a wonderful girl," Mosley said. "Smart as a whip. After she finished her MBA, she was going to come work for me at the bank. But of course, that never happened."

This time, the water in his eyes had nothing to do with his cold, and he had to clear his throat before he could continue. "I assume you've seen the police reports?"

I sat back down on the couch. "I have."

"Then you know that Joanna was having dinner with friends at Underwood's. They were all going to a concert and were running late, and she stayed behind to pay the bill. She left the restaurant to walk to her car a few blocks away, and that's the last time anyone saw her." Mosley closed his eyes. "The police found her body two weeks later near the restaurant."

He didn't say anything else, and for several seconds, the only sound was his raspy, congested breathing. He opened his eyes and cleared his throat again. "Joanna moved here from Cypress Mountain to go to college. She stayed with Jane and me in our apartment in the city. It was such a happy time for the three of us. The whole thing . . . it broke my wife's heart. Mine too. It sent Jane to an early grave."

I glanced over at Finn, who gave me a helpless shrug. He didn't know what to say to comfort his boss any more than I did.

Mosley blew his nose again and looked at Finn. "Go to my office. You'll find a cardboard box in the corner. Bring it in here, please."

Finn left the room and returned a minute later with a box that was eerily similar to the ones that Silvio had stacked up in Jade's office this morning. Finn nudged aside some of the mounds of tissues, careful not to actually touch any of them, and set the box on the coffee table.

"Go ahead," Mosley said. "Open it."

Finn pulled the lid off the top. Together, the two of us went through all the files and photos inside, while Mosley slumped on the couch across from us. Much of the information was the same as it had been in all the files we had on the other victims, right down to how useless it was.

"I did everything in my power to find the bastard who murdered my granddaughter," Mosley growled. "I bribed the cops to devote more manpower to the case. I brought in experts to examine all the evidence, what little there was. I even hired a profiler to try to learn more about the son of a bitch. Nothing worked."

I flipped through the files, scanning through all the information, photos, and reports. Mosley was right. He'd left no stone unturned in his search for Joanna's killer, and he'd kept meticulous notes of everything, including the hefty bribes he'd doled out. Private investigators, scientific experts, retired FBI profilers. He'd hired all those and more. Mosley had even had an independent forensic lab examine the traces of makeup left on Joanna's face. I made a mental note to show that file to Ryan when I went back to Jade's house. Maybe he'd be able to make more sense out of it than I could.

A thought occurred to me, and I set the last file aside. "Did you ask Fletcher to help you with this? Was this one of the many *favors* the two of you did for each other?"

For a moment, a brief smile lifted Mosley's lips. "Of course I asked Fletcher to help me. Who better to track down a killer than an assassin like the Tin Man? But he didn't find anything either. Not before he was killed."

This time, my eyes were the ones that watered. Finn's

too, but we both blinked back our memories of Fletcher and his own brutal murder inside the Pork Pit.

"I'm sorry that I can't tell you anything else," Mosley said. "Elissa is a wonderful girl. She doesn't deserve what's happening to her. Neither did Joanna."

I gestured at the files. "Can we take these with us? It's a long shot, but we might find something useful if we compare them with the files we have on the other victims."

"Take it all. If you think there's even a remote chance that you can find Elissa, take it all." Mosley blew his nose again. "And if there's anything that I can do to help, anything at all, just say the word. Anything I can do for you, I will."

"A favor from one of the most powerful men in Ashland? Careful," I drawled. "I might just take you up on that."

Once again, that faint smile flickered across his face. "My favor does come with one condition."

"What's that?"

His hazel eyes hardened, and he leaned forward and stabbed his finger at me. "You kill this son of a bitch. With no hesitation and absolutely no mercy. You do that, Gin, and you'll get all the favors you want from me."

"Is this the same deal that you made with Fletcher?"

"Yes."

"Then I accept."

"Good." Mosley leaned back against the cushions again. "What are you waiting for? Get out of here, and get to work."

I snapped off a salute to him. "Yes, sir."

Mosley harrumphed at my salute, but a small smile lifted the corner of his mouth.

Since Mosley was out sick, he asked Finn to go to First

Trust to check on a few things, while I grabbed the box of information on Joanna's murder. Once that was done, we left the dwarf to his cold and miserable memories.

Finn watched me slide the box into the front passenger's seat of my car. "Now what are you going to do?"

"I'm going back to the scene of the crime. The last crime, anyway."

"Northern Aggression?" Finn asked. "Why? The cops searched that whole place last night. Bria said they didn't find anything."

I slammed the car door shut with far more force than necessary. "Because we still have fuck-all nothing, as you so eloquently put it."

Understanding flashed in his green gaze. "You're getting desperate."

I sighed. "Of course I'm desperate. I don't want to go back to Jade empty-handed. I *can't*. We all know that this guy could kill Elissa at any second. And if I don't find something, some small clue, some tiny thread to follow, that's exactly what's going to happen. Sooner rather than later. And then, he'll kidnap another girl and do the same thing to her."

Finn slung his arm around my shoulders and gave me a hug. "We'll find this guy, Gin. We just need a little more time. Something will turn up. You'll see."

I forced myself to ignore the frustration surging through my body and smile back at him. "Yeah," I said, lying through my teeth. "You're right. We'll find him."

We said our goodbyes, and Finn headed downtown to First Trust bank, while I drove over to Northern Aggression. It wasn't quite noon yet, and all the lots around the club were empty, except for a single black Mercedes parked on the street a hundred feet away from the main entrance. The car had probably been left behind by someone too drunk to drive home last night, but I still raised my phone, zoomed in, and snapped a photo of the license plate.

I got out of my car and scanned the area, but everything was quiet, and I was all alone. It was far too early for the staff to be here, and I didn't see Roslyn's car either. She was probably still at home, sleeping in after dealing with the police late last night. So I wandered through the parking lots, not so much looking for clues as just soaking up the peace and quiet and going over everything that had happened. Thinking about everything that I knew about the Dollmaker and how I might find him before he murdered Elissa.

No realizations bubbled up in my mind, so I finally walked around the side of the building, turned the corner, and strode out into the middle of the cracked, dirty asphalt.

The three Dumpsters still marked the spot where I'd found Lacey Lawrence's body, although they'd been pushed apart and off to one side of the parking lot so that the police could better examine and process the scene. The cops had dutifully strung up yellow crime-scene tape all around the empty metal containers and the space between them, but the winter wind had torn most of the tape loose overnight, and the strings fluttered weakly in the steady breeze, like butterflies trying to escape a spider's sticky web. All of the garbage from the surrounding trash cans had been bagged up as potential evidence and taken to the police station last night, but the air still reeked of sour beer, rancid food, and cigarette smoke.

Despite the stench, I did a slow, methodical search of the entire area, peering into each and every one of the trash cans, standing up on my tiptoes so I could look into the Dumpsters, and crouching down and examining the spot where I'd found the girl's body. I even inspected all the cracks in the asphalt in the entire parking lot, just in case anything had slipped into one of the jagged openings.

Nothing—absolutely nothing.

All the garbage was long gone, and no blood stained the pavement where Lacey Lawrence had been found. I didn't find Elissa's purse, phone, or anything else that might have belonged to her, the dead girl, or the Dollmaker.

Disgusted, I got to my feet, lashed out, and kicked an empty beer bottle with a broken neck that had somehow escaped Bria and Xavier's garbage pickup last night. The bottle hit the side of a metal trash can and exploded on impact, showering the pavement with sharp shards. I looked around, searching for something else to break, something else to take my anger, disgust, and worry out on—

Skitter-skitter.

I froze, my gaze darting over to the trash can. But the bottle was as still and broken as before, the shards of glass gleaming in the weak sunlight. So what had made that noise?

Or who?

I palmed a knife, darted forward, and crouched down beside that closest trash can, making myself as small and invisible as possible. Goose bumps rippled up and down my arms, but they weren't from the cold wind. No, this particular sensation meant only one thing.

Someone was watching me.

My gaze darted from one side of the parking lot to the other, but I saw the exact same things as before. Cracked asphalt, empty trash cans, yellow crime-scene tape, a tall shadow at the corner of one of the Dumpsters—

Wait a second. That shadow hadn't been there before.

My eyes narrowed, and I focused on the shape, but it was just a slender shadow, a patch of pavement a shade darker than all the rest. It didn't tell me anything about whoever was lurking back there.

But someone *was* lurking back there, I was sure of it.

I crouched down a little more, but the angle was wrong, and I couldn't look underneath the Dumpster to see his shoes. I didn't know exactly who was back there—if it was the Dollmaker or some other enemy—but if he wouldn't come out and face me, then I'd just sneak up and stab him in the back.

Still holding my knife, I got to my feet and crept forward, making as little noise as possible, and headed toward the far right side of the Dumpster, at the opposite end from where the shadow was. I kept my gaze on the shadow the whole time, but it didn't move, not even an inch. Whoever was back there was as good at waiting as I was.

I reached the front corner of the Dumpster, but the shadow still hadn't moved. The only sound was the wind whistling through the parking lot, the cold gusts of air continually kissing my cheeks.

I drew in a breath and slowly let it out. Then I raised my knife and charged around to the back of the Dumpster.

Empty—the space behind the container was completely, utterly, depressingly empty.

No one was here.

I sprinted to the opposite end of the container, around the side, and back out into the parking lot beyond, but the shadow had vanished. I whirled around and around, looking in all directions, but I was all alone. If the Dollmaker had been here, he was gone.

"Dammit!" I snarled, stalking back and forth across the parking lot. "Dammit!"

Angry and frustrated, I whipped around and slammed my boot into the side of the closest Dumpster, right where the shadow had been. The wheels screeched in protest, but the container slid back a couple of inches, and a glimmer of gold flashed in the sun.

I blinked, wondering if my eyes were playing tricks on me, but they weren't.

Something bright and shiny was lying underneath the Dumpster, close to one of the front wheels.

Still holding my knife, I looked around again, just in case this was a ploy to get me to lower my guard so my enemy could get the drop on me. But I was as alone as before, so I sidled forward, crouched down, and reached underneath the Dumpster. Sure enough, my fingers closed over something cold, hard, and metal, and I pulled it out where I could see it.

A small gold tube glinted in the palm of my hand.

And not just any kind of tube—a lipstick case.

I sucked in a breath and got to my feet. I glanced around again, making sure that no one was sneaking up on me, then slid my knife back up my sleeve so that I could examine the tube with both hands.

I'd never seen this particular lipstick before, but the tube was solid gold, with sleek, wavy sides, telling me that it was expensive. I tilted the tube to the side and realized that the words *Glo-Glo* were stamped into the metal. That must be the brand name. I turned the tube up so that I could see the small print on the bottom that would tell me the exact color: *Heartbreaker*.

A cold, sick feeling flooded the pit of my stomach, but I uncapped the tube and slowly rolled it up, knowing exactly what I would find. Sure enough, the lipstick inside was blood-red.

The same blood-red that had been used to draw my spider runes on that dead girl's hands.

✳ 17 ✳

The sight of the blood-red lipstick—the Heartbreaker lipstick—punched me in the gut.

It was one thing to have seen my spider runes on the dead girl's hands. But to be holding the thing that they'd been drawn with, something so benign, so innocent, so ordinary . . . It was a painful reminder of just how sadistic the Dollmaker was—and just how much danger Elissa was in.

But I pushed my feelings aside and forced myself to examine the tube from all angles. And I noticed something odd: the lipstick hadn't been used. Not at all. If this were the tube that had been used on Lacey Lawrence, the lipstick would have been worn down, but this one was still smooth, sharp, and whole, as though it had just come from the store.

Maybe it had. This tube hadn't been here last night. Otherwise, Bria and Xavier would have found it. And I hadn't spotted it during my initial search either. I hadn't seen anything except that shadow, but I was more convinced than ever that someone had been watching me— and that that person had planted this lipstick for me to find. It was the only thing that made sense.

But who would do that? And why? Was it the Dollmaker, taunting me again? Had he been hiding behind the Dumpster, waiting for me to turn my back so that he could leave his sick little clue? Or was this the work of someone else, someone whose motives I couldn't even fathom right now?

My hand closed over the tube. As much as I wanted to hurl it to the ground and stomp it to pieces, I forced myself to slide the lipstick into my jeans pocket. I had to get this to Ryan. He could confirm for sure that it was the same lipstick used to draw the runes on Lacey Lawrence. Then maybe we could track down what store the lipstick had come from and exactly who had bought it—

In the distance, a car engine rumbled to life.

My head snapped around, and I thought of that black Mercedes that I'd seen parked on the street. Not left behind by a drunk driver after all.

I palmed my knife again, ran out of the parking lot, and sprinted around the side of the club, heading back toward the front of the building. I thought that the driver gunned the engine, although I couldn't be sure, given the steady *slap-slap-slap-slap* of my boots on the pavement and how loudly my heart was pounding in my ears. I broke free of the building and headed to my right toward the street where the Mercedes was.

Someone was sitting inside the vehicle now, although I

couldn't tell exactly who, given the dark tint on the windshield. I did have the impression that it was a man, although I didn't get a clear look at his features, which were hidden by a hat, his sunglasses, and the thick scarf he had wrapped around the bottom half of his face.

He spotted me too. For a second, I thought that he might gun the engine, jump the curb, and come roaring at me, trying to mow me down with his car. Instead, he threw the vehicle into reverse, wrenched the steering wheel, and whipped a beautiful U-turn right in the middle of the street. Three seconds later, he was speeding away in the opposite direction, and I knew that he would be long gone by the time I reached my own car.

"Dammit!" I snarled. "Dammit!"

For a mad, mad moment, I thought about chucking my knife down the street after the car. Not because I had any chance of hitting the vehicle but just to relieve some of the anger and frustration surging through me. But that would have been petty and pointless, so I forced myself to take deep breaths, slow my racing heart, and think things through.

Whether it was the Dollmaker or someone else, whoever had been watching me had wanted me to find the gold Glo-Glo tube. Someone had wanted me to know about the Heartbreaker color. Someone had deliberately left me a breadcrumb. Well, I was going to oblige the bastard.

Time to follow the lipstick trail.

I slid my knife back up my sleeve, got into my car, and cranked the engine. I also took a moment to pull the lipstick out of my jeans pocket and set it in the cup holder in the center console. The gold tube glinted in the sun, almost like an eye slyly winking at me over and over again, daring me to find out where it had come from. Well, at least I wouldn't be going back to Jade empty-handed. I had a clue, and I was determined to follow it.

Even if I still didn't know who had left it for me or why.

I pulled out of the parking lot and headed toward the one person who might be able to give me some answers about the lipstick: Jolene "Jo-Jo" Deveraux. Her salon was close to Northern Aggression, so I decided to visit her first and see what I could find out before I reported back to Jade.

Twenty minutes later, I steered up a driveway and squeezed my car in next to several others already parked. The front door was always open during business hours, so I let myself into the white plantation house and walked down the long hallway to the back of the structure, which opened into an old-fashioned beauty salon.

Cherry-red salon chairs were lined up in a row along one wall while stacks of glossy magazines and plastic pink tubs full of nail polish covered all the tables. A long counter ran along another wall, bristling with combs, curlers, scissors, styling irons, nail files, makeup brushes, and every other beauty tool known to womanhood. The air smelled of hair dye and other chemicals, although the harsh aroma was somewhat softened by the sweet vanilla that Jo-Jo infused into her homemade healing ointments, facial scrubs, and other beauty treatments.

Thursday was one of the salon's busiest days, since everyone was getting their hair, nails, and faces done for the weekend. Every chair in the salon was full, with several women reading magazines and letting their hair slowly set under the industrial dryers.

I headed over to the far corner of the room, where a middle-aged dwarf with perfect white-blond curls was painting the nails of a little girl who looked to be about five. The girl had on a poofy pink princess dress, along with a slightly askew silver plastic tiara and sparkly pink ballet shoes, as though today was a special occasion. Her mother sat nearby, waving her own freshly painted nails back and forth in the air to help dry them.

Jo-Jo looked up at the sound of my footsteps. So did Rosco, her basset hound, who was comfortably ensconced in his white wicker basket in the corner.

Her face creased into a smile. "Gin! What brings you here today?"

"I was wondering if you could help me with something."

"Of course," Jo-Jo said. "Just give me a few minutes to finish up with this little birthday princess."

She winked at the girl, who let out a pleased giggle. Jo-Jo bent over the girl's nails again, and I sank onto one of the sofas to wait. I eyed a stack of magazines on the table at my elbow, but they all focused on beauty tips, fashion, and hairstyles. Not exactly my milieu, but I picked up one and flipped through it just to have something to do. Beside me, two women in their early twenties with pink curlers in their hair chatted back and forth as they waited for Jo-Jo to get back to them.

"I can't *believe* that you talked me into competing in the Miss Ashland Pageant," one of the girls, a pretty brunette, complained. "If I'd known it was going to be this much freaking work, I would have told you no."

The other girl, an equally pretty redhead, rolled her eyes. "And I told you that it would be an easy way to get some scholarship money. So chillax already and enjoy being pampered."

The brunette huffed, crossed her arms over her chest, and slouched a little lower in her chair. "Well, I still say that our hunting trip to Cloudburst Falls next weekend will be *way* more fun than this."

I brought my magazine up to hide my grin. Beauty pageants one weekend, hunting the next. Ah, the wide and varied interests of Southern women.

I agreed with the brunette, though. Hunting was always much more fun. And I was going to bag a serial killer before all was said and done.

Jo-Jo finished up with the little girl and her mom, then checked and made sure that her other customers were okay by themselves for a few minutes. She crooked her finger at me, and we headed into the kitchen for some privacy. Rosco let out a loud *woof*, heaved himself to his feet, and followed us in hopes of scoring a doggy treat.

Jo-Jo went over to the fridge, pulled out a pitcher of sweet iced tea, and poured herself a tall glass. She offered me some, but I held up my hand, declining.

She took a long drink of her tea before setting it aside and staring at me with her clear, almost colorless eyes. "What's up, darling? What can I help you with? Does it have something to do with that poor missing girl? Sophia told me all about it when she came home from the police station last night."

"Yeah. I found something that I want you to take a look at."

I filled her in on everything that had happened, including the mysterious shadow lurking behind the Dumpster and the obvious clue that he'd left behind. I placed the lipstick on the butcher-block table between us.

"I figured that if anyone knew about this kind of makeup, it would be you. Have you ever heard of Glo-Glo lipstick? Do you know where they might sell it in Ashland?"

"Sure, I've heard of it," Jo-Jo replied. "It's a makeup company out of Bigtime, New York. They make good products. Lots of bright, vibrant colors at reasonable prices."

I tapped my finger on top of the lipstick. "All this gold doesn't look very reasonable to me. But of course, I'm no expert, which is why I came to the best."

Jo-Jo winked at me. "Well, you certainly did that."

She picked up the tube and examined it from all angles before pulling off the cap and examining the lipstick. She even went so far as to sniff the lipstick itself. After several seconds, she set the open tube back down on the table and held up her finger.

"Give me one minute. I'll be right back."

Jo-Jo left the kitchen and headed back into the salon. The second she was gone, Rosco crept even closer to me. The basset hound plopped down on the floor at my feet, let out a plaintive whine, and stared up at me with his big brown eyes. And he kept right on whining and wagging his tail, slapping it up against the side of my boot.

"All right, all right," I grumbled. "You win. You know a softhearted sucker when you see one, don't you, boy?"

Rosco *woof*ed his agreement.

I plucked the lid off a large blue and white container shaped like a dog bone. The bright color and fun style reminded me of that chocolate cake cookie jar that Elissa had given to Jade. And just like that, my light mood vanished. I grabbed a dog biscuit out of the container and tossed it down to Rosco to munch on.

"Here we go," Jo-Jo said, coming back into the kitchen. "I thought that I'd seen that fancy gold tube before."

She put an open catalog down on the table and tapped her finger on a product on one of the pages. "Heartbreaker lipstick. A special anniversary product from Glo-Glo. Apparently, it was the very first color the company ever produced. They've been selling it for years in regular, cheaper packaging, but for the anniversary, they decided to dress it up in that gold case. It's a nice red, and I thought about ordering a few tubes to resell to my clients, but the price is a little too steep for my tastes."

I blinked at the information on the page. "*Five hundred dollars?* For a tube of lipstick?"

"Like I said, a little too steep for my tastes, especially since you can still get the exact same color in the regular packaging for fifteen bucks a pop." She shrugged. "But we both know that there are a lot of folks out there with more money than common sense, especially in this town."

"So who would sell something like this? Where would you get it in Ashland?"

"Well, given the price, it's not the sort of thing that you can get just anywhere," Jo-Jo said. "The only place I know of that has been selling it is the Posh boutique in Northtown."

"How do you know that?"

"Several of the women who work at the boutique get their hair done here. One of them came in earlier this week, bragging about how she'd gotten her latest sugar daddy to buy her a tube of it."

I nodded. "Thanks for your help."

"You're quite welcome." She tilted her head to the side, looking at me. "So what are you going to do now?"

"Call Finn. He knows some of the folks who work at Posh. He should be able to get a list of everyone who's bought a tube of this lipstick in the last six months. After that, we'll see if anyone's name jumps out at us."

Jo-Jo nodded. She reached out and put the cap back on the lipstick, but she didn't give it to me. Instead, she started turning the gold tube around and around in her hands, and the pins-and-needles sensation of her Air magic gusted through the kitchen, pricking my skin with its sharp, sudden intensity. My spider rune scars itched and burned at the uncomfortable sensation of her magic, which was the complete opposite of my own Ice and Stone power.

In an instant, her eyes took on a bright, intense, milky-white glow. She might be staring at the lipstick, but she wasn't really seeing it anymore. She raised her eerie gaze to mine.

"Be careful, darling," Jo-Jo murmured. "I'm seeing storm clouds ahead for you. Some very dark, nasty ones. Swirling around and around, trying to consume you, trying to drown out all your light . . ."

In addition to healing people and smoothing out wrinkles with her Air magic, Jo-Jo's power also gave her glimpses of the future. I waited for her to elaborate, to be more specific, but she didn't say anything else. After a minute, the prickly feel of her Air magic vanished, and her eyes returned to their normal clear color.

Jo-Jo shook her head and finally held the lipstick out to me. "I'm sorry. I wish that I could tell you more, Gin."

"That's okay. Nothing else about this has been easy. Why should the future be any different?" I asked, not really joking.

I took the lipstick and held it up, staring at the smooth, shiny surface. The bright, glimmering gold was about as far away from Jo-Jo's dire prediction as you could get, but I knew better than to doubt her.

"Storm clouds, huh?" I murmured. "Funny, but I don't think that there are any other kinds of clouds in my life these days."

❋ 18 ❋

I left Jo-Jo's salon, went outside, and got into my car. I put the tube into the cup holder and texted Finn, asking him to get a list of everyone who'd bought a gold tube of Heartbreaker lipstick from the Posh boutique in the last six months. He hit me back a minute later, saying that he was on it.

I also texted Silvio, asking him to check and see if any other stores in Ashland sold the lipstick, just to cover all the bases. He too texted me back a minute later, saying that he would look into it, and he even sent me a little smiley face, telling me that he was happy to help. My assistant really did like this sort of thing. Then again, it wasn't the strangest thing I'd ever asked him to do. And it certainly wasn't the most dangerous.

I cranked the engine, steered down Jo-Jo's driveway, and left her subdivision behind. I'd just pulled out onto the main road when the car's sound system chirped with a new call. I hit a button on the steering wheel to answer it.

"Hello?"

For a few seconds, there was silence. Then a series of loud crashes and bangs sounded, along with several muffled shouts and the distinctive *tinkle-tinkle* of breaking glass. I glanced at the screen on my dashboard to see who was calling.

Ryan Colson.

I'd told Ryan to call if anything suspicious happened, but the noises coming out of the phone were downright violent. Someone had broken into Jade's house.

I floored the gas pedal, speeding toward her place. I thought about ending the call to dial Bria and tell her what was going on, but I wanted to stay on the line and hear what was happening.

Nothing—absolutely nothing.

After that first initial blast of sound, the noises stopped completely, and I didn't hear so much as a whisper of conversation in the background. Whatever was happening at Jade's house, it was now taking place away from the phone.

Either that, or Jade and Ryan were already dead.

I tightened my grip on the steering wheel, driving as fast as I dared on the curvy mountain roads. Still, it took me ten long minutes to reach the subdivision where Jade's house was, and my phone stayed silent the whole time. I made the appropriate turn and cruised into the neighborhood.

The first thing I noticed was the black SUV parked about fifty feet away from Jade's house.

The car itself wasn't unusual, but it was sitting down at the curb, instead of pulled up in someone's driveway. It was also parked the wrong way on the street, pointing out toward the subdivision exit, as though someone thought he might need to leave in a hurry and didn't want to waste precious time turning the vehicle around.

As much as I wanted to zoom up the driveway, leap out of my car, and bust into Jade's house, I forced myself to drive at a normal speed, just in case anyone was watching the street from inside the house. Sure enough, one of the curtains twitched, as though someone had pushed it aside just enough to peer through the crack in the fabric. On my passenger's seat, my phone was as quiet as before, although I could hear a faint hum through the car's sound system, telling me that the line was still open.

I reached the end of the street and made a right, as though I were going somewhere deeper in the subdivision. Really, all I wanted was to get out of sight of Jade's house. Since it was the middle of the day, the neighborhood was empty, with most folks at work and school. I steered my car up a driveway and parked in front of the first home I came to.

I picked up my phone, listening, but everything was as quiet as before. A fist of fear squeezed my heart tight. If there had been noise—yells, shouts, screams—I would have at least known that Jade and Ryan were still alive. The silence told me nothing.

So I ended the call and dialed Bria. It went straight to her voice mail, so I hung up without leaving a message and called Silvio. He picked up on the second ring.

"Calling so soon?" he asked in a dry, amused voice.

"You just texted me fifteen minutes ago. I haven't even had a chance to start looking into your lipstick question yet."

"Someone's in Jade's house."

"Who? How many are there? What do they want? Is it the Dollmaker?" His voice sharpened with every word.

I glanced around, making sure that no one was in the surrounding houses and watching me, but the neighborhood was as deserted as before.

"Gin?" Silvio asked. "How many people are there? What's going on?"

"I don't know, but I'm going to find out."

He protested, wanting me to wait for him to call the others and for everyone to arrive so that I would have some backup, instead of going into the house blind all by myself.

"No," I said. "Jade and Ryan don't have that kind of time. Whoever broke into her house has already been in there for almost twenty minutes. That's more than enough time to kill them or do whatever they came here to do. I'm surprised that they're still here."

Silvio sighed, realizing that I was right. "Well, at least promise me that you'll be careful. That you won't take any unnecessary risks."

Despite the tense situation, I still smiled, even though he couldn't see me. "There you go, trying to mother me again."

"Well, someone has to," he snapped.

"Thank you, Silvio."

"I'm on my way right now, and I'll call the others en route," he snapped again, although his voice was a bit less peevish than before. "Do me a favor. Don't die before we get there."

"Why, I wouldn't dream of it," I drawled.

I hung up with Silvio, palmed a knife, and got out of my car. Given the watcher at the front windows of Jade's house, I didn't dare use the street, so I walked around the side of the home I'd parked in front of, crossed the yard full of plastic castles, swing sets, and other toys, and slipped into the woods. It only took me a few minutes to work my way through the trees and back over to Jade's house.

I hunkered down just inside the tree line, watching the windows and glass doors on the back of the house. At first, I didn't see anything, but then a shadow moved into my line of sight, one that became clear as someone stopped in front of the doors, stepped up to the frame, and looked outside—a dwarf wearing a dark suit and clutching a cell phone.

Ryan had speculated that the Dollmaker was exceptionally strong, and dwarves were certainly that. Could this be him? Could this actually be the killer?

The longer I studied the dwarf, the more familiar his features seemed to me, especially his thin black mustache. I'd seen him before. I was sure of it. But where? When? I thought back, but I couldn't put my finger on how or when our paths might have crossed. I held my position, watching the dwarf, but after several seconds, he moved away from the doors.

But he wasn't the only one in the house.

Through the windows, I spotted at least two more

dwarves, also dressed in dark suits, moving from one room to the next, opening cabinets, looking in drawers, even standing on chairs so that they could peer into the air vents high up on the walls. They were obviously searching for something. But what? And why would they think it was in Jade's house?

Eventually, the dwarves headed back toward the front of the house, disappearing from my line of sight. The second they were gone, I sprinted from the woods, all the way across the yard, and over to the back corner of Jade's house. I pressed my body up against the brick and started counting off the seconds in my mind.

One . . . two . . . three . . . five . . . fifteen . . .

A minute passed, and no shouts of alarm, surprise, or warning rang out. The men hadn't spotted me, so I slithered forward, ducking down around the windows, still keeping my body pressed up against the side of the house. Now that I was closer, I could hear faint muttering, along with several thumps, bumps, and other crashing noises, confirming my theory that the men inside Jade's house were tearing her things apart.

I made it to the glass patio doors that led into the kitchen. When I was here this morning, the doors had been intact, but now the glass was completely busted out of one of them. This must have been how the dwarves had stormed into the house. Ryan must have heard the noise and dialed me on his phone.

I palmed a second knife and peered around the edge of the broken door, but no one was in the kitchen. In the front of the house, the crashes, clangs, and bangs grew louder and louder, as though the men were in a frenzy now, tearing through everything they could get their hands on, whether or not it was actually what they were searching for.

Go right ahead, boys. Make as much noise as you want. It will drown out the soft sounds of this Spider creeping into the house.

My knives still in my hands, I stepped through the busted door, moving slowly so as not to make my boots crunch any more than necessary on the broken glass. More noises came from the front of the house, but they dwindled and slowly faded away. I tiptoed through the kitchen, stepped into the hallway at the far end, and sidled along the wall until I could peer around the corner up ahead and out into the office beyond.

Jade and Ryan were sitting side by side on a couch along one wall, their hands tied in front of them with thick, heavy ropes. Jade had an ugly bruise on her left cheek, as though someone had backhanded her, while Ryan had multiple cuts on his face and a nasty, painful-looking black eye. Blood had dripped down his face and spattered all over the front of his dark blue sweater, and his knuckles were also bloody, bruised, and swollen. He'd fought back against the intruders. Good for him, although he'd gotten a vicious beating in return.

Battered though they were, the sight of them eased some of my own tense worry and dread. Jade and Ryan were still upright, still breathing, still alive, and I was going to make sure they stayed that way.

I tiptoed forward a few more steps so that I could see the other people in the office. There were four of them, all dwarves, all wearing dark suits. Your standard low-level muscle. But muscle for whom?

The men were picking through the wreckage of the office, particularly the corner where the boxes of evidence had been stacked. They'd torn the lids off each and every one of the boxes and had strewn all the documents, photos, and files across the floor, creating a thick carpet of paper. They'd also smashed several of the desks, chairs, and phones, adding more splintered debris to the mess.

One of the dwarves stepped in front of Jade and scowled at her. "Is this it?" he growled, sweeping his hand out over the mess. "Is this everything?"

Jade glanced at Ryan, who shook his head, telling her not to answer. The lead dwarf noticed the exchange, drew back his fist, and punched Ryan in the face, making his head snap back against the couch.

"That's it, Ken," the mustached dwarf said, pumping his own fist in the air. "Hit him again!"

"Happy to, Henry," the other dwarf drawled.

Ken punched Ryan in the face again, making him groan.

Ryan blinked and blinked, trying to shake off the hard blows. After a few seconds, he raised his head and glared at Ken. "Is that all you've got? My grandma hits harder than that."

"Wise guy, huh? I'll be happy to beat that right out of you." Ken grinned and drew his fist back again.

"Okay! Okay!" Jade held up her bound hands and tried to shield Ryan with them. "Stop hurting him. I told you before. All the files are here in the office."

Shock jolted through me. Files? The dwarves were here

for the murder files? That meant they had to be involved with the Dollmaker. I studied the four men, once again wondering if one of them might actually be the killer. As dwarves, they all had the strength necessary to beat and strangle someone to death, as Ken had already demonstrated all over Ryan's face. Still, they all looked like regular guys, all around five feet tall, with no odd or distinguishing features, except for Henry with his pitiful mustache. None of them looked like a cold-blooded killer.

Then again, I supposed I didn't look much like one either.

But the vibe just felt wrong. From what little I knew of them, serial killers liked to work alone. Besides, the Dollmaker had left precious little evidence behind, and nothing in the files pointed to his true identity. If he'd thought that Jade had any real clue as to who he was, then he would have come here himself, tortured her for the information, and killed her. He might have even painted her lips the same gruesome blood-red as all his other victims, since she was blond, just like all the other women.

But these run-of-the-mill goons were here instead of the man himself. Why? Had the Dollmaker sent them? Did they know who he really was? Or did they work for someone else entirely? Someone who had some other interest in the killer?

I shook my head, trying to clear away all the questions that circled around and around and ultimately went nowhere. I felt like I was trying to solve two separate jigsaw puzzles at once, only I didn't have enough pieces of either one to get a clear picture of anything—not one little thing.

But the intruders were one problem that was easily solvable. Even better, I could wing one of them and then squeeze that man for answers. Normally, I didn't hold back and take prisoners when my friends were in danger, but I'd make an exception, just this once, for Elissa's sake.

"I don't believe you," Ken growled. "There have to be more copies of this information. So where are they? Where are the files? And who have you told about them?"

Jade glared at him, her mouth a flat line in her face. "I'll tell you exactly where the copies of these files are—at the police station. Where did you think that I got them from in the first place? You idiot."

He glowered at her, but Jade lifted her chin, daring him to hit her again. After several seconds, he shrugged.

"I'm not worried about getting into the police station. We'll go right over there." Ken grinned. "As soon as we finish burning this place to the ground—with you and your boyfriend inside."

Jade gasped, and Ryan reached over and grabbed her bound hands with his own.

"It's going to be okay, Jade," he said. "You'll see."

Ken chuckled. "Sure, it will be. Just as soon as the two of you are extra crispy."

Their faces both paled, making him chuckle again. He turned to the other three men, who were kicking through the mess of papers on the floor. "One of you go into the kitchen and see if you can find some matches. I'll go siphon some gas out of the car to get things started in here—"

I didn't let him finish his gruesome sentence. Instead, I sprinted down the hallway, stepped into the office, drew my arm back, and let my first knife fly.

Ken saw me out of the corner of his eye and turned in my direction, but it was too late, and the blade hit exactly where I wanted it to, sinking into his left forearm. The wound was deep enough to make him howl with pain and stagger away from Jade and Ryan. The other three goons whipped around, eyes wide, shocked that someone else was in the house, but I was already moving forward.

The second dwarf raised his fists and lashed out at me; I ducked his slow, clumsy blow, came up inside his defenses, and stabbed him in the heart. He screamed and batted at his own chest, trying to dislodge the blade. I yanked it out and sliced it all the way across his throat in one smooth motion, cutting off his cries. He was dead before he even hit the floor.

I whirled around to face the third dwarf, Henry, the one with the mustache. He pivoted on his left foot and raised his right leg, trying to do some sort of fancy roundhouse kick to my face, like you would in a video game. I put my head down, charged forward, and rammed my shoulder into the side of his body, shoving him off balance. He staggered back, hitting one of the walls, and I followed him, slashing my knife all the way across his stomach.

Blood and guts sprayed everywhere, spattering all over the papers and photos still on the floor. Henry screamed and screamed, clutching his stomach and trying to hold his insides, well, inside, where they were supposed to be—

A pair of thick, strong arms closed around me from behind, and the fourth and final dwarf lifted me off my feet. Since my legs were already off the ground, I kicked out, driving my boots into Henry's bloody guts and making him scream again, even as his legs buckled and he crumpled to the ground.

I propelled myself backward as hard as I could, and the last dwarf couldn't hold me up in the air and keep his balance at the same time. He stumbled back, his foot slipped on some of the debris, and we both hit the floor. Since he was still holding on to me, I landed right on top of him. The dwarf yelped in pain and surprise, but he didn't let go. Instead, he tightened his grip, his hands like steel vises pinning my arms in place.

"Ken!" he yelled, his voice booming in my ear. "Kill this bitch!"

Ken, the first dwarf I'd attacked, yanked my knife out of his own forearm and headed toward us, murder glinting in his dark eyes.

I didn't have the strength to break the dwarf's grip, so I decided to make him wish that he'd never grabbed hold of me. I raised my knife and rammed it down into his right thigh, twisting and twisting the blade through all of his thick, hard layers of muscles. He bellowed with pain, right in my ear, but he still didn't let go.

Since my knife wasn't working as well as I wanted, I decided on an even more direct, painful approach. I reached for my Ice magic, slapped my other hand down on his crotch, and let loose with a sharp, cold burst of my power, right on his family jewels.

That *really* made him scream.

The dwarf's hands finally fell away from my arms. I rolled off him, ripped my knife out of his thigh, and stabbed it right back down into his chest. He screamed again, but he was a bleeding, half-frozen mess, out of the fight, and already closer to dead than alive.

Out of the corner of my eye, I saw Ken, the last dwarf standing, raise his foot back so he could kick me in the head. I yanked my knife out of his buddy's chest, lurched forward, and rolled out of the way of Ken's smashing wing tip. His shiny shoe slammed into his buddy's side hard enough to lift the other man off the floor, but the guy was already dead, so he didn't make a sound as he flopped back down to the ground again.

I got back up onto my feet, sizing up my last opponent, wondering how I could put him down without actually killing him. Unlike his buddies, Ken didn't rush blindly at me. Instead, he raised his fists, protecting his face, and rocked back on his heels, waiting for me to make the first move.

But Jade beat me to it.

She threw herself down off the couch and scrambled over to the mustached dwarf whose guts I'd sliced open. She shoved aside his bloody suit jacket, plucked the gun out of the holster on his belt, whipped it up, and aimed it at Ken.

"No!" I yelled. "Don't!"

Too late.

Jade pulled the trigger three times, sending three bullets straight into the dwarf's back. Ken yelled and arched back in shock. For a moment, I thought that he was going to fall right then and there, but he snarled, lunged forward, and lashed out with my knife, taking me by surprise and catching me across the stomach. I hissed at the sharp, stinging pain, whirled around, chopped the knife out of his hand, and shoved him away.

This time, Ken did crumple to the floor, snarling and sputtering curses all the while, although his legs didn't move along with the rest of his body. Jade's aim had been true, and it looked like all three of the bullets had punched into his spine.

"Why did you do that?" I yelled, dropping down beside Ken and rolling him over onto his back, hoping that he was still alive.

"I was trying to help you!" Jade yelled back.

"I wasn't going to kill *him*. We needed him alive." I bent down next to the dwarf. "Who sent you? Where is Elissa Daniels?"

I kept shouting the questions at him over and over again, but he just grinned, showing me a mouthful of bloody teeth. I leaned down, grabbed hold of his suit jacket, and lifted his chest up off the floor.

"Who sent you?" I yelled even louder, shaking him. "Where is the girl? Where is Elissa?"

Ken grinned at me again. "Wouldn't . . . you . . . like to . . . know . . . bitch . . ."

He rasped out a final breath, blood bubbling up out of his lips, and a familiar glassy sheen coated his eyes. His head lolled to one side, and I dropped him. There was no point in questioning him anymore.

Ken was gone—and so was any information he had about Elissa.

❋ 19 ❋

I rocked back on my heels and sat down in the middle of the mess on the office floor. The motion made fresh pain zip through the cut across my stomach, and exhaustion flooded my body. Not so much from the fight as from the fact that I hadn't gotten any information. The questions crowded into my mind about who had sent these men here and why. And once again, I had the nagging feeling that there was a lot more going on than just a kidnapped girl. But with all the men dead, no one was left to give me any answers.

Jade lowered the gun and slumped down onto the floor too, staring at Ken's body with a tight, strained face. "Why didn't you want me to shoot him?"

"Because we needed one of them alive. We needed to question someone about Elissa."

Anguish filled Jade's eyes. "I—I didn't think about that," she whispered. "He hurt Ryan and me. I didn't want him to hurt you too. I saw him holding that knife, and I just grabbed the closest gun and pulled the trigger."

"I know. And I'm sorry that I yelled at you. It's okay. Really, it is. We still have their phones and wallets and their car outside. We'll find something that will tell us who sent them after you."

Jade nodded and slowly set the gun down on the floor. She leaned over, holding out her still-bound hands to me, and I used my knife to slice through the thick ropes. Jade got up and went over to the couch where Ryan was still sitting.

"Are you okay?" she asked, putting a hand on his shoulder.

Despite his battered face, Ryan smiled at her. "We're alive, and they're not. That's what matters, right?"

Jade nodded and blinked back the tears in her eyes. I held out my knife, and she took it and used it to cut through Ryan's bonds. He leaned forward, rubbing first one wrist, then the other.

"So what happened?" I asked, still sitting on the floor.

Jade and Ryan looked at each other, then at me.

"Ryan was here in the office reviewing the files, and I was in the kitchen making some more coffee," Jade said. "The next thing I knew, one of the dwarves was smashing his gun into one of the glass doors and storming into the kitchen."

"I heard the noise," Ryan added. "So I called you. I ran into the kitchen to help Jade, but the men jumped me, and I dropped my phone before I could tell you what was going on. They hit me, dragged us in here, tied our hands, and started going through all the information on the Dollmaker." He glared down at the dead men on the floor. "They knew exactly who he was. They were here to destroy the files, to protect him."

"Did they say anything about him?" I asked. "Did they ever mention any names? Anyone they might have been working for?"

Jade and Ryan looked at each other again. Both of them shook their heads.

"They just talked to each other," Jade said. "They didn't mention anyone else."

I stared at each one of the dead dwarves. I didn't know Ken or the other two men. I was sure of that. But Henry, the last guy, the one with the scraggly mustache, looked familiar, although I still couldn't place when or where I might have seen him before. The dwarf had lost his phone during the fight, although the device had landed next to his hand. Something about Henry and his phone rang a bell in the back of my mind, and I found myself staring at the device, trying to recall where I had seen it and him before . . .

"Gin," Jade said in a sharp voice. "Gin!"

I must have zoned out for a second, because I blinked, and suddenly she was crouching down on the floor beside me, along with Ryan. I hadn't seen either one of them move.

"You're bleeding," she whispered.

I looked down. Sure enough, blood soaked the front of my sweater. I raised the fabric to reveal an ugly gash running across my stomach. I gingerly pressed on the wound and hissed at the fresh pain that spiked through my body. More blood oozed out of the gash and trickled down onto my jeans. Ken had cut me deeper than I'd realized.

"Gin?" Jade whispered again. "What do you want me to do?"

"Call Silvio," I said, my words slurring a bit. "Tell him that I parked my car at a house on the next street over. He'll get the healing ointment out of my trunk."

Jade crawled away from me, searching through the mess on the floor for a phone she could use.

"You need to lie back so I can put some pressure on that," Ryan said.

He helped me lie down on the floor and then put his hands on my stomach, applying constant, steady pressure.

"I guess this is a new experience for you, huh, Doc? Working on a living patient instead of a dead one?"

He smiled at me. "It's a welcome change."

I laughed and had to stop, as it made more pain shoot through my body, rising higher and higher with every beat of my heart, like a tidal wave about to drag me under.

"Just don't let me bleed out before Silvio gets here," I mumbled. "He'll never let me hear the end of it if I die on him . . ."

White stars exploded in my field of vision, along with a misty white fog that blanketed my mind.

"Gin? Gin!" Ryan shouted. "Stay with me!"

But his voice was faint and far away, and the tidal wave of pain rose again, higher and stronger than before. It crashed down on me, sweeping everything else away.

I was snared in a world of shadows.

As soon as the Fire elemental had sent her men after me, I'd staggered away from the edge of the trees and plunged into the heart of the woods, desperate to escape before they found and killed me.

And I'd become thoroughly lost in the process.

The dark, twisted shapes of the trees loomed like skeletal monsters all around me, making everything seem blacker and more sinister than ever before. I could barely see my own hand in front of my face, much less the gnarled roots that arched up from the forest floor to trip me or the rocks hidden in the leaves that stabbed into my bare feet like a hundred little needles, each one bringing a sharp sting of pain.

After tripping for the umpteenth time, I forced myself to stop and look around. Up ahead, more trees blended into a never-ending sea of shadows, one that I could easily become lost in forever. Behind me, several hundred feet in the distance, the Snow family mansion continued to burn, the orange-red flames looking deceptively bright, cheerful, and inviting in the black night.

I shifted on my feet and winced as another hidden rock poked into my heel. Stupid rocks. Stupid tree roots. Stupid everything. A harsh, bitter wail rose in my throat, but I swallowed it down. Crying certainly wasn't going to help anything. All it would do was tell the Fire elemental and her men exactly where I was. Not to mention Hugh, that creepy vampire. I couldn't let any of them find me.

So I bit my lip and considered my options. I could keep walking through the woods and wind up who knew where. It wouldn't be daylight for hours, and I could get so turned around in here that I'd never find my way out again, especially since I didn't have any food, water, or other supplies. Or I could walk back toward the flames, the mansion, and orient myself.

It was a big risk to take, especially since I didn't know where the Fire elemental, her men, and that vampire were. I hadn't seen any flashlights bobbing up and down in the woods, so maybe they were searching in a different area. Maybe they'd already passed me by. Maybe they'd already given up and left. Either way, my best chance to get away from them was to go back to the house. If I was lucky, I could slip down to the road and follow it . . . somewhere, anywhere *but here.*

So I turned around and trudged back toward the mansion, using the flames as a homing beacon to light my way. I'd been so panicked that I hadn't gone nearly as far as I'd thought, and I quickly made it back to the edge of the woods. I slid behind a tree, looking out at the mansion, but I didn't see anyone moving through the backyard or wandering around this side of the crumbled structure. My heart lifted. Maybe I could make it down to the road after all—

A hand clamped on my shoulder and spun me around.

A giant grinned at me, his crooked teeth gleaming in the ambient glow cast from the flashlight in his other hand. "Hello, little girl. I know someone who wants to talk to you."

Panic flooded my body, and fresh waves of pain exploded in my burned hands at the thought of facing the Fire elemental and her cruel magic again. I didn't think. I just reacted. I lashed out and kicked the giant in the knee as hard as I could.

I didn't do any real damage, since I wasn't wearing shoes, but the blow surprised him and made him lose his grip on my shoulder. I ducked under his arm and darted away.

"Hey!" he hissed. "Come back here!"

I expected him to start yelling that he'd found me, but the woods remained quiet, except for the continued spitting, hiss-

ing, and crackling of the mansion fire. The giant must have thought that he could chase me down himself.

He wasn't wrong about that.

I wove in and out of the trees, trying to disappear into the shadows, but something sliced into my bare feet with every single step, and I was limping along more than I was actually running. My heart pounded, sweat streamed down my face, and a stitch throbbed in my side, growing more painful by the second. Finally, that pain forced me to stop and catch my breath. I crouched down behind a large bush with snarled branches, squinting into the shadows, expecting the giant to come crashing through the woods at any second.

Think, Gin, think! I chided myself. The giant was much bigger and stronger than I was, and he probably had a gun too. I couldn't outrun him, so how could I possibly escape?

Not just escape. A sick realization filled the pit of my stomach. I needed to keep him quiet about seeing me too. I needed to silence him.

I needed to kill him.

I couldn't let the giant go back and tell the Fire elemental that I was still alive. That would ruin whatever small chance I had of escaping, of surviving. But how could I defeat him? What could I possibly do against someone who was so much bigger, tougher, and stronger than I was?

I forced myself to take in slow, deep breaths, trying to calm my racing heart and come up with a plan. Then I looked around again, trying to figure out where I was.

I'd learned my lesson before and had stuck close to the tree line this time instead of plunging deeper into the woods, but there was nothing that would help me. I couldn't even go much farther in this direction, since there was a canyon up ahead, one with sharp rocks on either side and all along the bottom. Far too many rocks for me to climb down, much less over and up again in the dark, without cutting myself to pieces. And that was if I didn't slip, fall, and break my neck outright.

I loved to tromp around in the woods, pretending that I was a great warrior on a grand adventure and an epic quest to save my kingdom. Mom had indulged me, letting me come out here whenever I wanted, but she'd always warned me not to go near the canyon. My heart squeezed at the thought of my mom, at the fresh, horrible memory of her charred, ashy body, but I forced the images away and thought. And a simple conclusion came to me.

If the canyon rocks could break my bones, maybe they could break the giant's too.

"Hey!" A voice sounded behind me. "You there!"

A bright beam of light slashed across my face, blinding me, so I threw my hand up and squinted against the glare. The giant had his flashlight pointed directly at me. My heart sank. No way he didn't see me. I was out of time, so I did the only thing I could.

I lurched to my feet and ran for the canyon, hoping that my desperate plan would somehow work . . .

"Gin? Gin, darling, wake up." A soft, soothing voice penetrated my nightmarish memory.

The phantom feeling of rocks cutting into my feet slowly faded away, and my eyes fluttered open. Jo-Jo was leaning over me, the milky-white glow of her Air magic wisping like hazy clouds through her eyes, while the afternoon sun made her white-blond curls shimmer like pure spun gold. It reminded me of the lipstick tube.

"How are you feeling?" she asked.

I glanced around and realized that I was still in Jade's house, lying on the same couch in the den where I'd slept last night. I slowly sat up, wiggling my fingers and toes, moving my arms and legs, and stretching and testing out my body. Except for feeling a little tired from the blood loss, I was in one piece again. Jo-Jo had used her Air magic to seal up the gash in my stomach.

"Okay, thanks to you."

She patted my hand. "Anytime, darling. Anytime. You sit still for a minute."

She left the den. I heard the faint murmur of conversation, and then Jade came rushing into the room, followed by Silvio and Jo-Jo, both moving at a much more sedate pace. Jo-Jo must have healed Jade too, since her face was now free of bruises.

Jade started to come over and help me up, but I waved her off. Silvio looked me up and down, but once he realized that I was okay, he sighed, shook his head, and started scrolling through screens on his phone. Jo-Jo stood in the doorway, watching me.

I got to my feet and took a step forward. I wobbled a little, but that was to be expected, given the painful injury I'd suffered. It would take my brain a little time to play catch-up with my body and realize that I was okay.

Jade frowned. "Don't you want to sit down? Shouldn't you be resting? You almost died."

"Actually," Jo-Jo drawled, "the wound was fairly minor, all things considered."

I snorted. "You mean that it wasn't nearly as horrific as some of the other things people have done to me over the years."

She grinned at my black humor.

"Perhaps you should take it easy," Silvio murmured. "Just for a few hours."

I snorted again. "Please. It's going to take more than a little knife wound in my stomach to slow me down. Besides, I can't sit on the sidelines now. Not when our killer has finally made some mistakes."

"Mistakes?" Jade asked. "What mistakes?"

"All those men he sent here to kill you. There has to be something in their phones and wallets that will tell us who this guy is and where he's keeping Elissa," I said. "So let's get to work, and get your sister back."

* 20 *

Despite continued protests from Jade and Silvio, I left the den and went back into the office in the front of the house. Ryan was there, sifting through the mess on the floor and trying to make some sense of the files and photos. He'd also been a recipient of Jo-Jo's healing Air magic, since all of the cuts and bruises that the dwarves had inflicted on him had vanished from his features.

"The others aren't here yet?" I asked. "How long was I out?"

Silvio checked his phone. "Only about thirty minutes. Don't worry. Everyone's on their way."

Jo-Jo had to leave to get back to her clients at the salon, but sure enough, Finn, Bria, and Owen all arrived a couple of minutes later.

"Are you sure you're okay, Gin?" Owen asked, his gaze dropping to the bloodstains on my clothes.

"I'm fine." I grinned. "Most of it's not even my blood."

He shook his head. "Only you would look at it like that."

Owen let out a tense breath, gathered me up in his arms, and held me tight. I hugged him back, listening to his strong, steady heartbeat. After a minute, he let me go, knowing that we all had work to do.

I walked to the next street over, retrieved my car, and parked it in Jade's driveway. I grabbed the Heartbreaker lipstick out of my console, along with a fresh set of clothes and a large black tarp from the trunk, and headed back inside the house.

Jade, Ryan, and Silvio were all still in the office, trying to wipe the blood off the Dollmaker files and put them back in some semblance of order.

Calling the cops would lead to all sorts of awkward questions about where we'd gotten the files, as well as potentially tip off whoever had sent these men after Jade, so Bria was here in an unofficial capacity. She moved from dead guy to dead guy, snapping photos of their faces with her phone, as well as grabbing all their wallets and cell phones.

That left Finn and Owen the not-so-pleasant task of hauling the dead dwarves out of the office.

"Why did *I* get elected to move the dead guys?" Finn sniped, reluctantly stripping off his jacket and rolling up his shirtsleeves. "My suit is way more expensive than Silvio's."

"I heard that," Silvio said, still sitting on the floor and going through loose papers.

"I meant you to," Finn snarked back.

Owen rolled his eyes. "Less talking, more lifting."

Finn and Owen picked up the dead dwarves one by one, hauled them through the house and out the broken kitchen door, and dumped them in the backyard. Once they were all outside, I unfolded the black tarp and covered up the dead men. Not the best way to hide multiple bodies, but it would have to do until later tonight, when Sophia could come over and properly dispose of them.

Once that was done, and Finn had finished grumbling about ruining yet another suit, I cleaned myself up and changed into my usual black assassin clothes, and we all gathered in the office again. Jade and Ryan told everyone about the attack. Then it was my turn. I showed the others the gold tube of lipstick and filled them in on the mysterious shadow and the clue that he'd left behind at Northern Aggression.

"May I see that, please?" Ryan asked.

I handed him the tube, and he uncapped it, rolled up the lipstick, and held it up where everyone could see it.

After a few seconds, he nodded. "Oh, yeah. That's the same color that was on the latest victim's hands."

"I thought so too."

"And you're sure that someone was creeping around the nightclub?" Bria asked. "That he deliberately left the lipstick there for you to find?"

"I'm sure."

"But how did he even know that you would go back there?" she asked. "That you would search the area where Lacey Lawrence's body was found again?"

I shook my head. "I don't know. But it's the best clue that we have besides the dead guys out back, so let's follow it and see if we can finally put a name to the Dollmaker."

Everyone took a different assignment. Bria called Xavier and asked him to discreetly run the dead dwarves' photos and IDs through the police databases to see if any of them had a rap sheet and who their known associates might be. Their SUV was registered to a shell company, so Silvio got to work figuring out who the car actually belonged to. Finn grabbed the men's phones to see if he could get any information off them, while Jade, Ryan, Owen, and I sorted through the files on the floor, trying to match everything back up together and seeing if there was anything else that we might have missed or overlooked.

Finn's phone chimed, and he pulled it out and looked at the message. "Hey, Gin. The manager at Posh finally sent me that info on the lipstick sales. I'll forward it to you."

A few seconds later, my phone chimed. I grabbed a pen and a piece of paper from the debris, sat down on a relatively blood-free patch of floor, and started going through the names, concentrating on all the men who had bought tubes of Heartbreaker lipstick.

To my surprise and disappointment, there were a lot of them. Dozens of men—or people with access to their credit cards—had purchased the lipstick, not to mention all the folks who'd paid cash, leaving behind no names at all. And there was no real pattern to the sales. Sometimes the boutique only sold one tube a week. Sometimes it sold ten.

However, I did find it extremely odd that the most recent tube of lipstick had been sold the very same day I found the dead girl at Northern Aggression. Whoever bought that particular tube had paid cash for it just after ten o'clock yesterday morning, right after the store opened, so there was no name or credit-card info. I doubted it was the killer, though. By that point, he would have had Lacey Lawrence for at least a few days, and he would have already had all of his supplies on hand, especially the lipstick, since it seemed like such a big part of his ritual. Still, I made a note of that purchase, reminding myself to come back to it later.

We worked in silence for about thirty minutes. Well, except for Bria, who murmured to Xavier about the dead dwarves, and Silvio and Finn, who typed and texted like their lives depended on it. Ryan and Owen sat on the floor in the middle of the office, putting papers and photos back into the correct case files and boxes. Jade helped them for a while, but she couldn't really concentrate. Eventually, she got to her feet and started pacing through the office, down the hallway to the kitchen, and back again.

I finished scanning through the last three months of purchases. I'd written down the names of all the men who'd bought tubes of Heartbreaker lipstick, but none of them jumped out at me. I sighed and scrolled down to the next section of information. Maybe the lipstick wasn't as big a clue as I'd thought—

Silvio's hands froze on his keyboard. The sudden silence startled me, and I looked over at him. My assistant leaned forward until his nose was almost pressed up against his tablet, and he kept peering at the screen, as if he wasn't sure that he was reading the information right.

"What?" I asked. "What is it?"

He kept staring at the screen, his lips puckered in thought. "The SUV that the dwarves were driving. It's registered to a shell company that's registered to another shell company . . . You get the idea."

"Yeah. So what?"

"Well, I finally found the owner of all those companies, and it's someone we're all familiar with."

"Who?" Finn asked in an eager voice.

Silvio looked over at me. "Damian Rivera."

This time, I blinked, wondering if I'd heard him right. "Damian Rivera? *My* Damian Rivera? Are you sure?"

He nodded. "I'm sure. He owns the company that car is registered to, which means that those are *his* dead dwarves lying under the tarp in the backyard."

"Dwarves . . ." I murmured, a memory swimming around in my mind, slowly coming into focus. "A dwarf with a bad mustache and a cell phone . . ."

"Damian Rivera?" Owen frowned, trying to place the name. His eyes widened when he realized exactly who we were talking about. "Isn't that the guy you spied on the other night, Gin? The one who's a member of the Circle?"

Finn shot his finger and thumb at Owen. "Got it in one, Grayson."

Jade stopped her pacing. "Who is Damian Rivera? And what is the Circle?"

The memory finally sharpened in my mind. I got to my feet, jogged down the hallway, and went out into the backyard. I pulled the black tarp off the dead men, bent down, and studied the face of Henry, the dwarf with the thin, scraggly black mustache, the one who had looked so familiar.

It was dark the last time I'd seen him, but I still recognized him as the guard who'd been patrolling Damian
Rivera's estate two nights ago. The one who'd been too focused on his video game to notice me. I'd let him live that
night, but here he was, dead at my hands after all.

Oh, the irony.

Hope and adrenaline lifted my heart. I let the tarp
drop back into place and jogged into the house and to
the office. By this point, all my friends were on their feet.

"Gin?" Ryan asked. "What are you doing? What's
going on?"

Instead of answering, I grabbed my phone and scrolled
through the rest of the purchase information from the
Posh boutique. My fingers twitched with anticipation,
but I forced myself to go slowly, carefully looking at every
single line in turn. Not on this screen . . . or the next
one . . . or the next one . . .

Finally, on the very last screen, I found his name, three
from the bottom of the list.

I let out a tense breath and held my phone out so the
others could see it. "According to this, Damian Rivera
bought half a dozen tubes of Heartbreaker lipstick from
the Posh boutique almost six months ago."

Ryan looked at me, picking up on my train of thought.
"That would be more than enough lipstick to account for
all the traces that I've found on the victims since then. He
must be using a new tube of lipstick each time."

Finn snapped his fingers as another thought occurred
to him. "And we already know that Rivera likes to beat
people. Silvio and I did tons of background on him. We
both saw the police reports of all those girlfriends and

servants he put into the hospital. Murder wouldn't be too much of a stretch from that."

I thought back to when I'd spied on Damian Rivera at his mansion. Hugh Tucker had shown up and told Rivera to take care of some problem before the Circle took action against him. What if that problem was Rivera being the Dollmaker?

According to what Tucker had told me, the Circle had eyes and ears everywhere, and I had no doubt that some of those spies were in the police department. Maybe someone had tipped off Tucker about Ryan, Bria, and Xavier's investigation. Brutally beating and strangling a dozen women—and probably more that we didn't know about—and leaving their bodies strewn all over Ashland was sure to attract unwanted attention sooner or later. And the members of the Circle prided themselves on their anonymity, on the fact that very few people knew that the group even existed. The hunt for a serial killer—especially one of their own members—could potentially shine all sorts of light on their shadowy operations, something that they would want to avoid at all costs, even if it meant getting rid of Rivera themselves.

Something about that last thought nagged at me, something about Rivera, Tucker, and the Circle. Something about Rivera taunting Tucker about his low status within the group. Something about Tucker's mysterious boss and how he gave all of them their marching orders. But I couldn't put my finger on exactly what it was . . .

"It's Rivera," Owen said. "It has to be. There are just too many things that add up and point right to him."

My thought, whatever it had been, vanished back

down into the bottom of my brain. Besides, it wasn't important right now. Finding Elissa was the only thing that mattered. After she was safe, then I would properly deal with Damien Rivera and ask him all my many, many questions about the Circle.

Jade's hands balled into fists, and rage sparked in her eyes. "Where does he live? Where is he holding Elissa?"

"Don't worry," I said. "We're going to pay him a visit and find out."

✦ 21 ✦

As much as we all wanted to immediately drive over to Damian Rivera's mansion, storm inside, and confront him, we all knew that we had to be smart about this.

For Elissa's sake.

If Rivera realized that we were onto him, if he thought that we had any clue as to what he'd done to all those women, he could easily kill Elissa, hightail it out of Ashland, and vanish. He had more than enough money and connections to disappear and live out his days on some remote tropical island, never to be seen or heard from again. None of us wanted that to happen, but we all realized that we were up against a ticking clock. All of his men were dead, and when they didn't report back to him in an hour or two, Rivera would probably realize that they weren't coming back at all, and he would act accordingly. We needed to be in position to rescue Elissa before that happened.

We trooped into the kitchen and gathered around the table there so that we could all have a seat and brainstorm together. Finn and Silvio called up all the information that they'd compiled on Rivera, swiping through screen after screen on their phones, trying to pinpoint exactly where he might be holding Elissa.

"He has properties all over the city, thanks to his dead mama's real-estate business," Finn said. "And these are just the ones that are officially on file. He could have more buildings off the books or under another name or company that we don't even know about."

"Finn's right." Silvio shook his head. "Elissa could be in any one of a dozen locations."

I stood up and started pacing around the kitchen, much the same way Jade had done earlier, trying to remember every little detail of Rivera and Tucker's conversation the other night. One of them had said something about a guest . . . a woman . . .

I stopped. No, not them, Bruce Porter. The dwarf was the one who mentioned that he'd set up Rivera's "guest" in his bedroom. What if he'd been talking about Elissa? That meant that she'd been at Rivera's mansion that night, and she might still be there right now.

"Forget about his other properties," I said. "Let's focus on the mansion."

I told the others my theory.

"That's kind of a slim thread to follow," Ryan said. "Do you really think that Rivera would be stupid enough to keep all the women he kidnaps and murders in his main residence? That wouldn't exactly fit in with how careful he's been about not leaving any evidence behind."

"Absolutely," I said. "Think about it. Damian Rivera is a mean, arrogant drunk. He thinks that he can do whatever he wants and that no one can touch him just because he's a member of the Circle. Besides, he's gone to a lot of trouble to kidnap all these women, hold them hostage, and make them perform in whatever sadistic fantasy he's dreamed up. He wouldn't want to risk stashing them someplace where he couldn't get to them in a hurry. He'll have Elissa somewhere close by, just like he probably had all the others close by. The mansion's our best bet."

The others agreed, and we moved on to exactly how we were going to get close enough to slip inside the mansion. If it had been anywhere close to dark, I would have gone in by myself, just like I had two nights ago. But it was three in the afternoon, which meant that there was still plenty of daylight and no shadows to hide in. I started pacing again, turning the problem over and over in my mind.

"We need to get Rivera out of the mansion, along with as many guards as possible," Bria said. "Fewer men means less security and less chance of something going wrong and Elissa getting hurt."

"But how do we do that?" Owen asked. "It's not like we can just call him up and ask him to leave so we can break in and search the place while he's gone."

An idea popped into my mind. The more I thought about it, the more certain I was that it would work. I went over, leaned down, grabbed Owen's face, and gave him a long, deep kiss.

After the better part of a minute and a couple of wolf whistles from Finn, I drew back, smiling at him. "You, Owen Grayson, are officially a genius."

Owen blinked a few times, trying to focus on my words. "I am?"

"You most certainly are." I kissed him again, then straightened up and looked at Finn. "I need a number for one of your contacts."

Finn sighed. "I'm not going to like this, am I?"

"Probably not."

I told him who I wanted to call. Finn was right. He definitely didn't like it, but he realized that it was our best option, so he hit a button on the speed dial and handed the phone over to me.

A thick, congested voice answered on the third ring. "Hello?"

"Hello, Mr. Mosley. This is Gin Blanco. Remember that favor you offered me earlier today? Well, I'm ready to cash it in."

Thirty minutes later, I was right back where I'd started two nights ago in the woods behind Damian Rivera's massive estate. Only this time, Finn, Bria, and Owen hunkered down just inside the tree line with me, while Silvio, Jade, and Ryan were waiting in Silvio's car down the street from the front of the mansion. Jade had wanted to come with us into the woods, but I'd finally convinced her that a small team was the best option for finding Elissa and getting her out of the mansion to safety.

As much as I wanted to confront Rivera, finding Elissa was our top priority. Once she was safe, though, all bets were off. I might be an assassin, but Fletcher had trained me to follow his code, one that didn't include torturing people. But I figured that the old man would be okay with me making an exception for Rivera for all those women he'd tortured and murdered. Besides, I still needed information about the mysterious leader of the Circle. Whether Rivera gave it to me willingly or screamed out the answers after I'd cut him up like a chopped salad, well, that was up to him.

I was hoping for option number two, though.

I scanned the mansion and grounds again. A sprawling two-story structure of gray stone, surrounded by acres of lawn, with Bruce Porter's caretaker cottage sitting off by itself at the very back of the property. Someone had finally gotten around to taking down all the holiday lights and removing all the snowflakes, white velvet bows, and other decorations.

According to Silvio, half a dozen dwarves were guarding the front of the mansion as usual, but no one was patrolling the grounds back here. I supposed that I shouldn't have been surprised by that, since I'd killed Henry. I was just hoping that Rivera hadn't noticed how long his men had been gone.

Bria and Owen peered through their binoculars at the back of the mansion, while Finn texted Silvio on his phone, letting him know that we were in position. I palmed one of my knives, focusing on the familiar, comforting weight and the spider runes in both the hilt and my hand pressing against each other. Someone had mockingly drawn my runes on the Dollmaker's latest victim, calling me out and daring me to find him. I still wasn't sure if it had been Rivera, but either way, he was going to be the one to regret it.

"Where do you think he's keeping Elissa?" Owen asked. "The mansion doesn't have a basement, so she has to be somewhere aboveground."

Bria lowered her binoculars, her mouth twisting with disgust. "You would think that one of the servants would notice something like that. Rivera holding a woman captive."

"Maybe they have," Finn said, still texting. "Maybe he pays them to look the other way."

"For every single woman he's kidnapped and murdered over the last two years? I don't care how well he pays his servants or his guards. Someone would have a conscience. Someone would have cracked and talked by now. At the very least, someone would have tried to blackmail him for more money to keep quiet." Bria shook her head, making her blond ponytail swing from side to side. "Something about this just doesn't feel right. We're missing something about this whole thing. Something big."

She was voicing the same concerns and questions that I'd asked myself a dozen times over the past two hours, ever since we'd begun focusing in on Rivera. But we were here, and it was too late to turn back now. I wasn't going to turn back now. I *couldn't*. Not until we found Elissa. And if we had to search every single square inch of the mansion, then so be it. I'd promised Jade that I would do everything in my power to find her sister, and

I was going to live up to that. Keeping your word was another part of his code that Fletcher had drilled into me, and I wouldn't be able to look at myself in the mirror otherwise.

"We think that Elissa is in the mansion," Owen said, lowering his binoculars. "But what are we going to do if she's not?"

I flashed my knife at him. "Then we'll grab Rivera, and I'll cut the answers out of him. He might be a serial killer, but I can get him to talk. Trust me."

"I'm okay with that plan," Owen murmured.

Bria nodded. "Me too."

Finn's phone lit up. He glanced at the caller ID and held up a finger, asking us to be quiet, before he answered. "Yes, sir? Of course, sir. Thank you, sir." He hung up and looked at me. "Mosley just made the call. Damian Rivera has been alerted to a very suspicious transaction on one of his accounts, totaling more than three million dollars. Mosley's asked him to come down to the bank in person so they can straighten it out."

I nodded. That was the favor that I'd asked of Mosley, given his position at First Trust bank.

Bria and Owen picked up their binoculars again and stared at the mansion, while Finn kept his eyes glued to his phone, waiting for an update from Silvio. I looked out over the lawn, but no guards appeared, not even Bruce Porter heading back to his caretaker's cottage.

Finn had already walked around the cottage and peered in all the windows, making sure that the structure was empty. Porter must be up in the mansion with

Rivera. Hopefully the dwarf would drive his boss to the bank and take at least a couple of men with them. The fewer guards here, the better it would be for us and especially Elissa.

A minute passed, then two, then three. Cold worry trickled down my spine. What if Rivera didn't take the bait? What if he didn't go to the bank? What if he didn't leave the mansion?

My hand tightened around my knife. Then I'd go in and confront him after all, no matter how many guards were in there with him—

Finn's phone lit up with a new message. "Silvio says a car just pulled out of the front gate. Porter's driving, and Rivera's in the passenger's seat."

I'd been hoping that they would take at least one more man with them, but this was the best—and only—chance that we had to find Elissa.

"Good," I said. "Let's go get our girl back."

Finn nodded and texted Silvio, telling him that we were going in. He put his phone away and pulled a silenced gun out from the small of his back. Bria and Owen both had similar weapons in their own hands. We all plugged transmitters into our ears so that we could talk to each other, checked to make sure that they were working properly, and headed for the mansion.

Since no guards were patrolling back here, we were able to sprint all the way across the lawn and over to the stone patio that surrounded the pool. We hunkered down behind the patio furniture and peered in through the windows. I spotted two women in the room where the giant Christmas tree had been, boxing up ornaments and other holiday decorations. I glanced in through the other windows, but I didn't see any more servants or guards.

"Remember," I whispered to the others. "We need to be as quiet and as invisible as possible. We get in, get Elissa, and get out."

Finn, Bria, and Owen all nodded back to me, and the four of us split up. Keeping low, Finn and Bria hurried over to a side door, which was unlocked, and vanished inside the mansion. Owen and I climbed up the same trellis that I'd used two nights ago to reach the second story.

I got to my feet, hurried over, and plastered myself against the side of the mansion. I waited until Owen was next to me, and then I eased forward and peered in through the window.

The white velvet bow had been removed from the frame, giving me a clear view inside. Rivera's office looked the same as before. Empty desk in the corner, fancy bar and shelves of liquor along one wall, photos lined up on the mantel, expensive antiques everywhere. Disappointment filled me. Now that we knew that Rivera was the Dollmaker, I'd half expected to see Elissa tied to a chair in the office. But of course things could never be that simple and easy.

Still, the office was empty, so I reached out and raised the window, which was unlocked. I held my breath, just as I had the other night, waiting for alarms to ring out, but none did. Rivera hadn't fixed his security flaw, and I was going to take advantage of it again.

Owen and I slipped inside the office, and I left the

window wide open behind us, just in case we needed to make a quick exit with Elissa.

"Where to now?" Owen whispered.

"Since she's not in here, Elissa is most likely to be in Rivera's bedroom. It's the biggest room in the mansion, besides this office. Let's go."

We crept over to the office door and stopped, listening, but no movement sounded on the other side of the thick wood. Owen twisted the knob and wrenched the door open so that I could peer out into the hallway beyond. It was empty, and I gestured for him to open the door the rest of the way. We slid out into the hallway and stopped, looking and listening, but the mansion remained quiet.

I frowned. Normally, the quiet would have been a good thing, but right now it bothered me. Rivera's perimeter men had been gone for more than two hours. You would think that someone would have noticed and tried to contact them by now. If my men hadn't returned from a job, I would have been doing everything in my power to track them down, in addition to circling the wagons and bringing in more guards. Maybe Rivera was too drunk to notice, or maybe he just didn't care what happened to them. Maybe his guards were as disposable to him as all the women he'd murdered.

Despite Mosley's ruse to get Rivera out of the mansion, I'd still expected the place to be crawling with guards, but it was as silent as a tomb. Weird. More worry and apprehension swept through me, but we were here now, and I wasn't leaving without Elissa, no matter what dangers we might encounter.

I gestured for Owen to stay behind me. He nodded,

and together we crept down the hallway, quietly opening every door and peering into every room we passed.

But all of them were empty, except for their fine furnishings.

My frustration grew with every single room we searched. The mansion was large, but it wasn't infinite, and we were running out of places to look. Finally, I reached the door to Rivera's bedroom, the last and final room on this floor. Once again, I stopped, listening, but I didn't hear anything.

I looked over at Owen, and he raised his gun and nodded, telling me that he was ready. I nodded back.

I tried the knob, expecting it to be locked, but it too was open, just like everything else in the mansion. Surely Damian Rivera wouldn't be so foolish as to kidnap someone and not keep her under lock and key, but apparently, he was. So I decided to roll with my good luck. I opened the door, and Owen and I swept inside the room, our weapons up and ready.

But it was also empty.

A massive four-poster bed dominated the space, black silk sheets trailing off one side and down onto the floor. Antique clocks, vases, and other knickknacks covered the nightstands on either side of the bed and the mirrored mahogany dresser that took up most of one wall. Empty champagne flutes and bottles littered the floor, and some stuck out from underneath the bed and the dresser. The air reeked of alcohol and cigar smoke, mixed with Rivera's nauseatingly sweet cologne.

But Elissa wasn't in here, and there was no sign that she had ever been in here. No ropes or other bindings perched on the nightstands, no women's clothes or accessories strewn across the floor, and, most telling of all, no golden tubes of Heartbreaker lipstick sitting on the dresser. Frustration surged through me, but I pushed it aside, hurried over, and opened the door to the walk-in closet, while Owen checked the attached bathroom.

But they were both empty too.

"Dammit!" I hissed. "She's not here. Finn, Bria, you guys got anything downstairs?"

Finn's voice crackled back to me a second later. "Nothing. No sign of Elissa anywhere. Just those two women still working on those holiday decorations. I'm sorry, Gin."

I sighed. "Yeah. Me too. Keep looking. Owen and I will do the same up here."

"Roger that." Finn signed off.

Owen and I searched the bedroom, but there was nothing out of the ordinary, except for all the empty bottles of champagne.

Owen shook his head. "Surely he doesn't drink all this by himself, does he? It's a wonder his liver hasn't exploded by now."

I let out a harsh, humorless laugh. "You should have seen him guzzling down booze in his office the other night. You'd think it was water and he'd just run a marathon the way he was swilling it down."

That bothered me too, more than anything else about this whole situation. Sure, Damian Rivera was arrogant, and he liked to hit people. But he was also a lazy drunk. He didn't seem to have the smarts to kidnap and kill so many women, much less to actually get away with it for so long without leaving any evidence behind. But I didn't have time to think about it right now, so we left the bed-room and searched the entire floor again, looking for any-thing that might lead us to Elissa.

But after ten minutes, I had to admit defeat. "She's not here," I said, talking to Finn and Bria through our earpieces again. "She's just not *here*."

"Yeah." Finn's voice was as sad as mine was frustrated. "There's no sign of her down here either. Let's meet on the patio and regroup."

Owen and I went back to the office to leave the same way we'd come in. I didn't want Rivera to know that any-one had been inside his mansion. At least, not until we'd found Elissa. Owen went over to the window and peered outside, checking to make sure that no guards had come around to the back of the house. But I lingered in front of the photos on the fireplace mantel, looking at them all again and hoping that I would find something, *anything*, that would tell me where Elissa was.

For some reason, I found myself studying that photo of Damian with his parents. In particular, his mother, Maria, caught my eye. The strange thing was, the more I stared at her, the more I realized that Maria Rivera looked exactly like Elissa and all of the Dollmaker's other vic-tims. Young, blond, pretty. But what made my heart drop and made a chill run down my spine was her makeup.

Her lips were painted a familiar, sickening blood-red.

Of course, she wasn't holding a tube of lipstick in the picture, but I knew—*I knew,* deep down in my bones—that she was wearing the Heartbreaker color.

Could this all be about Maria Rivera? Did Damian have some deep-seated mommy issues that had twisted him into a serial killer? Was he kidnapping women so he could kill his own mother over and over again? If so, why? What had Maria done to her own son that was so terrible? That made him want to beat and strangle her substitutes time and time again?

Owen noticed that I'd stopped in front of the mantel, and he came over to me. "What are you looking at?"

I pointed to the photo. "Who does she remind you of?"

He didn't see it for a moment, but then he leaned forward, his eyes narrowing with understanding. "Elissa . . . and all the other victims."

I nodded. "Yeah. Rivera is our guy. He has to be."

"So where is Elissa?" Owen asked.

"I don't know, but I'm not leaving here without her. C'mon. Let's go meet Finn and Bria."

Owen nodded and headed back over to the window, but I stayed where I was, still staring at that photo of Maria Rivera standing with Damian and his father, Richard, with Bruce Porter hovering in the background. It was your average family picture, completely innocent and innocuous. But once again, something about this whole situation bothered me, some nagging little thing that I couldn't quite put my finger on. I looked over the photo for a third time, but try as I might, I couldn't puzzle it out.

"Gin?" Owen asked. "You ready?"

"Yeah," I said, finally turning away from the photo. "Let's go."

* 22 *

Owen and I went back out through the open office window, crossed the roof, and climbed down the trellis. Finn and Bria were waiting by the pool, guns in hand, once again hunkered down behind the patio furniture.

"Now what?" Finn's green gaze darted back and forth, on the lookout for any servants or guards.

"Now we spread out and expand our search," I said. "Just because Elissa wasn't in the mansion, that doesn't mean Rivera doesn't have her stashed around here somewhere. Maybe he's holding her in one of the outbuildings. So let's split up again and look for her."

The others nodded, and Finn pulled out his phone and texted Silvio, telling him what we were doing next. Almost immediately, Finn's phone lit up with a new message.

"Silvio, Jade, and Ryan are still in position on the street outside the front of the mansion," Finn said. "Everything's quiet on that side of the estate, and none of the guards have moved away from their posts. We're still in the clear."

I nodded. "Let's get to work, then."

Finn and Bria went left, and Owen and I went right.

As with many such places in Northtown, Damian Rivera's estate was like its own little city. Several sheds and outbuildings surrounded the main structure on both sides, positioned in small clusters of trees to blend in with the rest of the immaculate landscaping.

Owen and I went from one shed and outbuilding to the next, careful to stay out of sight of the guards patrolling the front of the mansion. He kept watch while I slipped inside every structure that we came to and searched for Elissa. The sheds held everything from lawn mowers and other gardening equipment, to cleaning supplies for the pool, to red and green plastic tubs filled with all the holiday lights and decorations that had covered the mansion. We moved carefully, quickly, and quietly, looking at all the supplies, peering into the cobwebbed corners, and searching the floors for any trapdoors or sublevels.

But there was nothing. No women's clothes or accessories spread out across a table, no telltale footprints made by a woman's stilettos in the dust, no gold tubes of lipstick glimmering on a shelf. There wasn't a single sign of Elissa anywhere.

More and more frustration surged through me, burning like acid in my veins, and once again, I got the nagging feeling that I was missing something important, something obvious. Ten minutes later, Owen and I had cleared all the buildings on our side of the property, and we snuck back to the pool area.

"Finn, Bria, you guys got anything?" I asked through the transmitter.

Finn's voice crackled back to me a second later. "Nothing. Nothing at all, and we've looked everywhere on this side of the estate. I don't even see any ropes that might be used to tie someone down. If Elissa is here, then Rivera is doing a bang-up job of hiding her."

Even more frustration spiked through me, and I reached up and massaged my forehead, which was suddenly aching. "All right. You guys sneak out through the woods on that side of the mansion and go meet up with Silvio, Jade, and Ryan out front. Owen and I will make sure that we didn't overlook anything and go out through the woods in the back the same way we came in. We'll see you guys in a few minutes."

"Roger that." Finn signed off again.

Owen looked over at me. "We'll find her, Gin. I know we will."

I let out a long, tense breath. "I wish I had your confidence. It seems like all I've done the past few days is run around in circles, going nowhere fast."

He lifted his hand and cupped my cheek, his warm, strong fingers stroking my face. "You'll get somewhere. I know you will."

I grabbed his hand and pressed a kiss to his palm. "I love you for saying that, and I love you even more for actually believing it. So let's go over everything again. Elissa has to be here somewhere. She just *has* to be."

We left the patio behind and took the same route as before, avoiding the guards and working our way from one outbuilding to the next, checking to make sure that we'd looked absolutely everywhere. But we had, and there was nothing for us to do but head back across the lawn.

Ten minutes later, we were at the very back of the estate, getting ready to step into the woods, when a series of low mutters caught my ear. I stopped and turned around, scanning the grounds, wondering where the sounds were coming from, since we were several hundred feet away from the mansion now. And I realized that there was one place that we hadn't searched yet.

The caretaker's cottage.

My eyes narrowed, and I reached out with my Stone magic, listening. Sure enough, the stones of the cottage were the ones that were muttering, the harsh notes repeating over and over again, almost as if they were the words to a song ringing in my ears.

Blood, violence, pain, death . . . blood, violence, pain, death . . .

According to the info that Finn and Silvio had dug up, Bruce Porter had lived in the caretaker's cottage for years. As Rivera's head of security, Porter oversaw all the other guards and the servants. He would know every little thing that went on here, including his boss's proclivities. Porter probably wouldn't have any problem letting Rivera use his cottage, as long as the dwarf got to keep his cushy job. The building was also isolated enough to keep the other guards and servants from realizing what was really going on inside. That was why no one had talked, like Bria had thought they might.

Owen noticed that I wasn't following him, and he stopped and turned around. "What is it?" He raised his gun. "What's wrong?"

"The cottage," I murmured.

"But Finn looked in through the windows when we first got here," he said. "Elissa wasn't inside."

I reached out with my magic again, listening to the continued shrieks of the stone.

Blood, violence, pain, death . . . blood, violence, pain, death . . .

And I realized that the sounds were harsher, louder, fresher than they had been two nights ago. Emotional vibrations faded with time. They didn't grow stronger. Not unless someone was around to make the sounds increase with her sharp terror and stomach-churning fear.

"Gin?" Owen asked again.

Blood, violence, pain, death . . . blood, violence, pain, death . . .

"Elissa wasn't anywhere that Finn could see through the windows," I murmured again. "And he couldn't *hear* the stones. Not like I can. But she's in there. I know she is. C'mon."

I headed in that direction, with Owen following me. Through my earpiece, I heard Finn say that he and Bria were back safely at their car and would hold their positions until we met them, but I tuned him out, far more interested in what the stones had to say at the moment.

Owen and I crept back over to the cottage. Even though it was still afternoon, Porter had left a couple of lights on inside. I walked all around the structure, peering into every single window, but it seemed as empty as when Finn had checked it. Owen came with me, still watching my back. Eventually, we wound up back at the front of the cottage.

I tried the door, but it was locked. And not just a simple lock like those that had been on all the mansion doors. This one had three dead bolts all in a row. That was total overkill—unless you had something to hide.

Like the girl you'd kidnapped and were planning to murder.

"Gin?" Finn's voice sounded through my earpiece. "We have a problem. Rivera's car is pulling in through the front gate. He's already back from the bank. Looks like Mosley wasn't able to stall him as long as we'd hoped."

I checked my watch. We'd been searching for Elissa for more than an hour. It would take me several more minutes to make Ice picks and to actually finesse all three locks open, and Damian Rivera could come here at any moment to check on his hostage. So I decided to be direct about things. I gestured for Owen to stand back, and then I put my hand on the door, right over the locks, and blasted them all with my Ice magic.

Three inches of elemental Ice coated the dead bolts in a matter of seconds. The wood and metal shrieked and groaned in protest, almost as loudly as the stones were still muttering, but I ignored the sounds, sent out another wave of magic, and blasted right through the locks and all of the surrounding wood. Broken bits of metal flew through the air, along with long splinters and sharp, needle-like pieces of my elemental Ice.

The second the locks busted open, a loud alarm blared, and lights started flashing inside the cottage, which only made me even more convinced that Elissa was inside.

"What is that?" Finn yelled in my ear. "What did you do, Gin?"

"Just a little breaking and entering!" I shouted back at him over the continued din of the alarm.

"Well, I can hear it all the way out here on the street!" he yelled again. "Which means that the guards can hear it too!"

"Stay here," I told Owen. "I'll go inside and search for Elissa."

He nodded and raised his gun, his gaze locked on the mansion in the distance, where the interior and exterior lights were also flashing in time to the cottage's alarm system. He would watch my back and hold off the guards as long as he could, but I needed to do my part fast. So I put my shoulder down, rammed the door open, and hurried inside.

The front part of the cottage was one enormous open space that was a den, kitchen, and dining area all in one. I'd already seen all of this through the windows, so I moved over to a door that led into a bedroom and shoved it open. Elissa wasn't in this room either, so I wrenched open the closet door. That too was empty, so I headed into the attached bathroom. Still no sign of her, so I went back out into the main part of the cottage, looking around again.

Now that I was actually inside the structure, the stones' shrieks were harsher and louder than ever before, ringing in my ears right along with the alarm. This was definitely the place where Rivera held his victims for days on end before he beat and strangled them to death. But where was Elissa? If she was yelling at me to help her, I couldn't hear her over the alarm's constant blaring.

So I moved through the cottage again, searching everywhere, and counting off the seconds in my head. Owen and I probably had about five minutes before the guards would arrive in full force, and I needed to find Elissa and get her out of here before then.

I had started to go back into the bedroom to search in there again, even though I'd already cleared that area, when I noticed a crack in the stone floor, one that was peeping out from underneath the corner of a rug that I'd pushed aside with my boots when I first stormed in here. I glanced at the surrounding stones, but the crack didn't match the rest of the floor pattern.

So I slid my knife back up my sleeve, dropped to the floor, and ripped the rug aside. A secret trapdoor was set into the floor, complete with a large metal ring to open it. I grabbed the ring with both hands and pulled on it with all my might, but the thick door was far too heavy for me to open.

Since I didn't have the strength to pull up the trapdoor, I decided to go right down through it. I dropped back to my knees, slapped my palms on the floor, and blasted it with my Ice and Stone magic, just like I had done to the front door.

The floor was much harder and thicker than the wooden door had been, but I was motivated, and I forced my Ice magic down into the trapdoor, used my Stone power to crack it away, hooked my fingers into the jagged chunks of rocks, and tossed them aside as fast as I could. The sharp, splintered rocks cut into my hands, but I ignored the painful stings and focused all my magic on the floor.

Ice, Stone, blast, blast, grab, lift, throw away . . .

I repeated the motions over and over again until I'd blasted the entire trapdoor out of the way. I waved away a cloud of gray dust, leaned over, and peered down through the jagged hole that I'd made in the floor.

A glimmer of gold glinted in the dark space below.

For a moment, the odd, horrible thought filled my mind that I'd only discovered Rivera's stash of lipstick. But the dust cleared, and I realized that the golden glimmer was actually a strand of long blond hair.

I'd finally found Elissa.

* 23 *

I sat down, scooted over, and dropped through the hole in the floor. My boots hit hard-packed dirt, and I straightened up and glanced around.

The area was only about six feet high and twelve feet wide, making it bigger than a crawl space but not quite large enough to be a bona fide basement. A wooden ladder that I hadn't noticed before led up to what had been the trapdoor. Shelves lined the walls, but I didn't take the time to see what was perched on them. Dust hung in thick clouds in the air, the particles slowly drifting down and turning everything a dull, murky gray.

Elissa was sitting just to the right of the trapdoor ladder, tied to a chair, with heavy ropes binding her wrists and ankles. She wore a fancy red cocktail dress, along with matching stilettos, and someone had taken the time to curl her long blond hair into sleek waves that cascaded over her shoulders. She looked beautiful, and if not for the ropes, I would have thought that she was a model, patiently sitting and waiting to be called to some photo shoot.

Her head was bowed, her blond hair hiding her face from sight, and her entire body was still—much too still. My heart stopped, and my breath caught in my throat. I wondered if I was already too late, wondered if she was already dead, beaten and strangled by Damian Rivera like all those other women.

After several long, agonizing seconds, Elissa slowly lifted her head, shook her hair out of the way, and peered up at me, squinting against the harsh glare of the still-flashing lights in the cottage above. My heart started beating again, and my breath left my lungs in a rush. Alive. She was still alive.

But my relief was short-lived.

Elissa's face had been carefully, expertly made up with foundation, powder, eyeliner, and shadow, highlighting her green eyes and beautiful cheekbones. But the thing that made my blood run cold was her lipstick—Heartbreaker red, just like all the other women.

No cuts or bruises marked her skin, and no fingerprints ringed her throat. But that ugly stain on her mouth told me I'd gotten here just in time.

"Who are you?" Elissa's lips moved, forming the words, but her voice was so weak and low that I couldn't hear it over the blaring alarm.

"I'm a friend of Jade's!" I shouted, trying to get her to understand that I was here to rescue her.

Elissa's eyes widened. "Jade!"

I nodded, stepped forward, and palmed a knife,

quickly cutting through her bonds. Then I slid my knife back up my sleeve and helped her stand. Elissa wobbled, her body stiff from sitting in the same position for so long, but she gripped my arm and let me lead her over to the ladder.

"Go!" I yelled, although I wasn't sure that she heard me over the alarm. "Go! Go! Go!"

With shaking hands and legs, Elissa climbed the ladder. I hung on to the side and helped her. It seemed to take forever, but she finally crawled through the opening at the top about ten seconds later. I scrambled up after her, as nimbly as a spider climbing its own web, and pulled her up and onto her feet. Elissa wobbled again, a result of the towering high heels she was wearing, but she staggered across the cottage and out through the open front door.

Owen was waiting outside, his gun up and ready to fire. "They see us!" he yelled. "The guards see us, and they're heading this way!"

Sure enough, several dwarven guards armed with guns were up at the mansion, frantically running around the pool area and searching for who or what had triggered the alarm. Owen was right. A couple of them had spotted us and were yelling at their friends and pointing in this direction. The men began racing down the lawn toward us.

Owen stepped up and fired off several shots. Even though he was too far away to hit them, the gunfire still made the men stop and hunker down behind the bushes and trees for cover. But I knew that it wouldn't be long before they charged at us again.

"Don't let them take me back down there!" Elissa

sobbed, tears running down her face and ruining her perfect makeup.

I looked her in the eyes. "The only place you're going is back home to your sister. Now, do what Owen tells you, and everything will be fine. Do you understand?"

Elissa glanced from me to Owen and back again. She nodded, her head snapping up and down, ready to do anything to escape from this nightmare.

Out of the corner of my eye, I spotted the guards getting to their feet and creeping in this direction again. Owen noticed them too, and he fired off a few more shots. The men scattered again, but this time, they started darting from bush to bush and tree to tree, hopscotching down the lawn until they could get close enough to open fire on us. Time to go.

I handed Elissa over to Owen, then raised my hand to my ear, trying to hear over that damn alarm, which was still ringing as loudly as ever. I'd be surprised if they couldn't hear it all the way over in Cypress Mountain.

"Finn?" I said. "Finn? Are you still there?"

His voice crackled in my ear. "Of course I'm still here! What's going on?"

"We found Elissa, but the guards are heading toward us. I need you and Bria to come back to the woods to help Owen."

"On our way," Finn replied.

I looked over at Owen. "Go. Get her out of here. Now."

"What are you going to do?" he asked, worry flashing in his eyes.

I whipped up my knife. "I'm going to take out as many

of the guards as I can. Don't worry. I'll hold them off until you guys have a good head start, and then I'll be right behind you. Now, go. Go!"

He didn't like leaving me behind, but he knew that I could take care of myself and that getting Elissa to safety was the most important thing. Owen gave me a sharp nod, then grabbed Elissa's hand and pulled her away from the cottage toward the woods. She stumbled along behind him, moving as fast as she could.

The second that they disappeared into the woods, I turned back to the guards. With Owen and the threat of his gun gone, they left the trees and bushes behind and ran straight toward me. I palmed a second knife, so that I had one in either hand, and charged up the lawn to meet them.

Normally, people run away from goons with guns, so my unexpected sprint toward the dwarves made a couple of the men pull up short, raise their weapons, and take aim at me. But I didn't slow down, not even for an instant. Instead, I reached for my Stone magic and hardened my skin, turning it into an impenetrable shell—and not a second too soon.

Crack!

Crack! Crack!

Crack! Crack! Crack!

Bullets kicked up the dirt and grass at my feet and zinged through the air all around me. A couple even hit my body, but they bounced off my Stone-hardened skin and rattled away.

And then the men were on me, and I was on them.

I sliced my knife across the chest of the first guard who came at me, making him scream and stagger away. His buddies snapped up their guns and started firing at me again, but I kept my grip on my Stone magic, ignored the hard continued blasts of bullets against my skin, and waded right into the center of them.

My knives sliced every which way, the silverstone blades gleaming in the late-afternoon sun, and I cut into every single man I could reach. Blood spattered through the air like sheets of rain, the stench of it mixing with the acrid scent of gunpowder.

The guards quickly realized that I wasn't going to be felled by mere bullets, and they whirled around and ran away, trying to get back to the mansion so that they could regroup.

Too late.

As they ran, I summoned my Ice magic, shooting out spray after spray of deadly daggers, which punched into their backs, making them fall face-first onto the ground. The perfectly pruned grass quickly turned a dark, mottled black with blood.

In less than two minutes, it was over, and half a dozen guards littered the lawn, all of them bleeding out from the vicious wounds that I'd inflicted on them.

I glanced behind me, but Owen and Elissa were long gone, and I didn't hear any sounds of gunfire coming from the front of the mansion.

"Owen?" I said. "Owen, what's going on?"

A second later, his voice sounded in my ear. "Elissa is with Jade. Finn and Bria are here too. The only one we're missing is you."

A grin curved my lips. "On my way."

I turned to go, but one of the guards rose and grabbed my ankle. I tried to pull free, but he was a dwarf, with a strong, firm grip, despite the fact that his guts were leaking out all over the lawn. So I kicked him in the face with my other foot, breaking his nose with my heavy boot, and he screamed and slumped back down onto the ground. I stepped over his body, ready to head back to my friends—

"Well, this is a surprise," a voice slurred. "And way more exciting than my trip to the bank was."

I whirled around.

Damian Rivera stood on the edge of the stone patio. Wavy black hair, dark eyes, bronze skin, shockingly white teeth, expensive suit. He looked just like he had when I spied on him in his office two nights ago, and it was obvious that he'd been drinking just as heavily today as he had been then. A ruddy flush stained his cheeks, and his eyes were glassy and bloodshot at the same time.

He gave me a lopsided, goofy grin, as though it amused him to see his men crumpled all over the lawn like paper dolls that I'd shredded to pieces. Rivera didn't seem the slightest bit concerned by his moaning, groaning guards or the blood dripping from the knives in my hands. The longer he looked at me, the wider his grin became, as though he were actually pleased to see me.

After several seconds of grinning like a fool, his brow furrowed, and he snapped his fingers over and over again, as if trying to remember who I was or where he had seen me before. It must have come to him, because he snapped his fingers a final time, much louder than before, and stabbed his index finger at me.

"Gin Blanco, right?" he said in that same slurring voice.

I flashed my bloody knives at him. "The one and only."

Rivera nodded and grinned again, happy that he'd figured out who I was. "So you're the one who's been causing so much trouble lately." He shook his head. "You're really starting to annoy Mason. And let me tell you from personal experience, that's not something you want to do."

My eyes narrowed. Mason? Who was Mason?

Was he—could he be—was he the *leader* of the Circle?

My breath caught in my throat, but I forced myself to rein in my shock and surprise. Instead, I tightened my grip on my knives and slowly sidled toward Rivera, not wanting to startle him in his obviously drunken state.

"Gin?" This time, Bria's voice was in my ear. "What's going on? What's taking you so long? Are you in some kind of trouble?"

"Rivera's here," I muttered. "And he seems to be in a chatty mood. I'm going to ask him a few questions. I'll be there in a minute."

"You need to get out of there," she said in a worried voice. "Silvio says that three more SUVs are pulling up to the front of the mansion. Whatever alarm you triggered, it's summoned a lot more men."

I'd been so focused on taking down the guards that I hadn't noticed that the alarm had finally quit blaring. The lights in the mansion had also quit flashing. Someone had shut off the alert system. I wondered why, but this was too good an opportunity to pass up.

"All I need is one more minute," I said.

"And I'm telling you that you don't have one more minute. Get out of there, Gin. Get out of there now!" Bria yelled at me.

But I couldn't go. Not yet. I'd blown my cover with Rivera, and I couldn't leave him alive to tell Hugh Tucker that I'd been here and had killed his men. Tucker would realize that I'd identified Rivera as one of the Circle members, and the rest of them would start closing ranks. So I might as well stay and get the answers that I wanted— *needed*—about the Circle.

It was worth the risk.

"Tell me about Mason," I called out, as I crept closer to Rivera. "Is he your boss? Is he the one who runs the Circle?"

Rivera gave me another sloppy grin, but his eyes sharpened, telling me that he wasn't quite as drunk as I'd thought. "Wouldn't you like to know?" He frowned, as though some odd thought had just crossed his mind. "Although I'm wondering how you found out that *I* was a member of the Circle. That's most upsetting." He paused. "Isn't it, Porter?"

Porter. I'd forgotten all about Bruce Porter, but he'd driven Rivera to the bank, which meant that he'd come back to the mansion with his boss.

A shadow moved out of the corner of my eye, and Porter hurtled out from behind a bush, catching me square in the chest and driving us both down to the ground. My knives flew out of my hands, but I channeled my Stone magic into my fists, making them as hard and heavy as concrete blocks, and started pummeling Porter.

But he was a dwarf, and a tough one at that. Porter

grunted under my blows, but they didn't do much more than bruise his thick hide.

Then it was his turn to pound on me.

Thwack-thwack-thwack.

The dwarf hit me over and over again. My silverstone vest took the worst of the blows, but I still felt every hard, bruising punch. I tried to wriggle out from underneath him, but he locked his arms around my body and flipped me over, so that his back was pressing into the ground and I was lying on top of him, my arms and legs sticking up into the air like a turtle that was upside down on its shell and couldn't right itself. I couldn't even reach down far enough to touch and blast him with my Ice magic.

That was bad enough, but the view didn't make me any happier. By this point, the guards Bria had warned me about had made it around the side of the mansion and all the way back here. More and more men darted past Rivera to surround Porter and me, their guns drawn and leveled at my head.

Fletcher had a saying: *Arrogance will get you, every single time.* I should have listened to Bria and left while I had the chance, but I'd thought that I could get my answers and escape too. And what had my arrogance gotten me? Nothing but caught.

"Hit her with the stun gun!" Porter yelled, still holding on to me, even as I struggled against him. "Quick—I can take it!"

Uh-oh.

I reached for my Stone magic, ready to send it rushing out through my entire body and harden my skin again, but one of the men was quicker. He threw himself down onto the ground and slammed a stun gun into my side. Electricity surged through my body, hot and caustic, singeing every single one of my nerve endings and making me scream and scream.

In an instant, my vision went white, then gray, then utterly, finally black.

❄24❄

I headed for the canyon, running as fast as I dared through the dark woods.

Off to my right, the Snow family mansion continued to burn, but the flames were slowly weakening and taking their precious orange-red light along with them. Soon I wouldn't be able to see anything up ahead. With what little light there was I still kept tripping over rocks and tree roots, and my bare feet were a bruised, bloody mess that throbbed with every step.

Another rock stabbed into my big toe, making me hiss with pain and finally forcing me to slow down to a quick walk. I glanced back over my shoulder, but I didn't see the giant behind me, not even the yellow beam of his flashlight sweeping through the trees. I took another step forward and put my foot down.

But there was nothing there to hold me up.

My head snapped around, and I spotted the dark, gaping

chasm in front of me. At the last second, I managed to wind-mill my arms and lurch back away from the edge. My heart pounded, and cold sweat slid down my spine, as I realized how very close I'd come to falling to my death.

I carefully tiptoed forward and peered down into the canyon. But the distant firelight couldn't penetrate the ink-black shadows down there, and all I could make out were the vague, murky shapes of the stones below.

I thought back, trying to remember what the canyon looked like in the daylight. Wide and deep, with slick, jagged pieces of moss-covered rocks running down the sides and lining the bottom like spikes. But would the fall and the rocks be enough to kill the giant? I didn't know. I just didn't know—

Crack.

A branch snapped behind me. I whirled around, my eyes wide, my breath caught in my throat.

Crack.

Another branch snapped, followed by a muttered curse, and a bright beam of light sliced through the trees, quickly heading in this direction. The giant must be following the trail I'd left.

I whirled back around and stared down into the canyon again. Sure, I'd almost stepped off the edge, but I hadn't been watching where I was going. So how could I trick the giant into doing the same? Especially when he had a flashlight?

Think, Gin, think! I silently shouted at myself again, shifting back and forth on my feet, my fingers twisting in the ruined, tattered fabric of my nightgown—

My hands stilled, and I looked down. Despite the eerie gloom, I could still see my nightgown, since the fabric was so much lighter than everything else in the woods. What color was it? White? Blue? I couldn't even remember. But if I could see it, so could the giant, and maybe, just maybe, it could help me trick him.

I reached down, grabbed the bottom of my nightgown, and ripped a long, thin strip off it. At least, I tried to. The fabric didn't want to give, and fresh pain flared up in my burned hands, but I kept on tugging at it. Tears streamed down my face, and I had to grind my teeth to keep from screaming, but eventually, I managed to rip a piece off the bottom of the gown.

Crack-crack. Crack-crack.

Behind me, I could hear the giant getting closer and closer. There was no time to be picky, so I hooked the fabric on a bush that was right by the canyon's edge, arranging it so that it looked like I was hiding behind the thick branches. Then I moved away from the steep drop, darted around a tree, and hunkered down in the blackest shadows I could find.

I'd just settled into place when the giant charged into view. He swept his flashlight back and forth, and the yellow beam caught the piece of fabric that I'd hooked to the bush. The giant spotted it immediately.

"There you are!" *he growled.*

He charged forward, right by my hiding spot, and leaned down, as though he was going to snatch up that piece of fabric and me right along with it.

He never had a chance.

"What— Ahh!"

The giant ran right off the edge of the canyon, almost like a cartoon character would, and he screamed all the way down. A few seconds later, another sickening crack *sounded, louder than all the ones before. I shivered and wrapped my arms around myself, waiting, but the giant didn't make another sound, not so much as a whimper, and I knew that he was dead, his bones broken by the fall and the rocks below.*

But there were still other people in the woods.

Before I could even think about moving, more shouts rang out, and people crashed through the underbrush, heading in this direction. I hunkered down even lower, scooping leaves and dirt up over my nightgown to hide its pale color and making myself as small and invisible as possible.

Less than a minute later, another flashlight appeared, bobbing up and down through the trees, and a man stepped out of the shadows—Hugh, the vampire.

Unlike the giant, he was careful as he moved forward, slowly sweeping his flashlight back and forth across the ground. He too noticed the fabric strip hooked to the bush, but he realized that there was a steep drop beyond it, and he walked right up to the edge and stopped, shining his light down into the canyon below. After several seconds, Hugh crouched down and plucked the fabric off the bush, examining it with his light. His mouth puckered in thought, but he didn't move or mutter anything to himself.

He wasn't alone.

More faint crack-cracks *rang out, and another person moved through the woods in this direction—the Fire elemental. Through the trees, I could see the orange-red glow of her magic flickering all around her hand, since she was using her power as her own personal flashlight.*

"Hugh?" she called out, heading this way. "What's going on?"

The vampire got to his feet, tucked the fabric strip into his pocket, and stepped away from the canyon. He moved forward, meeting the Fire elemental halfway, about thirty feet from where I was still hiding. I squinted, but I couldn't make out her features, just the burning glow still flickering on her hand.

"What happened?" she demanded.

"What do you think happened?" Hugh snapped. "Your idiot bodyguard stepped right off the side of a cliff. He's lying at the bottom, squashed like a bug."

"Are you sure he's dead?" She started to walk past him.

Hugh stepped to the side, blocking her. "I'm sure. You've already lost one man out here. Call the others back, and let's leave. I'm tired of tromping through the woods in the middle of the night. Trust me. There's no one out here but us. I would have seen them."

The Fire elemental huffed, not liking to be told what to do, but she set off in the opposite direction, heading back toward the mansion. I thought that the vampire would follow her, but instead he turned around, scanning the woods, his eyes narrowing to slits and his nose twitching, almost as if he were sniffing the air like a dog. I remembered what my mom had told me about vampires, about how the blood they drank gave them enhanced senses. He might be able to see me after all, maybe even smell me too, even here in the deep, dark woods. I held my breath, not daring to move a single muscle . . .

And that's when I felt the spider crawl onto my hand.

Startled, I looked down. I didn't know what kind of spider it was, but it was a big, black blob on my hand, moving slowly, feeling along my skin with its hairy, prickly legs, carefully exploring this strange new territory. It must have been building a web or maybe even had a nest in the leaves that I'd disturbed.

As much as I wanted to scream and fling it away, I ground my teeth again and let it crawl around, hoping that it wasn't poisonous and that it wouldn't bite me. After what seemed like forever, the spider walked down my hand, crawled out to the tip of my index finger, and slid back down onto the leaves. I snatched my hand off the ground and cradled it against my chest. I looked up, wondering if I was alone yet—

The vampire was staring straight at me.

I froze again, my heart hammering up into my throat. Our eyes locked across the distance. No doubt about it. He'd seen me. Any second now, he would shout that he'd found me, and I'd have to run away again, run, run, run for my life—

"Hugh!" the Fire elemental snapped, her silky voice echoing through the trees. "It was your idea to leave, so let's go already!"

Instead of moving, he kept staring at me. I looked back at him, the two of us locked in a silent staring contest.

"Hugh!" she snapped again.

He looked at me a moment longer, then did the strangest thing. He pulled something out of his pants pocket and dropped it onto the ground. A second later, he turned and walked off into the woods.

I stayed frozen in place, still holding my breath, not daring to move a single muscle, thinking that it was some kind of trick. It had to be a trick, right? He wasn't just going to leave and pretend he hadn't seen me . . . was he? Why would he do that? Especially when the Fire elemental wanted to kill me just like she had the rest of my family?

But the seconds ticked by, and no one jumped out of the shadows at me. Not the vampire, not the Fire elemental, no one. But I still thought that it was a trick, so I started counting off the seconds in my head, waiting them out.

Five minutes passed. At least, that's how long I thought it was, although I had no real way of knowing. Still, no one approached me, and the woods remained utterly, eerily quiet. So I finally felt safe enough to leave my hiding spot, creep forward, and see what the vampire had dropped.

A hundred-dollar bill.

Not just one but a whole stack of them all rolled up together.

I frowned. The vampire had seen me. I knew that he had. So why hadn't he told the Fire elemental? And why leave this money behind? Was he . . . trying to help me? Why would he do that?

I didn't know, but I wasn't about to pass it up. I snatched the money off the ground. Then I got to my feet and headed back toward the dwindling bonfire of the mansion. My plan was the same as before. As soon as I was sure that everyone was gone, I'd walk down to the road and start heading toward the city. After I got to Ashland, well, I didn't know where I would go or what I would do, but one thing was for sure. I couldn't stay here any longer.

So I put my head down and started walking. I made it back to the mansion with no problems. The Fire elemental and her men were gone, along with Hugh, whoever he really was.

I let out a sigh of relief, stepped out of the woods, and headed for the road, forcing myself to keep moving forward instead of looking back at the ruins of my entire world. But

I couldn't escape it. Not with the ash still fluttering through the air like snow and the acrid stench of smoke coating everything, including me . . .

The stench woke me up. It was a harsh chemical odor but strangely comforting in a way, as though I'd sensed this same scent a hundred times before and associated it with a specific place. Someplace warm and inviting. Someplace safe. I drew in another breath, trying to figure out why it seemed so familiar. It almost smelled like some sort of . . . hair dye.

I relaxed. Owen and the others must have come back for me at the Rivera mansion. They must have fought their way through all those guards and pulled me out of there. I opened my eyes, fully expecting to see the warm, cozy confines of Jo-Jo's beauty salon.

But what I woke up to was another nightmare.

I was tied to a chair, my wrists and ankles lashed so tightly to the wood that I couldn't move them at all, no matter how hard I tried. And I definitely tried, straining and straining with all my might. I only stopped when the ropes started digging painfully into my skin, causing ugly burns, and I realized that I couldn't escape them. At least, not this way.

I was still wearing my black assassin clothes, along with my boots, but all of my knives were gone—the two up my sleeves, the two tucked into the sides of my boots, and the one in the small of my back. So I looked around, searching for my weapons.

I was in another cottage, although it wasn't Bruce Porter's caretaker cottage, since the stone floor here was still intact. I was sitting in the middle of a large den, halfway between a stone fireplace and a dark green leather couch. Several pieces of kindling were arranged in the fireplace, ready to be lit, with other, thicker logs stacked neatly in a nearby basket.

I glanced around the rest of the den. Brightly colored throw rugs, end tables, a bookcase bristling with paperbacks. The furniture was nice enough, although it had obviously been here for a while, given how well worn and old-fashioned it looked.

At first glance, everything seemed normal. Except for, you know, me being tied to a chair. Sadly, this wasn't my first time at that particular rodeo, so I moved on. I turned my head, scanning the kitchen area in the back of the cottage, still looking for my knives.

And that's when things started to get really, really weird.

A romantic table for two was set up in the middle of the kitchen. White tablecloth, two lit candles, a crystal vase full of red roses, fine china, a bottle of champagne chilling in a bucket. Someone had really gone all out.

I drew in a deep breath. In addition to the hair dye, I got a faint whiff of the food that had already been dished out on the two plates on the table. Lemon-pepper chicken, if I had to guess, along with honey-glazed carrots and mashed potatoes. A simple, elegant meal.

Still, the longer I stared at the table with its picture-perfect spread, the more my stomach roiled. It reminded me of the romantic dinner that Owen had surprised me with a couple of days ago. But there was no romance here—only death.

I listened, but I didn't hear anything but the faint

whistle of the wind swirling around the house. And the stones, of course. They shrieked with the exact same notes of blood, violence, pain, and death that the caretaker cottage had, telling me that I was sitting smack dab in the middle of the Dollmaker's lair. This was where he'd brought all the other women he'd kidnapped, and this was where he'd killed them all, when they didn't live up to the twisted fantasy that he'd so carefully crafted.

I wondered how it went exactly. If he complimented them on how pretty they were. If he expected them to make polite chitchat. If he force-fed them dinner while they were still tied up. If he flew into a rage when they stared at him with fear and horror. If he finally started beating them when he realized that the fault was with himself instead of them.

I didn't want to stick around to find out.

White lace curtains covered the windows, so I couldn't tell where I was, although it was dark outside. Given the lack of noise, the cottage was probably isolated, which meant that I needed to get out of here before Rivera came back. So I started struggling against my ropes again, harder than before. And just like before, I got absolutely nowhere.

Something moved out of the corner of my eye, and I turned my head, noticing another piece of furniture, a full-length mirror propped up in the corner by the fireplace.

For a moment, I didn't understand exactly what I was seeing in the mirror. Who was that strange-looking woman in the glass?

But then I realized that it was *me*.

That harsh chemical stench? It was hair dye, all right, just like I'd thought. And now I realized why the scent was so strong. It had been used on *me*.

Instead of its normal dark brown, my hair was now a bright, shiny, platinum blond that had been curled into loose waves that rested against my shoulders. He'd even taken the time to do my roots, so that I looked like a natural blonde. I didn't know whether to admire his effort or be disgusted by how far he would go to make me resemble his dream woman.

Yeah, disgust won out.

But the worst part was the fact that my face had been carefully made up—and my lips were painted a bright, glossy, familiar color.

Heartbreaker red.

I blinked and blinked, staring at myself in the mirror as if I could somehow change my own horrible reflection. My stomach roiled again, and hot, sour bile rose in my throat. Of all the things that I'd been subjected to over the years, all the beatings, all the fights, all the deadly duels, this was one of the worst things that I'd ever experienced.

I felt *violated* in a way that I never had before.

I wasn't Gin Blanco right now. I wasn't the assassin the Spider. I wasn't even a *person* anymore. I was a canvas, a doll, a plaything, primped and painted to Damian Rivera's exact specifications.

Bile rose in my throat again, but I swallowed it down, along with the primal scream of rage that went with it. I might have rescued Elissa, but it was obvious that Rivera was determined to make me his next victim. And since he'd already transformed me into his perfect woman, it didn't seem like he was going to keep me around for nearly as long as he had kept the others. That was me, Gin Blanco, classic overachiever, always on the fast track to death.

I had to get out of here before he came back. Since I couldn't break through the ropes myself, I looked around the cottage again, but my knives weren't in here, and I didn't see anything else that I could use to saw through my thick, heavy bonds. Even if I could have scooted myself all the way around the couch and over to the kitchen table, the china there looked far too old and delicate to be of any use. It would probably crumble to dust if I broke it.

Well, if I couldn't slice through the ropes, then I'd just break the damn chair and get out of my bonds that way. So I started swaying back and forth, trying to judge exactly how sturdy the chair was. The wood was thick, but it *creak-creak-creak*ed with every move I made, telling me that it would break if I put enough force into it. Now, how to do that? I could either use my Ice magic to freeze and crack the wood, or I could try to lurch to my feet, stagger over to the fireplace, and dash the side of the chair against the stone.

I decided on the second option, not wanting to waste my magic on something as simple as getting out of a chair. I had far better plans for my power tonight.

I'd used up some of my magic taking out the guards at the mansion, but Rivera had foolishly left my spider rune ring on my finger, and my matching pendant still hung from my neck, glimmering against the black fabric of my vest. He wasn't an elemental, so he hadn't sensed the reserves of Ice and Stone power rippling through the silverstone jewelry.

That mistake was going to cost him dearly. I was going to use every single drop of magic that I had left to kill him dead, dead, dead.

But first, I had to get out of the chair, so I drew in a breath and tensed my muscles, getting ready to surge to my feet—

A beam of light flashed across one of the windows. My head snapped in that direction, and I looked at the window, wondering if I'd imagined the light. But I hadn't. A second later, another beam of light appeared, and several sets of heavy footsteps *thump-thump-thump*ed on what seemed to be an old, creaky wooden porch attached to the front of the cottage.

The footsteps whipped back and forth, back and forth, from one side of the porch to the other, almost as if someone outside was pacing out his anger, anxiety, and frustration.

". . . bitch killed all my men . . ."

". . . can't believe you captured her . . ."

" . . . giving her exactly what she deserves . . ."

Muffled voices sounded outside, drowned out by the whistling winter wind. I couldn't make out all the words, but I recognized one of the voices as belonging to Rivera. Of course he was outside. He'd spent far too much time and effort turning me into his pretty little plaything not to want to finish acting out his delusional fantasy.

The voices stopped, the knob turned on the front door, and Rivera stepped into the cottage. He was still wearing the same expensive suit he'd had on before, and he looked as handsome as ever, right down to the stubble that darkened his jaw.

He studied me from head to toe, his black eyebrows arching in his face, as if what he saw surprised him. After a few seconds, he pulled a small silver flask out of his jacket pocket, unscrewed the top, and took a long, healthy swig of the contents. I could smell the caustic burn of alcohol all the way across the room, even stronger than the hair dye.

"Well," he slurred. "I see that you've been busy. You've only had her, what, three hours? And you've already got her all dolled up just the way you like 'em. That's quick work. Even for you."

I frowned, wondering who he was talking to. The things he was saying made it almost sound like . . . like he *hadn't* done this to me. Like he wasn't the one who'd dyed my hair, painted my face, and tied me down.

I thought back over everything that had happened over the past few days and all the clues that had pointed to Rivera—the lipstick, the men he'd sent to Jade's house, the threats that Tucker had made against him about dealing with his mysterious problem. And I realized that while those clues pointed to Rivera, they also led to another person. Someone else who also had access to all of those things.

All along, I'd thought that this whole thing was like two separate but connected jigsaw puzzles that I'd been trying to work at the same time. Well, all of the pieces had just snapped into place on one of them, and my heart dropped as I realized just how wrong I'd been about the Dollmaker.

Rivera turned toward the open door. "Aren't you going to come in and admire your handiwork?"

A shadow appeared in the doorway, and a man slowly stepped inside. The person who was the real Dollmaker.

Bruce Porter.

✳ 25 ✳

Suddenly, everything made sense. Why Rivera's credit card had been used to purchase the Heartbreaker lipstick. Why there hadn't been any trace of Elissa in Rivera's office or bedroom. Why the stones of the caretaker's cottage—Porter's home—had shrieked and wailed with such violent agony instead of Rivera's mansion.

Damian Rivera wasn't the one who'd abducted Elissa and killed all those other women. It had been Bruce Porter all along. He'd just used his boss's money, resources, credit cards, and manpower to help him do it and then cover his tracks after the fact.

The one thing that I still didn't understand, though, was Porter and his motivations. But it was obvious that he was the Dollmaker and that Rivera was indulging him, covering up his messes just the way Porter had covered up Rivera's drunken disasters for so many years. It wasn't even a real partnership as much as the two of them seemed to be codependent in a desperate, diseased way, each unable to function without the other.

"Aw, don't be shy, Bruce." Rivera took another hit from his flask and stepped aside so that Porter could walk closer to me. "You certainly weren't when you were making her look like *that*. You were smiling the whole time. Well, except for all the grumbling about having to dye her hair. I told you that you should have just slapped a wig on her and been done with things."

I shivered at the thought of the dwarf bending over me, his fingers in my hair, him touching my face, him carefully painting my lips the way he had done to so many other women before he killed them.

Porter crossed his arms over his chest and eyed me, disappointment flashing in his pale blue gaze. "A wig wouldn't have been the same." He shook his head. "The dye's not the same either. You know that they have to be natural blondes."

"So sorry to disappoint," I snarked. "Although I think that I can safely say in this case that blondes don't have more fun."

His eyes glittered with a hard, angry light. "I had a nice girl all picked out, and you just had to come along and ruin everything."

I bared my teeth at him. "What can I say? I'm an evil bitch that way."

"Yes, yes, you are," a third, familiar voice called out.

More footsteps sounded, and Hugh Tucker strolled into the cottage.

For once, I was almost happy to see him. The vampire might be a cold-blooded killer, but he wasn't the worst thing in the room. Not by a long shot. Rivera and Porter were tied for that dubious distinction.

Tucker moved over to the fireplace, away from the other two men, creating a clear divide between himself and the combined sickness that was Damian Rivera and Bruce Porter. Couldn't blame him for that. Then again, Tucker was his own special kind of disease.

As I studied the vampire, I once again thought back over everything that had happened the past few days, and another small puzzle piece clicked into place in my mind, one that made everything else snap into focus. Red-hot anger sizzled through me, and I grabbed onto that burning heat, riding the wave of searing emotion and slowly letting it cool, congeal, and harden into an icy block of rage, hate, and determination in my heart.

Tucker shook his head. "You just can't leave well enough alone, can you, Gin?"

"I could say the exact same thing about you."

His black eyes narrowed, but I didn't say anything else to fill in the real meaning behind my words. After a few seconds, Tucker snapped his fingers at the other two men.

"Leave us," he ordered.

Rivera straightened up to his full height and glared at the vampire, although his drunken wobble ruined his attempt to be intimidating. "You don't get to order me around, Hugh."

The vampire gave him a cold, thin smile. "Oh, I do tonight, Damian, when you've brought such unwanted attention to the group. He's not happy with you, letting your assistant go around town and murder all those innocent women. And he's especially not happy that the two of you were stupid enough to get caught and he had to send men to bail you out."

His words made me think about those three SUVs full of men that had showed up at Rivera's estate, the ones that had seemingly come out of nowhere, since they weren't part of his regular security team. The alarm that I'd tripped at Porter's cottage had signaled another alarm up at the mansion. That second alarm must have triggered some sort of Circle security protocol. That's where all the extra men had come from. I was sure of it. But the knowledge couldn't help me right now, so I filed the information away for another time.

Rivera airily waved his hand, dismissing Tucker's concerns. "Mason will get over it. He always does, just as soon as I line his pockets with more of my mother's money."

Once again, my ears perked up at that name. Mason had to be their boss, the man behind this sick, twisted curtain that was the Circle. For a moment, I savored the fact that I finally—*finally*—had his name. In fairy tales, names often had great power, like the miller's daughter saving her child by guessing Rumpelstiltskin's moniker. Well, names had power in Ashland too. Names led to records, and records led to homes, bank accounts, and businesses, all of which would eventually lead to a real, live person who I could find, drag out into the light, and kill.

But the longer I thought about it, the more the name Mason bothered me. A little warning bell chimed in the back of my mind. I'd heard that name before. I *knew* that I had. But where? When? Was he some Ashland mover and shaker Fletcher had mentioned to me? Some bigwig my mother had done business with? Or someone even closer and more personal than that?

Try as I might, I couldn't find the answer in the dregs of my mind, so I let it go—for now. Besides, at the moment, I did have the slightly more pressing problem of getting out of this cottage alive.

Rivera waved his hand again, as if he were going to keep talking about the mysterious Mason, but Tucker stared the other man down. The vampire didn't look at me, but his lips pressed into a hard, unhappy line. He realized how sloppy Rivera had just been, saying his boss's name out loud in front of me.

"Get out," Tucker snapped. "Now."

Rivera opened his mouth to protest, but Porter laid a warning hand on his shoulder, and the two men left the cottage, shutting the door behind them. Tucker tilted his head to the side, listening to the sounds of their footsteps on the porch. I thought back to the memory I'd had of him in the woods the night Mab killed my mother, how he'd been able to see and hear me even in the dark. He seemed to have more finely tuned senses than any other vampire I'd ever met. I wondered if it was a natural ability or if it came from all the blood he drank. Or maybe it was even a combination of the two.

Rivera and Porter must have stepped away from the cottage, because the sound of their muffled conversation faded away altogether. Only then did Tucker look over at me. I stared right back at him.

I thought that he would make some dismissive, cutting remark, but instead, he carefully studied me, as if comparing me with some other image in his mind. The prolonged silent scrutiny made me uncomfortable, although it didn't creep me out nearly as much as Porter's examination had. Then again, Tucker just killed people. I could understand that. But Porter's sadistic ritual? That was as strange to me as little green aliens falling from the sky.

After several seconds, Tucker shook his head, as if trying to clear away a bad, bad memory—or a ghost that haunted him still. But I knew from personal experience that ghosts didn't disappear that easily, and he couldn't help himself from staring at my dyed blond hair again.

"I never really noticed before now, but you look just like Eira. Even more than Bria does, in a way." He tried to make his voice low and emotionless, but he didn't quite succeed.

I thought back to what I'd overheard, how Damian had mocked the vampire about his feelings for my mother. I decided to twist that knife in even deeper.

"Well," I drawled. "You would know, since you were apparently in love with her."

Once again, Tucker's lips pressed into that thin, unhappy line at my exposing one of his deep, dark secrets, but he didn't ask me how I'd found out about his feelings for my mother. I didn't mind his silence, though. It was just more confirmation about what was really going on here.

And I realized something else. Damian Rivera had been right. No matter what had happened between them, no matter that she'd been murdered years ago, Tucker still carried a torch for my mother. I wanted to know why and exactly what there had been between them. But more than that, right now, I wanted to hurt him the same way that he'd hurt me by not saving her.

I glanced at the mirror again, my gaze fixed on my unnaturally blond hair. "You're right. I do look like her." I turned back to him. "Although I don't remember my mother looking like this. Do you know what I remember about how she looked? The one thing that sticks out in my mind above all others?"

"What's that?" Tucker asked, genuinely curious.

I stared him straight in the eyes. "Her dead, charred, ashy body the night Mab burned her to death. That's what I remember about how my mother looked, you son of a bitch."

Tucker flinched and actually swayed on his feet the slightest bit, as though I'd slapped him across the face and then punched him in the gut for good measure. I itched to do both of those things and more. So much *more*, including ramming one of my knives straight through his pitch-black heart over and over again, until there was nothing left of it and him but tiny bloody ribbons.

"My mother was a beautiful woman," I said. "Long blond hair, blue eyes, pretty features. So you can imagine how horrible it was to see all of that reduced to ash in an instant. Her hair, eyes, face, all gone and replaced by blackened skin and charred bits of bone. But do you know what the worst thing was? The one thing that still haunts me to this day? The one thing that still appears in my nightmares over and over again?"

For a moment, I thought that Tucker wouldn't ask me the inevitable question, but he slowly wet his lips, and I got the feeling that he just couldn't help himself. "What?"

"The charred stench of her burned, blistered skin. The ashy aroma that replaced her sweet perfume. The choking clouds of smoke that slithered down my throat and coated my lungs. You can't even fucking *imagine* it. Like a slaughterhouse that had caught fire and burned to the ground with all the animals trapped inside."

My voice was matter-of-fact and emotionless, but Tucker actually shuddered and turned away, as if he suddenly couldn't stand to see me looking so much like my mother. That cold rage in my heart thrummed with satisfaction. For the first time, I'd actually put a crack in Tucker's cool, detached armor.

I glanced at the mirror, which was angled so that I could still see his face. He dropped his head and closed his eyes, as if trying to banish the horrible images that my words called up in his mind. But he'd been there that night. He might not have seen my mother's body, but he'd witnessed the aftermath of Mab's Fire scorching through the mansion.

I wanted him to remember. I wanted him to think about it. I wanted the memories to haunt the bastard the same way they haunted me.

A long silence followed. Neither one of us spoke. If only I'd had one of my knives, I would have cut through my ropes, risen from the chair, and stabbed him in the back.

But if wishes were horses, I'd have a yard full of prancing ponies by now.

Finally, Tucker opened his eyes, cleared his throat, and faced me again. "I tried to save your mother. Truly, I did. I gave her every opportunity."

"To do what? Fall in line with the rest of your Circle cronies? Do all the horrible things that they ordered her to? To be their little lapdog, just like you are?" I barked out a harsh, humorless laugh. "Doesn't seem like much of an *opportunity* to me. More like a prison. But then, you would know, wouldn't you, Tuck?"

My cruel words finally snapped him out of his memories and his soft sentiments, whatever they were, and his face hardened back into its usual detached mask.

"You're the one who's tied to a chair, Gin. Not me. I'd say that you're the prisoner here."

I shook my head, deliberately making my freshly dyed blond hair fly around my shoulders. "Nah. I'm not a prisoner. I don't take orders from anyone; you can't say the same. I'm my own person, but you'll never be that again."

Tucker's eyes glittered, and I saw the silent agreement in his black gaze. He shrugged his shoulders, not quite dismissing my words. "Either way, one good thing has come out of all of this."

"What's that?"

He flashed me a smile, showing off the fangs that glinted in his mouth. "You won't be a thorn in my side anymore."

I gave him an amused look. "Why? Because you think

that Rivera and Porter are actually going to kill me? Think again, pal."

His smile widened, and his black eyes warmed just the faintest bit. "You have your mother's confidence—and her stubbornness too."

It was by far the nicest thing he'd ever said to me, but anger spiked through me at his words. He made it sound like some sort of shortcoming on her part, and mine too. "I know."

"Yes, you do know, don't you?" he murmured. "And sadly, little Genevieve, it's going to be the death of you, just like it was for her."

I started to ask him what he meant, but Tucker gave me another long, measuring look, then opened the door and left me behind.

Tucker stepped onto the porch and out of my line of sight, although he left the door open behind him. A few seconds later, more footsteps *creak-creak-creak*ed on the wood. Rivera and Porter must have come back from wherever they'd gone and rejoined the vampire on the porch.

"Kill her," Tucker ordered in a clear, strong voice that carried into the cottage. "And try to get it right this time. I'm tired of cleaning up your messes, Damian."

I heard more footsteps, heading for the far end of the porch. After a few seconds, the footsteps faded away, as if Tucker had stepped off the porch and out into whatever landscape lay beyond. And I realized that the vampire was leaving. He was actually leaving without killing me.

Tucker was no fool. I wasn't a scared little girl stumbling around the woods like I had been the night of my mother's murder. He knew exactly how dangerous I was and that I would fight until my very last breath. But instead of ending me himself, he'd walked away and left the job up to Rivera and Porter. If there was one thing that I knew about Tucker, it was that he always had a reason for his actions, no matter how twisted they were. Hmm.

The other two men stepped back inside.

Rivera glanced over at me, making sure that I was still securely tied up, and took another long hit from his silver flask. He held it up to his ear and shook it, but the container was empty. His nostrils flared with anger that his precious booze was already gone.

"I need a refill," he growled. "You heard Tucker. Kill her. And be quick about it. It won't be long before her friends realize that she's still on the property and come back searching for her."

Still on the property? So we were still on the Rivera estate. But where? I'd reviewed every single inch of the grounds when I'd been planning to break into Rivera's office, and Porter's caretaker cottage had been the only one clearly marked on the property. So where was this second cottage located? I didn't know, but fresh hope filled me. All I had to do was get out of my bonds and out of the cottage. Once I was outside, I could figure out exactly where I was and escape. Then I would find my friends, and we would come back here together, finish what we'd started, and put these bastards in the ground for good.

"Of course," Porter murmured in a neutral tone, more than accustomed to dealing with Rivera's drunken demands.

Rivera rolled his eyes, knowing that he was being handled. He stomped out of the cottage and slammed the door shut behind him. He crossed the porch, and the sound of his staggering footsteps faded away. No doubt Rivera was on his way back to his mansion to get his much-needed refill and drink the rest of the night away.

That left me alone with Bruce Porter.

I thought that he might immediately come over and start beating me, as both Tucker and Rivera had ordered. I tensed, ready to reach for my Ice and Stone magic and use it to blast right out of my chair and the ropes still tying me down.

But Porter had other plans. He grabbed one of the chairs from the kitchen table, brought it over, and put it down directly across from me. He sat down, leaned back, and made himself comfortable. Once he was settled, he looked at me and smiled.

And just like that, the Dollmaker finally revealed his true self.

Oh, Porter looked exactly the same as before. Gunmetal-gray hair cropped close to his skull, pale blue eyes, deep lines grooved into his ruddy skin, strong, compact, muscular body in a dark, subdued suit.

But from one second to the next, his entire demeanor changed.

Gone was the dour, serious head of security, the man who stood quietly in the background and waited for others to tell him what to do. Now his eyes were brighter, his smile wider, his posture far more natural and relaxed. He looked . . . happy.

No, I realized, not happy. Giddy—giddy that he was about to act out his sadistic dream yet again.

Well, I hoped he enjoyed it, because his dream was quickly going to turn into the worst fucking nightmare of his life.

"Now we can finally get started," Porter chirped in a high, almost manic voice that was completely different from his usual soft tone. "It's been so long since I've had a special guest here. You can imagine how excited I am."

"Oh, yeah," I drawled. "It's been less than a week since you kidnapped a woman, dolled her up, brought her here, and beat and strangled her to death. Can't imagine how you've lasted so long without all of *that*."

Anger sparked in the dwarf's eyes that I wasn't playing along with him, but he forced himself to dampen it down. He'd gone to too much trouble to kill me just yet. His gaze flicked over to the fireplace, and I spotted a photo sitting on the mantel, one of Maria Rivera.

It was the exact same photo that I'd seen in Damian's office, the one of him standing with Maria and his father, Richard. At least, it used to be the same photo. Someone had cropped both Damian and his father out of the picture, leaving only Maria, with Porter now standing right beside her instead of off in the distance like he was in the original photo. So I'd been right when I'd thought that this was all about Maria. I'd just associated her with the wrong man.

"So this is all about her?" I asked. "You kidnapped and killed all those women trying to find a replacement for

Maria? Let me guess. You were in love with her, and it didn't end well."

Porter kept staring at that photo, his expression softening with fond memories. "My father worked for hers, and my family lived here in this cottage. The two of us grew up together. I loved her from the first moment I saw her, ever since we were kids. She was always so beautiful, so elegant, so classy. Nobody had style like Maria did."

"So what happened?"

I was totally stringing him along, trying to keep him talking long enough for me to figure some way out of here. Even with my magic, it would still take me precious seconds to break free of my chair and the ropes that tied me down. Given his dwarven strength, Porter could easily kill me with one blow if he hit me in just the right spot. I needed to find some way to incapacitate him first. Then I could work on getting out of my chair.

Porter kept looking at the photo of Maria. "When we were eighteen, I told her how I felt about her and asked her to run away with me." His smile vanished, and the happy light was snuffed out of his eyes. "But she didn't want to run away. She said that she didn't want to leave her parents behind."

More likely, she didn't want to leave their massive fortune behind, but I kept my mouth shut, still analyzing my situation. For as strong an elemental as I was, my Ice magic was useless right now. An Ice dagger wouldn't help me cut through my ropes, and since my hands were tied down, I couldn't even raise my wrist and send a spray of them shooting out at Porter.

"So you loved Maria, but she wouldn't go with you," I

said, just to keep the conversation going, just to keep him prattling on about the past. "And eventually, she married Richard Rivera."

"It wasn't her fault," he growled. "It was her parents. They never liked me."

Couldn't imagine why.

"They made her marry Richard. But he didn't love her. He didn't appreciate her. Not like I did. All Richard was interested in was drinking and having affairs and spending her money. He broke Maria's heart over and over again." Porter shrugged. "So I finally killed him when Damian was a teenager. Made it look like a car accident."

That got my attention, and I looked at him again. "Does Damian know that you murdered his father?"

He airily waved his hand the same way that Damian had done earlier, dismissing his own evil deed. "Of course not. I covered my tracks very well. I always do. Besides, the boy was better off without him."

"So you killed Damian's father and had Maria all to yourself again."

Porter nodded, smiling widely again. "For a while, everything was wonderful. Of course, I gave Maria plenty of time to mourn. I'm not a complete monster."

Oh, no. Not a complete monster.

But I held my tongue and went back to my own problem of how to escape. Since I'd ruled out using my Ice magic, I focused on my Stone power. But it wouldn't help me cut through my ropes any more than my Ice magic would. So I asked him some more questions, trying to buy myself some more time to figure this out.

"And what about Damian? What does he think about

your obsession with his dead mother and all the women that you kill in her place?"

Porter snorted in disgust. "Damian's always been far too interested in his booze and broads to think about anything else, including his mother. He's just like his father that way. As long as I keep him happy and cover up his drunken messes, he lets me do as I please. He understands that I know what's best for him."

I wondered if Damian was really as self-centered and oblivious as Porter thought. Or maybe Damian realized that if he didn't go along with the dwarf that he would end up dead in a supposed car accident just like his father had.

"But finally, I got tired of waiting for Maria, and I told her that now that her parents were gone and Richard was dead, it was finally time for us to be together." Porter shook his head. "But she didn't react the way I expected. Not at all."

This time, I couldn't keep my mouth shut or keep the sarcasm out of my voice. "Let me guess. Maria said that she only thought of you as a friend. That she just didn't love you and that the two of you were never going to be together the way you wanted. Maybe she even tried to break it to you gently, but that's when you finally snapped."

Something else occurred to me, something that I'd read in the information that Finn and Silvio had compiled for me on the Rivera family. "Maria died in a car accident too, didn't she? Several years ago. Let me guess. More of your handiwork."

Porter shook his head. "I didn't *mean* to hit her. It just

happened. She just made me so *angry,* saying that she could never be with me. That I was just a friend. That she appreciated my service and my loyalty, but there could never be anything more between us. Why couldn't she see how much I loved her? Why did she have to make me kill her? Why . . ."

He kept right on talking, but I tuned him out, much more interested in what the stones of the cottage suddenly had to say. All around us, they started muttering, responding to Porter's dark, dark rage.

Blood, violence, pain, death . . . blood, violence, pain, death . . . blood, violence, pain, death . . .

The shrieks were even stronger here than they had been at the caretaker's cottage, the agonizing notes so sharp and loud that it seemed the emotional vibrations were slowly tearing the stones apart one molecule at a time. Of course, that wasn't really happening, since emotions, no matter how strong and intense, couldn't break apart solid stone.

But *I* could.

I needed to incapacitate Porter, and what better way to do that than by using my Stone magic to drop his own house of horrors right on top of his head? That would be some poetic justice, Spider-style. So I concentrated on all those plaintive shrieks and wails, listening to the mutterings and using the sounds to seek out the weakest points in the stones that made up the cottage.

There—right *there.*

The mutterings were particularly harsh and loud in the upper section of the fireplace, right above the mantel where Porter had put that doctored photo of him and

Maria. Of course, the emotional vibrations would be concentrated there, since Maria was the focal point of Porter's obsession. Even better, I could see a faint spiderweb pattern of cracks starting from that point in the fireplace and running all the way up to the ceiling.

I glanced from the cracks to Porter and back again, calculating distances and angles. I needed to get him to move just a little bit closer to me, so that he would be directly in the line of fire, so to speak. But that would be easy enough to accomplish. All I had to do was attack him with words the same way that I had Tucker. So I fixed my attention on that one weak spot in the fireplace and started gathering up my Stone magic. I'd only have one shot at this, and I had to make it count.

"And do you know what the worst part was?" Porter said, still continuing his rant. "Maria was ready to move on. She told me that she'd already made plans with someone else and that she was on her way to meet him. I stood there and watched her curl her hair and put on her makeup while she told me all about it."

Well, that explained the makeup. He was trying to re-create that one fateful moment, only with the outcome that he wanted instead of what had really happened.

"She put on her lipstick last, then looked at me in the mirror and smiled, asking me to be happy for her." Porter snarled. "As if I could ever be *happy* when she was with someone else. Why did she have to do that? Why couldn't she just love me as much as I loved her?"

"Oh, I don't know," I said, my voice dripping with venom. "Maybe because she realized how obsessed you were with her. Maybe because she was tired of you always watching her, not to mention following her around all the time. Or maybe she just wanted you to go away and give her one fucking moment of *peace*. Did you ever think that *you* were the problem, not her?"

Porter blinked and blinked, as if such disturbing thoughts had never occurred to him before. "But . . . but I *loved* her."

I let out a harsh, mocking laugh. "You didn't *love* her. You *stalked* her, you *hunted* her. And when she wouldn't play along, when she wouldn't give you what you wanted, you finally *killed* her. Maria's gone, and you have no one to blame but yourself. And now you keep trying to recreate these feelings you had for her with other women. Well, guess what, Bruce? None of the poor girls you brought here and murdered loved you either. And Maria? I imagine that she pitied you more than anything else."

I paused, getting ready to twist my verbal knife in even deeper, just like I had with Tucker. All the while, I kept gathering up my Stone magic, getting ready to hurt Porter with it even more than I was hurting him with my sharp, taunting words.

"Nah," I said. "Maria didn't even pity you. She just made *fun* of you. She probably laughed and laughed at you behind your back with all her rich, snooty friends."

"Shut up," Porter growled. "Maria never did anything like that. She would never be so cruel."

"She would have been *exactly* that cruel," I snapped right back at him. "How could she not laugh at you? The silly little servant boy who thought that he actually had a chance with the rich, pretty princess? Just hearing your stupid sob story makes me want to laugh."

I stared him right in the eyes and started chuckling, making the sounds as low, harsh, and mocking as possible. Trying to make him forget about everything else except how angry he was with me.

And it worked.

Porter's blue eyes narrowed to slits, a red flush crept up his neck, and his hands clenched into fists. And I knew that I was seeing exactly what all those other women had seen right before he killed them. They'd said the wrong thing, they'd ruined his fantasy, and he'd flown into a rage and killed them, just as he'd killed Maria when she finally rejected him.

I let my chuckles fade away. "Face it, Bruce. Maria never cared about you, not one little bit . . ."

This time, I was the one who went on a rant. More and more hateful words spewed past my lips, each one more poisonous than the last, even as I gathered up more and more of my Stone magic, getting ready for what was to come. My words and power mixed together, each one fueling the other.

That flush crept up to Porter's cheeks, staining them a dark, mottled red, and pure murderous rage glinted in his eyes. His entire body tensed, and his hands were fisted together so tightly that his fingers had gone white from the strain. But I kept right on talking, taunting him.

"And you know what else?" I said. "You didn't bring all those women here because you thought you loved them. Not really. You brought them here because you wanted to hurt them the same way that Maria hurt you. Because deep down, you *like* hurting women. Because you wanted all the fucking *power* over them that you never had over her—"

And he finally snapped, like a rubber band stretched to its breaking point.

Bruce Porter let out a harsh primal scream, surged out of his chair, and threw himself at me.

And that's when I finally unleashed my magic.

✲ 26 ✲

My Stone magic roared out of my body like an invisible lightning bolt, and I focused all my power, all my energy, on that one weak spot above Maria and Porter's doctored photo on the mantel. As soon as my magic hit all those tiny spiderweb cracks, the stones blasted out of the fireplace like missiles, all aimed directly at Bruce Porter.

The stones slammed into the dwarf, knocking him away from me and down onto the floor. Porter yelped in surprise and tried to get up, and I used my magic to blast another wave of stones out of the fireplace and straight into him, knocking him back down to the ground. He yelped again, but instead of trying to get up, he curled into a ball to protect himself from the heavy chunks of rocks and sharp, flying shrapnel.

I'd managed to take down Porter, at least for a few minutes, so I looked over at the fireplace again, this time focusing on a much lower stone in the wall.

"Come on, baby," I muttered. "Come to Gin."

My heart pounded, sweat streamed down my face, and tremors shook my body from head to toe from concentrating so hard and long on that one spot. Even though I'd been practicing using my Stone magic in just this sort of pinpoint-precision way, getting one single stone to shoot out of an entire wall of them *and* go exactly where I wanted it to taxed even my great elemental power. But this was my best—and only—chance of escaping, so I cleared my mind, concentrated even more intently on that spot on the wall, and let loose with another hard, forceful wave of magic.

CRACK!

That single stone shot out from the wall, zoomed across the room, and slammed straight into the side of my chair. The heavy rock punched right through the wood, shattering the entire left side of the chair. The brutal blow knocked me over onto the ground, and my head smacked against the floor, making me see white stars. But my left hand was free now, so I pushed the pain away, grabbed a long, jagged piece of stone from the floor, and used it to saw through the ropes on my right wrist and my ankles.

And not a moment too soon.

Porter finally realized that I wasn't targeting him anymore, and he got up onto his hands and knees and shook off the stones that had landed on top of him, like a dog flinging water out of its fur. He had a large purple knot on his forehead, and several bloody gashes streaked down the side of his face, but he was by no means out of the fight and not even close to being dead.

I staggered to my feet, and Porter did the same. His head whipped left and right, taking in my destruction of his precious cottage. By this point, the fireplace was little more than a crumbled heap of stones, and deep, ugly cracks zigzagged through the entire ceiling and down into the walls. Gray dust covered everything, including that photo of him and Maria. It lay in the rubble in front of the fireplace, the silver frame busted to pieces, the glass shattered, and the actual picture inside reduced to tatters.

"You bitch!" he screamed. "You've ruined it! You've ruined *everything*!"

"You're damn right I did," I snarled.

Porter charged at me again, but I whipped up my hand and sent a spray of Ice daggers shooting out at him. He lurched out of the way but tripped over the rocky rubble and fell back onto the floor. But even that had little impact, given his thick, strong dwarven musculature, and he let out a loud growl and started to get right back up again.

I couldn't let him get his hands on me, so I darted past him, threw open the cottage door, and sprinted outside. A wooden porch was attached to the front of the house, just like I thought, and I ran across it, pounded down the steps, and raced out into the darkness beyond. But I didn't go far.

"Come back here!" Porter yelled.

Instead of responding, I whipped back around so that I was facing the cottage again, snapped up my hands, and let loose another wave of my Stone magic.

And this time, I collapsed the entire fucking house right on top of him.

The cottage might have been perfectly pristine and

preserved on the inside, but the outside was old, weathered, crumbling, and covered with dead kudzu vines. I hammered at the structure again and again, cracking the walls and roof with my Stone magic and forcing my Ice power into all those open spaces. Then I used both my Stone and my Ice magic to widen those cracks and break away even larger chunks of rocks. Forget finesse. I battered the structure as hard and fast as I could with my power, and thirty seconds later, I was finally rewarded.

Crack!

Crack! Crack!

Crack! Crack! Crack!

The front wall exploded, as though blown apart by a series of bombs. Without that support, the roof caved in, and the other walls crumbled under the suddenly unbalanced weight. Less than ten seconds later, the entire cottage folded in like a house of cards right on top of Bruce Porter. But I kept right on unleashing wave after wave of magic, crushing every single stone that I could and burying the dwarf in this horrible place where he had killed so many innocent women.

Finally, when the house was just a pile of dusty, rocky rubble, I let go of my magic and lowered my hands. I wiped the sweat off my face and drew in long, deep breaths, trying to calm my pounding heart. All the while, I stared at the cottage, looking and listening for any signs of life. But the only sounds were the continued *crack-crack-crack* and *scrape-scrape-scrape* of the rocks breaking and sliding together, as what was left of the house slowly settled. I reached out with my magic again, this time listening to the stones themselves, but their mutterings were more relieved than agonized now, as if they were glad that no one else would have to suffer within their shattered walls. The sounds comforted me.

Now that I'd buried Porter, it was time to figure out exactly where I was, so I peered into the darkness. I had no idea what time it was, and there was no moon or starlight to help me. Thick, heavy clouds cloaked the night sky, and it had snowed sometime while I'd been unconscious. A dusting of flakes coated the ground, brightening the landscape just a bit. While I stood there, more and more flakes started falling, and I even thought that I heard a faint rumble of thunder in the distance, like thundersnow. I remembered what Jo-Jo had said about storm clouds being in my future. I shivered—and not entirely from the cold.

Rivera had said that we were still on his estate, and I thought back to the property maps that I'd analyzed when I was scouting out his mansion. Some noise sounded in the distance, and I tilted my head to the side, trying to figure out what it was. It took me a few seconds to realize that it was the Aneirin River. Suddenly, I knew exactly where I was. When Finn and I had been here, I'd noticed an old, crumbling cottage off in the woods in the distance—the cottage that I had just reduced to rubble.

I thought about what I knew of the rest of the area. If I headed toward the sound of the rushing water, I would eventually reach the cliffs that overlooked the river. From there, I could better orient myself and hike out of the surrounding woods. After that, all I had to do was get to a road or a phone, and I could let the others know where I was—

A body slammed into me from behind, knocking me down to the ground. Rough hands flipped me over onto my back, and Bruce Porter locked his hands around my throat.

The dwarf looked like, well, like a house had fallen on top of him. Gray dust and dirt covered him from head to toe, his suit hung in shredded tatters from his body, and the cuts on his face, hands, and arms all dripped blood. He seemed like an angry ghost come back to get his revenge on me.

His hands tightened around my neck, and I quickly grabbed hold of my Stone magic again, hardening my skin so that he couldn't cut off my air any more than he already was.

"You bitch!" Porter growled. "You think you can run away from *me*? You think you can reject *me*? I love you! I've always loved you! Why can't you love me back? Why?"

He wasn't even talking to me anymore. He wasn't even trying to kill *me* anymore. Not really. For Porter, this was still all about Maria, and I was just unfortunate enough to be her latest substitute.

Since I didn't have my knives, I reached for my Ice magic, created a sharp dagger, and stabbed him in the bicep with it, just trying to get him to loosen his grip on my throat. He grunted with pain, but he didn't let go, so I blasted the wound with my power, driving hundreds of tiny Ice needles deep down into his muscles.

That was finally enough to get him to lose his grip, at least with that one hand. I rammed my elbow up into his face, breaking his nose. He grunted again and rolled off me. I scrambled away from him and got back up onto my own feet.

And so did Porter.

Despite the bloody cuts on his face, the bruises covering his body, and the needles of Ice sticking up out of his arm like he was part porcupine, the dwarf got right back up. Even worse, he seemed just as strong as ever before. He didn't teeter, didn't stagger, didn't even wobble, not the slightest, tiniest bit. It was like he didn't even *feel* any of his injuries. Maybe he didn't, given the snarling curses spewing past his lips and the determined rage glinting in his eyes. Or maybe he just didn't care about anything other than killing me right now.

I'd never much cared for zombie movies, but I was starting to feel like I was trapped in one, because Porter just wouldn't *die*. I'd collapsed an entire house on top of him, and he looked like it had just been a warm-up bout for the main event. If I'd had my knives, I could have eventually inflicted so many wounds on him that he would collapse and die from the blood loss alone. But I didn't have my knives, and I didn't have an easy way of killing him without getting dead myself, especially given how much damage he could inflict on me with his bare hands, something that he seemed very eager to do.

Porter growled and charged at me again, determined not to let me—or the ghost of Maria that I represented—get away.

So I did the only thing I could.

I sidestepped him, whirled around, and ran away.

I left the clearing in front of the cottage behind and darted into the woods like a deer being chased by a hunter. That's exactly what I was at this moment.

"Come back here, you bitch!" he roared, charging through the trees behind me.

I forced myself to run faster, my boots kicking up sprays of snow and slipping on the slick, frozen leaves underneath. And of course, I hooked my foot on a gnarled root and stumbled right into a tree. I managed to turn my body so that only my left shoulder hit the thick, solid trunk, instead of my face, but the hard blow still sent a wave of pain shooting through that entire side of my body. I ignored the pain, yanked my foot free, and kept going.

The whole time that I ran, slipping and sliding through the patches of snow, I tried to think of some way that I could kill Porter before he killed me. But without my knives, my options were severely limited. I'd exhausted my Ice magic with that last blast of needles in his arm. Even the cold reserves stored in my spider rune pendant and ring were gone. All I had left now was my Stone power, and precious little of it, but that magic wouldn't actually let me cut Porter down.

Another tree root clutched at my boot, tripping me again, and I forced myself to slow down before I fell and broke my ankle. If that happened, I was truly done for.

A stitch throbbed in my left side, and I stopped and ducked behind a tree. I wiped the cold sweat off my forehead and sucked down breath after breath, trying to slow my racing heart. After a minute of that, I made myself breathe in and out through my nose, so that I could listen and try to figure out where Porter was. But I didn't hear him crashing through the trees after me, and only the steady rush of the river broke the snowy quiet.

I focused on the sound of the rushing water. It was much louder here than it had been outside the cottage, and I pushed away from the tree, trying to figure out how close I might be to the Aneirin River. A minute later, I stepped out of the woods. About fifty feet ahead of me, the ground dropped away completely, and I realized that I was looking at the cliffs that lined the river, the same ones that Finn and I had come across two nights ago.

And I suddenly realized how I could kill Porter once and for all—or at least take him down with me.

Instead of heading back into the woods, I left the trees behind and walked forward until I was standing by the edge of the cliffs. I peered down, but it looked the same as before. A hundred-foot drop, with a rocky shore below and the black ribbon of the river running alongside it.

More snow started to fall, turning into a steady shower. I stepped away from the edge, looking right and left through the thick, swirling flakes, but this spot was as good as any to make my last stand, so I turned around and faced the woods again. And then I stood there and waited, just waited for Porter to find me.

It didn't take him long, since he knew the area a lot better than I did. Three minutes later, he ran out of the woods into the snow-dusted clearing in front of me.

"Maria, there you are," he called out. "I knew that you couldn't get away from me."

Instead of offering up some fresh, cruel taunt, I shook my head, so that my dyed blond hair fell forward, covering most of my face, including my smeared, runny makeup. I also reached up and started curling a strand of it around my finger over and over again, playing along with Porter's fantasy and giving him something to fixate on.

"Why would I run away from you, Bruce?" I crooned. "I was waiting here for you. It's been such a long time since I've seen you."

I had no idea what Maria Rivera's voice had sounded like, so I made my tone low and breathy, without a trace of malice or sarcasm. It was the same tone that I'd heard Finn use when he was wooing a new client. And it actually seemed to work, because Porter nodded his head, agreeing with me.

"I know now that we belong together," I said in that same breathy voice. "I'm sorry that it took me so long to realize it. I've been such a fool."

For a moment, confusion filled Porter's face, and I wondered if I'd gone too far, if I'd deviated too much from his memories of Maria and how she'd rejected him. But then his bloody, dusty face split into a wide smile, and he walked forward.

"You don't know how long I've waited to hear you say that," he said, his voice taking on the same high, giddy note that he'd had in the cottage earlier.

I smiled back at him and slowly raised my arms out to

my sides, as if I was inviting him to come over and give me a hug. That was *exactly* what I wanted him to do.

"I know, baby," I crooned again. "And I'm so sorry. I've been wrong about so many things, including you. *Especially* you."

Porter nodded. "That you have, Maria. That you have."

"Well, why don't you come over here and let me make it up to you? I promise that I'll make it worth your while." I let out a soft giggle and batted my gunky eyelashes at him, as though I really were trying to seduce him. The thought made me sick, and I had to grind my teeth to hold a fake smile on my face.

He walked a little closer to me and then a little closer still, his shoes crunching through the snow. The sounds reminded me of bones breaking, but I forced myself to keep smiling and keep my arms raised, even though I was leaving myself totally open and exposed to him.

Porter stopped right in front of me, and I peered at him through the screen of blond hair that still hid most of my face. He smiled at me for a second longer, then lunged forward and locked his hands around my throat.

"Did you really think that I would ever mistake *you* for *her*?" he snarled, tightening his grip. "She was the love of my life. You? You're nothing but a damn *nuisance*."

I laughed in his face, although it came out as more of a choking, wheezing sound.

"What's so funny?" he growled. "Why are you laughing at me again? Why?"

Instead of trying to pry his fingers off my neck, I reached down and pulled him even closer. "I might be a nuisance, but I'm the nuisance who's just killed you, you sick son of a bitch."

He frowned, wondering what I was getting at, but I threw my head back and screamed as loudly as I could. The sharp, sudden sound made him flinch, and he shifted on his feet, just the slightest bit. I slammed my boot into his ankle, pulling him off balance. Porter staggered forward, and I used his own momentum to help me backpedal, dragging him along with me. He cursed, realizing what I was up to, but it was already too late.

Gravity is a bitch, and so am I.

With one final burst of strength, I kicked us both over the edge of the cliffs.

❋ 27 ❋

As we fell, I grabbed hold of every single scrap of Stone magic that I had left, every ounce of power that was still inside my body, plus what was stored in my spider rune pendant and ring. In an instant, I sent that magic surging out through my entire body, using it to harden every single part of me, from my dyed blond hair to my head to my arms, chest, legs, and feet. I also flipped us over in midair, so that Porter was on the bottom of our free fall.

"Wha—wha—aaah!" The dwarf's words dissolved into one solid, unending scream.

I grinned and held on to him even tighter.

We seemed to fall forever, but less than five seconds later, we hit bottom.

Crunch-crunch.

Porter hit the ground first. An instant later, I slammed into him. The weight of my body, made much heavier by my Stone magic, drove his that much deeper into the ground—right on top of all those sharp, jagged rocks that lined the riverbank.

Porter punched into the rocks like a water balloon. *Splat.* I heard the *crunch-crunch-crunch* of his bones breaking, along with a loud series of *snap-snap-snap*s, as though all the vertebrae in his spine were exploding one after another.

I also felt every bit of the brutal impact, and the sudden sharp ache in my chest told me that I probably had a couple of cracked ribs. My brain rattled around inside my skull, meaning that I probably also had a serious concussion. But still, I'd take that over trading places with Porter any day.

I might not have had my knives, but I'd made my own body into a weapon, and Porter was dying as a result.

For a minute, maybe two, both of us were too stunned to move, so we lay where we had landed, him on the rocks and me on top of him, my fingers still fisted in his tattered suit jacket. Finally, Porter coughed, spraying blood everywhere. The drops stung my face with their wet, shocking warmth, and still more of them soaked into my fake blond hair. The sharp, coppery stench drowned out the chemical odor of the hair dye.

I groaned and slowly rolled off him, flopping down onto a small patch of snowy mud. Rocks sliced into my side and back, drawing blood and making me hiss, but I welcomed the pain. It told me that I was still alive.

For another minute, I lay there, surfing the waves of pain until they died down to a more manageable level. Then, just as slowly, I pushed myself up onto my elbow. It took me another minute to get my breath back enough to sit up the rest of the way and another minute still before I was able to glance over at the dwarf, even though he was right next to me.

Porter looked like he had broken every single bone in his body. His arms and legs were stuck out at impossible angles from the rest of his torso, and hard lumps jutted up against his skin from where the shattered bones had been forced so far out of place. His spine must have been crushed too, because it didn't seem he could move a single muscle, not even his head to look over at me.

But believe it or not, he was still alive.

His eyes were still open and blinking, so I leaned over where he could see me. Slowly, his blue gaze focused on my gray one. He coughed again, more blood bubbling up out of his mouth, although the rest of his body didn't actually move with it.

"You know what, Porter? You actually got one thing right," I said, my words slurring a bit from the concussion.

"What's . . . that?" he rasped.

I leaned down so that my face filled his entire vision. "Blondes really do have more fun."

A low rasping sound rippled out of his throat. It almost sounded like a laugh of agreement. Then he coughed again, and a familiar glassy sheen covered his eyes.

I sat there and watched Bruce Porter, the Dollmaker, die.

Despite the fact that I was more or less in one piece, I didn't have the strength or energy left to try to get to my feet, much less find a way out of here. So I rifled through

Porter's pockets, hoping that he had his phone on him and that it had somehow survived the fall. My fingers wrapped around a hard plastic case, and my heart rose. I pulled it out of his pants pocket and held it up where I could see it. The screen was cracked in three places, but the phone turned on.

It took me several tries, and I cut my fingers on the broken glass, but I finally managed to punch a number into the phone. And when it actually started ringing? I'll admit it. A couple of tears slid down my face that had nothing to do with my concussion or cracked ribs.

"Gin?" Owen answered on the first ring, his voice sharp with worry. "Is that you?"

"Yeah, it's me."

I told him where I was—or at least where I thought I was—on the Rivera estate. After that, there was nothing to do but wait.

Owen stayed on the phone with me the whole time, talking to me, telling me that he and the others were on their way and that everything would be all right. But the phone was on its last legs, and his staticky voice cut in and out, so I gave up trying to talk back to him. Plus, my brain felt like it was stuffed full of wet cotton, and everything seemed far away.

Eventually, I was too tired to even sit upright anymore, so I lay down on my back in the cold mud and rocks with the phone wedged up against my ear, listening to the *crackle-crackle* of static. If nothing else, maybe the phone would stay on long enough for Finn and Silvio to track it back to me.

For the longest while, I drifted in and out of consciousness. Concussion and cracked ribs aside, it wasn't so bad, really. Porter might be a bloody, broken mess, but his body was warm enough next to mine to keep me from freezing to death before Owen and the others found me. Plus, it was quiet here, and the only sound was the steady rush of the river a few feet away. I didn't even mind the cold sting of the snowflakes hitting my cheeks one after another.

I didn't know how much time passed, if I slept or just passed out, but eventually, I found myself staring up at the night sky. The storm clouds were still up there, but the snow had tapered off to light flurries.

That was the only reason I could see the man standing over me.

He was bundled up and dressed all in black, from his toboggan to the scarf wrapped around his face to his long coat and boots. A small black bag dangled from his right hand, reminding me of a doctor's satchel. Something about how he was dressed seemed familiar, although my head was hurting too much for me to figure out what it was right now.

"Owen?" I rasped, thinking that he'd finally arrived.

But the man didn't answer me. Cold unease trickled down my spine. Owen would have already been holding me tight, telling me that everything was going to be okay, but this man kept his silence and his distance. I didn't know who he was or what he wanted, but if he thought that I was an easy target just because I'd jumped off a cliff, well, I'd show him just how wrong he was.

The man kept staring down at me, and I crawled my

hand through the cold mud, searching for a loose rock or a broken piece of driftwood that I could use as a weapon.

The man bent down. For a second, I thought that he was going to lean down right next to me, but he maintained his distance. A familiar *clank-clank* sounded, like metal scraping against metal. Then he straightened up and stared down at me again.

I blinked, and suddenly, the man was gone. I rolled my head from side to side, peering into the snowy dark, but I didn't see him anywhere. I would have thought him a figment of my imagination except for one thing: the black satchel now sitting on the ground next to me.

I still didn't have the strength to sit up, but I wormed around in the mud until I could reach out, grab the satchel, and drag it over to my side. My fingers were so cold and stiff that it took me a couple of tries to unhook the clasp. But I finally managed it, reached down, rooted around in the bag, and came up with . . .

A knife.

I squinted at the weapon in my hand. It blurred in and out of focus, but I knew that shape, that length, that weight. More important, I could feel the symbol stamped into the hilt pressing into my palm: a small circle surrounded by eight thin rays.

Not just any knife—*my* knife.

I used the tip of the knife to jiggle the satchel. Sure enough, more *clank-clank*s rang out, telling me that more knives were in the bag, probably the other four that I'd been carrying when I was captured. I wondered what Rivera and Porter had done with my knives and especially why the man in black would bring them to me. I didn't know, and right now, I didn't care.

I dragged the satchel even closer and hooked my arm through the loops, so that I wouldn't lose it and no one could take it away from me. Then, my knife in my hand, I closed my eyes and drifted off again . . .

"Gin!" a voice shouted. "Gin!"

My eyes snapped open. Once again, a man dressed in black was standing over me. But this man dropped to his knees in the mud right beside me, and Owen's face came into focus right above mine, his violet eyes filled with worry.

"Hey," I rasped. "There's no need to shout. My hearing is just about the only part of me that's working properly right now."

He laughed at my black humor, then leaned down and pressed a gentle kiss to my cold lips. He pulled back, and I realized that my friends were gathered around me in a tight circle—Owen, Bria, Finn, Silvio, and Jo-Jo. They were all staring down at me, horrified expressions on their faces, their gazes fixed on the makeup smeared all over my face and especially my unnatural blond hair.

"Where's Jade?" I asked. "And Elissa?"

Jo-Jo dropped down beside me. "They're at the salon, along with Sophia and Dr. Colson. Now, we need to take you there too, darling. I'm going to heal you up enough so that we can move you." She took my hand, sympathy filling her eyes. "I won't lie, Gin. This is going to hurt."

I grinned up at her. "Do your worst. After the night I've had, it will feel like a picnic."

She smiled back at me, then gently pried my knife out

of my cold, stiff fingers. She handed it over to Finn. He eyed the satchel, obviously wondering where it had come from, but he slipped it off my arm and put the knife in the bag with all the others.

"All right, then. Here we go, darling," Jo-Jo said.

She smiled at me again, and then her eyes began to glow a milky-white, and her Air magic gusted over me.

The sharp, pricking pins and needles of Jo-Jo's Air magic flooded my body, filling in the cracks in my ribs, soothing out all my many bumps, cuts, and bruises, even easing the pounding pressure and cottony, disconnected feeling in my head. She was right. Getting everything healed hurt just as much as hitting the ground had, and I had to grind my teeth to keep from screaming. Owen held my hand through the whole thing. He didn't wince, not even once, despite the intense pressure I was putting on his fingers.

Finally, about ten minutes later, Jo-Jo's eyes cleared, and the uncomfortable sensation of her Air magic vanished. I lay in the mud another minute, just getting my breath back. Then I held my hand out, and Owen helped me sit up and eventually stand on my own two feet. But I wobbled so badly that he scooped me up into his arms. Still, I felt much better than before, and I could actually focus again.

I looked down at Bruce Porter—or what was left of him. The dwarf was in the same position as before, his body broken from the fall and his sightless eyes staring up into the night sky. But what made my stomach twist was his mouth. He'd coughed up so much blood that his mouth was a dark red stain against the rest of his face, almost as if he'd painted his own lips with Heartbreaker lipstick.

I shivered, and Owen pulled me a little closer.

"What do you want to do about Porter?" Silvio asked.

I didn't even have to think about it. "Leave him. Out here in the open, just like he left all those poor girls. The bastard doesn't deserve a proper burial."

And that's exactly what we did. One by one, we looked at the Dollmaker a final time, then turned and left him behind, as bloody, broken, and dead as his victims.

* 28 *

I didn't remember everything that happened after that. Just bits and pieces. Owen carrying me along the river-bank. Jo-Jo keeping a close eye on me, making sure that I was healed well enough to keep going. Bria, Finn, and Silvio asking me questions. Me babbling and babbling, trying to tell them what had happened. I didn't know if they understood everything I said, but I thought they got the gist of what had gone down with Tucker, Rivera, and Porter.

"Rivera," I said at one point. "We need to go back to the mansion. We need to get Rivera before he gets away . . ."

"Don't worry about Rivera," Bria said in a grim voice. "I'm working on a warrant to arrest that son of a bitch, and Xavier is watching the mansion. Rivera's not going anywhere."

"But we have to get him now . . ."

"No, darling," Jo-Jo said in a firm voice. "We have to get you out of here. Rivera can wait."

I'd never been able to argue with Jo-Jo, and I was still a little out of it, so I fell silent. But my mind churned, plotting the best way to go after Rivera as soon as possible.

Eventually, the high, jagged cliffs dwindled down to a small hill, and we were able to climb back up into the woods and leave the Rivera estate far, far behind. Owen tucked me into his car, and the next thing I knew, Bria was helping me get into the shower, and I was crawling into bed in one of the guest rooms at Jo-Jo's house. I fell asleep almost immediately, and for once, no nightmares disturbed me.

Sometime late the next morning, sounds started intruding on my peaceful slumber. Namely, the bedroom door opening and someone tiptoeing inside, trying to be quiet, although he stepped on a creaky floorboard, totally ruining the surprise. I rolled over onto my side and opened my eyes to see Owen standing by the foot of the bed, holding a tray full of food.

"Hey," I said, my voice still thick with sleep.

"Hey, yourself. It's almost noon, but I thought you might want some breakfast."

I thought of the meal that Bruce Porter had laid out on his kitchen table last night. "Just as long as it's not lemon-pepper chicken."

Owen frowned, not understanding what I was talking about. But I didn't want to ruin the lighthearted mood, so I decided not to fill him in on that particular detail.

Not yet anyway. I propped some pillows behind my back so that I could sit up.

Owen bowed low, then set the tray down on my lap and gave an elaborate flourish with his hand. "And breakfast is served, Madame."

"You've been hanging around Finn too long."

He grinned. "Maybe, but it seemed like the appropriate thing to do."

"Just don't go around talking about yourself in the third person. Or with an English accent."

"I'll try to refrain from that." He paused and added a suave note to his voice, doing his best impression of Finn. "Although it will be hard, considering how absolutely, incredibly, adorably *awesome* I am."

"You are adorably awesome, especially when you're bringing me food," I teased.

Owen winked and saluted me with his hand. "Happy to oblige, ma'am."

He settled himself on the bed next to me, and the two of us dug into the breakfast that he'd prepared. Blueberry pancakes, applewood-smoked bacon, and a light, refreshing fruit salad made with strawberries, white grapes, kiwi slices, lime juice, and a drizzle of sourwood honey for extra sweetness.

Finally, we finished our meal, and Owen addressed the elephant in the room.

"Do you want to talk about it?" he asked, his gaze flicking to my still-blond hair.

"Not really, but I guess I should."

Owen removed the tray from the bed, sat back down

next to me, and put his arm around my shoulders. I told him everything that had happened last night, much more coherently than I had done before, from waking up in Porter's cottage, to using my Stone magic to escape, to throwing myself and the dwarf off the side of the cliffs.

"But what about your knives?" Owen asked. "How did you get them back? And why were they in that black satchel?"

"I'm not sure. That part is still a little fuzzy."

I wasn't lying. It *was* still a little fuzzy, although I thought that I knew exactly who the man in black was. But I had no way of confirming my suspicions at the moment, so I kept my theory to myself.

Owen looked at me, concern filling his face. "Are you sure that you're okay, Gin? Last night, everything that Porter said and did, that had to be horrible, even for you."

"Okay?" I shrugged. "I don't know about that. But I'm as well as can be expected. I'm just glad that we were able to save Elissa."

"She owes you her life," Owen said.

I winked at him. "And I owe you mine."

"Nah," he said, winking back at me. "You saved yourself, just like you always do."

I leaned over and put my head on his chest, listening to his heartbeat. "Maybe. But it's still nice to know how much you care."

Owen wrapped his arms around me, pulled me even closer, and pressed a kiss to my forehead. "I'll always be here for you," he said in a hoarse, ragged voice. "When you were missing, when we couldn't find you . . . my heart was just . . . *gone*."

"I know," I whispered back. "I know."

And we stayed like that, holding each other close, for a long, long time.

It took some doing, but I finally managed to convince Owen that I was fine and that he should go into work. He reluctantly agreed but made me promise to call him if anything happened. But nothing was going to happen. At least, not until I figured out the best way to get close to Damian Rivera. No doubt he'd doubled or even tripled his security by now, but a few extra guards weren't going to stop me from finally asking him all my many questions about the Circle.

Owen left, and I took a long, hot shower to ease some of the lingering aches and pains in my muscles. Then I put on fresh clothes and headed downstairs.

Since it was Friday, I expected the salon to be full of customers, but only four people were in the room: Jo-Jo and Sophia, along with Jade and Elissa.

Elissa perched on one of the cherry-red salon chairs. A hot-pink cape was draped over her body, and her long blond hair was lying wet, flat, and straight against her head. Jade sat in the chair next to her sister, while Jo-Jo stood at the counter, sorting through some scissors, looking for just the right pair. Sophia relaxed on the floor next to Rosco's basket, stroking the basset hound's long, floppy ears while he grunted with pleasure.

At first glance, everything seemed normal. But Elissa's face was pale and strained, and Jade glanced over at her sister every few seconds, as if making sure that she was really here and that she hadn't vanished again. Jo-Jo was right. Damian Rivera could wait. At least for another hour or two. Making sure that Elissa was okay was the most important thing right now.

"What's going on in here?" I drawled, leaning against the doorframe.

All four of them looked at me, and Rosco let out a loud *woof!* of greeting. He was the only one who didn't do a double take at my dyed hair.

Jade cleared her throat and gestured at her sister. "We crashed here last night. We just got up a little while ago and had some breakfast. Since we were already here, Elissa wanted to get her hair done before we go back home. Jo-Jo was nice enough to close the salon down for the rest of the day just for us."

Jo-Jo smiled at the two of them. "It's no problem at all, darling. I'm happy to help in any way that I can." She finally picked out a pair of scissors, along with a wide-toothed comb, and went over to stand beside Elissa. "All you have to do is tell me what you want, and I'll work my magic."

Elissa nodded, and Jo-Jo turned her chair around so that Elissa could see herself in the mirror over the counter. She wasn't wearing any makeup, so she didn't look anything at all like she had when I found her in that secret chamber, but she still flinched, as though it hurt to look at her own reflection.

"It's okay." Jade got up, went over to her sister's side, and squeezed her hand. "Just take your time."

Elissa kept staring at herself in the mirror. For a moment, I thought that she wouldn't be able to get the words out, but she drew in a breath and started talking.

"He . . . he liked brushing my hair," Elissa said in a

soft, hesitant voice. "He would brush it and brush it and tell me how pretty it was, how much he loved it . . ."

Her voice trailed off, and a horrified shudder rippled through her body. It took her several seconds before she could look at herself in the mirror again.

"I want you to cut it off," she said in a slightly stronger voice. "A cute bob or something like that. I just—I just want it *gone*."

Jo-Jo nodded. "I can do that, darling. No problem. Anything else?"

Elissa glanced over at Sophia, who was still petting Rosco. Her gaze focused on the Goth dwarf's black hair. "Can I dye it too? Some other color? Just for a little while?" she asked, looking up at Jade.

Jade gripped her sister's hand a little tighter. "You can dye it any color you want to, sweetheart."

Elissa hesitated. "Can we do some streaks too? Maybe hot pink or something like that? If it's not too much trouble?"

"Hot pink? Now you're speaking *my* language." Jo-Jo winked at her in the mirror. "And darling, nothing is too much trouble for you today."

Jo-Jo started cutting off Elissa's hair, chatting with her about her college classes, her favorite movies, and other safe, normal topics. Elissa's responses were short and clipped at first, but Jo-Jo could make anyone feel at home, and she slowly got the girl to relax and open up a little bit more.

"I'm going to get some water," Jade said. "If that's okay?"

Sophia pointed to the doorway. "Sure. Bottles in the fridge."

Jade nodded and jerked her head at me, and I followed

her into the kitchen. She grabbed a bottle of water out of the fridge, but she didn't actually open it.

I crossed my arms over my chest and leaned back against the counter. "How is she?"

"Physically, she's fine," Jade said. "Emotionally is a whole other story. I made an appointment for her to speak with a therapist later on today. But she wanted to get her hair done first. I'm going to let her do whatever she needs to in order to try and recover from this."

I nodded. "That's probably the best thing you can do for her."

In the salon, Jo-Jo kept up a steady stream of conversation, still talking to Elissa about her classes. Every once in a while, Sophia would chime in with her raspy voice. Rosco barked another loud *woof!* and Elissa let out a small, hesitant laugh, gently chiding the basset hound for lying down at her feet in hopes of getting a tummy rub.

"Did she tell you what happened the night that Porter grabbed her?" I asked.

Jade let out a tense breath. "It happened just like you thought it did. She saw Porter carrying that other girl and went around to the back of the nightclub to make sure the girl was okay. She realized that something was wrong and started to call the police, but by then, Porter had seen her, and it was too late. Elissa said that the last thing she remembers is him punching her in the face. She woke up in his cottage. She said that Porter brushed her hair and made up her face over and over again, like she was his own personal doll. You can imagine how terrifying that was."

My hand crept up to my own hair, and I fiddled with

one of the blond locks for a few seconds before I realized what I was doing. I dropped my hand back down to my side. "Yeah."

Jade finally cracked open her water and took a long sip before setting it down on the counter. She fiddled with the bottle for several seconds, sliding it back and forth, before pushing it aside for good. She raised her head and looked at me again.

"Bria told me what happened. How you wouldn't give up searching for Elissa. How you stayed behind so that Owen and the others could get her to safety. What Porter did to you later." Her voice dropped to a ragged whisper, and tears streamed down her face. "But you did it. You brought my sister back to me. That means everything to me. More than any favors we could ever trade, more than any deals we could ever make. I'm in your debt now. Whatever you need, Gin. Whatever I can do for you, you just name it, and it's yours. Today, tomorrow, always."

I could have told her that she didn't owe me anything, not one damn thing, but Jade had her pride, and I knew how important this was to her.

"All right, then. I'll hold you to that. After all, a favor is a favor, right?"

I smiled at her, and Jade wiped the tears off her face. She darted around the table, yanked me into her arms, and gave me a tight, fierce hug. A small, choked sob escaped her throat, and her entire body trembled. She started to pull back, but I could tell that she was on the verge of breaking down completely, something that she didn't want her sister to see. So I tightened my arms around her, telling her that it was okay to let go, that I had her, that I was here for her. Another sob rocked her body, and I felt more of her tears soak into my shirt.

I stood there and held Jade while she silently cried.

An hour later, Elissa's long blond locks had been transformed into a sleek black bob with hot-pink streaks, much to her satisfaction. Since we were all gathered in the salon again, I asked Jo-Jo to dye my hair back to its natural dark brown. I didn't want to be reminded of Bruce Porter any more than Elissa did.

Jo-Jo finished with me, went over to the sink, and washed her hands, while I sat in a chair and toweled off my wet hair. Elissa was in the backyard playing with Rosco, while Jade stood by the double doors, watching her sister.

"Are you sure that you want to go back home today?" I asked. "Especially given the, ah, mess in your backyard?" I arched my eyebrows, and she realized that I was talking about the four dead dwarves.

"Actually, Sophia took care of that earlier today," Jade said.

I glanced over at the Goth dwarf, who'd moved from the salon floor over to one of the sofas and was now reading a Karma Girl comic book.

Sophia lowered the comic and gave a modest shrug. "I do good work." Then she grinned and went right back to her reading.

I turned back to Jade. "But what about all the damage in your office?"

"Silvio's been over there all day working on that, along

with Finn and Ryan," Jade said. "I told Silvio that I could get a cleaning crew to come in, some of my own people, but he insisted on doing it all himself."

That sounded just like my assistant. "Of course he did."

Jade waved her phone at me. "Silvio texted me a few minutes ago, saying that all the files had been boxed up and that Ryan was taking everything back to the police station where it belongs. Besides, I think it would be good for Elissa to sleep in her own bed tonight. Give her a sense of normalcy."

I nodded. "If you need anything, anything at all, you or Elissa, just call me."

She nodded back at me. "I will, Gin. Thanks."

Jade knocked on one of the doors, and Elissa came back inside with Rosco. The two of them packed up their things, said their good-byes, and headed home.

They hadn't been gone five minutes when a car rumbled to a stop in front of Jo-Jo's house. The front door banged opened, and Bria stormed into the salon, a grim look on her face.

I sighed and lowered my towel. "Now what's wrong?"

"Damian Rivera is dead."

Shock jolted through me. "What do you mean, he's dead? He was fine last night. Drunk and delighted that Porter was going to torture and kill me."

Bria flopped down in the chair next to mine and ran her hand through her hair in frustration. "Xavier and I got the call right before our warrant came through. Rivera was beaten to death inside his office. A maid found him when she went in to clean this morning."

"But how—" The answer came to me in a flash. "Tucker," I muttered. "He must have realized that I'd survived. He knew that I'd go after Rivera, so he went back and killed Rivera so that I couldn't get anything out of him about the Circle. Dammit. I knew that I should have gone after Rivera as soon as Jo-Jo healed me last night. Dammit!"

Anger surged through me, and I threw my towel across the room. Somewhat comically, it hit the patio doors and harmlessly bounced off, falling to the floor. Jo-Jo gave me a look, but Sophia kept right on reading her comic book, ignoring my temper tantrum. Rosco put his head down and let out a whimper from his basket in the corner.

I slumped back down in my salon chair. Every time I thought that I was getting closer to learning more about the Circle, Tucker was right there to cut me off again. And he said that I was a thorn in *his* side. Bastard.

"Don't blame yourself, Gin," Bria said. "There's nothing you could have done. Rivera died sometime during the night, not this morning."

"During the night? What time?"

She shrugged. "Ryan won't know for sure until he does the autopsy, but he estimated sometime around midnight."

"And what time did you guys find me on the riverbank?"

"Before then. About eleven o'clock," Jo-Jo chimed in. "Why do you ask?"

I shook my head. "No real reason."

But my mind churned, thinking about everything. Given the estimated time of death, Tucker had killed

Rivera after I'd battled Porter. The vampire must have been lurking somewhere in the woods and realized that I was still alive and that Porter was dead. I hadn't been in any shape to go after Rivera then, but Tucker would have known that I'd hunt Rivera down the first chance I got. Tucker could have easily told the other man to leave Ashland, but instead, he'd gone ahead and killed Rivera himself.

Why? Why would he do that?

The more I learned about Hugh Tucker, the less sense I could make of him.

"I know you're upset, Gin," Bria said. "But it's not your fault that Rivera's dead and we can't question him about the Circle."

I waved my hand, cutting her off. "No. I'm not upset. Not really. Sorry I lost my temper. I know you're right. So let's look on the bright side of things."

Bria arched her eyebrows, surprised by my sudden change in attitude. "And what is that?"

I grinned. "Tucker saved me the trouble of going over there and killing Rivera myself. Why, you might even say that he gave me the day off."

❖ 29 ❖

Given my nasty fall off the cliffs, Jo-Jo insisted on checking me out one more time. She gave me a clean bill of health, and I left the salon and went back home to Fletcher's house.

Finn and Silvio were both there waiting for me, sitting in the den, with stacks and stacks of papers spread out all around them and covering every available surface, from the couch cushions to the coffee table to the open space in front of the fireplace.

"Finally! I thought you were *never* going to get here. We've been working for *hours* already," Finn said, the words rushing out of his mouth without him even stopping to take a breath.

He reached over, grabbed a large mug, and took a long swig. I could smell the strong scent of chicory coffee all the way across the den. From the bright glaze in Finn's eyes, it looked like he'd had at least a pot of the stuff already—maybe more.

"What's going on? I thought that you guys cleaned up all the Dollmaker files and sent them back to the police station."

"Oh, we did," Silvio said, his demeanor much calmer than Finn's. "But we decided to start on a new project."

"And what would that be?"

Finn rolled his eyes and took another swig of coffee. "Figuring out who *Mason* is, of course. You know, the name that Rivera dropped to you last night? The one that you kept repeating over and over again in your concussed state? The guy who is probably the leader of the Circle?"

"That's what this is all about?" I asked.

"Of course," Finn chirped. "Not that we've been getting anywhere, though. Do you know how many people named Mason—first and last—there are in the Ashland area? Hundreds of them, maybe even thousands. And Mason may not even be his real name."

He tossed up a wad of papers in indignation, then glared at them as they drifted down to the floor around him like square snowflakes.

Silvio cleared his throat. "I think what Finn is trying to say is that even with the name, we're still looking for a needle in a haystack." He gestured at all the papers. "A very large haystack."

I could see that, but my throat still closed up to think that they'd cared enough to start searching anyway, without my even asking them to. It took some of the sting out of the fact that Tucker had gotten to Damian Rivera before I did. Still, that little warning bell clanged in the back of my mind again.

Mason. Where did I know that name from? And why did I get the sinking feeling that learning the answer would only cause me more heartache?

"Gin?" Silvio asked. "Are you okay? Is something on your mind?"

I pushed my worries away and plastered a smile on my face. "I'm fine. I was just thinking that I have the utmost faith and confidence in y'all. If anyone can track down this Mason fella, it's the two of you."

Finn snorted. "Faith? Faith is all well and good . . ." He deliberately let his voice trail off.

I sighed, knowing what was coming next. "But?"

"But dinner would really help. With dessert." He waggled his eyebrows. "Lots of dessert."

I rolled my eyes, leaned over, and ruffled his hair.

"Hey, now!" Finn smoothed his dark brown locks back down into place. "Don't mess with the 'do."

I ruffled his hair again, just because I could. "Tell you what. You guys take a break, go into the kitchen, and see what's in the fridge that you might like me to whip up. Deal?"

"Deal!" Finn chirped again, grabbing his mug and surging to his feet. "I need more coffee anyway."

"I doubt that," Silvio muttered, but he too got up, grabbed his own mug, and headed into the kitchen after Finn.

While the two of them argued about who was going to get the last cup of coffee, I headed over to the fireplace and stared at the framed drawings on the mantel of my mother's and sister's runes, the snowflake and the ivy vine, representing icy calm and elegance. I also reached out with my magic, listening to the stones that made up the fireplace and the surrounding walls. They murmured back to me, echoing my own anger, grief, and sadness that my family was gone, that they had been taken away from me so suddenly, so brutally, so cruelly.

I wondered how many times Bruce Porter had stood in front of his own mantel, staring at that doctored photo of him and Maria and thinking about the past. The ironic fact that I was doing more or less the same thing as a serial killer wasn't lost on me.

In a way, I supposed that I was just like Porter, forever dwelling on the past, obsessed with it even, and still snared in all the consequences of so many people's dark deeds, including my own. But my obsession was for learning the truth, for getting answers, and for finally making the people who'd murdered my family pay for their crimes.

"I'll find Mason sooner or later," I said to my mother's photo. "No matter who he is or where he's hiding. And then I'll kill him for what he did to you and Annabella. I promise you that."

I ran my fingers over her snowflake pendant a final time, then left the den and headed into the kitchen to see what Finn and Silvio had come up with for dinner.

Over the next few days, things slowly returned to normal. I ran the Pork Pit during the day and searched for information on the Circle and the mysterious Mason at night, along with the rest of my friends.

Bria and Xavier were assigned to investigate the murder of Damian Rivera, but it turned out to be an open-and-shut case. Tucker hadn't just killed Rivera. The sly vampire had actually left a note behind—and he'd blamed the whole thing on Bruce Porter.

Tucker had typed up the note as though he were Porter, and in it, he'd confessed to being the Dollmaker. He claimed that Rivera had found out what he'd done and was going to turn him into the police, so Porter had killed his boss instead. And here was the real kicker. The note claimed that Porter was so distraught by what he'd done to Damian that he'd thrown himself off the cliffs at the edge of the Rivera estate. So in one fell swoop, Tucker killed Rivera, blamed Porter for it, and closed the entire case by claiming that Porter had committed suicide.

I had to admire the vampire's efficiency, if nothing else.

Of course, Bria and Xavier did a thorough search of the entire Rivera estate, including Porter's caretaker cottage. They found a secret drawer in the bottom of Porter's dresser that was full of locks of blond hair, each one tied off with a different-colored ribbon and all from the women he'd murdered. I didn't like the fact that Tucker had twisted the story around to suit his own needs, and also those of the Circle, but at least the victims' families got a little bit of closure, knowing that the person who'd killed their loved ones couldn't hurt anyone else ever again.

Including Stuart Mosley.

Four days after the fight at the Rivera estate, the dwarf came to the Pork Pit at about two o'clock in the afternoon. He shrugged out of his long gray overcoat, hung up his matching hat, and sat on a stool at the counter next to Silvio, who was typing on his tablet like usual, still in hot pursuit of the mysterious Mason. The two of them exchanged polite nods, and Silvio went back to work.

"Mr. Mosley," I said. "You're looking much better today."

And he truly did. His silver hair was neatly brushed, his Rudolph-red nose had returned to its normal color, and his hazel eyes were sharp and clear instead of tired and watery. Plus, he was wearing a suit instead of the rumpled pajamas he'd had on the last time I'd seen him.

Mosley harrumphed. "Yes, according to Finn, I am not a germ-infested, snot-ridden mess anymore, so that's a definite improvement."

I laughed, pulled my order pad out of the back pocket of my jeans, and grabbed a pen from the top of the cash register. "So what can I get you?"

"I'm not here to eat."

"Oh?"

Mosley glanced around the restaurant, which was largely empty, since the lunch rush had already come and gone. Only two spots were occupied.

Jade Jamison sat at a table across from Dr. Ryan Colson. Given the way the two of them kept staring at each other, smiling and laughing, I'd say that they were on an unofficial date, whether they realized it or not. Jade saw me watching them, and I flashed her a thumbs-up. She grinned back at me, and a faint blush colored her cheeks. She leaned forward and focused on Ryan again.

I wasn't the only one who noticed Jade and Ryan together. From a nearby booth, Elissa Daniels stared over at her sister, a faint smile lifting her lips.

Jade had been calling me every day with updates. Elissa was seeing a therapist and trying to cope the best she could with everything that had happened. Bria had been able to keep Elissa out of the official police investigation, so no one knew that she'd almost been the Dollmaker's next victim. The last thing she needed right now was to be hounded by the news reporters who had been covering the story nonstop.

Jade had told me that Elissa just wanted things to go back to normal—or as normal as they could be—so I'd decided to help with that. Three other girls were sitting in the booth with Elissa: Eva Grayson, Owen's sister; Violet Fox, her best friend; and Catalina Vasquez, Silvio's niece.

Eva, Violet, and Catalina had all been through some pretty horrific things themselves, and I thought that the four of them might be able to help each other. That they might be able to talk about things together in a way that maybe they couldn't with the older people in their lives. At the very least, Eva, Violet, and Catalina could show Elissa that this too would eventually pass, that the pain and fear would slowly lessen, and that there were still plenty of good things and people left in the world, instead of just the nightmare that she'd experienced.

Plates of food were spread out across the table, along with their laptops and textbooks. Ostensibly, they'd come here to study, although they didn't seem to be getting any work done. Eva was doing most of the talking, throwing her hands up into the air as she told some story, with Violet and Catalina both chiming in occasionally. Elissa sat there, nodding her head instead of talking, but every once in a while, her eyes would brighten, and she would smile a little at something one of the other girls said. You couldn't get more normal than gabbing with some new girlfriends. I just hoped that it helped her.

Mosley looked over at Elissa. "She seems to be doing well."

"As well as can be expected, I suppose."

Elissa noticed Mosley sitting at the counter. She hesitated, then raised her hand and waved at him. He waved back at her, a strained expression on his face. Elissa went back to her conversation with the other girls, and Mosley turned around and faced me again.

"I reached out to Ms. Jamison as soon as Finn told me what happened," he said. "Jade told me that they were coming here today. I didn't want to intrude on Elissa's recovery, but I wanted to see her for myself. Make sure that she was really okay. Physically, at least. I've also set up a trust to pay for whatever she needs now and in the future."

"That was nice of you."

He shook his head. "No, it's not. Not since all of this is my fault."

"How do you figure that?"

"If I hadn't gotten sick that night, Elissa would have been at that charity dinner with me," Mosley said. "She never would have gone to Northern Aggression, and Bruce Porter would never have gotten his hands on her."

"No," I said. "He would have kidnapped some other poor girl, someone whose sister *didn't* come to me for help, and we might never have found her, much less stopped him for good. Believe me, Mr. Mosley, I am well acquainted with guilt. None of this is your fault. It's all on Porter. He's the one who chose to kidnap and kill all those women."

"Including my Joanna." His voice dropped to a hoarse whisper.

I didn't say anything. Nothing I could say would take away Mosley's grief over his granddaughter's murder.

He stared down at the counter for several seconds, slowly tracing his fingers back and forth along the smooth, shiny surface, lost in his own thoughts. Finally, he cleared his throat and looked up at me again.

"There's no need to stand on formality. You can call me Stuart." His mouth quirked with a bit of amusement. "After all, you have seen me in my pajamas now."

"Only if you call me Gin."

He nodded and steepled his hands together, finally getting down to business. "Seeing Elissa isn't the only reason that I came here today. I wanted you to know how grateful I am for everything that you did for her, my granddaughter, and all of Porter's other victims. I only wish that I'd been able to get my hands on him myself."

For a moment, his face darkened, and cold, calculating rage glinted in his hazel eyes. And I realized that Stuart Mosley was not a man you wanted to mess with.

He looked at me again. "I also came here today to tell you that my offer still stands."

"And what offer would that be?"

"Any favor you want, any boon or consideration that you, Finn, or the rest of your friends need. I am not without money, resources, and influence."

First Jade, now Mosley. I should take down serial killers more often. Everybody wanted to do me favors now.

I wasn't about to pass up this opportunity.

"I have questions. About Fletcher. And the Circle. Did he tell you about them?"

Mosley nodded. "Yes. Fletcher didn't tell me much about what he was up to or about the group itself, but I'll be happy to answer what I can. Perhaps over dinner one day soon?"

"I'd like that."

He smiled at me. "I would too."

"But first things first." I stabbed my pen at him. "You need to order some food. Fletcher would never forgive me if I let one of his friends leave without a good hot meal."

Mosley chuckled, thinking that I was joking. But when he realized that I was serious, he ordered a platter of pulled barbecue chicken, along with baked beans, a garden salad, and a basket of Sophia's homemade sourdough rolls. I also threw in a heaping serving of blackberry cobbler with vanilla-bean ice cream for dessert.

Some more folks came in to eat, and we were suddenly busy again. Sophia helped me fix Mosley's food, and I'd just set it on the counter in front of him when the bell over the front door chimed. I looked up to call out a greeting to my new customer, but the words died on my lips when I realized who it was.

Hugh Tucker had just strolled into the Pork Pit.

* 30 *

I had two knives in my hands before Tucker took another step into the restaurant. Silvio was also on his feet, his tablet clutched in his hand as though he planned to brain the other vampire over the head with it. Sophia was at the far end of the counter at one of the cooking stations, but she had a death grip on a cast-iron skillet, ready to wade into the fray.

Mosley turned his head, wondering what had alarmed the three of us. I didn't know if he recognized Tucker, but his eyes narrowed, and he tightened his grip on the knife and fork in his hands. Everyone else was still absorbed in their food and conversations, and they didn't notice the sudden tension in the restaurant.

Tucker held up his hands and slowly walked toward the cash register where I was standing. "I'm not here to fight. I just want to have a simple conversation."

I gripped my knives a little tighter. "And what's to stop me from cutting you down right here, right now?"

He glanced around. "Well, all of these nice folks, for one thing. You wouldn't want to ruin their meals, would you?"

He was right. More than two dozen people were in the restaurant, chowing down on their barbecue and side dishes. They hadn't come here to witness a murder, and I wasn't about to subject them to that, especially not Elissa, after what she'd just been through. No matter how badly I wanted to kill Tucker.

"Plus," he continued, "I have someone stationed outside the restaurant with a gun aimed right at you. Just for some added insurance."

I glanced out through the storefront windows. I didn't see anyone lurking on the sidewalk, but that didn't mean they weren't out there, maybe sitting in a car at the curb. Not that a gun would do them much good outside, since the windows were bulletproof. But if a fight broke out inside the restaurant and my customers started fleeing out the front door, the shooter could always decide to target them instead of me. So as much as I hated it, I had to play along with Tucker. Besides, I thought that I knew exactly why he was here, and part of me wanted to see if I was right.

"Fine," I snapped. "What do you want?"

He tilted his head at an empty booth in the back corner of the restaurant. "Why don't we go over there and discuss it? Away from prying eyes and ears?"

He looked at Silvio, who shrugged back at him. Thanks to his own enhanced vampiric senses, my assistant would still be able to hear our conversation no matter how softly Tucker talked.

"Lead the way," I said.

"So you can stab me in the back with one of your knives?" Tucker laughed. "I don't think so. Why don't you put those away so we can have a civilized conversation like normal people? And I do hope you know that it's not a request."

He gestured with his hand, and I had no choice but to slide my knives back up my sleeves, step out from behind the cash register, and head over to the booth. I started to sit down, but Tucker called out behind me.

"Other side, please. I prefer to sit with my back against the wall. Plus, I wouldn't want Ms. Deveraux getting any bright ideas about sneaking up behind me and whacking me on the head with her lovely skillet."

I ground my teeth. That had been exactly what I was hoping would happen, but I glanced over my shoulder at Sophia and shook my head, telling her and Silvio to stand down. Sophia went back to her cooking, while Silvio sat back down on his stool. Mosley relaxed a bit too, although he kept glancing in this direction.

Once I was sure that my friends were going to hold their positions, I did as Tucker had commanded and sat down in the booth. He unbuttoned his dark blue suit jacket and slid into the opposite side.

He stared at me, and I looked right back at him. His gaze focused on my hair, once again its usual dark brown color and pulled back into a ponytail.

"You dyed your hair back already."

"You sound disappointed. Why? Because I don't look quite as much like my mother anymore? You should be careful about dwelling on the past, Tuck. One day you might wake up and be just like Bruce Porter."

He arched his eyebrows, but he didn't respond to my taunt.

I leaned forward and fixed my cold gray gaze on his inscrutable black one. "Actually, I'm glad that you came by today."

"Really? Why is that?"

"Because I have something that belongs to you."

I started to drop my hand down under the table, but Tucker waggled his finger at me. "Ah-ah," he warned. "Slowly, Gin. Slowly."

I rolled my eyes, but I did as he asked. With slow, exaggerated movements, I reached into my jeans pocket, pulled something out, and set it on the table between us.

The gold tube of Heartbreaker lipstick glinted in the sunlight streaming in through the storefront windows.

Tucker stared at the lipstick a moment, then arched his eyebrows again. "And why would you think that belongs to me? I am many things, Gin, but I am not into women's makeup."

I sat back and crossed my arms over my chest. "Because you set this whole thing up, you sneaky son of a bitch."

"I have no idea what you're talking about."

I snorted. "Oh, that's *rich* coming from you."

Tucker crossed his arms over his own chest, mimicking my hostile posture. "Please. Enlighten me."

"I'll readily admit that I have the world's worst luck," I said. "But I thought that it was a very strange coincidence that I found a woman's body at Northern Aggression the very same night that I went there looking for a missing girl. I really should have known by now that there are no coincidences. Especially where you're concerned."

Tucker kept staring at me.

"You see, I heard that little chat you had with Damian Rivera in his office several nights ago. You were telling him to clean up his mess—or else—but you weren't talking about Rivera's habitual drunkenness and DUIs, were you? You were talking about the fact that Bruce Porter was a serial killer and the police had discovered a pattern to all these pretty blond girls being murdered and dumped all over Ashland. Care to tell me which one of the cops on your payroll tipped you off about the Dollmaker investigation?"

Tucker didn't say anything, and his face remained as impassive as ever, so I continued.

"But you knew that I was there and that I was listening to every single word that you and Rivera said, since I'd left the window open on my way out of the office. Given your freaky vampire senses, you probably heard me out on the roof too. And Rivera royally pissed you off when he mocked you about being reduced to the Circle's errand boy. But Rivera was right about how powerless you were compared with him. You couldn't act against Rivera yourself. Not openly. Not without the rest of the Circle's approval. So you decided to use me to do your damn dirty work for you."

My accusation hung in the air between us like a storm cloud crackling with lightning, and I could almost see the wheels turning in Tucker's mind as he debated how to respond.

"While I'm highly flattered that you think that I'm some sort of genius criminal mastermind, I really have no idea what you're talking about, Gin." Tucker tapped his fingers on the table. "I certainly didn't tell Bruce Porter to kidnap and murder all those poor women."

"No," I said. "But you were the one who drew my spider runes on the dead girl Porter dumped at Northern Aggression."

Tucker's fingers stilled, and surprise flashed in his eyes before he could hide it. He hadn't thought that I would figure it out. I'd been right when I felt I was trying to solve two separate but connected puzzles. One had been figuring out that Porter was the Dollmaker. And the other one was about Tucker giving me the one clue that had led me straight to Rivera.

"Now, I don't know exactly what happened. If you followed Porter from the mansion that night and realized that he was dumping a body at the nightclub, or if you found out about the dead woman some other way. But you wanted to get rid of Porter and Rivera, and it was too good an opportunity to pass up. So you drew my spider runes on that dead girl's palms, knowing that someone in the police department or coroner's office would recognize the symbols as my personal rune. You also realized that Bria would find out about the marks sooner or later, that she would tell me, and that I would be pissed off enough to investigate."

Tucker didn't say anything, but his mouth quirked up into the faintest smile. That was all the confirmation I needed.

"But you still had another problem to solve. Porter had

been very careful, and nothing linked him or Rivera to any of the victims. You had to point me in that direction somehow, so you decided to leave a little clue behind for me to find." I tapped my fingernail against the top of the gold tube. "A very expensive brand of lipstick that you somehow knew that Porter used in his ritual."

Tucker eyed the lipstick, but he still didn't say anything.

"But then you had *another* problem. Where to leave the lipstick so that I would find it. You checked with your sources, probably the same cop who tipped you off about the Dollmaker investigation, and you heard about Elissa Daniels. You realized that Porter had grabbed her and was going to make her his next victim. Now, I don't know if you found out that she was Jade's sister or if you just followed me back to Jade's house when I drove her home from the police station. But that night, you broke into Jade's house, getting as far as opening the kitchen door. I imagine that you were going to leave the lipstick behind somewhere in the house for me to find. But I heard you creeping inside, and since you couldn't afford to be seen, you slipped away."

He tipped his head at me. "It seems that I'm not the only one with good hearing."

I ignored his compliment. "But you still needed to plant the lipstick *somewhere*. So I imagine that you started following me around, waiting for your chance. Somehow you realized that I was heading back to the scene of the crime at Northern Aggression. You managed to get there ahead of me, and you finally planted the lipstick for me to find. But once again, I almost caught you, and you had to leave in a hurry. But you didn't really care, did you? Because you knew that I would find the lipstick and that I would trace it back to Rivera. Then one thing would lead to another, and I would most likely kill him and Porter and solve all your problems for you."

A faint smile lifted Tucker's lips. "That was the idea, although Damian almost ruined everything by sending his men over to Ms. Jamison's home. I didn't realize that he had his own sources in the police department or that he would be smart enough to send his men over there to destroy any files she had. Still, you killed them in the end, and the men were another link back to Damian, so it all worked out for the best."

I shook my head. "I have to hand it to you. Clever, Tuck. Very, very clever."

He gave a modest shrug. "I do try to be efficient about these things."

White-hot rage burned in my heart that he had so thoroughly used me, along with more than a little embarrassment, especially since I hadn't realized what was really going on until I'd been tied to that chair in Porter's cottage. The only saving grace was that I'd rescued Elissa. But the real irony of the situation was that I probably wouldn't have been able to save her if Tucker hadn't manipulated me. Without that lipstick trail to follow, I never would have connected Rivera and Porter to the Dollmaker, and I never would have found Elissa in time. So as much as it pained me to admit it, I owed Tucker.

At least enough to let him walk out of here alive today.

"How is Miss Daniels, by the way?" Tucker's black gaze

flicked past me, and I knew that he was looking at her on the other side of the restaurant.

"She's still alive," I snapped. "Not that you really care."

He shrugged again. "No matter what you think about me, what Porter did to those women was an abomination. I wanted to stop it the moment I learned about it."

"So why didn't you?"

His mouth puckered, as though he'd bitten into something rotten. "Let's just say politics and leave it at that."

"Politics? Really?" I snorted. "Is that why you went back to the mansion and beat Rivera to death?"

For the first time, a genuine smile played across his face, although his black eyes remained stone-cold. "Oh, no. That was just *fun*. Believe me, Damian had it coming. He'd hurled one too many insults my way over the years, when he was nothing but a lousy drunk. The only useful thing about him was his massive family fortune, and his problems were starting to outstrip even that."

I could almost sympathize with him there. I would have enjoyed hurting Rivera too. I waited for Tucker to go on, but he didn't elaborate, and I knew that he wouldn't say any more about Rivera. So I decided to change course.

"Tell me one thing," I said. "Since we're having such a civilized conversation."

"What?"

"Why didn't you kill me when you found me lying next to Porter on the riverbank?"

Tucker blinked, as if he hadn't expected me to remember that. I'd thought that the man in black had seemed familiar, and later on, after Jo-Jo healed my concussion, I'd remembered that he'd been bundled up just like the man in the car that had driven away from Northern Aggression. Once I'd realized that Tucker was the one who'd planted the lipstick at the nightclub, the connection had been obvious.

"I didn't think that murdering you when you couldn't fight back was very sporting," he murmured. "Besides, you'd done the hard work of killing Porter. I figured that you'd earned a brief reprieve."

"Is that also why you brought my knives to me?"

He shrugged again. "Damian gave the knives to me after Porter took them off you. I had no use for them."

"No, I suppose you didn't," I said. "But do you know what's really funny? How many times you've tried to kill me versus how many times you've helped me. I'd say they're about even now."

He frowned. "What do you mean?"

I might not have one of my knives in my hands, but I could still hurt him. "I'm talking about the night that Mab burned my family's mansion to the ground. How you saw me in the woods but pretended you didn't. How you dropped some money on the ground and just walked away."

The vampire shifted in his side of the booth, actually looking uncomfortable, as if I'd caught him doing something that he didn't want anyone else to know about—ever.

All around us, people ate their food, sipped their drinks, and carried on with their own conversations, but a tense silence fell over our booth. I kept quiet and waited, hoping that I'd rattled Tucker enough to get him to start talking, but of course I hadn't. Frustration, anger, and annoyance rushed through me at his continued silence.

"Why did you come here?" I snapped, tired of Tucker and all his damn mind games. "What do you want?"

For a moment, I thought that he wasn't going to answer, but he finally looked at me again.

"You were right. I did realize that you were spying on us in Rivera's office that night." Tucker drew in a breath and slowly let it out, as if he was dreading what he was about to say. "I came here because I wanted to explain about your mother."

I couldn't have been more shocked if he'd lunged across the table and slapped me across the face. In an instant, all my frustration, anger, and annoyance crystallized into cold, cold rage. On top of the table, my hands curled into fists, my nails digging into the spider rune scars embedded in my palms.

"Really?" I snarled. "You want to explain about my mother? Well, maybe you should start by saying why you didn't save her. Why you let Mab Monroe and the rest of your precious Circle fucking *murder her*."

For the first time since I'd known him, Tucker's face twisted with regret. Once again, I thought that he wouldn't answer me, but to my surprise, he began to speak in a flat, emotionless voice.

"Ashland society is a very tight-knit circle, as I'm sure you know," he began. "My family used to be one of the wealthiest and most respected in the entire city, at least until my father gambled everything away. He was a drunk, you see, just like Damian Rivera, although Damian was at least smart enough not to spend all of his mother's money."

He smiled, but it was a dark, humorless expression.

"But my father insisted that we keep up appearances and maintain the same lifestyle that we'd always had, even though doing so put us deeper and deeper in debt. He too was a member of the Circle, but without any real money to his name, he quickly fell through the ranks, losing all his power and position, until the others regarded him as little more than a pet. And then, when he died, *I* became their pet, forced to pay off his many debts."

"Their servant," I said.

He nodded, not bothering to deny it. "Everyone treated me that way, except for your mother. Eira was always kind to me, even when we were kids. She was the only one of them who ever treated me like an equal." He paused, as if he was having difficulty getting his next words out. "I loved her for that and so many other things."

I asked the question that had been bothering me for days now. "And did she love you back?"

He gave me a sad smile. "She actually did, once upon a time. But my Circle duties took me away from Ashland. I wanted to stay, to be with her, but of course, I couldn't exactly say no in my position. And by the time I came back, she had married your father."

"So you missed your chance with her."

"I did. I regretted it, of course, but she seemed happy, so I moved on."

He waved his hand, but I could hear the lie in his voice. He hadn't moved on any more than I had from her murder.

"So you wished my mother well in her marriage, and then, years later, you let Mab Monroe burn her to death. Some love story."

Tucker actually flinched at my words, but he quickly smoothed out his features. "Once I realized what was going to happen, I tried to persuade Eira to leave Ashland, to flee, but she wouldn't hear of it. She thought that she could take on the Circle and win. She was wrong about that. And so are you."

He leaned forward, his black eyes glittering in his face. "You asked me why I came here. Well, consider this a warning, the only one you will ever get from me. You're right. I wanted Damian and Porter dead, and you helped me make that happen. So I covered up your involvement in this whole messy affair. Think of it as a quid pro quo."

So that's why he'd gone to all the trouble to write Porter's fake suicide note. He almost made it sound like he was protecting me. But I knew better. He was protecting his own ass.

"But?" I asked the inevitable question.

"But if you continue your investigation into the Circle, the other members will eventually notice, and they will take appropriate steps to deal with you. And not just you but your friends and family too. Owen Grayson, Finnegan Lane, the Deveraux sisters, Bria. Everyone you love and care about." He snapped his fingers. "They will kill them all, just like that, just like they killed your mother and sister."

"And will you be the one leading the charge, Tuck?" I asked in a soft voice.

"Of course. That's my job." His mouth twisted. "And a good pet always obeys his master's orders."

This time, I leaned forward, letting him see the cold, hard determination in my wintry gray eyes. "I'm not going to stop. I will *never* stop until I find out who every single member of your cursed Circle is. I will kill them all, one by one, until I find your boss. And then I'll kill him too. Consider that *my* warning to *you*."

He stared at me, a sad smile tugging at his lips. "You really do have your mother's stubbornness. It's going to be the death of you, little Genevieve. Just as it was the death of her."

"Genevieve Snow died the night my mother and sister did," I snarled.

He gave me another sad smile. "And so did I."

Tucker slid out of the booth, got to his feet, and buttoned his suit jacket, putting his armor back on in more ways than one. He gave me a deep, respectful nod before striding over to the front door, opening it, and stepping out into the cold winter sunshine.

❈ 31 ❈

I sat in the booth and watched the vampire walk down the sidewalk and out of sight. The second Tucker was gone, Silvio left his stool at the counter and hurried over to me.

"Do you want me to follow him?" he asked. "Try to track him or his car? I can still catch him."

I shook my head. "No. He's not my problem, and he's not my enemy. Not today, anyway."

Silvio looked at me. "I heard what he said about your mother. About his . . . feelings for her. Does Bria know?"

I shook my head again. "No. Owen knows, but I haven't told Bria yet. But I will. Tomorrow. Tucker, the Circle, searching for Mason. Everything will go back to normal tomorrow."

"And what about today?" Silvio asked in a quiet tone.

I looked out over the restaurant, my gaze going from one person to another. Sophia standing by one of the stoves, stirring a pot of baked beans. Mosley finishing up his meal. Jade and Ryan with their heads close together, talking and laughing. Elissa, Eva, Violet, and Catalina chatting away in their booth. All the other customers enjoying their barbecue.

"Today? I'm going to enjoy what I have."

Silvio nodded and went back over to his stool. I got to my feet, walked over to the counter, and stepped behind it.

I needed to make one more vat of Fletcher's secret barbecue sauce today, among other things, and I quickly lost myself in the comforting rhythms of cooking, cleaning, and cashing out customers. All the while, though, I kept thinking about everything that I had to do next, my mind spinning one strand after another, stringing them all together into a web of certainty.

I'd told Silvio the truth. Today I would enjoy and be grateful for everything that I had. The restaurant, my friends, my family, Owen.

But I'd also told Tucker the truth too. I would never give up my quest to find out more about my mother and what had led to her murder, and I wouldn't back down from the powerful people who'd taken her away from me.

So tomorrow I would start figuring out a way to keep my friends and family safe during my upcoming war with the Circle.